Praise for *Crackenback*

'*Crackenback* is a strong, multi-layered work of crime fiction with good lashings of Australiana, wit and enough tension to cause an emotional avalanche.' *The Manning Community News*

'A nail-biting cat and mouse game in play.' Living Arts Canberra

'I did enjoy this one; empathetic characters, wonderful settings and a gripping narrative.' Reading, Writing and Riesling

'Lee Christine is certainly making her mark in crime fiction with memorable characters involved in cracking good plots set in the stark beauty of the Snowy Mountains in the heart of winter—the perfect time to commit a seriously good crime.' Blue Wolf Reviews

'Lee Christine has produced a novel of great merit. *Crackenback* builds on the success of *Charlotte Pass* and in its place we have another absolutely thrilling read.' Mrs B's Book Reviews

Praise for *Charlotte Pass*

'This intriguing, page-turning mystery will have you gripping the handle of your hot beverage of choice, if not spilling it entirely.' *Tas Writers*

'Ice, snow, fog and darkness set the scene in Lee Christine's chilling delve into the niche genre of romantic alpine crime.' *Newcastle Weekly*

'This is a murder mystery in the classic tradition, revealing a cast of characters from the past and slowly revealing secrets and connections. And this comes interwoven with a side serving of romance for the present day characters.' *NZ Booklovers*

'Not afraid to tug at your heart strings in one paragraph and have you gasping in shock at the next, this is a confident and assured book that will keep you guessing until you reach its nail-biting conclusion.' *The Manning Community News*

Lee Christine is the author of six romantic suspense novels. Her first crime novel, *Charlotte Pass*, was published in 2020 and was a finalist for Favourite Romantic Suspense Novel in 2020 Australian Romance Readers Awards. Her second crime novel, *Crackenback*, was published in 2021, and her third, *Dead Horse Gap*, is soon to be released, publishing in February 2022.

Lee lives in Newcastle, NSW, with her husband and her Irish Wheaten Terrier, Honey. To read more about Lee Christine, visit http://leechristine.com.au.

LEE CHRISTINE

Crackenback

ALLEN&UNWIN
SYDNEY • MELBOURNE • AUCKLAND • LONDON

This edition published in 2022
First published in 2021

Allen & Unwin
83 Alexander Street
Crows Nest NSW 2065
Australia
Phone: (61 2) 8425 0100
Email: info@allenandunwin.com
Web: www.allenandunwin.com

A catalogue record for this book is available from the National Library of Australia

ISBN 978 1 76106 638 2

Set in Sabon LT by Midland Typesetters, Australia
Printed and bound in Australia by the SOS Print + Media Group

10 9 8 7 6 5 4 3 2

For Douglas

For Douglas

Prologue

The Philippines

He sits up at the distant whine of an approaching vehicle. Few come along here, and he has memorised the distinctive sounds of the regular ones.

Scrambling over the weakened bodies of the other men, he peers out into the darkness through a gap in the rusty corrugated-iron wall. The sky is lighter than when he'd last woken, roused from sleep by the gnawing pain in his side. He puts his ear against the corroded tin. There is no mistaking the occasional misfire of the engine, and the grating sound of the changing down of gears.

He sits back on his haunches. He can just make out the shadowy shapes of the prisoners inside the shed, their emaciated bodies curled into the foetal position. Outside the shed door he hears the guard move. Tall and skinny, the guard is quieter than the ones approaching in the car, and marginally kinder.

Reaching out, he gropes for Goose's bony shoulder. 'Wake up. They're back.'

Weeks have passed since their captors were last here, and he has no way of knowing if progress has been made.

He rouses Shady first, then, holding his breath against the stench of Viggo's infected foot, nudges the Swede in the back. He would have killed them both months ago, but Shady is the only one who speaks native, and their chances of release are better with the Swede alive.

The vehicle turns into the driveway, the fleeting sweep of headlights sending cockroaches scuttling for the soggy corners. He moves aside so Shady can get close to the gap in the wall and listen.

The engine cuts. Doors slam in quick succession. Shady presses his ear to the hole.

Although the voices are muffled, he recognises the inflections, the dynamics and the pitch, tuning into their emotions like a dog trying to read signals from its owner. A nasally voice laced with frustration rises above the others. The squat man with the wide-set eyes.

'He's saying they've gone quiet,' says Shady, translating. 'There's been no communication for a month. The guard's telling them about Viggo's foot now. He's saying he needs medical treatment.'

The squat man speaks again, his tone more belligerent. Shady interprets, his voice low and quiet. 'Food, hush money, even this shit garage. It's costing them, he says.'

A quieter voice, more tempered. It's the thick-set one with a taste for fake designer sportswear. 'What's he saying now?' he demands, grabbing Shady's arm.

'That they should cut their losses and let us go.'

Hope swells inside his chest, but then the squatty one speaks again, his voice drowning out the others. 'He's disagreeing,' reports Shady. 'He's saying they need to send a message, a strong one.'

Raised voices as the men continue to argue.

Then suddenly, Shady abandons his post, stumbling and crawling in panic to cower in the corner furthest from the door.

Coward.

The strong beam of a Maglite shines through the holes in the corrugated iron where the nails have rusted away.

'Goose. Get up the back,' he hisses.

Goose moves close to Shady. The Swede has woken, and whimpers at the familiar sound of the key being inserted into the padlock.

Chains rattle and the door flies open.

He looks up. A blinding beam of light arcs through the air then crashes into his temple. He slumps sideways, pain exploding throughout his skull a second before his vision turns black.

A hoarse scream. Somewhere.

A chorus of frantic begging.

Acid surges into his throat.

Crying sounds as one of the others is dragged away.

He rolls onto his stomach, muscles straining as he attempts to lever himself off the ground.

A shot rings out in the darkness.

One

'Mummy!?'

Eva Bell straightened up from the bed she'd just made. 'I'm in the Wisteria Suite, Poppy.' She smoothed her hand over the lilac quilt cover, then plumped up the pillows. Poppy's quick, light tread was accompanied by much clinking and jangling.

'You have your own percussion thing happening there,' Eva said, turning as her three-year-old daughter appeared in the doorway. Poppy's forearms were decorated to the elbow with Eva's silver bracelets and an assortment of coloured bangles. The multiple neck-laces she wore reached to the knees of her Minnie Mouse leggings. 'You've been raiding my jewellery box again.'

Poppy climbed into an armchair covered in a floral wisteria print. Silvery rays of late-May sunshine streamed through the window behind her, bringing out the hint of auburn in her golden curls.

'Where did the turtle come from?' Poppy asked, holding out her wrist so Eva could inspect a heavily laden charm bracelet. 'I can't remember. Was it the Gollygus, or something like that?'

'Close. I brought it home from the *Gal-ap-a-gos* before you were born.' Eva rubbed her thumb over the small gold charm. 'This little

5

turtle is actually a really old tortoise. I can show you where the Galapagos are on the globe, if you like.'

'Okay.' Poppy slid off the chair and slipped a small hand into her mother's. 'Gal-ap-a-gos,' she sounded out the name as they walked to the door.

'That's it.' As she left the room, Eva glanced back to admire her work. Five years ago, the rooms at the Golden Wattle Lodge had been plainly furnished and identifiable only by the number on each door. Choosing an individual theme for each suite had been the top priority in a long list of changes Eva had made, and it had immediately added character to the place. The lodge was now a popular choice in the Thredbo area regardless of the seasons.

With another housekeeping task ticked off her list, she adjusted her stride to match Poppy's shorter one as they made their way along the hallway. All three suites on the east side of the lodge were now ready for the first guests to arrive in late June. That only left the three on the west side, which hopefully she would get to this afternoon.

At the end of the hallway, Eva shut the door behind her and stepped into the warmth of the spacious lounge room, thankful the guest rooms could be closed off from the general areas of the lodge. 'It's warmer now,' said Poppy.

'The heating isn't on in the rooms,' Eva said. 'No use wasting money when there's only you and me here. And I was working, so I was warm.'

On her right was the staircase leading to an equipment room, laundry and garage on the lower level. Running her hand along the bannister, Eva bypassed the stairs, Poppy skipping along beside her.

'Okay, let's have a look at this globe.' She crossed the lounge room, glancing briefly into the lobby with its curved reception desk and double glass doors leading to the vestibule beyond. The lobby was deserted now, the front doors locked, but in a few weeks' time it would be buzzing with excited guests checking in for their winter holiday.

Eva smiled as they went over to the small bookcase tucked in a corner of the room. The globe sat top centre, the lower shelves crammed with a variety of paperbacks and magazines. She was spinning the globe, looking for the islands off the coast of Ecuador, when the downstairs door flew open with a bang.

'Helloooooo! Are you there, Eva?'

Eva looked around. 'Bede?'

'Yeah, it's me. Sorry, the wind caught the door.'

'No worries. Come on up.'

The downstairs door slammed closed, but not before a blast of frigid air swept up the steep stairs. Eva put the globe back in its place and smiled at Poppy. 'I'll show you where the Galapagos Islands are later, okay?'

'You're allowed to use the front entrance, Bede,' Eva said as their nearest neighbour appeared at the bottom of the stairs.

'Didn't want to tramp dirt through your fancy foyer.' Puffing a little, he arrived at the top and dragged off his beanie. 'Good to see you both.'

'You too.' Despite the puffing, Bede had barely aged in the five years Eva had known him; his short-cropped hair now had a little more salt mixed in with the pepper, but he still had the slightly squishy dad bod of a man comfortably into his fifties and not fond of exercise.

She waited while he unzipped his parka and shrugged it from his shoulders, then asked, 'How was your son's Byron Bay wedding?'

'Beautiful. Worth the rush I'm now in getting ready for the opening weekend.'

'Lucky the season was delayed a few weeks.'

'I reckon.' His gaze shifted to take in the spacious lounge room. 'Geez, you've made some great improvements to this place. Your landlord will be loving you.'

'He's been great. He's in full support of anything that will improve the building.'

Eva looked at the room again with fresh eyes. A wagon-wheel chandelier with candle-shaped lights hung from the exposed beams, while burning logs cast a soft glow from a fireplace built entirely of river stones. The fake bear skin she'd brought home from Canada was spread on the floor between the hearth and a wooden coffee table. Atop the coffee table was a Mayan chess set with intricately carved wooden pieces, which Eva had picked up in South America.

Bede took a piece of red river gum from the wicker basket and added it to the fire. 'You know, I thought you were making a mistake when you ripped the old fireplace out of the wall and built this big one in the middle of the room.'

'Really? I didn't know that,' Eva said with a smile.

'Yeah. No, it's worked a treat.'

'Well, I didn't want an awful internal wall cutting the room in half and the wall wasn't structural, so putting the fireplace in the centre was a good compromise. I was thinking of my feet, too. With the dining table on the other side, it's closer to the kitchen.'

'Bora Bay!' Poppy yelled triumphantly. She was holding up her heavily braceleted wrist to show off a tiny seahorse charm.

Bede leaned over and peered at the bracelet. 'What have you got there, munchkin?'

'Mummy said Bora Bay. She's been there, and to lots of places.'

Bede straightened up and winked at Eva. 'The perks of working on a fancy yacht, cooking for rich people.'

Eva averted her eyes, trying not to think of how quickly things had turned sour on that last voyage. Eva smiled and ruffled Poppy's hair. 'No, I said *Byron* Bay, sweetie. Bora Bora is different.'

'How did you know that seahorse was from Bora Bora, Poppy?' Bede asked.

'Mummy told me. I 'membered.' Poppy looked up at Eva and she nodded.

'What a clever girl,' Bede laughed.

'Okay,' Eva said with a smile. 'How about you put all my jewellery back where it belongs?' She slanted a look a Bede. 'Do you have time for coffee, or is nine-thirty too early?'

'I reckon you could twist my arm.'

Eva watched Poppy run off towards their room before leading Bede out to the galley kitchen. 'Let me know if there's anything I can do, Bede, if you're pressed for time.'

Bede had helped her out several times during her first snow

season when she'd literally been learning on the job. Everything that could go wrong had gone wrong back then, and it had been Bede who'd shown her how to replace a blown fuse, maintain the septic system and hook up the portable generator. Waiting around for her Canberra-based landlord to organise tradesmen would have sent her out of business. Mutual support from the mountain community was the way things functioned in this harsh environment where Antarctic winds downed trees and knocked out electricity. By the time the roads were ploughed, and the tradies turned up, the water in the pipes could have frozen.

'Just let me know if you're going into Jindabyne,' Bede said. 'That'd save me a trip. How're your preparations going?'

'I have half the guest suites made up. Once the rest are done, I can start planning the menus and ordering the food.'

'You're ahead of me,' he said, leaning against the square wooden table where Eva and Poppy ate their meals away from the guests. 'I doubt my chef's capable of thinking even a day or two in advance. Geez, he's a temperamental bugger, always flapping around in a rush at the last minute.'

Eva busied herself brewing the coffee. She knew what Bede meant. She'd helped his chef out of a few tight spots. 'I'm the furthest away from the village,' she said, 'so I can't afford to be disorganised. I'm counting on guests' return business to keep me afloat.'

'Your cooking will do that,' Bede said as they carried their coffees into the lounge room. 'How was business over summer?'

'Up on last year.' Eva took a sip of her espresso. 'It's growing . . . steadily.' She sank onto the leather sofa with a sigh. 'Have you thought any more about opening up the Willy Wagtail year-round?'

'No, I want to spend a couple of months with my boy in Mullumbimby, and I'm loathe to give up my fly-fishing time. Still, every year it's getting harder to make my money in four short months. I'd only open year-round if you agreed to come and manage it for me. I need someone I can trust.'

'I know.' It wasn't the first time Bede had extended the offer, but Eva had decided long ago she would always be her own boss.

Occasionally, the wanderlust would bite, though, and she'd find herself envying Bede's greater freedom. But all it took was one sweeping gaze around the idyllic home she'd created for herself and Poppy and the wistfulness would disappear.

For a while they sat companionably, quietly enjoying their coffee and the revived heat of the fire. Finally, Bede broke the silence. 'How're your bookings?'

'I'm around seventy-five percent occupancy for the season. You?'

'Getting close.' Bede drained his cup then sighed in appreciation. 'That's a top blend. Which one is it?'

'Oh no you don't,' Eva said with a laugh. 'I'm not giving away *all* my trade secrets.'

'You're killing me.' He handed her his cup with a good-natured smile. 'Well, I'd better be off. I just wanted to call in and say g'day, see how you two were getting along.'

'We mightn't be able to see you through the trees, but it's nice to know you're there, Bede.' Eva followed him to the coat-stand as Poppy emerged from their private room. 'Say goodbye, Poppy.'

'Bye, Bede,' she said, before yawning suddenly. 'Mummy, I'm tired.'

'How about you have a nap? It's only ten o'clock but you've been up since six,' Eva said, rolling her eyes at Bede.

'See you, munchkin. And try and give your mum a sleep-in sometime.' Bede pulled on his jacket. 'Don't come downstairs, Eva. I can see myself out.'

'I have to come down anyway, I have clothes in the dryer.' She made sure Poppy was heading to their room before following Bede down the stairs.

'Feels like the temperature's dropped again,' he said, turning left into the hallway and heading for the side exit door.

'Get going then. Don't forget to call me if you need anything in town.'

'I will.' Bede dragged on his beanie and gloves before turning up his collar and opening the door. A rush of frigid air made Eva's eyes water. 'Yep, there's snow on the way,' he said, raising a hand in farewell.

Eva locked the door with a violent shiver. When guests were staying, she would leave it unlocked twenty-four–seven so they had unlimited access to the mountain bikes, skis and snowboards stowed in the equipment room next to the laundry. In the evening, too, guests would often stroll down to the village for a nightcap, or to catch the in-house band at the Willy Wagtail. Most of them returned to the lodge after she and Poppy had gone to bed, and an unlocked back door meant a good night's sleep for the two of them.

Eva hurried back along the hallway, pausing briefly at the bottom of the stairs to listen for Poppy. All was silent. Eva could only hope she was already napping after her early rising.

There were three doors on her left: the laundry, the equipment room and the internal access to the double garage. Opening the laundry door, Eva switched on the light, then propped the door open with the metal doorstop.

She was pleased to find the dryer had finished its cycle, saving her a second trip downstairs, and as she dumped the warm clothes into the washing basket, she wondered if she'd been a bit mean not telling Bede which blend of coffee she used. This was Thredbo, after all, not the cutthroat world of Michelin-star restaurants. But then she smiled, imagining how horrified Bede would be if she told him the price.

She was halfway through folding the laundry when an insistent knock on the side access door startled her. She hurried to unlock it, ready to greet Bede for the second time that morning and demand to know what he had forgotten this time.

The man burst in so quickly that Eva had no time to react. Tall, scruffy beard, the front of his jacket caked in blood, he towered over her, his shadowy face concealed by an oversized hood. He dropped a small backpack and the swag he was carrying to the floor, before locking the door behind him.

Eva stepped backwards in the narrow hallway, heart pounding, her throat muscles paralysed with shock. She opened her mouth to speak, but no words came out.

'Eva, it's me.' The man dragged the hood back from his face. 'Eva?' His voice was low and urgent. And familiar.

She took in his bedraggled appearance, recognition finally dawning. It had been four years since she'd last seen him, and if she'd passed him in the street she wouldn't have known him. 'What's happened to you?' Eva whispered, the rough concrete wall pressing against her back and chilling her spine.

He glanced up the stairs. 'I saw that guy leave. How many others are here?'

'There's only me. We're not open yet.' Eva's voice sounded distant, strange.

'Where is she? Is she here?'

A bolt of terror stole Eva's breath at his mention of Poppy. She looked at the smeared blood, the matted hair, the cuts and bruises across his knuckles. 'Let me call an ambulance, or I can drive you to the hospital. You need medical help.'

'No.' He shook his head, his breathing growing more and more laboured. 'Do you have a first-aid kit?'

Relief engulfed her when he didn't press her further on Poppy. She nodded. 'Upstairs.'

He picked up his things and gestured towards the stairs with his chin.

Eva pivoted slowly, watching him over her shoulder. He was thinner, less bulked up than he'd been in the past. She ascended the stairs, her legs shaking at the unexpected intrusion.

As they reached the lounge room, his swag and backpack hit the floor again. Left arm pressed against his middle, he limped from window to window, testing the locks before pulling the heavy drapes closed. The room dimmed, illuminated only by the glowing log Bede had added to the fire, and a single strip of sunlight shining through a gap where the curtains didn't quite meet.

'What are you doing?' Eva asked, trying to stem her panic. She reached out with shaking hands and curled her fingers around the back of an armchair to anchor herself.

He turned, staggering a little. 'Where's your mobile?'

She moved away from the chair, anxiety churning her stomach. 'It's in the kitchen. You can have it. Take it with you.'

He remembered the way, moving around the fireplace to the rear of the building, which overlooked the driveway winding around the trees from Crackenback Drive below. Eva shadowed his tall frame, desperate to understand what was happening, but loath to wake up Poppy.

He shouldered his way through the single swinging door to the kitchen, where her phone lay in clear view on the stainless-steel benchtop.

'Please,' she said, 'if you won't let me help you, then call someone who can.'

He looked up from inspecting her phone. 'I need a sewing needle.'

Eva frowned. Was he planning to stitch himself up in her kitchen? 'There are repair kits in the bathrooms,' she said, turning away. 'I'll get one.'

'Wait!'

Eva froze. A floorboard creaked behind her and the air stirred. She wheeled around, stumbling as she backpeddled away from him. He reached out, his fingers close to her face, his body reeking of blood, wet earth and body odour. 'Give me your earring.'

Understanding dawned. He didn't want to use her phone. He wanted to shut it down. 'Just do as I say, Eva, and give me the damn earring.'

She raised her hands, fumbling with the small butterfly clip before sliding the pearl stud from her ear and dropping it in his hand.

Without taking his eyes off her, he ran a thumb down the side of the phone then guided the sturdy post into the miniscule opening. When the tiny drawer slid open, he picked out the sim card with his nails and shoved it in his pants pocket.

Eva ran to the far end of the bench and snatched the hands-free phone from its cradle. 'Get out!' she cried, terror weakening her voice when she longed for it to be strong. Not that it mattered; she could scream the lodge down and no one would hear her. 'There's an SUV in the garage. Go now, or I'm calling triple zero.'

'I just need shelter, and your computer,' he said, yanking the landline from the wall socket.

Eva's mind flashed back, and she was on the yacht. She backed away, bumping into the cupboards. She gasped and swung around, grabbing hold of the bench to steady herself. She blinked hard. There was no heaving grey ocean beneath her.

'Your computer?' he said.

Eva's heart bounced around in her chest, every instinct urging her to flee. But her overwhelming urge to protect her child kept her motionless. If only Bede would come back, or a delivery person would ring the doorbell. Someone. *Please.*

'*Eva!*'

'It's on the d-desk,' she stammered, her entire body beginning to shake. 'In the lobby.'

His eyes cut swiftly to the door and then back at her. 'Go on,' he said.

Eva led the way back through the lounge room, hands clenching and unclenching at her sides, eyes shifting from left to right searching for something, anything she could use as a weapon, but there were only throw rugs and scatter cushions. A few offcuts of firewood were within reach, but she wouldn't stand a chance with him so close behind her.

In the lobby, he hurried past her to move behind the reception desk, wincing as he leaned over to look at her laptop. 'What's the password?'

Eva shook her head defiantly, her insides quaking. 'Not until you tell me why you're here.' With Poppy asleep only metres away, her best chance of getting him out of the lodge was to reason with him.

'*Password?*' he growled.

'GoldenWattle2,' she blurted out. 'Capital G and W. Two's a digit.'

He worked the touchpad, then began to type, his fingers a blur over the keys. He closed the lid, then quickly scanned the desk drawers and opened the one with a lock. 'Where's the key for this drawer?'

She told him it was in the top drawer, and when he'd locked the computer away and stashed the key in the same pocket as her sim card, he came out from behind the desk. 'Okay. I need that first-aid kit.'

'Not until you tell me what you're going to do.' Eva forced the words though wooden lips, needing him to say it aloud, to confirm the one horrifying thought she couldn't let go of.

He'd come for Poppy.

When he didn't answer, she couldn't stand it anymore. 'Please, don't take her away from me,' she begged, her voice breaking. 'I'll do anything.'

He paused, and for the briefest second something like under-standing flashed in his eyes. 'Then tell me where the first-aid kit is.'

'It's in there.' She pointed to the general restroom on the other side of the lobby.

'You're coming too,' he said, placing a hand in the middle of her back and propelling her forward.

'Please, don't do this!' she cried, stepping into the bathroom ahead of him. 'We can work something out.'

He closed the door then turned to face her, cutting off any chance of escape from the confines of the small room. 'I'm not here for the kid.'

Two

Police Headquarters
Parramatta, Sydney

At 8 am Detective Sergeant Pierce Ryder knocked on Inspector Gray's door, then listened for the invitation to come in. Gray rarely opened the door himself, only moving from behind his desk to stand at the window overlooking Marsden Street. For those summoned to his office, there was no way of knowing how long the wait would be, but you bloody well better be there when he called your name to enter.

'Come in, Ryder.' Inspector Gray's voice drifted through the heavy wooden door with the authority of a high-school principal.

Ryder let himself in. Sure enough, Gray was standing at the window, gazing outside, as though he were imprisoned in his own office.

Gray turned around as Ryder came further into the room, his bushy eyebrows raised in enquiry. 'Any progress on the Hutton case?'

Ryder didn't sit. Gray rarely extended the invitation; if he did, it usually meant unwelcome news was on the way. 'We've been trawling through the case notes of his first two victims and re-interviewing people when necessary. I'll have a formal progress report ready in the next day or so.'

'You and Detective Flowers arrested the Charlotte Pass killer in record time, but the Hutton case seems to be moving as fast as Sydney's peak-hour traffic.'

'New information has been hard to come by. We haven't had a credible sighting of him since last year. I'm hopeful of a breakthrough any day, especially now the reward money has been increased.' Ryder's voice rang with a confidence belying his frustration.

'Let's hope you're right. And the new recruit? Has she arrived?'

'Yes, sir. Detective Flowers has been showing Detective Sterling around the office. I'm giving a general overview of the Hutton case for her benefit in ten minutes. The whole task force will be there.'

Outside, a cement truck roared past, probably on its way to one of the many construction sites around Parramatta.

'So, you have a woman on the team now, Pierce. Don't ask for any more.'

Ryder frowned. 'Any more women?'

'Any more detectives.' Gray moved to put his mobile phone on his desk, and for the first time Ryder noticed a limp in the Inspector's stride. 'We have too many crimes to solve and not enough police officers. The government's bolstering our numbers, but most of them are still at the academy, and the ones who are out are too green. Our resources are stretched to breaking point.'

Ryder nodded. 'Our team might be small, but we're hard working and highly skilled.'

'You'll need to be. Right now, we have no other option.'

There was a pause as Gray picked up a memo from his desk and scanned it. He glanced up at Ryder. 'How do you think she'll go?'

'Detective Sterling?'

'Hmm. The sergeant at Taree said she had some problems fitting in up there.'

It was the first Ryder had heard of it. Maybe the old boys' club up the coast had closed ranks. He watched as Inspector Gray put the memo back on the desk. 'I don't think she'll have any problems on my squad,' Ryder replied.

'I'm glad to hear it. We don't need any more personnel on stress leave.' Gray raised a hand, a signal he was satisfied with what he'd heard. 'Let me know how you go.'

Ryder left the office and headed for the elevator, then changed his mind and retraced his steps. The Inspector's admin assistant, whom he'd known for ten years, worked at a desk recessed into a small alcove off the corridor. It would only take a minute for Ryder to have a word. He stopped in front of Vivien's desk, trying not to look too impatient while he waited for her to stop typing. When she took off her headset, he gestured towards the Inspector's door. 'Is he okay?'

Vivien peered at him, her red-framed glasses the same shade as her lipstick. 'You noticed?'

'Bit hard not to. He's limping, like he has gout or something.' Ryder wasn't one to pry into his colleagues' personal business—he did that for a living—but he liked the Inspector and his intuition told him something was up.

Vivien glanced down the corridor as though her boss might come rushing out of his office and overhear them, unlikely as that was. 'He needs a double hip replacement,' she whispered.

'Oh. When's he being operated on?' And who would take on the role of acting inspector while Gray was on leave?

'That's the problem,' said Vivien. 'He can't take time off while the Chief Inspector's on leave, so he's putting up with it. He rarely sits down because it's so painful to get up out of the chair again. Have you noticed how he stands, braced against the window?'

'Yeah, I was wondering what he found so interesting out there.'

Vivien picked up her headset. 'Well, now you know. There's nothing interesting out there at all.'

Ryder bade farewell to Vivien then took the stairs to the floor below where Mitchell Flowers and Nerida Sterling were deep in conversation at Flowers' desk. 'Sorry to keep you waiting,' Ryder said. 'Has Daisy shown you around?'

Sterling frowned and looked at Flowers for a few seconds before understanding dawned on her face. 'Oh, Detective *Flowers*?'

'Yes, sorry,' Ryder said. 'A friend of mine gave him that nickname, and it's kind of stuck.'

'Yes, Sarge, he's given me the grand tour.' Sterling lisped every so often when pronouncing her s's. It had taken Ryder a while to realise she wore clear braces. She stood and straightened her suit jacket. Keen blue eyes shone from an open, friendly face; her blonde hair styled into a no-nonsense short bob. 'And I've met most of the task force already.'

'In that case, let's get started on this recap. It's almost eight-thirty.'

Ryder picked up the files from his desk and headed for the larger meeting room. He hit the switch and the fluorescents flickered on, casting an artificial glow around the windowless room with a whiteboard its sole decoration. Standing behind the chair at the head of the table, Ryder watched as one by one the detectives filed in, clutching coffee mugs, water bottles and mobile phones and took their places around the table.

Ryder sat down and ran his eye over the squad. Next to him was Detective David Benson, who'd recently transferred from Queanbeyan while his wife and kids remained at home. Along from Benson was Detective Geoff O'Day. Both men had worked on the Charlotte Pass case, and while Ryder hadn't agreed with some of the gung-ho decisions Benson had made back then, he hadn't lost faith in his ability, and he'd always respected O'Day's attention to detail. Flowers was sitting next to Sterling down the other end of the table, chatting away and showing her his friendly side. On Ryder's right, Detective Ray Brown peered at him over the top of his black-framed glasses.

When everyone was settled, Ryder attached three images to the whiteboard. 'This is a police sketch of Gavin Hutton,' he began, tapping the first. Hooded eyes stared straight ahead, limp dishevelled hair partly obscuring a lean face with an unshaven jaw. 'This sketch was compiled over time from descriptions given by credible witnesses. Hutton could look like this when he's hiding out. In contrast, the second and third images are CCTV shots from the Sydney and Goulburn crime scenes. You should be familiar with them as they've appeared in every newspaper and on every television screen in the country.' Ryder pointed to the images. 'In these photographs, Hutton's hair is shorter, and he's dressed in nondescript clothing to blend in. Plain pants, T-shirt and jumper.'

Ryder turned away from the board and looked at Sterling. 'Hutton was a corporal in the Australian Army. He was discharged in 2012 and upon his return to Australia from Afghanistan, he moved in with a woman he met online, Kimberley Dickson. According to Dickson, Hutton was cagey about his family, saying only that his parents had died and sharing nothing of his family life. She found him to be a loner, not interested in getting to know her friends or keeping in contact with his old school friends or army buddies. Like many former soldiers, he struggled adjusting to civilian life.'

Ryder sat and opened his file and located Kimberley Dickson's statement. 'Dickson said he was restless and bored and appeared to miss the action that came with doing dangerous work overseas. After a difficult eighteen months, the relationship was going nowhere. Dickson admitted to being relieved when Hutton received a job offer in Zimbabwe, working as part of a security team guarding a mine specialising in rare earth minerals.'

Sterling put up her hand. 'What are rare earth minerals?'

'Lithium, cadmium, terbium to name a few. They're used in mobile phones.' Ryder went on: 'Hutton's skills as a former soldier were always going to be highly valued by western companies operating in unstable and dangerous foreign countries. We don't know where he went after he left Zimbabwe. We assume he worked in other hotspots around the world, maybe in the Middle East. We do know from a Qantas flight manifest, and the withdrawal of his entire savings from his bank account, that he was back in Australia by September 2017.'

Ryder looked up. 'Any questions so far?'

When no one spoke, he continued: 'Hutton resurfaced as the prime suspect in the murder of Dominic Burrows in mid-2018.' He stood and attached a photograph of Burrows to the whiteboard: a pale-skinned, emaciated young man, his body ravaged from long-term drug abuse. 'Burrows, originally from the Gold Coast, was living on the street and in squats around Central Station in Sydney. He was found beaten to death in a park adjacent to the station. He was a regular at a nearby injecting room and several food kitchens.' Ryder sat and flicked through the file. 'The woman who runs Nana's Soup Kitchen . . . ?'

'Nanette Roxby,' said Brown, pushing his black-framed glasses higher on his nose.

'Thank you. Nanette Roxby saw Burrows arguing with another man who'd been into the kitchen a few times. Called himself Ben. The argument was serious enough for Nanette to give them both a warning.'

Ryder paused to look at the detectives gathered around the table. Sterling was leaning forward, her hands clasped and resting on the table, her full attention on Ryder. Flowers was lounging in his chair but listening intently. Benson and O'Day were staring at different spots on the tabletop, while Brown sat with his arms raised, his fingers locked behind his head. Not too bad for a task force who'd heard these facts many times over.

Ryder took a breath. 'Altercations in soup kitchens aren't unusual, but when we showed Nanette Roxby the CCTV footage from the area the night Dominic Burrows was murdered, she identified one of the men close to the crime scene as Ben from the soup kitchen.'

'How did you find out this "Ben" was Gavin Hutton?' asked Sterling.

'Two people came forward,' put in O'Day. 'A man who'd served with him in the army, and a woman who'd fostered him for eighteen months during his teenage years. Details are in the file.'

'Does Hutton have a record?' Sterling asked.

'Only a few appearances in the Children's Court,' said O'Day.

'Two different blood types were found at the crime scene,' Ryder said. 'Burrows' and one other unidentified blood type which we strongly suspect is Hutton's. Both have been added to the blood type database, but we haven't had a match so far.'

'Could Hutton have a drug problem, too, and he killed Burrows for his next hit?' asked Sterling.

'The second blood sample, if it is Hutton's, showed no trace of drugs,' said Benson. 'Only Burrows' did.'

Sterling nodded and Ryder went on: 'Hutton vanished after the Burrows murder. Then, in March 2019, a gym proprietor, Fergus Suter, was murdered in Straker Park in Goulburn. Beaten to death.' The image Ryder put on the whiteboard could have graced the cover of a men's health magazine. Clear-eyed and smiling into the camera, Fergus Suter stood knee deep in the surf, his blond hair lifted by a gentle breeze, his casually folded arms showcasing well-defined muscles. 'Suter closed the gym at nine pm, called in to the Snake Pit Hotel for a beer before heading home—but never made it.'

'Both murdered in parks,' Sterling said thoughtfully.

Ryder nodded. 'The CCTV footage outside the hotel captured a man following Suter. Cameras further down the street near a convenience store showed the victim and the perpetrator only moments apart. They were both heading in the direction of the park. Fergus Suter's body was found early the next morning by a group of cyclists. The assault was vicious, his injuries similar to those of Dominic Burrows. Unfortunately, only the victim's blood was found at the scene this time, but facial matching confirmed the man caught on the CCTV cameras was Gavin Hutton. From our enquiries, we learned that Hutton, again using the name Ben, booked several personal training sessions with Suter prior to the gym owner's death.

Flowers sat straighter in his chair. 'Even if we apprehend Hutton, we can't pin Suter's murder on him without supporting forensic evidence.'

'*If* we apprehend him?' said Benson, his tone unusually scathing. '*When* we apprehend him.'

Flowers shrugged. 'Just saying. The CCTV footage puts him in the area, that's all.'

'Did anyone else hold a grudge against Suter?' asked Sterling.

'No debt, no grudges, no jilted lover,' said Ryder. 'His boyfriend, William Guthrie, lives in Canberra through the week, so they saw each other at weekends.'

Sterling frowned. 'A gay hate crime or jealous ex-lover?'

'I'm working on that line of investigation,' said Brown.

'William Guthrie has a rock-solid alibi,' said Ryder. 'He was on an assignment for the Department of Defence in Canberra when Suter was murdered. By all accounts, Suter was a well-liked member of the community with no enemies.' Ryder shook his head. 'Both these murders were brutal, their faces beaten beyond recognition.'

'Who's Dominic Burrows' next of kin?' asked Sterling.

O'Day frowned. 'We've interviewed his uncle Michael Joseph a few times.'

'That's right,' said Ryder. 'Burrows' parents live in Queensland. They were estranged from their son. His closest family contact is his mother's younger brother, who lives in Sydney. Michael Joseph works as a consultant and used to help his nephew out from time to time. We never found any leads to follow up—'

'Sarge?' Flowers interrupted. He had his phone to his ear and was scribbling in his notepad. 'Two calls just came in on the hotline.'

'Who from?' asked Ryder.

'A Jervis Bay resident was coming out of the water after an early morning swim when he saw a man fitting Hutton's description rolling up a sleeping bag as though he'd spent the night on the beach. Local police haven't had any luck locating him yet.'

'And the other one?'

'One of Hutton's old teachers at Martinsfield High School. He recognised his name, not his picture. Apparently, he was overseas on long service leave when we visited the school. He only learned about Hutton when he got back.'

'Okay. Well, this is good news; it's more than we've had in weeks.' Ryder spoke to Flowers: 'You and Sterling come with me. Everyone else, keep going with what you were working on. Thank you.'

As the task force members began to disperse, Ryder took the photographs down from the whiteboard before following them out of the room.

'Flowers, head down to Jervis Bay,' he said when they were back in the general office. 'Find out if this is a credible sighting. Someone besides the swimmer could have laid eyes on this bloke. Hopefully, by the time you get there the local police might have picked him up.'

'Yes, Sarge.' Flowers began to gather his personal items, looking excited to be unchained from his desk.

'Speak to the locals, especially fast-food outlets, service stations and caravan parks where he could have used the facilities.'

'Sarge, you don't need to keep telling me—'

'All right, on your way then. It's already gone nine o'clock.' Ryder turned to the new recruit. 'Sterling, you can come with me. There's no better way to get up to speed than on the job. We'll talk to this school teacher, and while we're in the area we'll catch up with Hutton's former partner, too.'

'That's Kimberley Dickson, right?'

'Right.' Ryder smiled. He had a feeling Nerida Sterling was going to fit in just fine.

Three

A bitter wind brought the first snow flurries to the mountains mid-morning, gusting through Thredbo and turning the landscape white. On the far edge of the village the thick gums surrounding the Golden Wattle Lodge bent in unison, while a low-hanging branch scraped ominously against a windowpane.

Inside the lodge, relief flooded through Eva's body. *He's not here for Poppy.* Keeping as far away from Jack Walker as possible in the confined bathroom, she pressed her palms against the cold white tiles and watched his every move. If he wasn't here for Poppy, he had to want something from her.

'Gavin Hutton,' Jack said as he filled the basin with water. 'Do you recognise that name?'

She nodded.

He unzipped his jacket, then lifted his stained sweater. Blood seeped from a five-centimetre gash close to his navel. 'He did this. Slashed me with a knife.'

Eva stared at the wound and then swallowed hard to steady herself. 'Where were you?'

'Between Leatherbarrel Creek and Tom Groggin campground.'

Eva pictured the well-known camping areas, roughly half an hour's drive from Thredbo. On foot, it would be a three-to-five hour hike, depending on fitness levels and the weather.

'Gavin Hutton is wanted by the police,' she said, never imagining that news of a killer in the Kosciusko National Park could come as such a relief, but for some inexplicable reason Gavin Hutton was behind Jack bursting into her lodge that day. Compared to what she'd been thinking only moments earlier ... Eva relaxed, moved away from the wall a touch. 'What were you doing out there?'

He flicked off the tap, braced a hand either side of the basin and then plunged his face into the water. Eva watched, memories flooding back. She'd seen him do the same thing when he'd been here before, though Jack Walker had looked a lot different back then.

He straightened suddenly. Eyes closed, his hair plastered to the sides of his head, he ran a washer over his face then raked his fringe back. Blue eyes met hers in the mirror. 'What was I doing? I was hunting him.'

Eva stayed quiet, watching as he grabbed a hand towel and dried his face and neck. Then he took a cotton ball and antiseptic from the first-aid kit he'd found in the vanity and applied it to the wound. He gave a violent jerk, his sharp intake of breath hissing through his teeth.

'You have to report it to the police,' she said. 'You have to tell them where Hutton was when he attacked you so they can catch him.'

'I don't have to do anything,' Jack said firmly, fixing her with a steady gaze despite his clear discomfort.

'But it's the right thing to do,' she argued. 'My sister's boyfriend is the lead detective on that case. You should let them handle it.'

He was silent for so long Eva wondered if he'd heard her. He continued to apply the antiseptic, the only sign of pain the sudden pallor of his skin.

'Did the army send you?' she asked. It made sense. Jack had told her he was a former commando with the Royal Australian Signals Corp when he booked out the lodge four years ago, using it as a base to train a group of former soldiers in Thredbo's back country, readying them for risky security work overseas.

'The army has nothing to do with it, and the police don't have a clue.'

'And you do?' Eva shot back, frustration roaring to the surface. His head snapped up. 'Yes, I do.'

'Then explain how you got into a fight with a serial killer. For the love of God, the average person doesn't do this kind of thing.'

'Hutton's no serial killer. Lust drives serial killers. Hutton wants revenge—trust me.'

Trust! Eva almost laughed in spite of everything happening around her. The last time a man had told her to trust him, that he would sort things out, she'd ended up locking herself in her cabin every night. 'You said Hutton wants revenge. Revenge for what?'

Jack released the plug, the water draining noisily into the pipe. Then the bathroom turned quiet; the silence broken by the distant sound of a tinny children's song.

'Poppy!' Eva cried, wrenching the door open and going out into the lobby as her daughter came in from the lounge room, her Rock-a-Bye Bear clutched in her arms. The little girl's cheeks were flushed pink, her eyes bleary with sleep.

Eva scooped Poppy up, holding her small, warm body close as her mind ricocheted in ten different directions. She'd always hoped that one day Poppy would meet her father, but never had she imagined it happening like this.

'Hello,' Poppy said, swivelling around in Eva's arms to look at Jack. 'Did you fall off your bike?'

He moved into the doorway and stared at the little girl. 'Nope,' he said, focusing intently on his daughter. 'I was mountain climbing . . . out there.'

'I fell off my bike once and got stitches.' Poppy began to struggle in Eva's arms, wanting to get down. 'Where are all the other guests?' the little girl demanded.

Eva set her daughter down reluctantly, but kept a firm hold of the child's hand.

'There's only me,' Jack said, his eyes softening a little. 'I came early because I hurt myself.'

Poppy stuck a finger in her mouth and pushed out a cheek. 'You mustn't be very good at climbing.'

27

'Hmm . . . I need practice.'

'Take your finger out of your mouth, Poppy,' Eva said, tugging on her daughter's hand.

'Mummy.' Eva felt a drag on her shirt tail. Poppy cupped a hand over her mouth and beckoned for her mother to come closer. Keeping Jack Walker firmly in her sights, Eva leaned down to hear what Poppy had to say.

'He's dirty. Where's his clean clothes?'

Eva took her first full breath in what felt like forever. Thankfully, the mix of soil and blood just looked like dirt to Poppy. She straightened slowly, a plan taking shape in her mind. If she could get Poppy downstairs, they could be out in the yard in a matter of seconds. With Jack nursing an injury, they had a reasonable chance of making it through the trees to the Willy Wagtail.

'I'll get you some clothes from the laundry,' she said to Jack. 'There's a ton of comfortable stuff in the cupboard down there. It's amazing what people leave behind.'

Tightening her grip on Poppy's hand, Eva spun around and headed for the stairs. Heart pounding, she half-carried half-dragged Poppy along with her. She hadn't gone more than ten steps when she sensed movement behind her, a rustle of clothing, a soft expletive. Ignoring Poppy's protests, Eva swung the child onto her hip. She reached for the bannister, her fingertips almost touching the polished wood when Jack grabbed her arm and pulled her to a sudden stop.

'I tell you what. Leave Poppy here with me and you go down to the laundry and get the clothes.' Even in the shadows Eva could make out the challenge in his eyes. 'We'll wait up here. Poppy can tell me all about how she came to fall off her bike.'

❄

The few minutes spent in the laundry were the longest of Eva's life, even more so than the time confined to her tiny cabin below the waterline during that final, fateful voyage on the yacht. Back then, she had been responsible for just herself. Now, there was a life more

28

important than her own. Fingers trembling, she rifled through the cupboard and found track pants and a hoodie that looked about the right size. Straining her ears for sounds from upstairs, Eva cast her eyes around the small room, looking for a weapon, struggling to hear over the blood surging in her temples. Jack had to be having some kind of meltdown to be talking about Gavin Hutton seeking revenge. Revenge for *what*? If a killer was in the national park, the thing to do was call the police and get the hell out of Thredbo, not cut off all connectivity to the lodge.

I'm not here for the kid.

How could she be sure of that? How could she be sure he was safe to be around?

Leave Poppy here with me.

Eva pivoted, scanning the contents of the airless room, devoid of natural light. Detergent. Ironing board and iron. The washing she'd left half-folded in the basket when she'd gone to open the door.

Was he taking Poppy right now? Leaving in her car? Eva tried pushing the unbearable thought aside, but her mind wouldn't let it go. With the walls closing in on her, she scanned the room again, her gaze falling on the metal doorstop she'd chosen because of its decorative flower shape. Scooping it up, she ran her thumb across the sharper edge of the wedge and then buried it under the bundled-up clothes.

Leaving the light on, she began to climb the stairs, her fingers curled around the metal flower in her hand.

'Kill the light,' he said gruffly.

Eva stopped and looked up, her legs going weak with relief. Two shadowy figures, one tall, one tiny, waited at the top of the stairs.

'It's on a timer,' she lied, continuing her climb, her body vibrating with tension.

Three steps to the top now. Two. One. For God's sake, *breathe*.

'*Mummmeeee*,' Poppy whined, her bottom lip quivering, eyes shifting between Eva and Jack. 'I wanna drink.'

Schooling her face into a calm mask, Eva gripped the doorstop under the clothes. 'Did you put my jewellery back where it belongs?'

29

Anything to get Poppy away from the menacing presence of Jack Walker.

'I put them on the bed,' Poppy stammered, her little body taut with anxiety.

Steeling herself against what she was about to do, Eva said sternly, 'Do as I ask please, Poppy, then I'll get you a drink.'

For a moment, she feared Poppy was so shocked by her tone that she wasn't going to move. But then the little girl reluctantly obeyed, the Rock-a-Bye Bear still clutched in her arms.

Eva turned slowly to face Jack Walker.

He held out a hand, palm upwards.

Eva stared at it, her heart in her throat.

'You can give me what you're hiding now,' he said quietly.

When she didn't move, he thrust a hand beneath the clothes and pulled the metal doorstop from her grasp. Eva gasped and dropped the clothes.

'You don't want to do that,' he said, weighing the heavy item in his hand.

Pent-up fury drove strength into her body, and she advanced on him. 'What do you expect me to do?' she cried, striking out and bashing her fists against his chest. 'You have no right!' Eva shoved him hard, swinging upwards and striking the underside of his chin with her knuckles. Pain radiated through her hand, but she continued to claw at him, grabbing handfuls of his sweater. 'No right!'

'Ah!' He brought his free arm up to his middle, his face twisting in pain.

Eva stepped back, gulping in great breaths of air. Tears welled but she blinked them away. 'Why should I believe you?' she said, her voice breaking. 'You come in here . . . close everything down . . . and tell me it's about Gavin Hutton wanting revenge.'

'It is.' He bent over slowly and picked the clothes up from the floor.

'Why disconnect everything?' she asked, puffing from the adrenaline.

'Because I don't trust you not to call the police,' Jack replied, turning to head slowly back towards the bathroom. 'They'll bring in the dogs and choppers, and Hutton will disappear like all the other times the police thought they had him.'

'So?' Eva followed, the knuckles on her right hand beginning to throb. 'What do I care if they come in all guns blazing and scare him off? As long as he's nowhere near us.'

'You need to care.' He opened the door wide, then crouched down and shoved the metal wedge under the door. 'Stand in the doorway where I can see you,' he said, straightening with obvious pain and grabbing hold of the vanity unit for support. Bracing his hands on the granite top, he breathed heavily.

'How is it that you know so much about this man, and yet you say the police know nothing? And why are you locking everything up here when he's probably gone deeper into the national park?'

Jack turned his head and looked at her, still leaning heavily on the vanity. 'Because he knows this place. He's stayed here before.'

Shock stole Eva's breath.

'He was a participant on one of my courses.' Jack straightened. 'Years ago, before you took over the lease on this place.'

'Okay, so even if he was here years ago, we know that he hides away from people now. Why would he risk being caught coming here, close to the village, when there are so many other remote properties in the mountains that are empty?'

'Because he knows I'm onto him. And he knows where I'll be.'

'Here? In the Golden Wattle?' Anger flared deep inside Eva again. 'If what you're saying is true, and I'm not sure how much I believe you, all you've done is put Poppy and me in danger.'

'You and Poppy will be safest here, with me. Look, I know what he's doing, and he didn't entirely get the jump on me, I did some damage to him, too.' Jack ripped open some plaster strips and started to apply them as makeshift stitches to the wound. 'You may be right, though,' he said between gritted teeth. 'Gavin Hutton mightn't be here just yet, but he will be, in time.'

31

Four

Jack picked up the soiled cotton balls and empty packaging and threw everything into the waste basket. The cut was painful, but it was a flesh wound and would begin to heal quickly. He'd kill for a hot shower, but he couldn't take the time now. The child was in the lobby, upset, but it was impossible to hear what the problem was over the furry singing thing.

Eva appeared in the doorway and looked right at him. The child was on her hip, her face streaked with tears, her chubby arms wrapped tightly around the toy. When she caught sight of Jack, she let it fall to the floor and buried her face against her mother's neck.

'She's wants a drink,' Eva said, her voice ringing with challenge. 'Stop me if you have to.' She walked off, leaving Jack alone in the bathroom.

A wave of dizziness hit him, and he leaned against the bathroom wall. When his vision righted, he changed into the clean track pants Eva had brought him and slid his feet back into his boots. Exhausted by the exercise, he waited, taking deep even breaths until he was able to raise a foot and rest it on the toilet lid. Sweat poured from his forehead as he fumbled with his laces.

Eva wasn't going to let him walk all over her, and why would she? They'd only known each other for five days, and that was more than four years ago. Every six months he transferred money into her account and then waited for the inevitable email asking him to stop. The only contact they had was the photograph she emailed him twice a year, on Poppy's birthday and at Christmas.

When both boots were back on, he gladly rid himself of the filthy shirt. The area around the wound was swollen and angry, but already the artificial stitches had started to work, holding the skin together and helping the blood to congeal. As he'd done many times before when he'd been on active duty, Jack tore open a gauze packet and placed a soft square of it over the wound before securing it with strips of surgical tape.

A second wave of dizziness flooded over him, and he leaned forward, bracing his hands on either side of the basin. Staring in the mirror at a leaner, dirtier reflection of himself, he tried to remember when he'd last eaten.

When his head cleared, Jack picked up the striped hoodie. He was fit, and his body would quickly make up the lost blood. But he needed a meal, painkillers and antibiotics to stave off infection—and, most of all, sleep.

He was sliding his arms into the sleeves when he heard them coming back. Eva was trying to pacify the little girl. 'I made dumplings for lunch. They're your favourite.'

After weeks in the back country existing on tinned food, chocolate and energy bars, the thought of dumplings had Jack salivating like Pavlov's dog. But as vital as it was to build his strength, he couldn't think of food right now. He needed to check the security of the lodge again in case he'd missed something in his haste. Steeling himself against the spreading ache in his abdomen, he leaned over and picked up the little girl's teddy bear. A few specks of dirt clung to its fur, and he hurriedly brushed them off before they could leave a mark.

Jack stepped out of the bathroom in time to see a juice popper fly across the lobby.

'She's not usually like this,' Eva said defensively as juice began to seep onto the tiles. 'It's you.'

He propped the bear on top of the reception desk. 'I'm going to take another look around.'

A handful of dying embers winked at him from the fireplace, a faint aroma of powdery ash wafting in the air. Pausing by the bannister, Jack looked down the shadowy staircase to where a faint wash of light was visible. The laundry light was clearly not on a timer. From memory, there were two more internal doors in addition to the laundry further along the hallway. One led into the garage, the other into some kind of storage room. The external door where he'd forced his way in was where they were most vulnerable.

At the windows, he parted the drapes again and made sure the locks were in good condition. He would check the windows in the suites later when he'd regained a bit of strength, but those rooms were high off the ground and had no direct access to the verandah at the front due to the natural slope of the land.

Back in the lobby, he was pleased to see that things had calmed down. Eva had wheeled the swivel chair out from behind the desk and Poppy was spinning it around giving her bear a ride. A light still shone from the bathroom where his putrid clothes lay in a heap on the floor. He caught Eva's eye as he moved past her to the front doors. Like many dwellings built in cold climates, the lodge had a vestibule, the extra room between two sets of double doors the most effective way to stop heat from escaping and cold getting in when guests were coming and going.

Satisfied that the sturdy outer doors were deadbolted, he was pushing his way through the glass-panelled inner doors when the sound of an approaching vehicle pulled him up fast. A truck in low gear was revving up the driveway.

❄

Eva hovered by Jack's shoulder while he shifted the curtain aside and peered at the vehicle. 'It's a faded burgundy four-wheel drive with a trailer,' he said.

Eva pushed in front, forcing him to take a step backwards. This was her life, her lodge. Jack Walker had burst in here unannounced, with a story of Gavin Hutton and revenge. How could she be sure

34

he wasn't weak and dehydrated from lack of food and water? Dehydration caused delirium. Worse still, he could be in the middle of a psychosis.

'It's probably Randall,' she said, putting her eye to the break in the curtain. 'It is. He's delivering the firewood.'

'Why's he stopping there?' he asked, moving up behind her again and peering over the top of her head.

'I keep the wood in the extra car space underneath so it stays dry. He always stops there and backs the trailer up.'

Jack pulled her away from the window. 'What's the normal routine?'

Normal routine? She wrenched her arm from his grasp. 'For God's sake, we're not the army.'

'Does he come in here first, or do you go out and meet him?'

'Most of the time I'm so busy I don't even realise he's arrived until I hear him under the house, or when he comes into reception to get his money.'

'You pay him cash?'

'Yes. He's a pensioner earning a few bucks on the side.'

'Does he use the bottom door like the other bloke did?'

Eva stared at his unreadable face. There was a faint bruise close to one temple, a vertical scratch on his neck. 'You mean Bede?'

He gave a careless shrug. 'If that's his name.'

'Yes, that is his name.'

'I need to know. That bottom door is where you're most vulnerable.'

She swung away, angry at his interrogation and eager to get back to Poppy. 'Randall always comes in the front doors,' she said over her shoulder, uneasy at how closely he was shadowing her. 'I pay him in notes from the petty-cash tin. That's the one you locked away in the drawer with my laptop.'

In the lobby, she watched as Jack dug in his pocket for the key and unlocked the drawer. Poppy had gone from spinning the bear in circles to wheeling the chair around the lobby like a pram. How was it that their lives had changed so much in an instant? One minute, she'd been looking forward to the snow season and happily chatting to Bede about his son's wedding, and the next . . .

'Take the exact amount with you to the door, and carry Poppy on your hip. She'll play up if you leave her with me.'

'I wonder why,' Eva muttered, reaching into the drawer for the tin. 'How long is he likely to be down there?'

She put the tin on the desk, the loose change rattling inside. 'Depends on how much firewood I need.'

'Act naturally, but get rid of him. If he's inclined to chat, apologise and say you're in the middle of something.'

'You know what?' she said, fumbling with the latch. 'How about you give me one good reason why I shouldn't just open up that door and ask Randall to call the police?'

Annoyance flashed in his eyes. 'Because the cops won't move quick enough to catch Hutton. They'll just scare him off. Good enough reason?'

Eva shoved some notes into the back pocket of her jeans and lowered her voice to a whisper so Poppy couldn't hear. 'That's preferable to being held hostage in my own home.'

Jack closed his eyes for a second before opening them wide as though he were clearing his vision. Then he moved to the glass front doors and waited, listening for Randall's approach.

'If they don't apprehend Hutton, he's always going to be a threat. The safest place for you and Poppy right now is here with me.'

'The safest thing is to call the police and then *leave*,' argued Eva. 'If Hutton's coming here, I can't think of a better reason to get in the car and get the hell out. You said yourself he wants revenge and he's coming after you.' Eva looked at her daughter, knowing she would give her own life to protect her. Poppy took a small sip from the juice box, the plastic straw turning orange. Then the little girl leaned forward and spoke in the bear's ear before holding the straw to its mouth.

Eva looked back in time to see that Jack had also been watching Poppy. 'That's where you're wrong,' he said, lowering his voice. 'It's true that Hutton wants revenge, but he's not coming after me. He's coming after you.'

Five

'Both Hutton's parents were heavy users—booze and drugs,' Ryder said, glancing at Sterling as he drove along the congested Woodville Road. 'There was neglect and domestic abuse during his formative years. At seven, he was made a ward of the state. Every foster parent—and there were many—described him as difficult to handle. They all said he was a loner, distrustful of people, quick to anger.'

Beside him, Sterling shook her head in resignation at the sad yet all too familiar story as Ryder took the turn-off onto the Hume Highway.

'He left school halfway through year eleven and joined the army. He served in Afghanistan mostly.'

'Was he violent towards Kimberley?'

'She said he wasn't, but admitted they argued a lot.'

'What about his extended family?'

'We haven't found any yet.'

A few moments of silence followed, and then Sterling spoke again. 'You said in the meeting that Hutton emptied his bank account after flying into the country.'

'That's right. He only uses cash. There's no paper or electronic trail to follow. That is what's making locating him so challenging.' Ryder checked his side mirror and changed lanes. 'We're waiting

37

for the company he worked for in Zimbabwe to release his file.' He glanced at the new recruit. 'Ever tried dealing with Zimbabwe?'

She smiled a little. 'Haven't had the pleasure yet.'

There was a brief pause.

'So, are you a Taree native?' Ryder asked.

'Wingham.'

'Ah, I've been up to Wingham Brush a couple of times.'

'It's a beautiful part of the world.'

The quiet conviction in her voice had him wondering how she was coping with life in the emerald city. Sydney wasn't for everyone. Ryder checked his speed, his thoughts shifting to Benson. The detective's jovial demeanour had been in short supply in recent weeks, and the thought that he might request a transfer back to Queanbeyan made Ryder nervous—Inspector Gray had made it perfectly clear they wouldn't have the numbers to replace him.

'I read in your application that you're a keen water skier,' he said to Sterling, shaking away thoughts of Benson. Ryder always found the information listed under 'leisure activities' the most interesting part of a resume. Every applicant was 'hard working, motivated and enjoyed new challenges', but you could tell a lot about a person by what they did in their spare time. 'Did you grow up skiing on the Manning River?'

'Yep. I had hopes of turning professional, but I wasn't quick enough.'

Ryder nodded, pleased to see Sterling remained alert throughout the conversation, eyes scanning the heavy traffic and nearby surroundings. 'My girlfriend was a ski patroller for many years,' he said.

'Snow skiing is a completely different technique to water skiing.'

'So she tells me.'

'What does she do now?'

Ryder glanced at the dashboard's digital time display, a twinge of worry unfurling in his stomach. 'She works as a rep for one of the big ski brands.' Vanessa had a long drive ahead of her from Mount Beauty today. He would be glad to see her safely back in Sydney tonight. 'Are you hoping to do some water skiing while you're stationed down here?'

'I am. I have a caravan and a boat on the banks of the Hawkesbury.'

'The Hawkesbury? That's a long commute.'

Sterling laughed. 'Oh, no, I've rented a unit in Parramatta, about five minutes from the station. I'll only be up at the Hawkesbury on my days off. A friend of mine owns a property with a river frontage.' She glanced at him uncertainly, as though wondering how much she should tell him. 'He's a driver, like me, in the bridge to bridge.'

Ryder couldn't hide his surprise. 'You're a speedboat driver?'

She gave him a wry look. 'Like many who didn't make the grade.'

'That's interesting.'

'It's a lot of work, training with the skier behind the boat,' she said.

'And a lot of responsibility, too, for the skier's safety.'

Sterling turned away to gaze out the window again. 'Yeah, there's that as well,' she said quietly.

Five minutes later, he pulled the unmarked car into the high-school carpark. A white sign with an arrow pointed the way to the principal's office.

'Takes me back,' said Sterling as they set off down the pathway. 'I spent a bit of time in the principal's office myself.'

Ryder smiled, surprised at her openness. A bell rang, its long, high-pitched wail cutting through the air like a siren.

The reception area hadn't changed since his visit last year. The school crest was mounted above the desk, while framed awards lined the walls, testament to students' academic achievements, prize-winning artworks and champion sports teams. Two girls sat quietly together. One looked ill, like she might be waiting for someone to come and collect her. Her friend was lending support. A boy sat nursing his right hand, his nose bloodied, his lower lip swollen as though he'd been in a fight.

Ryder and Sterling remained standing.

Before too long, the receptionist appeared with the principal in tow. Meredith Evans wore her suit jacket slung around her shoulders like a cape, her dark hair styled into a heavy bun. 'Detectives,' she said, glancing at them briefly.

Before Ryder could answer, she spoke to her charges: 'Ryan, I'll deal with you shortly.' Then to the girl who was clearly unwell: 'Rebecca, your father is on his way to pick you up. If you could go and wait in the sick bay, please.' And, finally, to Rebecca's friend: 'Maddison, run down to the history staffroom and fetch Mr Carmen. Tell him he's needed urgently in the principal's office.'

＊

Ryder figured Matthew Carmen had to be nearing retirement age. He watched as the history teacher with scruffy grey hair and beard settled himself into the principal's chair. After apologising twice for the meeting room being unavailable, Meredith Evans finally left them alone.

'Mr Carmen, thanks for calling the hotline,' Ryder began before introducing himself and Sterling. He lifted up his mobile phone. 'I'd like to record what you've got to say about Gavin Hutton, if that's okay by you.'

'That's totally fine,' the history teacher said. He shifted around, straightening his brown tweed jacket and looking out of place in the principal's chair. Ryder brought up the recording app on his phone, understanding Carmen's nervousness—the teacher was about to give the police information about a wanted killer.

Ryder put his phone on the desk. 'Just take your time and tell us what you know about Gavin Hutton.'

The teacher licked his lips. 'I remember him being a troubled youth when I taught him years ago. He had a quick temper in the playground, and on the footy field. I used to coach the school side in those days, and I had him for modern history as well. Every so often he wouldn't show up. He'd just go AWOL for a week. I remember calling his foster parents and they said it wasn't unusual. Apparently they'd notified the police the first few times but eventually gave up. I got the impression they thought getting on his back about it would only make things worse.'

'We've heard the same story from every foster family he was with. He'd disappear periodically, then suddenly reappear.'

Carmen nodded. 'For a while there, I thought I was getting somewhere with him. I'd been an army cadet, and in those days I was still in the reserves. I felt the army would be good for him, straighten him out, instil in him what he lacked, which was discipline and a respect for authority.'

'Seems he took your advice,' Ryder said.

'He did. He dropped out of year eleven and enlisted. I felt like celebrating at the time, it seemed like a massive victory, but now . . .' Matthew Carmen gave a regretful shake of his head, the weight of his actions clearly troubling him. 'Perhaps encouraging him to join the armed forces was a mistake. I worry it could have desensitised him further.'

'What about friends?' Ryder asked. 'Was there anyone he was particularly friendly with?'

Carmen shook his head again. 'No one in particular. He used to spend a lot of time at the boxing gym down by the railway line, though. He could have been friendly with someone down there.'

'The gym in Martinsfield?'

'Yeah, I recommended he try out the gym. He'd been teaching himself hand-to-hand combat skills from a book he'd borrowed from the library.'

'Is the gym still there?'

'Yep, I walked past it the other day.'

Ryder switched off the recording app, trying to curb his excitement over the new lead. 'You've been extremely helpful, Mr Carmen.'

'I hope so.' The teacher looked at his watch. 'If it's okay, I might head off. I'm already late for second period. God knows what they'll be up to.'

Ryder smiled. 'We'll check out that gym, and if you think of anything else, please get in touch with us immediately.'

They filed out of the office, retracing their steps through the now empty reception area. 'We contacted his classmates last year, but he never kept in touch with any of them,' Ryder said to Sterling as they walked back to the car. 'Same with his army regiment.'

'He destroys all his relationships?'

'Sadly, I doubt he ever really learned how to make them in the first place.'

'Do you know where he went whenever he disappeared?' she asked.

'Nope, we keep running into dead-ends.'

'Maybe he was looking for his parents.'

Ryder nodded. 'That's one theory. They died within a few years of each other, both from a drug overdose. Their bodies were so debilitated from the effects of long-term substance abuse, it's difficult to know from the toxicology reports . . .' Ryder hit the key fob and the car lights flashed.

'Difficult to know what?' Sterling asked when they were back in the car.

Ryder placed his hands on the steering wheel and looked straight ahead to where two boys were playing handball on the pathway. 'Whether or not his mother and father were his first two kills.'

❋

Ten minutes later, Ryder parked in the narrow laneway that separated the railway line from a group of rundown buildings. The tempting aroma of banana bread drifted towards him from the nearby rustic cafe as he locked the car.

'That's cool,' said Sterling, pointing to a ramp at the front, whose decorative railing was made of repurposed steel and fashioned into a chunky steampunk design.

'The cake smells pretty good, too,' said Ryder with a smile.

They passed an artist's studio with dirty barred windows on either side of a graffitied roller door. Bald plaster busts peered out from behind the vertical bars like prisoners drawn to the light.

Further along they came to the gym's entrance, it's opening hours scrawled on a piece of plyboard and nailed to a wooden door with flaking green paint. Inside, Ryder waited for his eyes to adjust to the shadowy interior. A boxing ring stood in the centre of the space while around the perimeter various lengths of rope hung from overhead beams, a few with punching bags attached. An old split-cycle air conditioner laboured away on one wall, while rows of free weights and bar bells lined the other.

Ryder kicked aside a blue exercise ball and headed towards the ring where two men were sparring. Neither fighter looked up, too intent on ducking and weaving and landing the next punch. Above the ring, a metal fan rotated on slow.

'Morning fellas,' Ryder said loudly. 'Detectives Ryder and Sterling from Sydney Homicide.'

The men stilled and lowered their fists, their skin covered in a slick sheen of sweat. The shorter man was thickset, white and middle-aged. The younger man was of islander appearance and looked to be in his late teens.

Ryder opened his suit coat and flashed his badge.

'Go and cool down, Troy,' the older man said, pulling off his gloves and scooping up a towel from the corner of the ring. 'How can I help?' he asked, climbing through the ropes.

'We're looking for the owner?' said Ryder.

'You found him.' The man towelled himself off as he came towards them. 'Pete Hoffman,' he said between deep breaths. 'What's this about?'

'We're making enquiries about a man who used to come here.'

'Oh, yeah? How long ago?'

'Twenty-two years.'

Hoffman shook his head. 'I've only owned the place for eleven.'

'Who was the previous owner?'

'Old Clarey Amos. He started this place fifty years ago. Still comes in most days.' He tilted his head towards the rear of the property. 'He's out the back now.'

'Must be our lucky day,' said Sterling.

'I wouldn't count on it, he's got dementia; too many blows to the head in his fighting days.' Hoffman slung the towel over his shoulder and led the way towards the back of the gym. 'His long-term memory's not too bad, though.'

With the exception of a new-model laptop and laser printer, the gym's back room could have been an office graveyard. Two old

IBM golf ball typewriters sat on a ledge beside a photocopier of the same vintage and an antique duplicating machine. A sturdy black telephone with a straight cord and a silver dialling mechanism was among a pile of later-model phones in various colours, all with spiral cords. Everything in the room was coated in a generous layer of dust.

Ryder looked at the black-and-white photographs on the walls. Boxers stared menacingly into the camera; each with fists raised in a high guard to protect their face. None of the half-hidden faces were familiar to Ryder, but he guessed the old bloke searching through a filing cabinet at the back of the room would know.

'Clarey,' Hoffman called out.

'Who wants to know?' The old man swung around, his body stooped, tufts of white hair sticking out from beneath a newsboy cap. 'What can I do ya for?' he asked, his gaze taking in all three of them.

Ryder stepped forward and introduced himself and Sterling.

'Come to arrest me, have ya?' the old man asked, looking them up and down.

Ryder smiled at the old-timer. 'Are you confessing to a crime?'

Clarey's smile showed a disturbing number of missing teeth. 'Not today.'

'We'd like you to have a look at a few photographs, Mr Amos,' said Sterling. 'You might have seen this man's face already on the TV or in the newspaper.'

'Don't read the paper, don't watch the telly either.'

The old man's glassy-eyed stare hardly filled Ryder with confidence. 'We're going back twenty-two years,' he said. 'A former teacher told us he used to train here after school.'

Clarey frowned. 'We've had thousands through here since then.' He took the pictures from Sterling and held them at arm's length, the way you did when you needed reading glasses. 'What's he done?'

'Committed serious crimes,' said Sterling. 'Do you recognise him?'

'Is this him now?'

Ryder nodded. 'These are the most recent photos we have.'

Clarey shook his head. 'Nah, no idea. What's his name?'

'Gavin Hutton.'

Clarey blinked, and he squinted harder at the image. 'Strike a light,' he said softly.

'He was good at hand-to-hand combat,' Ryder pressed, afraid Clarey's memory might suddenly desert him.

'Too right he was. He showed promise but the poor bugger never had any money. I said if he cleaned up the gym, I'd train him for free.'

'That was good of you,' Ryder said, wondering whether Clarey Amos would have offered the same deal to a less talented fighter. 'Did he have any mates here, people he used to hang out with?'

'Never saw any. He always seemed to be on his own.'

'Would there be anything in the old newsletters?' asked Hoffman from the doorway.

Clarey gave him a blank look.

Hoffman shrugged. 'I thought he might be in one, if he competed.'

'I don't need 'em,' the old man scoffed. 'I can see from this that it's Hammer.'

'Hammer?' Ryder asked. '*Hammer Hutton*? Was that his fighting name?'

'Sure was.' Clarey gave Ryder a direct look, his eyes suddenly clear and focused. 'The ref had to stop every bout before he beat his opponent to a pulp.'

❄

Ryder pulled into the car dealership on Parramatta Road and climbed from the vehicle as the promotional banners scattered throughout the property flapped like wet sails in the stiff breeze. A portly salesman looked up from where he'd been polishing the bonnet of a midnight-blue sedan and ambled towards them. Ryder flashed his badge, stopping the bloke in his tracks. He pointed Sterling towards the service centre, up one end of the red-brick building away from the sparkling new-car showroom at the other end.

Kimberley Dickson was sitting behind the counter, a telephone receiver pressed to her ear, her dyed burgundy hair pulled severely back from her face. She looked up, eyes widening in alarm as Ryder stepped through the automatic doors. Covering the mouthpiece, she spoke to the bespectacled man beside her. 'This one's for me, Sean,' she said, signalling towards Ryder with her eyes. 'Can you take over this call for me?'

Despite his curiosity, the service manager picked up Kimberley's transferred call without protest.

Gavin Hutton's heavily pregnant former partner led them outside and around the corner of the building, moving with the tell-tale gait of a mum-to-be. 'We can talk here,' she said, casting her eyes up and down the cement path running the length of the building. 'No one's having a smoko right now.'

A year ago, the mere mention of a cigarette would have set off a craving in Ryder, to say nothing of the unpleasant aroma of stale butts wafting from the metal disposer on the wall. Thankfully, he'd kicked that habit to the kerb.

'What are you doing here?' Kimberley asked, clearly upset by their presence. 'Couldn't this have waited until after work?'

'We've had a call to the hotline,' Ryder said evenly. 'A reported sighting of Gavin.'

She groaned, eyes scanning the area. 'I'm permanent here now. I'm going on maternity leave next week. The company can't know about him. They'll fire me.'

'That would be unfair dismissal,' put in Sterling.

'Oh, get real,' Kimberley retorted. 'You think they'll worry about that when he could turn up here with a gun?' She rubbed a hand across her swollen belly, her eyes clouded with worry.

'We've had a reported sighting at Jervis Bay,' Ryder said quietly. 'Do you know if Gavin had any ties to the place?'

She shook her head. 'I don't even know where that is.'

'It's on the coast, near Nowra. Take your time. Might he have gone down there to visit friends or to fight?'

Her eyes snapped to his. '*Fight*?'

Ryder had been a cop long enough to know that the woman's surprise was genuine. 'He was a talented amateur boxer; his fighting name was Hammer Hutton.'

'Hammer Hutton,' she mouthed the words quietly to herself. 'I didn't know that. Maybe he thought it would frighten me.'

Ryder waited, giving her time to think. He knew that people's memories were notoriously unreliable. You could ask the same question a week apart and get two entirely different answers. 'Think, Kim. Jervis Bay. Could he have gone down there for work?'

She frowned. 'Is that anywhere near Berry—'

'Yes,' Sterling said quickly. 'It's about half an hour away.'

'Do you remember him going there?' asked Ryder.

'Well, that's the only place I ever remember him going for work. He did a course down there.'

An image of the picturesque rural village with its cafes and galleries formed in Ryder's mind. 'What kind of course?'

'Security.' Kimberley put her hand on her back and shifted uncomfortably. 'But I thought it was more than just Berry, something like Berryman . . . or Berryville.'

'Not Berridale?' Ryder asked.

'Yes, that's it. Is Berridale near Jervis Bay?'

'No, it isn't.' Ryder looked at Sterling, barely able to contain his excitement. 'But it is in the Snowy Mountains.'

'Can I go now?' Kimberley asked.

'One more thing. What company ran the course? Did he sign up online?'

'I have no idea. All I know is that the people doing the course had to leave their cars in Berridale and travel together from there. I don't know where they went after that. Gavin wasn't a talker, Detective, and we were almost over as a couple by then. He moved overseas pretty soon after that.' She checked the time on her watch. 'Look, I have to get back to work. They'll be wondering what's going on.'

Ryder nodded. 'Thank you for your time.'

They accompanied her back to the office, and Ryder waited until the curious manager was within earshot before giving Kimberley

47

LEE CHRISTINE

his card. 'Take this. I'll arrange for an hourly patrol to drive past your place. We've had reports of other letterboxes being broken into in your suburb. If we're unaware of a problem, we can't do anything about it, so thanks for alerting us.'

Kimberley turned it over in her hands before looking up at Ryder, her eyes shining with gratitude. 'Thank you for coming out. I was . . . worried about identity theft.'

'Well, mostly they're after credit cards,' Ryder said. 'If you're not due for a new one, I don't think you'll have much of a problem.'

'Good luck with the baby,' Sterling added as they turned and left the office. When they were outside, she looked at Ryder. 'What's the significance of the Snowy Mountains?'

'We've had credible reports of a man squatting in barns and sheds along the Alpine Way in the Snowies,' said Ryder. 'Several cars were broken into, but only cash, sleeping bags and first-aid kits were taken. Credit cards and other valuables were left behind, which sets them apart from other break-ins.'

'And Hutton uses cash only, no cards?'

Ryder was pleased at how closely the new recruit was paying attention. 'Right.'

Sterling paused before they got in the car. 'Smart lady, Kimberley Dickson, playing along with you like that.'

Ryder eyed the bumper-to-bumper traffic crawling along Parramatta Road, relieved they were only a few minutes from the station. 'Yep. She might not know where Jervis Bay is, but she's one hell of an actress.'

48

Six

'I've turned around.' Flowers' voice resonated from the speaker as Ryder pulled into the carpark at police headquarters. 'I was at Bulli when the sergeant at Jervis Bay called and told me not to bother coming down. Turns out it wasn't Hutton—it was a Norwegian tourist. Our May weather is warmer than Bergen in the height of summer apparently, perfect for sleeping on the beach.'

'Did he resemble Hutton at all?' Ryder asked.

'Around the same height but that's about it. The poor bloke had never heard of Gavin Hutton. He had no idea what was going on.'

'I'm as sick of these false sightings as you are,' Ryder said. 'But trust me, one day it'll be him. He can't hide forever.'

'Learn anything at the school, Sarge?' Flowers asked.

Ryder brought him up to date, recounting their trip to Martinsfield High School and then on to the gym where a young Hammer Hutton had turned his body into a lethal weapon.

Flowers gave a low whistle. 'Fergus Suter wouldn't have stood a chance against Hutton. We know Suter treated his body like a temple, but Dominic Burrows was high on meth. He would have taken it to Hutton with the superhuman strength they get from that drug.'

'Probably why the crime scene was a bloodbath. And that's not all . . .' Ryder summed up their conversation with Kimberley Dickson.

'A security course in Berridale?' Flowers mused. 'Why didn't she tell us about that before? I remember us asking her if Hutton had been to the Snowy Mountains.'

'I don't think we mentioned Berridale specifically. Anyway, I've been telling Sterling about the reported sightings last year, and how the trail went cold.'

'We did arrest the Charlotte Pass killer, though, so not all was lost,' said Flowers, his voice ringing with pride.

'A band is only as good as their last album, Flowers,' said Ryder.

'You'll have to get used to the music references, Sterling,' Flowers said with a sigh. 'Sarge is a frustrated rock star.'

❄

Ryder and Sterling had just arrived back at the station when a call came through from Vanessa. Ryder stopped by the water cooler in the corridor and put her on hold. She knew from experience he wouldn't keep her waiting long.

'Why don't you start searching online security courses, Sterling, particularly in New South Wales? Once you have a list, start calling around and asking if Hutton was a former participant.'

Sterling gave him a quick nod. 'Will do, Sarge.'

Ryder watched as she disappeared into the general office area then hit the hold button on his phone. 'Hello, Vanessa, are you still there?' he asked.

He heard her laugh. 'You're having a good day. I can hear the smile in your voice.'

'That's because I'm talking to you.' Holding the phone in one hand, he filled a plastic cup with water from the cooler and turned his back as a uniformed cop hurried past him. 'Where are you?'

'Khancoban. I've just stopped for a quick coffee.'

Ryder checked his watch. 'You've made good time. It's only eleven-thirty.'

'Yeah. I'm feeling a bit tired now, though. It's been a busy couple of days.'

'You've been doing a lot of long-distance driving.'

'I know, and I'm not used to it. I was thinking I might call into Eva's at Thredbo for a coffee, and if I don't get my energy back, I'll stay at the lodge overnight. I've bought something really cool for Poppy, too. I'd love to give it to her.'

'That sounds like a great idea. What did you get?'

'It's a surprise. You'll love it, Pierce. I'll take a photo and show you when I get home.'

Ryder smiled. He was picturing Vanessa, drinking coffee in a sun-filled country cafe, her long hair pulled up into a high ponytail. 'You drive safely, and let me know what you decide about tonight.'

'I will, Detective,' she laughed. 'I'll keep in touch.'

'Be safe, Vanessa.'

'You too.'

Ryder disconnected the call, sculled his water and threw the cup in the bin. He was almost at the door to the general office when it flew open to reveal a wide-eyed Nerida Sterling.

'I was coming to get you, Sarge,' she said in a rush, her lisp in full flight with her rising agitation. 'Jindabyne Police are on the phone.'

❄

Ryder summarised the Hutton update as best he could for Inspector Gray. 'A couple of campers in the Kosciuszko National Park called the Jindabyne Police. They reported smelling smoke when they woke up this morning. Anyway, these blokes are pretty experienced—they know campfires are illegal in the park—so they went looking for the source.'

Gray closed his eyes for a long second and rested his forehead in his hand. 'Thank God someone has a brain cell. The last thing we need is another bushfire.'

'They found the remnants of a small campfire and, worryingly, blood pooled on the ground and a pile of bloodied leaves. They had a scout around in case anyone was injured, but eventually went back to their camp. A couple of our boys up in Jindabyne are taking a look around there now.'

'So why ring Homicide? People go missing in national parks all the time.'

'I know, but it's almost winter, and it was about this time last year we had all those calls about a man sleeping in barns and sheds on outlying properties. The local boys up there know to contact me if anything out of the ordinary happens. What if this person, someone who is game enough to light a fire in the national park, is the same bloke who broke into those cars and squatted on private property? He could be making his way to lower ground again now it's winter.'

'Has anyone been reported missing?'

'No.'

The Inspector huffed. 'You can't assume that every lost or injured hiker is Gavin Hutton, or that he's responsible for every car break-in around the area. Bullocks Flat's notorious for it. Opportunists know the cars are there for a while.'

'These break-ins happened along the Alpine Way. And there's more, sir.' Ryder took a deep breath. 'We've just learned that Gavin Hutton did some kind of security course near Berridale before he went overseas. The signs are there. He's familiar with the Monaro area.'

The Inspector raised a bushy eyebrow. 'Go on, get to the point.'

'Sterling's searching for possible training companies. I'm just about to call the National Parks and Wildlife's central office to see if a permit is needed for that sort of business, so we can track down the company.'

The Inspector turned towards the window. 'You said this morning you were confident of a breakthrough. Is this it, do you think?'

Ryder hesitated, reluctant to commit. 'It's a strong lead, Inspector, and we haven't had one in a while. The National Parks central office could take weeks to get back to us. I think we should visit the local office in Jindabyne. They're the ones who have face-to-face contact with the people running these businesses.'

'You want to break with procedure and go down there? Without a body?'

Ryder paused. 'I already have two bodies. I don't want any more.'

❄

Ryder called Flowers the moment he left the Inspector's office.

'Hey, Sarge?'

'Call into your place, Flowers, and pack a bag.' Ryder looked at his watch. It had just gone midday. 'Meet us at the Big Merino in Goulburn at, say, two-thirty?'

There was a surprised pause, then Flowers said, 'Okay. Where are we going?'

'Bring your heavy-weather gear, Daisy, and you might want to grab a final turmeric latte. We're heading back to the Snowy Mountains.'

Seven

Eva bundled Poppy into her puffer jacket, then slid the white beanie with the fluffy pink pompom over her soft curls. 'We won't be outside for long,' she said. 'We're just going to say hello to Randall.'

Eva slipped on her jacket, the fingers on her right hand stiff and sore from where she'd hit Jack on the chin. It took three attempts to close the zipper.

Conscious of Jack's hulking frame behind the door that remained closed, Eva settled Poppy onto her hip, and opened the adjacent door to a sub-zero howl of wind and the sound of stones crunching beneath Randall's boots.

'Ah, I wasn't sure if you were home.' He climbed the three steps to the verandah and approached the lodge's entrance, snow flurries speckling his beanie and jacket.

'Hello, Mr Randall,' Poppy piped up before Eva could speak. 'Bede ... got married where Mummy's seahorse came from, and then the other man fell off the mountain and came to our place ...'

'Oh, no, Bede didn't get married, it was his son,' Eva interrupted Poppy's rambling recount of their day and twisted her lips into a smile. 'How are you, Randall?'

She surveyed the clearing from the doorway, her heart thumping uncomfortably. It was large enough for over-snow vehicles to drop guests off once the driveway became inaccessible to cars. Now it was covered in a layer of snow that would be gone within the hour if more didn't fall. Beyond the clearing, the tree-covered terrain sloped upwards towards the Thredbo ski slopes and beyond to the white-capped mountains of the Crackenback Range.

'Can't complain, Eva.' Randall stroked his white bristles and winked at Poppy. 'I called a couple of times to let you know I was on my way, but it went straight to voicemail.'

Eva nodded, her mind frantically searching for an excuse. Her regular contacts like Randall knew she returned calls promptly. 'Oh, sorry, I . . . um . . . I have a new phone,' she said, willing her honest little daughter not to pipe up and contradict her. 'I've been trying to set it up.'

Randall chuckled. 'Funny, isn't it? Those young people working for the telcos tell you how easy it is. "Just put everything up in the cloud," they say, "then download it onto the new phone. *Easy*."' He chuckled again. 'No, thank you. I'll hang onto my old flip phone.'

A movement in the thick line of gum trees drew Eva's attention. There was something or somebody in there, beyond the wooden barbecue tables and benches that stayed outside all year-round. Poppy's swing, fixed to one of the sturdiest gums, swayed back and forth in the wind. It hadn't been the swing she'd noticed, though; it was something else. Eva shivered, straining to see any further movement, aware of Jack as he listened to everything she and Randall said, his back to the unopened door beside her.

'Temperature's dropping,' said Randall, looking skywards while Eva pulled the money from her back pocket and gave the notes to Poppy.

'You can give them to Randall,' she said.

Poppy took the notes and held them out.

'Oh, twenty is enough. You only needed a top-up today.'

Eva pointed to the twenty-dollar note, hoping Randall didn't see the tremor in her hand. 'Give Randall that one, darling,' she said.

Eva scanned the clearing again, searching for whatever had been moving out there. It was probably just a wombat, or one of the eastern grey kangaroos that occasionally drifted with their mob past her lodge. But Jack's presence had her on watchful tenterhooks for human danger. And if it were human, they could have used the lonely trail that led through the trees to the Willy Wagtail, or the second trail linking the Golden Wattle with the ski runs.

'Thank you, sweetheart,' Randall was saying, holding up the twenty-dollar note and smiling at Poppy. 'You didn't have to raid your moneybox, did you?'

Poppy gave him a bashful smile and shook her head.

'Okay, Eva, I'll be on my way. I'll see you in a fortnight,' Randall said, heading off down the verandah stairs.

'Randall?' His name burst from her lips before she could stop them. This could be her last bid for escape.

'Yep?'

You and Poppy will be safest here, with me.

Eva hesitated, a pulse fluttering in her throat. Despite every logical thought urging her to act, gut instinct prevented her from speaking.

A rabbit shot out of the trees and hopped into the clearing. Poppy squealed in her ear and yelled, 'Bunny!'

Eva put a hand to her chest and smiled weakly. 'Oh, never mind, it's just a rabbit.'

Randall looked towards the animal, then raised a hand. 'Cheerio then, ladies.'

Eva stepped backwards into the lobby, and Jack locked the door. 'Quick thinking with the new mobile,' he said, listening for the sound of Randall's footsteps dying away.

'I was lucky. I'm not a natural liar.'

'Really?' His eyes narrowed. 'That light is still switched on in the laundry.'

Eva swallowed. 'I want the full story from the start,' she said, setting a struggling Poppy on the floor and praying her intuition hadn't deserted her. 'Don't leave anything out.'

'You'll get it, but I'm not talking in front of her.' He dug into his pocket and took out her sim. 'Randall said he called you. We need to check your voicemail to see if anyone else has.'

'Mummy, I'm hungry,' Poppy whined.

Eva looked at her watch, surprised to see it was almost 12.30 pm. 'Okay, let's take off our jackets first. Then we'll have some lunch.'

While Jack slid the sim card back into her phone, Eva began to heat up the dumplings in the steamer. When the phone had booted up, he plugged in the password and showed Eva the screen.

Three calls. The first recorded a number only, the second was from Vanessa and the third showed no caller ID.

'Do you recognise the number?' he asked.

Eva shook her head. 'It could be Randall's.'

With the dumplings steaming and the phone on loudspeaker, they listened to her voicemail announce three new messages.

'Hello, Eva,' Randall's voice came through the speaker. 'I'm dropping firewood off to Bede today. I thought I may as well top-up your supply while I'm out that way. Anyway, it doesn't matter if you're not home, I'll get the money next time. Thanks.'

The next voice message was from Vanessa. 'Hi, Eva, it's me. I've stopped at Khancoban on my way back to Sydney. I was thinking I might call in for a coffee and maybe stay over if I'm too tired to drive. Happy to be bumped if you've got a hot guy there, though.' Vanessa chuckled at their in-joke. Her younger sister knew full well Eva wasn't interested in any kind of relationship when Poppy was so young, but it didn't stop her teasing Eva. 'Anyway, I should be there in about an hour and a half.'

Eva looked at Jack in alarm. 'What time did that message come through?'

'An hour ago,' he said, glancing at the oven clock. 'She's half an hour away. I don't care what you tell her, just put her off.'

Eva's mind scrambled for excuses while she returned Vanessa's call. But, no matter how good the excuse, there was a chance her sister would pick up on the strain in her voice.

'Hey, Eva. What are you up to?'

Eva took a deep breath. 'Oh my God, Vanessa, I am *crazy* busy. Sorry I missed your call.'

'You sound stressed. What's going on?'

57

Eva set the microwave for one minute and closed the door loudly, hoping the kitchen noises would back up her lie. 'You remember that cooking class I held here over the Jazz Festival weekend?'

'Yep.'

Eva banged a plate down on the stainless steel benchtop, hoping Vanessa would put the agitation in her voice down to stress. 'Well, I decided to hold another one. I mean, I'm organised, and the season opening is still a few weeks away.' She paused. 'I thought why not.'

Vanessa laughed. 'And now you're regretting it?'

'A bit.' She hurriedly grabbed a jar of peanut butter and spread it onto a slice of bread. 'I mean, I can't complain, it's good money, but—' Eva closed her eyes, wretched at having to lie to her beloved younger sister—'the lodge is full. I don't have a free room.'

'That's fine. Don't feel bad, Evie. I crash at your place all the time. I'll book a room in Jindy if I get tired.'

'Promise me you will? I'm sorry.' At least that sounded heartfelt.

'Hey, don't stress. I was hoping to give Poppy a pair of skis I bought for her, but it can wait until next time. Oh my God, Evie, they're pink, and soooo cute.'

Despite the tension in the kitchen, Eva couldn't help but smile at the excitement in her sister's voice. From the moment Poppy had been born, Vanessa had been waiting for the day she could put her niece on a pair of skis. Eva set the slice of bread in front of Poppy, who was already sitting up at the table, and then looked over at Jack. 'I know she'll be safe with you, Vee. I wouldn't trust anyone else to teach her.'

'The most important thing is, we have to pick our day. Warm, sunny and no wind. We want her first experience to be a good one. How is my favourite niece?'

'She's fine. She's eating a sandwich.' Eva swallowed the lump in her throat, reluctant to let her sister go but knowing she must. 'Okay, I have to run. We're just taking a quick break. I'll give you a call when I can.'

'Sounds good. See ya.'

Eva hung up. Jack was at the sink. 'Would she call in unannounced to help you out?' he asked after he'd drained a glass of water.

She shook her head. 'It's not in Vanessa's nature to arrive without calling first.'

'I hope you're right. If she did, she'd wonder where all the cars were.'

Eva looked at him in dismay. She hadn't thought of that. Vanessa would know right away that Eva had lied.

'Is Auntie Nessa coming?' Poppy spoke around the bread in her mouth. 'What did she get me?'

'It's a surprise and, no, she can't make it today unfortunately.' Eva turned away from the disappointment in her daughter's eyes.

Jack pointed at the phone. 'Ring the voicemail again.'

Eva skipped the first two calls this time. Jack was standing, head lowered, his hands braced on the kitchen bench. The voicemail service announced the third message. Jack straightened and together they stared at the phone.

Silence. Then the tiniest shift of sound, like someone was listening on the other end. Then the call ended.

'Get many calls like that?' Jack asked.

'The odd one. Do you . . .' Eva lowered her voice so Poppy couldn't hear what she was saying. 'Do you think it could be him?'

'It's unlikely he'd have a phone. He flies under the radar. I'm not discounting it, though. He could have stolen one.'

'Tell me what he's like,' she whispered. 'Physically and mentally? Does he look different to the police sketch?'

'You'd recognise him, especially now you're on the lookout. He's leaner but he's retained most of his strength. Mentally . . .' He paused to consider her question. 'I had reservations about him when he was here doing the course. He wasn't a team player, and he had a chip on his shoulder the size of Uluru. Former soldiers are often complex, but their skill set is in high demand.'

Jack Walker would know all about that, Eva thought. 'What kind of a job did Hutton want?'

'A high-paying one overseas, protecting oil and gas plants, airstrips and mines. They're mostly American-owned companies, sometimes Australian.'

Eva shook her head. It was going to take more than a quick conversation in the middle of the kitchen to get to the crux of this story. She glanced at Poppy, thankful she was still eating her sandwich.

'I know he was offered work in Zimbabwe,' Jack said. 'After that, I dropped out of the industry, so I wasn't in contact with him.'

Eva tried to hide her surprise. 'I assumed you were still running those courses, that you'd chosen to stay at a different lodge. I mean, it would have made sense.'

He shook his head. 'The course I ran here was the final one. When you came to Sydney to tell me you were pregnant, I'd just signed a contract for a new job.'

Eva tried to hide her surprise. So much for all those times she'd kept an eye out for him when she'd been in Jindabyne.

Suddenly, his face drained of colour. He pulled a chair out from the table and sat down heavily opposite Poppy.

'How long since you've eaten?' Eva asked, alarmed at the fresh sweat breaking out on his face.

Jack shook his head. 'I can't remember.'

Eva took half the dumplings out of the steamer and put them on a plate. They'd only take seconds in the microwave. Hurrying, she grabbed one of Poppy's juices from the fridge.

'Mummy?'

'Yep?' She inserted the straw and put it down in front of Jack. 'Drink that.'

The microwave beeped.

'*Mummy?*'

'Hmm?' Eva took the plate from the microwave and put it on the table. The last thing she needed was Jack passing out in the middle of the kitchen. She stilled, watching him as another thought popped into her mind: if he did pass out, she could call the police and an ambulance, then escape in her car.

But what if he's telling the truth?

He blinked hard, then opened his eyes wide as though trying to clear his vision. No, whatever was going on, she needed to stay calm. In his current state, he didn't pose a threat to them, and it was important she find out the whole story. Finally, he reached out and picked up one of the dumplings.

'Mummeeeee!' Poppy howled, her lower lip quivering as she stared at Jack. 'Why did you just give him my food?'

'What? Oh, Poppy.' Eva picked up her daughter and rocked her. The little girl buried her face in Eva's neck and sobbed her heart out. 'It's okay. There are more in the steamer. I think he just needs some sugar. How about we get him some of your sultanas?' she said with false brightness. 'Would you like some, too?' She carried Poppy into the walk-in pantry. 'I know they're in here somewhere.' Damn! Where were they?

'Eva?'

She wheeled around. Jack was hunched over the table, his eyes closed, his head supported in his hands. 'I don't need sultanas. I need paracetamol, ibuprofen and antibiotics if you have any,' he said quietly.

Repositioning Poppy on her hip, she began a thorough search of all the medications she kept locked away out of Poppy's reach. 'I have some. People are always getting injured down here and asking for them.'

'I'm sure there's some leftover antibiotics in my ensuite,' she said, putting the tablets on the table. She watched as he burst open blister packs of painkillers and washed them down with orange juice. 'I'll get them.'

Murmuring soothing words to Poppy, Eva made her way through the lounge room, which was becoming shadowy and quiet and much colder as the temperature plummeted without the warmth of the fire she'd shared with Bede only three hours ago.

'Here we go,' she said, opening the door to their rooms and putting Poppy down. Spacious enough to accommodate both her queen-sized bed and Poppy's single bed comfortably, it was the only suite located at the front of the lodge. She ran her eyes over the familiar room, comforted by its soothing ambience, the colourful bedspreads with their wildflower print, the antique dressing table with the wooden jewellery box that Poppy had raided earlier, and the giant panda sitting on the cane chair in the corner.

She went into the ensuite, retrieved the packet of antibiotics from the cupboard and returned to the bedroom.

'Feeling better now?' she asked, engulfed with love for her tiny daughter.

Poppy nodded, her eyes red from crying, her soft cheeks still damp with tears. 'I want Bunce,' she said, pointing to the soft pink teddy bear Vanessa had given Poppy for her first birthday.

'Sure. Let's get him.' Eva walked over to Poppy's bed and scooped up Bunce the bear.

'There you go.' She put the bear into her daughter's arms, relieved to see a hint of a smile on Poppy's face as she hugged the toy. Eva knew she needed to make things as normal as she could for Poppy, or this situation could have a devastating effect on her. Living in the lodge was challenging enough for a three year old, and Poppy had needed to adapt to a lot of comings and goings in her home life that other children weren't faced with. The seasonal changes and busyness of lodge life meant it was difficult for Eva to keep her in a routine. The Golden Wattle could be full of rowdy ski parties in winter, and mountain bikers and bushwalkers in summer. Of course, there were plenty of families, too, with kids of all ages for Poppy to play with, but they were mostly transitory; there for a week at a time and then off home again. And as close as they were to Eva's parents and to Vanessa and Pierce, until Poppy went to primary school in Jindabyne, Eva would be the only constant in her young life.

'How about we close the curtains and make our room cosy for your afternoon nap later?' she murmured to Poppy, who'd climbed onto her bed. The side window of their suite looked over the driveway that led into the garages where Randall had left the firewood. Their front window faced the clearing where the rabbit was now nowhere to be seen. The sky was an ominous leaden grey, the cloud cover so thick and low it was dark enough to be late afternoon rather than lunchtime. 'The snow's getting heavier,' she said to Poppy. 'Do you see how big those flakes are now?'

Poppy nodded, but she gave the falling snow only a cursory glance.

Eva reached up and pulled the heavy curtain across the side window, blocking out the view of the driveway. 'We don't want a draft coming in through the windows.'

It was when Eva was drawing the curtain across the front window that she noticed something in the snow cover in the clearing that hadn't been there when she'd spoken to Randall earlier. Leaning closer, she peered through the thin layer of condensation, a sign the outside temperature was dropping. The wind had picked up, too, strong gusts rattling the windows and slamming tiny shards of ice into the glass.

Eva squinted harder. What *was* it she could see down there?

It was then she realised that it was a set of footprints, partially obscured by the fresh snowfall. They were leading from her front verandah to the trail to the Willy Wagtail. Or was it the other way round? From this distance it was impossible to tell which direction the person had been travelling in.

Eva tightened her grip on the packet of antibiotics. Randall had stuck to the landscaped gravel path before coming up onto the verandah and then he'd gone back the same way. He'd had no reason to cross the clearing. Both Bede and Jack had avoided the front entrance and used the bottom door.

A strange feeling that someone was watching her made her step away from the window. Was someone out there now, looking up at the lodge, waiting?

A faint noise behind her made Eva freeze, the hairs on the back of her neck standing on end.

Slowly, she turned around.

Eight

Memories of the last time he'd been in Eva's room stormed into Jack's mind as he waited in the doorway. The perfectly made bed that they'd messed up night after night four years ago had an updated doona and a pile of matching cushions. The single bed beside the queen, with its fluffy animals in lieu of cushions, definitely hadn't been part of the furniture.

'Is everything all right?' he asked. She was watching him warily, her arms wrapped protectively around the child. 'You were gone a while.'

'Did you think I was going to do a runner?'

He shrugged. That was exactly what he'd thought.

'I found the antibiotics,' she said, her shoulders lowering like she'd exhaled some of the pent-up tension. 'They're not long out of date, so they should be fine.'

'Thanks.' He turned to go, expecting her to follow, but when he looked around, she'd put the child down on the bed. Poppy began to play with one of her fluffy animals. Eva moved towards the window.

'Did you come to the front door today?' she asked, a frown line creasing her forehead. 'Before you knocked on the bottom door, I mean.'

'No.'

'I think you should take a look at this.'

Jack walked briskly to the window. Eva shifted aside so he could peer through the glass.

'Look at the clearing beyond the entrance. Can you see footprints? A lot of snow has fallen, so they're hard to see.'

From where he was standing, Jack could see the wooden steps leading up to the verandah. Sure enough, there was a set of footprints in the snow heading towards the opposite end of the building.

'I was closing the curtains when I saw them,' she said. 'They weren't there when I went out to pay Randall. I would have noticed them.'

Randall had retraced his steps back to his car, passing directly below where they were standing now. 'What about Bede?' he asked. 'Does he ever use the front door?'

Eva shook her head. 'Never.'

'You were right to show me,' he said, drawing the curtain across the window. 'They either went around behind the lodge or they headed off into the trees. Or, they came from that direction and walked to the bottom of the stairs, and maybe up onto the verandah.'

'It's hard to know which way they were going without seeing the prints up close,' Eva said. 'Occasionally we get people cutting across the clearing, but . . . .'

Jack spun around and headed for the door. 'They don't come that close to the lodge?'

'Exactly.'

He could hear her behind him, coaxing the child off the bed and back into her arms before closing the bedroom door.

'Where are you going?' she asked when they reached the lounge room.

'To check the place out again. Those two other doors under the stairs, one goes into the garage, right?'

'Yes, the other is an equipment room. There are some metal racks in there, that's all.'

'And the garage is unlocked?'

She nodded, real fear in her eyes now.

'Okay, stay here by the fire and let me do this alone,' he said. 'I won't be long.'

Eva nodded.

Jack went to the top of the stairs, then paused to look back at Eva. As he watched, she picked up a piece from the chess set and gave it to Poppy.

'Horsey,' said Poppy, jumping it over its fellow chess pieces.

Moving more easily now the painkillers had kicked in, Jack checked the bottom door first. When he was satisfied the lock hadn't been tampered with, he doubled back to the laundry. The door had stood open earlier when Eva's so-called timer light had been spilling its beams out into the hallway. He hadn't heard it close from upstairs since then, but that was hardly surprising. Most likely it had drifted shut after Eva had taken the doorstop to clobber him with.

Even so, he was on high alert as he turned the handle and burst into the room. It was a standard laundry with one entrance, and empty. He opened the cupboard door. Nothing inside but extra towels and a pile of clothes similar to the ones he was wearing.

Switching off the light, he moved out into the hallway again and towards the two doors located at the rear of the stairs. He opened the first one. A sensor light came on. The room was a concrete box, no windows, bare except for the ski racks Eva had told him about.

Next was the internal access to the garage. Putting an ear to the door, he listened for movement from the other side. All was quiet, though he could tell from the bitingly cold draught at his feet that Randall hadn't put the roller door down after leaving the wood. Slowly, Jack opened the door. Again, a sensor light flickered on as the bracing air cleared Jack's head. Casting his eyes around the garage, he took note of the wood stacked in a neat pile in front of him and the late-model SUV parked nose-in on the other side. A range of handheld garden tools hung from a peg board on the wall beside a pair of skis mounted on brackets. On a bench fixed into the wall was a hedge trimmer, a drill set and a leaf blower.

Jack stepped through the doorway and did a circuit around the woodpile, checking under the car and making sure the vehicle was locked. Locating the door control panel on the wall, he pressed the button and stood looking out onto the driveway until the roller door had fully closed.

He turned to go when his attention was drawn to a bulky control panel for an alarm system mounted on the wall beside the door. At a guess, it looked to be around thirty-five years old, and had probably been installed when the lodge was built.

'All good so far,' he said when he arrived back in the lounge room. Eva was standing by the fireplace, clutching a heavy brass fire poker, her eyes following his every move. Jack was pretty confident she wasn't going to use it on him, and given the lioness look in her eyes, that was a massive relief. Poppy was still playing with the chess set.

Jack went through to the lobby and checked the bathroom, vestibule and the front-door deadlocks. Back in the lounge room, he examined the window locks again; they were the only ones with direct access to the verandah. 'I'll look at the suites now,' he said.

His memory was serving him well. There were doors on either side of the lounge room. Both led into a narrow hallway that in turn gave access to the suites: three on either side of the building, the windows at first-floor level due to the slope of the land. Only the lobby, the lounge room and Eva's suite at the front of the lodge had views over the clearing.

Jack tested the window locks, scanned the snow on the ground for footprints and noted which rooms had ceiling access.

'All secure,' he said when he joined her. 'How many magic buttons do you have for the garage?'

'Two. One's in the car. I keep the spare in the safe.'

'Good. That alarm system—are you able to isolate sectors of the building?'

Eva shook her head. 'No. It's really old. I used it a few times when I first moved in but gave up. It's no use when guests are in-house, and even when there's only Poppy and me, I don't bother with it. It has a tendency to malfunction in bad weather.'

'Sounds like it's more trouble than it's worth. My main concern is that external bottom door.' The one he and Bede had used. 'How many people have a key to it?'

'My cleaner has one, and the guests get one with their room key.'

'On the same keyring?'

'Yep. They're hanging on the board behind the reception desk.'

Jack had seen the board. 'A physical key is not a secure system. Not by a long way.'

'Most of the lodges work that way except the bigger ones that stay open twenty-four seven. The guests take the key with them. If they come in after Poppy and I have gone to bed, and the door is locked, they can let themselves in.'

Jack tensed. 'Have you had any keys go missing?'

'Of course. People lose them all the time. I've had guests ring me up apologising because they've found a key in their jacket pocket when they've got home. Some have mailed them back to me.'

'You need better security,' he said. 'When this is over, have a keypad lock installed on that bottom door and make sure you change the code every week. Got it?'

She gave a brief nod. 'Got it.'

Poppy raised her hands, wanting to be picked up. 'Mummy, I'm sleepy.'

'Okay, come on.' Eva lifted her up with a tired sigh, kissing Poppy's forehead as she laid her head on her mother's shoulder. 'How about you watch a movie in our room?' she asked. 'Like you do when I'm busy with guests?'

The little girl lifted her head, suddenly wide awake. '*Moana*?'

Eva smiled. '*Moana* it is.'

❄

Jack took two pieces of wood from the basket and arranged them inside the fireplace along with kindling and crunched-up newspaper.

'It's important we keep the fire going,' he said when Eva came back. 'If Hutton does turn up, he'll watch the place for a while and try to work out how many people are here.'

'You have to tell me why he's after *me*,' she said, folding her arms and standing closer to the fire. 'Do you realise how crazy all this sounds?'

'Yeah, I do,' Jack said, picking up the firelighter from the mantelpiece.

'What does he think I did to him?' she asked.

'*You* didn't do anything.' He set the newspaper alight and waited until he heard the first pop as the kindling caught fire. 'I did.'

'What did you do?'

'It's a long story, and not a good one. His plan is to punish me by getting to you and Poppy. That's his modus operandi.'

'How do you know it is?'

'Because he's done it to others.'

'But we're not even—' Eva waved a hand backward and forward between the two of them '—together.'

'He doesn't know that.'

She frowned, tired circles under her eyes. 'How did he even find out about me? We've only seen each other once in four years.'

'I know, and I get how confusing this is for you.' God only knew it had taken him long enough to work it out. 'He tracked down a close friend of mine, Julieann.'

'Who's Julieann?'

Jack nodded at the couch. 'There was a day when I was twelve that changed my life. You might want to sit down while I tell you a story.'

69

Nine

Jack sprinted barefoot down the bush track that ran parallel to the train line. He kept to the higher side of the track, steering clear of the grassy tufts in the hollows, his feet finding the footfalls in the hard earth without him needing to look. He knew every rock to push off, every branch to duck under, and the exact spot from which to launch himself across the metre-wide ditch so he nailed the landing on the other side. Excitement spurring him on, he waved at a neighbour walking his greyhounds, then tore past the corner pub with its cream-and-green ceramic tiles and black wrought-iron verandah, where two old timers sat in the same positions every day.

'Mum!' he yelled before he'd reached the gate of the tiny miner's cottage. Barely puffing, he leaped onto the porch before charging through the front door. 'Mum, guess what?'

His mother appeared at the end of the hallway, still in her supermarket uniform of black pants and green blouse.

'Sam's mum asked me to go to One Mile Beach with them for two weeks in the Christmas holidays.' Jack glanced into the living room as he hurried down the hallway. His father and grandfather were sitting in their usual spots in front of the television, having finished their shifts at the colliery. Side by side, they were surly and silent, the only sound the familiar voice of the race caller coming from the television. 'Can I go, Mum? Please?'

'Who's going, love?' asked his mother in her soft Irish accent.

'Just Sam and his mum. His dad's still at sea. They're taking the caravan.'

Jack could barely control his excitement. Staying on the beach for two whole weeks with his best mate. It would be so much fun, so much better than spending the holidays watching people go in and out of the pub, or hanging around with the high-school boys while they talked about how they were going to hot up their cars when they were old enough to buy one. There wasn't even a council swimming pool nearby. Last Christmas holidays, he'd caught the train into Newcastle practically every day so he could swim at the beach.

'Well, you should be okay with Sam and his mum, but you'll have to ask your father.'

Jack nodded. He knew better than to interrupt his father while he was poring over the form guide and watching the races, though. He'd wait until after dinner to ask.

✳

Jack blinked, his body relaxed, his limbs tired from days of swimming. He frowned at the blurry face in front of him and then sat bolt upright, gazing at the unfamiliar surroundings.

Sam was standing beside Jack's camp bed in the annexe attached to his parents' caravan. 'Wake up, lazybones,' he said, laughing at Jack's confusion. 'The fish'll be biting.'

Jack scrambled out of his sleeping bag. They'd dressed in preparation the night before so they didn't wake up Sam's mum stumbling around in the dark at dawn. All Jack had to do was find his thongs and he would be set to go.

The annexe was stuffy, but the air outside was cool and salty. Carrying their rods and their pre-prepared esky, they made their way through the darkened park, careful not to trip over any tent ropes. When they arrived at the beach access, Jack switched on the torch. An animal darted across the sandy path to hide in the tussocky grass. Sam laughed and said it was probably the resident goanna. By the time they baited their rods, the first rays of pre-dawn light had appeared on the horizon. Leaving the esky further up the beach, they kicked off their thongs and tramped towards the breaking surf, the sand cool between their toes.

'I think it's low tide, so we should stand about here,' Sam explained, pointing to a darker patch of water beyond the breakers. 'There are some deep holes just out there and dawn is the best time to catch whiting. They feed before sunrise, so there are a lot of them out and about.'

Wading in until he was shin deep in water, Jack cast his line as far as he could, hoping it had travelled beyond the breakers. It would be nice for Sam's mum if they came home with a good catch. Maybe she'd even freeze a few so he could give them to his mum at the end of the holiday. Jack liked Sam's mum. She always said nice things about Sam's dad, like how she missed him when he was away, and how she was looking forward to him being home again. Not like Jack's parents, always bickering about who was better, the English or the Irish. Jack couldn't see the point of it all when they were living in Australia.

Suddenly, a strong wave almost knocked him over.

'Whoa!' Sam yelled. 'Maybe I got the tides wrong. Better get further up the beach.'

Jack pushed his way out of the surf, holding his tackle aloft.

'I'll have to have a think about this,' said Sam as they dropped everything beside the esky. He put his hands on his hips and surveyed the beach, looking for the best spot for them to re-cast their lines.

Jack pulled a smelly piece of seaweed off his ankle and tossed it as far down the beach as he could. 'At least we can see better now.'

'Help! Help me!' came a distant cry.

'Where did that come from?' Sam spun around and looked back towards the caravan park.

'Help!'

'Out there!' Jack pointed at the water where a swimmer was flailing about in the surf. He lost sight of them for a few seconds, then the figure surfaced again.

'Help m—' The swimmer was hit by another wave, their scream cut short.

Jack took off, shedding his clothes as he went. Beside him, Sam was doing the same. 'You go for help,' Jack yelled, sprinting towards the surf. 'I'll swim out.'

He didn't stop when he reached the water's edge, racing through the shallows then diving under an oncoming wave. Surfacing, he dragged in a breath, saw a close set of breakers bearing down on him, and struck out towards the first one. It broke, engulfing him in a surge of white water. He plunged below the turbulence, resurfaced and swam on to meet the next one. A wall of water rose in front of him, its suction dragging him towards the trough. Jack dived deep and touched his fingertips to the sand before the wave began to lift him skywards. He burst through the crest an instant before the wave broke, releasing its energy and thundering onwards towards the shore.

The swimmer was beyond the breakers, a flash of yellow, a hand in the air. Then they sank below the surface. Jack struck out, felt the drag of the undertow and relaxed, allowing the current to carry him closer to the struggling swimmer.

When Jack reached the woman, she was exhausted from fighting the rip. 'Turn over and float,' he cried, fearful she'd drag him under or he'd lose sight of her. 'I won't let you go. Help is coming.'

To his relief, the woman did as he asked. Hooking his left arm under her shoulder, he cupped her chin in his hand and kept her head close to his. He floated beside her, spitting out salt water every time it washed into his mouth.

'What's your name?' he asked.

'Julieann.'

'I'm Jack,' he said, frog kicking every so often. 'Just float, look at the clouds and breathe.'

As he held her up in the surf at One Mile Beach listening to the two jet skis roaring towards them, Jack knew he'd saved a life . . . and it felt good. He wanted to do it again.

It wasn't the accolades, the news coverage, the front-page headlines or the bravery award he was to receive. It was the chance to make plans for a better life, an escape from becoming a third-generation miner.

When he learned that Julieann worked as a marriage counsellor in Maitland where he was to attend high school, suddenly it didn't seem so bad that he and Sam would soon head off to different schools. Even the extra travel time didn't worry him.

Sometimes, if Julieann had a gap in her appointments, she would take Jack for a milkshake after school. They would often talk for over an hour. She was at the school gate taking photos before he left for his year twelve formal. She came to his graduation from Duntroon, his grandfather's funeral and his father's, and she talked to him at length about cultural identity when his mother decided she needed to return to Ireland.

In moments of reflection, Jack was inclined to wonder where he would be now if he and Sam hadn't gone fishing for whiting that morning. In that moment in time, a friendship had been forged. Julieann Bower was destined to become the greatest influence on Jack Walker's life.

*

'Did this Julieann tell him about me?' Eva asked, looking up at him, the firelight making patterns on her face.

Jack nodded. 'Unintentionally. Hutton talked his way into her apartment about a month ago, saying something about a strata inspection. Julieann retired to Shoal Bay a few years ago. There was a photo of you and Poppy there, the one where you're standing in the clearing with this place in the background.' His relief that Julieann was unharmed had quickly given way to an abject horror and fear that Hutton had learned he had a daughter. 'I always send her a copy of the latest photo.'

There was a long silence. Jack didn't say anymore. It was a lot for her to digest.

'He recognised this place?' she said eventually.

He nodded. 'Yeah.'

'Do you think he was going to hurt Julieann?' she whispered.

'I'm certain he changed his plans when he found out about Poppy.'

Eva covered her mouth to stifle a cry. The happy strains of a Disney song filtered into the room from where Poppy was watching *Moana*.

Jack watched as she stood up, and he shifted out of the way when she began to pace in front of the fire. Then as suddenly as she'd started, she stopped, leaning over and returning the chess pieces to their rightful places on the board.

When she didn't say anything, Jack went on. 'Hutton gets revenge, but not by killing the people he thinks have wronged him. That would be too quick. He punishes them for life by taking a family member, someone close. Julieann became suspicious when he kept asking questions. She called me right away and said he looked like the wanted man on the news. That's when I started to figure out what was going on.'

Eva picked up a throw rug that had slipped off the arm of the couch and fallen onto the floor. 'We have to go to the police.'

Though she spoke with conviction, Jack could see her fingers tremble as she folded the ends of the rug together. He took two steps towards her, careful not to crowd her but leaving Eva no option but to look at him.

'Listen to me,' he said gently. 'In any other situation I'd agree with you, but this is different. Hutton needs to be stopped, or you'll spend the rest of your life looking over your shoulder. If you go to the police and they don't apprehend him, they'll put you and Poppy into protective custody.' He spread his hands and looked around the room. 'You won't be able to stay here at the Golden Wattle. You'll be separated from your family and friends. Your sister. Eva, you and Poppy will be completely alone.'

Ten

Vanessa called as Ryder left Goulburn. Up ahead, he could see the back of the other unmarked car, with Sterling now riding in the passenger seat. 'Hey, Vanessa. Where are you?'

'That's the first question you always ask. Are you keeping tabs on me, Detective?'

'Never.' He took a tentative sip of the boiling-hot coffee he'd bought from the fast-food outlet at the Big Merino, hoping it had cooled to a more palatable temperature. If there was one thing Ryder hated, it was burning his mouth.

'You sound like you're in the car?' she said.

'I am. I'm coming your way.'

'You *are*? Where are you going?'

'Jindabyne. So we can meet up there tonight.'

There was a pained groan. '*Oh, no!* We're going to pass each other on the highway.'

Ryder's heart sank. She must have decided to push on to Sydney after all. 'I called you a couple of times. I couldn't get through; your line was busy.'

'I know. I saw the missed calls. I was talking to Eva, and then a whole lot of work calls came through. I'm on the outskirts of Canberra.' There was a short silence, then: 'Well, that sucks.'

'It's my fault. I should have left a message and said we were coming down. I had Sterling in the car with me.' Ryder sighed.

'Oh, well, it was a nice thought, and it can't be helped,' she said, but he could hear the disappointment in her voice.

'I didn't want to talk in front of her as it's her first day. We just met up with Flowers at the Big Merino. She's gone in his car now.'

'Oh, okay. Never mind, Pierce. What's taking you back to the Snowies?'

'The Hutton case.'

There was a pause, then: 'Oh, God. Has there been another murder?'

'Not this time, thankfully.'

'It must be a strong lead for you to be going down there.' Ryder heard the hesitancy in her voice. While he didn't share the more sensitive details of his cases with Vanessa, she knew how important the Hutton case was to him.

'It's more than we've had in a long while. I'm just sorry we're going to miss each other. I was hoping you'd decided to stay at Eva's. I was about to give her a call. We need a place with three rooms.'

'Oh, Pierce, Eva's booked solid. She's teaching one of those intensive cooking classes again. She sounded super stressed when I talked to her.'

'Okay, well, the Golden Wattle is out. I'll get Sterling to start ringing around.'

'Let me know where you end up. I'll message you when I'm back at the apartment. Stay safe, Detective Ryder.'

'You too.'

'Oh, Pierce?' she said before he could hang up. 'Watch out for black ice on the road. The snow was beginning to bucket down on the Alpine Way. Do you have snow chains?'

'Don't need them. We're in the unmarked four-wheel drives.'

Ryder parked the four-wheel drive beside Flowers' vehicle, holding the door firm against the wind while he climbed out. The freezing gusts slapped him in the face, reviving him after the warmth of the car. He slammed the door closed and fetched his black overcoat from the back seat. He hadn't needed it since his last visit down here.

Sterling had found them three loft-style apartments overlooking Lake Jindabyne, which was convenient for their appointment at the National Parks and Wildlife office in the morning. Ryder needed to talk with the local boys up at Jindabyne Police, too.

'Are we putting our gear in the rooms now?' Flowers asked, coming over to talk to him. 'Or do you want to eat first? It's almost four.'

Ryder's stomach grumbled. They'd skipped lunch, opting for takeaway coffee at Goulburn. He pointed to the group of shops and restaurants across the road. 'Let's see if one of the cafes over there will make us something.' He slipped on his overcoat and turned up the collar, knowing once he got inside into the warmth, he wouldn't want to go out again.

They found a corner table at an Italian restaurant in the Nuggets Crossing complex where the chef agreed to make them a late lunch/ early dinner.

'I'm starving,' said Flowers, rubbing in hand sanitiser before pulling out a chair and sinking into it. 'I think I'll have the pizza that's on the specials board outside.'

Ryder smirked from behind his menu and looked at Sterling. 'Flowers is into whole foods, free from all additives and preservatives and cooked from scratch, except when he comes down here.'

'Can you blame me, Sarge? It's just so friggin' cold.'

They ordered ginger beer all round, and it became clear to Ryder that Sterling, despite being dragged off to the Snowy Mountains on her first day, had struck up a good rapport with Flowers on the way down in the car.

'So, let's think about what we learned today,' he said. 'How does that change what we know about Gavin Hutton?'

'We can assume his victims didn't stand a chance if he can fight like that,' said Flowers.

'True. Which means he's going to be difficult to apprehend if he poses a direct threat to us.'

An uneasy silence fell over the two Detective Constables. Ryder wasn't sure what action Sterling had seen, but he knew Flowers had never had to discharge his weapon. 'Okay, what else?'

'He was a student on that course,' said Sterling, 'so, maybe he has a contact, or contacts, down here somewhere.'

'Yep. He could be more familiar with this area than we previously thought. It adds credibility to last year's sightings.'

'Don't you think it's odd that we haven't heard from any of the other participants on that course?' asked Flowers. 'Surely one of them would have recognised Hutton's face from the TV. That photo has been on every channel.'

Ryder thought for a minute. 'Not necessarily. There might only have been a handful of students, and they could be anywhere now.' He took a slice of herb bread from the basket that had arrived on their table.

'I'd be tempted by that reward,' mumbled Flowers.

'Perhaps Hutton is not entirely without empathy,' offered Sterling. 'We know he wasn't violent towards Kimberley Dickson. And you heard what she said this morning, Sarge, when she found out he'd been a boxer.'

'What'd she say?' asked Flowers around a mouthful of bread.

'We told her his nickname had been Hammer Hutton and she said, "I didn't know that. Maybe he thought it would frighten me."'

Ryder nodded. 'We know that serial killers lack empathy and don't form emotional attachments. Now, Hutton's by no means perfect, but he did form some kind of emotional attachment to Kimberley, and maybe to the history teacher we spoke to as well.'

'So, he mightn't be a serial killer?' asked Sterling.

'When *anyone* kills more than once, we have to assume we have a serial killer on our hands, but his attachments to Kimberley and the history teacher are something we can keep in mind, Sterling.'

'Aren't serial killers born?' asked Flowers.

'Usually they are.' Ryder paused as their meals were put in front of them. 'We also know Hutton hides away, and calls himself Ben while disguised. And don't forget about his parents' deaths. We can't prove he wasn't responsible.'

'Okay, but let's say he *didn't* murder his folks,' said Flowers. 'What made him suddenly beat a man like Dominic Burrows to death?'

'And why go to the trouble of disguising himself as "Ben" if it wasn't a targeted kill?' added Ryder.

'And he did the same thing when he murdered Fergus Suter,' Sterling said, her eyes widening.

Ryder nodded. 'That's right. He booked several personal-training sessions and paid in cash. Some serial killers carefully select their victims, while others kill randomly. Detective Brown has been looking for connections between the two victims and Hutton, but we've had no luck yet.'

Before Sterling could ask another question, the waiter was back. 'Would anyone like cracked pepper?' he asked.

From that moment all talk ceased as the three of them started on their meals.

After they'd finished eating, Sterling pushed back her chair. 'You'll have to excuse me. I'll be back in a sec. I have something caught in my braces.'

'Sure,' said Flowers, jumping up from his seat so she could get past. 'I'm always getting food caught in the wires on the back of my teeth.'

'It's so annoying, isn't it?' Sterling said with a smile.

After she left, Flowers sat down and grinned at Ryder. 'I like her. She seems nice.'

'So, you have problems with your wires, too, hey Daisy?' Ryder grinned, happy to give Flowers a bit of stick while the new recruit was absent.

'Don't you?'

'Never needed braces. I've been perfect since the day I was born.'

'Oh, that's right, I forgot.' Flowers pointed a spoon at him. 'You're starting to sound like Lew, you know. Do you think you'll have time to catch up with him while we're down here?'

Ryder nodded. 'We'll see.' It would be great to see his best friend, the former Inspector he'd worked under for many years. He hadn't seen Lew since he'd come out of retirement to help them with the cold case up at Charlotte Pass. To Ryder's surprise, Lew and Flowers had hit it off straightaway.

The front door opened, and another frosty blast of air blew into the restaurant. Flowers looked up. 'Why are so many people here already? The season doesn't open for another few weeks.'

'Cross-country skiers don't use lifts, and according to Vanessa, once there's enough snow on the ground the snowboarders hike up the slopes.' Ryder pointed beyond the carpark and Kosciuszko Road, where dense black clouds hovered low over the moody grey waters of Lake Jindabyne. 'We should get going. Those clouds are full of snow and it's already starting to dump.'

❄

Ten minutes later, they were standing on the kerb beneath a bare poplar tree, Ryder's face beginning to numb. The temperature had dropped at least five degrees since they'd arrived. Fog lights reflected off the wet shiny roads. Most of the vehicles crawling past had chains attached to their tyres.

Back at the car, Ryder lifted his overnight bag from the boot and glanced at the ice forming on the windscreens of vehicles parked nearby. 'You'd better set your alarms half an hour earlier,' he said. 'It's going to be fun scraping that off.'

Once check-in was done, Ryder gave Sterling the files for Dominic Burrows and Fergus Suter. 'We've given you an overview of the cases, but I'd like you to have a detailed look through the documents on file. It's always good to have a fresh pair of eyes go over them.'

'Will do, Sarge.'

Ryder looked around the lounge area of The Loft Apartments. 'Good job, Sterling, finding the accommodation. This is very pleasant.' Large photographic prints of the Kosciuszko National Park hung on the exposed brick walls, and comfortable-looking sofas were scattered around. 'I'll probably pick up a snack later and take it to my room. I'll leave you two to your own devices. We've had a full day already.'

'Okay, Sarge,' said Flowers. 'See you in the morning.'

Ryder raised a hand in farewell and went to find his room. It was up a set of stairs, across a mezzanine landing that looked down onto the reception area where Flowers and Sterling were still talking. 'I must be getting old,' he muttered as he unlocked the door, wishing Vanessa were there to share the enormous loft-style room that opened up in front of him.

He put down his bag and walked towards the full-length glass doors that opened onto the balcony. Snowflakes fell like a curtain of white, so heavy they obscured the view of Lake Jindabyne beyond the balcony rail. The circular outdoor table, cane chairs and wooden handrails were already covered in a thick layer of snow. There'd be no beer drunk al fresco tonight.

Ryder drew the curtains and turned to take a closer look at his digs. There was an open-plan kitchen with a fridge, a four-seater table and a sofa. He picked up his bag and climbed the stairs to the loft, where he kicked off his boots and eased himself onto the bed. Resting against the mountain of feather pillows, he reached back and locked his hands behind his head. As he stared at the ceiling, he wondered where in the Snowy Mountains Hutton was hiding out that night. One thing was for sure, it would be very cold and very lonely.

Much like the cell that one day Ryder would put him in.

Eleven

The wind had died down, but outside the snow continued to fall, muffling all sound and wrapping the lodge in a calm quiet, at odds with Eva's growing anger.

'So, Poppy and I are in this situation because of you?'

Jack nodded but offered no apology, which only fuelled her anger.

'Why are you so certain you can deal with him but the police can't?' she rushed on, searching her mind for a way out. 'And if you won't call them, then call somebody else. What about those commando army mates of yours? Call *them*. Tell them to get up here and to bring their guns. I don't *care*. I just want Poppy safe.'

'I want that too.'

'So, what are you waiting for?' She clenched her fists at her sides. 'You're injured. How can you possibly—'

'Because I'm her father,' he said harshly. 'No one is trained better than me. No one will protect her more than *me*.'

Eva fell silent, shocked at the emotion in his voice more so than his words. 'That's a turnaround,' she said eventually. 'Four years ago you said you didn't want to be involved in her life.'

'No, I said it would be *better* if I wasn't involved. And I was right. Look what's happened, and I haven't even been here.'

Eva sank down on the couch again. What was the use of talking about the past when it couldn't help the present? They needed Poppy safe and Hutton caught. They both agreed on that.

'Hutton's not stupid,' Jack said, glancing at the clock on the mantel. 'I've been here for six hours now. If he's out there, and he sees police or other reinforcements turning up, tonight, tomorrow, whenever . . . he'll slink away. He might wait a year, or two, five even, before turning up again. Will you ever be able to sleep at night?'

Eva shivered, chills tingling up and down her spine despite the heat of the fire. She hated the thought of living in fear, of looking over her shoulder, of being too terrified to fall asleep. How would she cope when Poppy went to school, or over to a friend's house to play, or was invited to a birthday party? How could she let her daughter out of her sight knowing it might be the last time she ever saw her?

Eva buried her face in her hands, feeling as though she might be sick. The thought of protective custody was equally horrific, a half-life lived in the shadows.

She lowered her hands and sighed. 'What happened on that course that made Gavin Hutton hate you so much?'

'Nothing.' He took a deep breath. 'Our paths crossed a few years later after Hutton had been working security at a mine in the Philippines.'

'You were in the Philippines?'

'No, I was in Sydney. I flew over.' He hesitated for several long seconds, as though trying to anticipate her reaction. 'I work in ransom insurance. Hutton was kidnapped. I was the best man to take that contract as I knew him. It's a small industry.'

His answer was so unexpected, it took a few moments for the words to sink in. Eva shook her head in bewilderment. 'Ransom insurance? What does that even mean?'

'It's a type of insurance that companies take out in case their employees are kidnapped, which happens in certain parts of the world more often than we'd like.'

'Do they have to take out that kind of policy?'

'No, but it makes sense for companies operating in countries controlled by rebel groups, mafia or criminals. I mean, these groups are solely motivated by money. I'm talking countries like Somalia, Mali, Yemen and Afghanistan. Being insured increases the hostage's chance of survival.'

'What's your role?'

'I'm the negotiator.' He shrugged as if it were no big deal. 'I negotiate a price. I don't meet these groups face to face. That's the job of other members of the crisis response team.'

Eva shook her head. 'What other members?'

'We don't always work with the same team. It depends on locality and who's available. There's always a hostage retrieval expert, and a guy who does the money drop, but that doesn't happen very often now. It's more common for the money to be paid out through ATMs.'

ATMs? Eva stared at him. She'd seen movies about hostage negotiators, but this was no movie, this was real life, and this hostage negotiator was Poppy's father. 'Isn't the government supposed to do that?' she asked, trying to hide her astonishment.

Jack shook his head. 'They get involved when a citizen is arrested and jailed overseas under foreign laws. We don't deal with judicial systems; these are criminals who control large tracts of land.'

'I know about cartels from when I was cooking on the yacht. We sailed through the Panama Canal once and into South America. They made sure we were aware of the risks—just the general ones, like being careful travelling into the country areas because sometimes they aren't as safe as the cities.' Eva shifted restlessly. How ironic that the unwanted attention of the owner's brother had been a bigger threat to her safety than any criminal cartel. After that, she'd sworn she would never put herself in a situation where she was trapped again, and yet here she was.

'Right, so you know,' Jack said. 'Some governments are able to keep law and order in their cities but are short on manpower in the outlying areas. Criminal organisations can take control out there, and unfortunately that's where a lot of these companies are located.'

LEE CHRISTINE

'What did you mean when you said, "We don't deal with judicial systems?" Who is "we"—the insurance company?'

He shook his head again. 'We're private consultants with different specialties. The insurance company puts together a team when someone is taken.'

Eva continued to stare at him. She had no idea of the kind of life Poppy's father led; how could she? She sent him photographs. He deposited money into her account, which she'd put away for Poppy's education. That had been the extent of their relationship, until now.

Eva's head hurt. She massaged her temples with her fingertips, trying to work it out. 'Gavin Hutton is alive, though, so he survived the kidnapping. I don't understand why he would be trying to get back at you now?'

'Because I didn't negotiate his release.'

Eva paused, surprised. 'Why not, if that was your job?'

Jack's jaw tightened, and he turned to face the fire—but not before Eva caught the gleam in his eye. 'He had no family to raise the ransom.'

Eva frowned. 'But you said he was insured by the company. What does his family have to do with it?' She didn't care if he had to answer a thousand questions. All this had happened, and Poppy was now in danger, because of him.

'When someone is taken, I go to the family.' He warmed his hands then turned around to put his back to the fire. 'They raise as much money as they can for the ransom. They re-mortgage their homes, sell cars and other furniture, borrow from relatives. I negotiate a price. The other team members take it from there. If it turns out the worker was insured, the insurance company reimburses the family.'

'So, the insurance company doesn't pay the money directly to the kidnappers?'

He shook his head. 'That's our job.'

Negotiation, money drops, hostage retrieval. What sounded like a Hollywood movie were elements of Jack Walker's specialised, high-risk day job where the stakes were life and death. Finally, Eva was

86

beginning to understand why he thought he was better equipped than the police to handle things here.

'Often the family raises extra money, but in Hutton's circumstances the policy was capped. I couldn't go any higher. We were negotiating with a group of thugs who didn't know how things work. A lot of the time, we know which group we're dealing with, and how they operate. Those groups know they'll get an insurance payout, so it's in their best interest to return the hostage in good health. That wasn't the case this time. They were in bad shape.'

'So, how did Hutton even know you were involved?'

'I was on site at the company offices with the others, representing the insurance company. There was a debrief after they were released. We needed information from them, details about the kidnappers to enter into our database—in case we had to deal with them again.'

Eva could only nod.

'I'd had extensive telephone communication with the leader, and I'd met Hutton before, right here in this lodge. The hostages had to undergo medical checks. The Swedish guy was the worst, that's why they moved to get him out. The Swedes negotiated a payout for the entire group. That meant we had to reimburse them for the amount they paid for Hutton.'

Eva sat stunned. To think that since Poppy's birth she'd longed for Jack to be part of his daughter's life. She understood now why it was better that he wasn't.

When she looked up, he was watching her. 'It's a business,' he said simply.

A harsh, grinding sound cut through the silence followed by a heavy thump. They swung around looking towards the front of the lodge. Jack was halfway to the window when the grinding noise came again . . . louder and longer.

'It sounds like snowboarders,' Eva said, joining Jack at the window. 'It is. There must be enough snow up top for them to get all the way down.'

Sure enough, two young men decked out in dark jackets and baggy pants were resting on snowboards in the clearing. As they watched, the young men began to whoop and laugh with delight.

'Here comes another one,' Eva said, spotting a flash through the trees close to the bottom of the track.

A third rider appeared, well-balanced, his head protected by a helmet similar to those worn by the other two. Heading in a straight line towards one of the wooden picnic tables, he lined it up and jumped, riding it for the entire length of the seat, the friction making the hideous scraping sound they'd heard from inside the lodge. At the end, he launched himself into the air before landing in the snow with a solid thump.

'Normally, I'd ask them to stop doing it because they damage the picnic tables, and when guests are here I worry they'll fly into the clearing and knock someone over.' Eva checked her watch. 'It's five past four. It will be dark by four-thirty. They won't be here much longer.'

Jack let the curtain fall back into place. 'Let them hang around as long as they want. If Hutton is out there somewhere, they'll be a deterrent. At this stage, the longer I have to recover the better.'

'Mummy?'

Eva swung around to see Poppy standing near the leather lounge rubbing her eyes.

She picked Poppy up, her heart aching with love for her young daughter. 'Did you fall asleep in the movie?'

Poppy shook her head and smiled. 'It's over. I love the baby piggy.'

Eva held Poppy tight and inhaled the sweet smell of her hair. 'I love the baby piggy, too.'

'Eva?'

When she turned around, Jack tilted his head towards the lobby. 'I need to do something.'

'What?'

He looked at Poppy before answering. 'Two of the suites have manholes,' he said quietly. 'I'm going to lock the doors from the outside.'

A chill ran down Eva's spine, the thought of Gavin Hutton coming down through the ceiling too horrific to contemplate. 'Let's hope the snow keeps falling overnight, then,' she said. 'It builds up on the roof and quickly turns to ice. When he falls off and lands on his head, that will be the best deterrent of all.'

Jack Walker smiled, and for the first time since he'd burst into the lodge, Eva recognised the laconic grin she'd found so irresistible all those years ago. Then it was gone.

'I'll get the keys,' he said, all business again.

When he disappeared into the lobby, she headed for the kitchen. 'How about some dinner?' she asked, trying to sound like nothing abnormal was happening in their lives.

She had no luck tempting Poppy to eat, and eventually she gave up and offered her another juice popper. Over the past few hours, the stakes had grown exponentially, so the sugar content in the juice was the least of her worries. Setting the kettle to boil, she dropped a teabag into a large mug. Poppy wasn't the only one who'd lost her appetite.

'Help yourself to the frozen dinners in the freezer,' she said when Jack reappeared. 'Five minutes in the microwave.'

'Thanks,' he said, fetching more painkillers from the cupboard.

Eva looked him up and down. 'You look like you could use a good feed,' she said, noticing how loose the clothes were on him as she sipped her tea.

'Mummy, can I have a biscuit?' Poppy asked, pointing to the biscuit barrel, and knocking the popper off the table in the process.

'You haven't eaten dinner,' Eva said wearily, picking up the juice box and putting it on the bench.

'Do you know why they call these poppers?' Jack asked.

Eva stilled, the mug of tea halfway to her lips. It was obvious from his lighter, more conversational tone that the question hadn't been meant for her. Slowly, as if it were no big deal, she turned around. Jack was holding the popper, and for the first time since he'd burst into the lodge, he spoke directly to his daughter. 'Do you know?'

Poppy bit down on her lip and shook her head.

'Don't worry. I'll clean up the mess,' he said with a sideways glance at Eva.

'Are you going to make a mess?' Poppy demanded with a nervous giggle.

Jack shook the juice box. 'Depends how much is left.'

Poppy's eyes rounded as he blew air into the straw—stopping when the box had expanded to its full capacity. A corner of his mouth curved as he pulled out the straw before putting the juice box down on the floor. 'Big bang coming.'

Poppy was half out of her seat, leaning over the edge of the table, her eyes gleaming with anticipation.

Jack lifted one foot and brought his heel down hard on the juice box. It split with the bang of a champagne cork, spraying droplets of juice across the floor. Poppy jumped violently, her eyes wide, her mouth forming an O. For an awful second Eva thought she was going to burst into tears, but then she dissolved into fits of giggles, a high-pitched infectious sound that soon had Eva and Jack smiling.

'That's why they call it a popper,' he said, grinning.

Poppy slid off her chair and jumped on the flattened box with both feet.

'It only works once,' said Jack, 'and I've had lots of practice popping them in the school playground.'

'Okay, I think it's time for you to have a bath and go to bed, missy. Say goodnight.'

Poppy brushed her hair out of her eyes. 'Goodnight.'

Jack nodded, his eyes on his daughter. 'Goodnight, Poppy.'

❄

Eva sat on a low stool beside the bath and watched over Poppy while she played with her plastic toys. For a few brief moments in the kitchen she'd forgotten about Gavin Hutton and his plans for Poppy and her, but now the looming darkness beyond the windows had her dreading the night ahead.

'Mummy, how did he . . .' Poppy frowned. 'What's his name again?'

Eva swallowed, her heart aching for her little daughter who was so innocently unaware that Jack was her father.

'What's his name?' Poppy demanded, splashing the water so all the plastic ducks capsized.

Definitely not *Daddy*. And while it was fine for Eva to call him Jack, her intuition warned her it would be safer for Poppy to think of him as another guest, in the event he disappeared again when all this was over. If that happened, they could both revert to calling him Mr Walker, which is how Poppy referred to most guests.

'You mean Walker?' Eva asked, deciding his last name was a good compromise.

Poppy nodded. 'How did Walker bust that juice?'

Eva explained how the popper had burst, making Poppy laugh all over again as though it had just happened. When the bath water began to cool, Eva lifted her out, towelled her dry and helped her put on her pyjamas.

'Can you read *Winnie the Pooh*?' Poppy asked, when she'd finished brushing her teeth.

'How about we read it in my bed and you can sleep with me,' Eva suggested, needing and wanting Poppy as physically close to her as possible tonight. 'I think it's going to be cold.'

Ten minutes later, lulled to sleep by the familiar story and the cosiness of the electric blanket, Poppy was fast asleep.

Eva closed the book, her mind replaying the moment Jack had burst in that morning and taken her devices. He had expected her to call the police. Any sane person would have. In the confusion and panic, she'd feared he was here to take Poppy, but now Eva had settled down, she realised there had been a total absence of the usual markers leading up to such a frightening event. Danger signals that were sadly reported in the media every week. Threats, attempts at control, escalating emotional and sometimes physical abuse over time. Nothing like that had ever happened between her and Jack. Other than the bank deposits, she'd heard nothing from him.

But now he was back.

For a very good reason.

Eva slipped out of bed, careful not to wake her daughter. She needed to know what Jack's plans were for keeping them safe overnight. Despite the smile he'd given Poppy at the time, she hadn't missed the grimace of pain when he'd stomped down hard on that juice box.

He was in front of the fire.

Eva folded her arms and walked towards him, the air in the lounge room chilly after the warmth of her bed.

'I was hoping you'd come back out,' he said. 'Do you have a rollaway bed?'

She nodded. 'I have two. One in each storage closet, in the hallway. You'll find sheets, blankets and pillows in there, too.'

'Right here is the best place for me to set up. I can see straight through the lobby to the front door, to the top of the stairs, and I can see your door over there. I can also stoke the fire.'

'What are your plans, you know, if he . . . gets in? What do you think he'll do?'

'He won't. He can try, but the place is totally secure. Any confrontation between me and Hutton is likely to happen outside.'

'And if you don't win this so-called confrontation outside?'

He was silent for a while, as if contemplating how best to answer. 'I'll win it. I trained him how to survive out there, after all.'

'You're confident, even with that injury?' She looked pointedly at his abdomen.

'The more days I can hole up here, the better I'll be when he shows up.'

Eva dragged her fingers through her hair. 'I get everything you say, but I want Poppy out of the lodge. I'm prepared to stay with you here, and fight for her life, and mine, to have Hutton behind bars, and Poppy and me . . . free. But she has to be moved out of danger. I know any number of people who'll take her at a moment's notice.'

Jack swallowed, and firelight reflected in his eyes. 'The thing is, I don't know which of the two of you he wants to harm. He does his research, I know that. He found Julieann. He'll track down whichever of the two of you he wants to find. I can protect you both *here*, but not if you split up.'

The final hope she'd been clinging to melted like snow in springtime. She didn't want the police to put them in protective custody, nor did she want Gavin Hutton to go to ground only to resurface in years to come and resume this crazed plan for revenge. It had to be this way. There was nothing left to talk about.

She turned to leave.

'Lock your door, Eva,' she heard him say.

❄

Eva woke suddenly, her body curled protectively around Poppy. She lay still, staring at the darkness, waiting for the sharp crack that had woken her to come again.

When her eyes had adjusted and she could make out the dark shapes of furniture, she straightened her legs and rolled over. The hands on her bedside clock glowed 2.09 am.

Heart pounding, she slipped out of bed and put on her dressing gown, then padded to the door in socked feet. Putting an ear to the door she listened, praying Poppy wouldn't wake up.

Crack!

Eva jumped, her heart beating so hard she could feel it pulsing in her throat. Laying a hand on her chest, she breathed a sigh of relief. It was a log splitting on the fire, an unusual sound at this time because she was always so careful to put it out before they went to bed.

Crack!

Eva frowned, wondering how on earth Jack could sleep with that going on right next to him. Or maybe he was awake. Somehow, she'd managed to sleep five hours, a feat she would have thought impossible when she'd first laid her head on the pillow.

Stealthily, she unlocked the door, opening it wide enough so she was able to stick her head out. A fire roared in the grate, the kindling popping and cracking as though Jack had recently added fuel, but the rollaway bed was empty save for a pile of blankets, as was the couch. She stepped outside the room and pulled the door closed before heading to the kitchen. Neither she nor Poppy had eaten dinner, and Poppy was certain to wake up soon feeling hungry. Maybe some warm milk would do the trick until morning.

The kitchen was in darkness. Thinking he must be checking the doors and windows again, she grabbed a banana for herself, then set about heating some milk in the microwave before tipping it into a keep cup for Poppy.

Back in the lounge room, the fire burned just as brightly but there was still no sign of Jack. It was then Eva noticed that the door leading into the hallway was open. Had he gone to check the suites down that side of the lodge? Worry churning her stomach, she walked across the room. Pausing in the doorway, she looked down the length of the hallway to where the door to the Wisteria Suite stood open. Maybe he'd needed to use the bathroom, but if that were the case, he was taking a long time. And then, just as they'd been spiralling all day since Jack's arrival, her thoughts began to escalate into panic. What if he'd burst open that injury when he'd stomped on the popper and couldn't stem the bleeding?

Moving quietly down the hallway, she approached the door, conscious of a noise coming from inside the suite. The sound of running water. Jack was taking a shower.

Eva retraced her steps, slipping into her bedroom and locking the door with relief. Leaving the milk and banana on the bedside table, she slid into bed beside Poppy without bothering to take off her dressing gown. Curling her arm around her daughter, she thought about the footprints in the snow and sighed. She had no chance of going to sleep until she heard Jack come back and resume his watchful position.

Twelve

Ryder sipped his coffee and looked at the view, the TV muted while he waited for the 8 am news bulletin to air. Outside, ploughs rumbled along Kosciuszko Road, their blades pushing the fifty centimetres of snow that had fallen overnight into banks on the kerb.

His phone buzzed as a text message came in; Vanessa saying good morning and hoping he slept well.

A photo came through next. Ryder chuckled at the tiny pink skis with a psychedelic flower design, propped against the lounge in their Sydney apartment. So, this was the surprise present Vanessa had wanted to give to Poppy yesterday afternoon.

A longing stirred deep in Ryder's soul. He typed in a text saying what a lucky girl Poppy was to have Vanessa as an aunt, and perhaps one day they would have a child of their own to surprise. He'd been a father once, and he'd loved every minute of it. He rubbed the area over his heart, the part that always hurt whenever he thought of Scarlett. Was it too soon to broach the subject with Vanessa? At thirty-nine he wasn't getting any younger, but it wasn't all about him.

Ryder looked up at the print on the wall—brumbies cantering through snow gums. In a year or two Vanessa's parents would retire, and she would move west to take over the family farm, something she'd always longed to do. And while becoming a country cop would be a career killer for him, he would do it for Vanessa. Maybe then

95

would be the right time to start a family. Ryder deleted the last part of his message and hit the send arrow. It was too important a subject to bring up in a text.

He was tipping the dregs of his coffee into the sink when his phone buzzed for the third time, notifying him of a new email. It was from the rare earth mine in Zimbabwe where Gavin Hutton had found work after completing the course down here in the Snowies.

Ryder took a breath and opened the email. *Here we go. Finally!*

He scanned the two short paragraphs. *We thank you for your email requesting the personal details of our past employee ... are pleased to provide you with the following ... Please find attached ...*

Ryder scrolled down and opened the attachment. While he waited for it to load, he checked the time—8.20 am. Zimbabwe was eight hours behind Australia, meaning it would be around midnight there. Ryder frowned. Someone working the night shift. It was a twenty-four hour mine.

The attachment filled the screen and Ryder skimmed the information they had on Hutton: his last known address in Australia, a list of vaccinations he'd had before he'd left, contact details and telephone numbers for his accommodation in Zimbabwe. Then Ryder stopped scrolling, his heart tripping as he read the words listed in the Emergency Contact column.

Trevor Dylan Swan
431 Blueswater Road
The Entrance NSW
Relationship to employee: Brother

With an unsteady hand, Ryder jotted down the mobile number listed for Trevor Swan before calling it.

Optus advises that the phone number you have dialled has been disconnected. Please check ...

Ryder rang the number a second time to make sure he hadn't punched in the wrong digits. When the automated message started again, he ended the call and rang Flowers.

'Morning, Sarge.'

'Get up here now, Mitch, and grab Sterling on the way. We've got a new lead.'

❄

Ryder was on the phone to Sergeant Ted O'Neill of The Entrance Police when Flowers and Sterling arrived five minutes later.

Ryder beckoned them inside as he continued the conversation. 'It's a boarding house, you say?' he asked, turning the phone onto loudspeaker.

'Four thirty-one Blueswater Road is.' Sergeant O'Neill's sleepy, considered drawl rang throughout the room.

'Can you send a couple of officers around to keep an eye on the place for a few hours? The address is from 2014 when our suspect, Gavin Hutton, was working in Zimbabwe. Swan could have moved since then. The mobile number noted down has been disconnected.'

'I might be able to do better than that for you.' There was a soft chuckle. 'We've been to that boarding house a couple of times in the past. It might only take a phone call to the owner to find out if Trevor Swan is still a tenant.'

'A phone call might be best, Sergeant, and let's keep the Gavin Hutton connection to ourselves for now. If Swan is still living there, I don't want him spooked. It's critical we talk to him.'

'I'll make a call and get back to you. I can always bring him in and hold him until you get here. Just say the word.'

'I appreciate that, Sergeant,' said Ryder. 'You can get me on this number.'

Flowers gave a low whistle as Ryder killed the call. 'Hutton has a brother?'

Ryder nodded. 'He's listed as the emergency contact on Hutton's employee record at the Zimbabwe mine.'

'We didn't know he had a brother?' asked Sterling.

Ryder shook his head. 'He wasn't listed on Hutton's parents' death certificates.'

'Or on Gavin's birth certificate,' added Flowers. 'But he wouldn't be, if Gavin was the firstborn. And from his surname, it seems Trevor has a different father.'

'There could be any number of reasons why Trevor's name wasn't noted on the death certificates,' said Ryder. 'I've seen death certificates where "unknown" is noted in the children's column. Right now, our priority is finding him.'

'I agree,' said Flowers. 'We can start the paper trail now we have his name.'

'I'm wondering if that's where Gavin went when he disappeared all those times,' mused Ryder, 'to see his brother.'

'Well, Swan hasn't come forward,' said Flowers, 'so the reward money hasn't tempted him to dob in his brother.'

'What do you need me to do, Sarge?' Sterling asked.

'Yes . . . Sterling, good morning by the way.' Ryder gave her a brief smile and scribbled down Trevor Swan's name and address on the hotel notepad. 'Apply for a birth certificate and check if he has a record. The agencies take varying amounts of time to get back to us, as you know, although the tax office is usually pretty quick, so they could be helpful. Anyway, you know the drill. Find out as much as you can about Trevor Swan. Flowers and I will keep in touch.'

❋

'I would have liked Sterling to come with us,' Ryder said as they headed across the road to the National Parks and Wildlife office. 'We get enough desk work at Parramatta.'

'At least she'll be warm in her loft.' Flowers shivered and looked down as something crunched under his boot. 'What's all this white stuff on the road?'

'Salt. It helps melt the ice.'

'Does it do any good?'

'It might stop you from falling on your arse,' Ryder said with a laugh.

They made their way through the outdoor carpark, teeming with SUVs, four-wheel drives and the odd sedan. They paused as a misted-up wagon reversed out of a car space, chains rattling, engine spluttering, clouds of water vapour belching from its exhaust. Further up the rise, a ute turned into the carpark, the build-up of snow on its cabin roof so thick it looked like icing on a cake.

They came to a large wooden building with a high gable roof. Inside, it was modern Australian with lots of wood and an impressive cathedral ceiling. The central heating was set to a comfortable temperature. A young man with fair hair tied neatly into a ponytail asked if he could help them.

'Detective Sergeant Ryder and Detective Constable Flowers from Sydney Homicide,' Flowers began. 'We have an appointment with Ms Patricia Franks.'

'Hello, that was me you spoke to yesterday,' the young man said. 'I've only been here for a while, so I thought it would be better if you talked to Patricia. She's been here forever.'

Ryder nodded. 'Thanks.'

'Sure, I'll go get her.'

A tall, slim woman who looked to be in her forties emerged from a back office in under a minute. She walked briskly towards them, straightening her long knitted scarf so it hung evenly around her neck.

'Geez, from what he said I thought she was going to be eighty,' Flowers said under his breath.

'Good morning.' Patricia Franks beckoned for them to shift along to the far end of the counter where it was more private. She rubbed her hands together as though she'd just walked in and hadn't had time to warm up yet. 'Bit chilly this morning.'

Ryder made the introductions.

'Pleased to meet you,' she said. 'I read the message. You're looking for information about a security course that was run in the national park?'

'We're not sure if it was conducted in the park or a surrounding area,' Ryder said. 'We're told the participants left their cars in Berridale and travelled together from there.'

'Hmm.' Patricia Franks shook her head. 'That's not much help. A lot of tour companies meet their groups in Berridale and bring them the rest of the way by minibus. Parking can be difficult once you get up here, and if there's snow like today you need chains and antifreeze. Much easier to leave the cars lower down.'

Ryder nodded. 'Makes sense.'

Franks clasped her hands together and leaned forward. 'What else do you know about the course?'

'We're pretty sure it was designed to get people ready for employment in the security industry. It would have been around 2013 to 2014.'

'So, it's not operating now?'

'We don't know, it could be.'

'Security work?' Franks thought for a few moments, her mouth pulled into a straight line. 'Mostly what we have now are outdoor adventure experiences, and the people or companies who run them need a permit and public liability insurance to operate. I can give you a list of the businesses that are currently trading.'

'That would be great,' said Flowers.

'Now, security work. Do you know what that would involve, something that might jog my memory?' she asked.

'Would it involve weapons, Sarge?' asked Flowers.

Before Ryder could answer, Franks jumped in. 'The only people who are allowed to discharge firearms in the national park are the army mountain unit, when they're training in the back country. And that's a very delicate arrangement between us and the Department of Defence. We acknowledge that it's necessary for them to train out there, but it's important they minimise the impact on the alpine environment. Actually . . .' She paused for a few moments to think. 'There *was* a company that ran more extreme courses, not with firearms, though.'

'How extreme?' asked Flowers.

'Canyoning and caving—we have a system of caves in the park. Ice climbing, they do that around the area of the Blue Lake, mountaineering, abseiling, that kind of thing. Oh, and reading maps and compasses, orienteering, because they used to camp out for a couple of nights in the back country.'

Flowers raised his eyebrows. 'That does sound extreme.'

'Well, more so than the usual fly fishing and white-water rafting.' Franks' dark eyes twinkled. 'Personally, I'd rather a butterscotch schnapps in front of the fire, but those courses were popular with certain people . . . people who stood out.'

'In what way?' asked Ryder.

'Well, most people down here are fit and outdoorsy, but these men were more military types. I guess that's what I'm trying to say. I do remember the man who used to teach them.' She frowned, 'Gosh, I can picture him. What *was* his name?' She shook her head in dismay. 'The business name escapes me, too. Look, I haven't seen him for a few years. He could have let the permit lapse, or maybe he sold the business.'

'Could you do an archive search for us?' asked Ryder. 'Not just that particular company but all outdoor training courses going back to 2013?'

'I can do that. You might have to give me a while, though. It could take a few hours.'

'That's okay.' Ryder handed his card to Franks. 'We might get that list of companies from you now.'

'The ones who hold a current permit? I'll do it right away.'

'Let's hope she finds something in the archives,' Flowers said when Franks had left. 'It would be good to talk to the bloke who led those expeditions.'

'He mightn't even remember Hutton. He hasn't called the hotline.'

'Neither have any of the other students in the group.'

'Maybe they're all working overseas,' said Ryder. 'Or dead, if they're into that sort of stuff.'

When Franks returned with the printed list of companies, they thanked her for her help and headed towards the automatic doors.

'Sterling will be able to exclude some of these companies pretty quickly,' Ryder said as they crossed the carpark. He shuffled through some advertising pamphlets he'd picked up at the Visitors Centre on the way out. 'For instance, this one specialises in school groups only, and this one has something to do with the Duke of Edinburgh Award program.'

They crossed the road back to the apartments and walked towards the two unmarked four-wheel drives parked side by side in the carpark. 'Just as well we have four-wheel drives,' said Flowers. 'I've never fitted a car with chains before.'

'Only half the cars have them on now. The ice must have melted.' Ryder dug in his pocket for his phone and checked the screen, anxious to learn whether Trevor Swan still lived in the boarding house at The Entrance. 'There's no word from Sergeant O'Neill yet,' he said.

'I'll run the list up to Sterling,' said Flowers, handing Ryder his car key. 'She can start ringing around.'

'Where's the scraper?' Ryder queried.

'Driver's-door pocket,' Flowers called over his shoulder.

Ryder had removed the worst of the ice from the windscreen by the time Flowers returned. 'Sterling got anything yet?' he asked.

'Not yet. She's glad to have that list to work through,' said Flowers when they were in the car.

An icy blast hit Ryder's face as Flowers turned the engine over.

'Sorry, Sarge,' he mumbled, snapping closed the vents and turning the heater to high. 'Might have been easier to walk than defrost the car.' He started fiddling with the demister as the windows began to fog up.

Flowers drove steadily once he had vision through the windscreen, the wipers cleaning away the remaining ice. Out on Kosciuszko Road, a portable electronic sign warned of black ice on the road.

The interior had barely started to warm up when they turned into a regular Jindabyne street and stopped outside a flat-roofed, single-storey house. Only the blue-and-white checked sign standing in the front yard identified the building as a police station.

Melting snow dripped from the eaves as Ryder pulled off his gloves and stepped inside. While Flowers spoke to the junior female officer behind the counter, Gavin Hutton's face taunted Ryder from the 'Wanted' poster displayed on the waiting-room wall. Within minutes, Sergeant Thalia Cooper appeared and led them down a corridor to her uncommonly tidy office.

'You didn't waste any time getting here,' she said, eyeing them with wary acceptance as he and Flowers sat facing her across the desk.

'We're chasing another lead,' said Ryder, then recapped the purpose of their visit to the National Parks and Wildlife office.

'I've been here for six months,' she said, staring at them from under a bluntly cut fringe. 'I'll ask a few of the boys who've been here long-term if there was ever an incident report involving this security company you're looking for. One of them might remember something.'

Ryder nodded. 'Thanks ... and for contacting us about the campfire that was lit in the national park.'

She nodded, twisting the wedding ring on her finger. 'There's a note to flag you personally if anything out of the ordinary turns up. Sadly, someone lighting a fire in the park isn't unusual, but a whole lot of blood at the scene is.'

'Where exactly in the park was this?' Ryder asked.

'Down near Leatherbarrel Creek, not far from the border. Are you familiar with that area?'

Ryder shook his head. 'No.'

'There's a small camping ground there, close to the Alpine Way, but this was further in.' She pushed back her chair and stood up. 'Won't be a sec.'

She returned moments later carrying two large plastic evidence bags, both stuffed full of a mix of soggy and dry leaf matter. 'I'm sending these off to forensics this morning. I'm really hoping we don't find a body out there.'

'Would you mind sending them to Harriet Ono in Canberra?' Ryder asked. 'I've used her in the past. She's excellent.'

'I can send them to anyone you like.' Sergeant Cooper jotted down Harriet's name on her pad.

Ryder picked up one of the bags and turned it over in his hands, the plastic still cold from the fridge. Many of the smaller leaves had been drenched in blood, while larger foliage was marked with splatter patterns. Others contained streaks of blood as though they had been used to wipe something. Smaller particulates and specks of dried blood had worked their way into the corners of the bag. The second bag looked much the same.

'Do you think someone skinned and cooked an animal?' Flowers asked.

'I'm hoping someone's killed a rabbit and nothing else.' Sergeant Cooper shook her head. 'Although campers don't tend to kill anything, not even feral animals. Still, it would be a better outcome than a native animal or a human. We found blood in two separate spots, hence the two evidence bags.'

'That's a lot of blood for a rabbit,' said Flowers.

'Was anything else found at the scene?' asked Ryder.

'No. The fire was small, and nothing was left behind.'

Ryder nodded. 'Okay. Let us know if anyone's reported missing.'

'You'll be the first to know, Detective.'

'There is one other thing, Sergeant Cooper,' Ryder said. He had always suspected Hutton moved around the country by stealing cars, changing the plates, and probably torching the vehicles and leaving them in bushland. The reward for information leading to Hutton's arrest was worth so much money it would make hitch-hiking, public transport and even walking risky for him. Ryder only had to look at the number of false sightings to know the community was on the lookout.

'Are you able to get me a list of burned-out vehicles found in the Monaro district going back to 2017?' Ryder asked. 'Or should I contact Queanbeyan for that?'

'I can put in a request for that information,' Cooper said. 'It'll save you having to deal with two different stations.'

'We'd appreciate that.' Ryder pushed back his chair and stood up. 'Thank you, Sergeant. It's a long shot that the person who lit that fire is Gavin Hutton, but if you could cc me in on the blood analysis, that would be great.'

Sergeant Cooper nodded. 'Will do, Detective.'

Thirteen

Eva woke at 7.30 am to the sounds of Jack moving around in the lounge room. Careful not to wake Poppy, she slipped out of bed and into the ensuite, dressing quickly in her standard winter 'uniform' of black leggings, a long knitted jumper and white sneakers.

The fire burning throughout the night had kept the lounge room toasty warm. Drawing closer to the heat, Eva held out her hands to warm them. Jack was nowhere to be seen, but the rollaway bed was standing near the doorway at the top of the stairs. The blankets, folded with an army-style neatness, were stacked on a nearby chair.

Flexing the fingers on her tender right hand where it had connected with Jack's chin, she headed towards the kitchen. Cooking sounds greeted her as she pushed open the swing door.

'Oh, good, you're awake,' he said.

Eva stopped so suddenly her rubber sole stuck to the floor and made a high-pitched squeak. His hair was short, a bit unevenly cut, and the facial growth was gone.

'Want some omelette?' Jack asked, the piercing blue eyes she remembered so well clear and alert this morning.

She looked with interest at the omelette rising in her largest pan. 'Okay.'

'I've used a lot of your eggs. The protein will help repair muscle.'

'Help yourself to whatever you want.' She glanced sideways at him, surprised to find his hair was dark blonde. Apart from when he'd shown up yesterday, she'd only ever known him with his head shaved.

'There's no sign of Hutton.' He lifted the edges of the omelette with an egg slide. 'We've had about fifty centimetres of snow overnight. That, and the injury will slow him down.'

Eva breathed a sigh of relief. The longer Hutton took to get to the lodge, the stronger Jack would be. She took two plates from the cupboard and put them on the benchtop, then switched the kettle on to boil. 'How's the . . .' She baulked at saying 'stab wound' and settled for 'injury'.

'Better.' He cut the omelette into pieces and slid some onto her plate. 'I've checked around the property. Nothing's disturbed. The only tracks outside were made by small animals.'

Eva sat opposite him at the table as she'd done every morning after . . . oh, God. She fumbled with her cutlery, conscious of the heat in her face. The man sitting opposite her was unlike the one who'd burst into the lodge yesterday, and everything like the one who'd walked into her kitchen four years ago and asked if they could have more bread.

Poppy's father.

'How come it all went wrong?' she blurted out.

He looked up from his omelette, his eyebrows raised.

'The negotiation process, with Hutton.'

He put down his cutlery and swallowed before answering. 'It didn't, not from the insurance company's viewpoint at least. We worked within the parameters we had. Personally, I was disappointed that I couldn't negotiate a release, but the Swedes did, so that was a relief. When a group's taken, there's cooperation between the stakeholders.' He cut another slice of omelette and stabbed it with his fork. 'As far as the hostages go, no one can predict what their state of mind will be after they're released. It's like war.' He chewed slowly, watching her.

Eva cut a small piece of omelette and ate it. 'You're right,' she said.

'I am? About what?'

'It's very eggy.'

This time the half-smile reached his eyes. 'You don't have to eat it.'

Eva laid down her fork and went to make tea while he demolished the rest of his breakfast. 'I was thinking about this last night,' she said when she sat down again, 'and I'm not defending Gavin Hutton, not in the least, but why wouldn't the government have stepped in? Didn't he fight for this country?'

'Hutton did serve, and I get where you're coming from, but the government stepping in is not the answer. If the press and general public start lobbying for the release of hostages, it plays right into the kidnappers' hands. They love that kind of publicity. That's how millions of dollars are exchanged, and before you know it, another person is kidnapped. Huge payouts increase the odds of more Aussies being kidnapped. They become a target.'

Eva frowned, trying to understand the murky world in which Jack operated. 'So, insurance is the only way companies can protect their workers?'

He nodded. 'Usually it's high-profile execs flying around the world who are most at risk. Hutton was a security officer at a mine in the Philippines. He was snatched by a bunch of opportunists, along with some other people who were out on the town one night.'

A jazzy ring tone filled the kitchen as Eva's phone lit up on the bench. They both jumped up from the table at the same time. Eva looked at the screen in dismay. 'It's Bede.'

'Let it go to voicemail.'

'He probably wants to know if I'm going into town. I offered to pick up anything he needed.'

At the beep, Jack played back the message. 'Hey, Eva. I'm sending a couple of new boys around with a broken drill bit. Can you see if you've got one the same size we can use? Thanks. Oh, and I told them to put those ski racks out for you while they're there. Sorry to bother you so early.'

The doorbell rang before Jack had even hung up.

'Shit!' Eva said. 'Sometimes messages take a while to come through when the reception's patchy. I'll get the drill pack from the garage.'

'No, come with me.' He was already heading for the door. 'We'll send them down to the bottom entry.'

Eva followed him across the lounge room, fingers of early-morning sunlight shining between the gaps in the curtains. The doorbell rang a second time, the melodic notes echoing throughout the lodge. Eva glanced at the door to her suite, which remained firmly closed. Hopefully, Poppy would sleep a bit longer.

They crossed the lobby, pushing through the glass doors and into the vestibule. Eva shivered in the cooler air.

'Yes?' Jack called out in the low, authoritative tone that had terrified her yesterday, reassuring now the lodge's fragile defences were being breached.

'Hey,' a young male voice resonated through the door. 'Bede sent us over to pick up a drill bit.' Some indecipherable mumbling followed, then laughter.

Eva watched, stomach churning with nerves as Jack unbolted the deadlock and swung the wooden door open. Not that she expected Hutton to come charging in the moment the door was open, but she couldn't stop herself scanning the clearing and the trees beyond for anything unusual. *Someone* had left those footprints in the snow yesterday.

Bright light blinded her. She threw up a forearm, blocking out the reflected rays from the snow's surface. Squinting, she peered past Jack's shoulder. Without sunglasses, it was impossible to see if anyone was lurking beyond the two young men standing at the door.

'Morning, fellas,' said Jack.

'Hey.' The taller one looked Jack up and down with interest. The other young man was shorter and thicker set. Both wore beanies pulled low over their foreheads, baggy pants and jackets, and lace-up boots. As Eva's eyes adjusted to the glare, she could make out two snowboards propped against the steps.

'So, you have power-tool problems?' Jack asked.

'Not me man, him.' The taller one looked at his shorter mate and gave a goofy laugh. 'Broke the bit, drilling into a brick wall at the Willy Wagtail.'

The shorter guy sniggered, looked down at his feet and shook his head. 'Such a lame name for a ski lodge.'

'Okay.' Jack took the broken bit from the shorter one. 'Might be best if you go around to the bottom door.' He pointed along the front of the building. 'See you downstairs in a minute.'

Jack closed the door and locked it, then looked at Eva. 'I don't think we have too much to worry about with these two.' He paused for a few seconds. 'Do you think Bede will ask them if they put the racks out?'

Eva bit her lip. 'I reckon he will.'

'Then let's do it, so we can get rid of them. We don't want Bede sending them back.'

'Mummy?'

Eva swung around at the sound of Poppy's voice.

'You're awake,' she said, watching the little girl skip towards them.

'I dressed myself,' she said proudly, twirling around.

'Good job.' Eva had to stop herself chuckling at the outfit Poppy had selected. She wore the unicorn onesie Eva had bought for her to sleep in, and pink plastic gum boots. A red and white polka dot skirt was pulled on over the top of the onesie. 'We're going downstairs,' she said, lifting Poppy up. 'You'd better come, too.'

Eva followed Jack, relieved to see him moving with more agility than yesterday.

'Wait here,' he said when they reached the bottom. 'The drill pack's in the garage, right?'

Eva nodded. 'On the shelf next to the peg board.'

'You slept for ages,' she said to Poppy as the garage light flickered on, illuminating the area under the stairs. Outside, the scrape of a snowboard on ice told her the boys from Bede's lodge had arrived.

Jack was back with the drill pack in less than a minute, opening the door to the equipment room and shoving the doorstop underneath to hold it open. 'I'll stay at the entry while they bring the racks out. It's a chance for me to check down the side of the building from ground level.'

Eva watched as he opened the external door and handed the drill pack to one of the boys, opening the pack and showing them the bit size they needed.

That downstairs door, that's where we're most vulnerable.

'Watch as you go in, fellas,' Jack was saying. 'The entry's as slippery as an ice rink. I'd give you a hand, but I've got a rib cartilage injury.'

'How'd ya do that?' the taller one asked.

'Skiing in Niseko.'

'I hope to get to Japan one day.' The shorter one came in first, stomping clumps of snow off his boots. Cocking his head towards the equipment room he looked at Eva. 'In there?'

'Yes. They're really heavy.'

They brought the smaller rack out first. 'Where do you want it?' the shorter one asked.

'One either side of the verandah steps. Thanks.'

They returned swiftly, huffing and puffing from the exertion while Jack stood sentinel at the door. The larger rack was next. As they manoeuvred the splayed legs through the doorway of the equipment room, Eva retreated along the passageway towards the garage and set a struggling Poppy onto the floor.

'Put it down for a bit,' the taller one said in a rush. Grimacing from the effort, his face flaming, he pulled in some deep breaths.

'Careful not to jam your hands,' Eva warned, as they prepared to lift it again.

'Yeah, it's tight,' huffed the shorter one. 'I'm glad I'm wearing gloves.'

There was a scrape of metal against concrete as the legs and the top of the rack wedged between the walls.

'This happened last time,' Eva said, letting go of Poppy's hand. 'You need to tilt it, this way.' She demonstrated, holding her left hand slightly higher than the right.

Jack glanced over his shoulder, his brows pulled together, an irritated expression on his face. Eva wanted to tell these two to forget all about it so they could lock up the lodge again, but the rack was stuck in the middle of the passageway, blocking access to the laundry and garage. 'Last year they lifted it higher. The passageway's not square. It's narrower at the bottom.'

They did as she instructed, lifting it about half a metre and tilting it in the right direction. Carefully, they started to move again. With a sigh of relief, Eva turned to get Poppy.

The passageway behind her was empty, as was the room where the ski racks had been.

'Poppy?' she called, her heart leaping. There was no way she would have gone into the garage; Eva would have heard the door close.

'Poppy?' she called louder, unable to keep the note of panic from her voice. 'Jack!' she cried, trapped behind the metal rack and the two snowboarders. 'Where's Poppy!'

Fourteen

'Where do you think you're off to?' she heard Jack ask.

'She's up here,' one of the snowboarders said over his shoulder. 'She crawled past between me and the wall when we lifted the rack up.'

Relief turned Eva's legs to water. She watched as Jack scooped Poppy up in his arms. Poppy grizzled at her plan being thwarted, then squealed with delight as Jack lifted her higher in the air before settling her onto his shoulders. Holding Poppy's gumboots, he stepped outside into the snow as the snowboarders finally reached the end of the passageway.

Eva rushed through the doorway, slipping and sliding in her inadequate sneakers, desperate to have Poppy close to her again. Only once before had she lost sight of Poppy, in a department store in the city. One moment she'd been there, the next she'd vanished. It had taken Eva's panicked cry for the little girl to give up her hiding place among a row of thick winter coats hanging on a circular rack. The last few minutes had been every bit as terrifying as the incident in the department store ... the added threat of Gavin Hutton amplifying Eva's fears.

Despite her lack of outdoor clothing, she plodded through the snow to where Jack stood a short distance away. At the forefront of her mind was the relentless fear she was destined to live with should Jack fail to apprehend Hutton.

'Mummy, look at me,' Poppy cried, her small hands buried in Jack's hair.

'I can see you,' she snapped, anger welling to the surface now Poppy was safe. 'You scared me,' Eva said, her voice catching. 'How many times have I told you not to run away from me? What if they'd dropped that rack on you?'

'Hey, she's all right,' Jack said, his eyes on the two boys as they lugged the ski rack around to the front of the lodge.

'Sorry, Mummy,' Poppy said, looking down at Eva, her eyes full of contrition.

'It's okay,' she said with a smile. She shouldn't have let go of her daughter's hand, but she'd been anxious to help so the boys could leave as quickly as possible.

'The only tracks out here are made by our two removalists,' said Jack. 'There's no sign of anyone else.'

'Not even the bunny?' asked Poppy in dismay. 'I was looking for him.'

'Is that why you ran out here?' Eva asked, looking up at her daughter, who seemed perfectly at ease sitting on Jack's shoulders in her skirt and unicorn onesie. She glanced at Jack. 'We saw a bunny in the clearing when we talked to Randall yesterday.'

'I can see everything up here,' Poppy bellowed, rocking backwards and forwards on Jack's shoulders. 'Maybe I'll see him hopping around.'

The snowboarders were making their way back, looking every bit as relieved as Eva felt that the job was done.

Jack shifted Poppy's hand from his left eye up to his forehead and spoke to them. 'Were you fellas sliding down that track yesterday, and grinding across the picnic tables?'

'Yeah, that was us, sorry,' the taller one mumbled as he bent to pick up his snowboard. 'Bede let us off early. We won't do it again.'

'We don't mind if you do. Eva thought she heard someone outside, that's all. You might give us a heads-up if you see someone hanging around, okay?'

'Sure man, will do,' he said.

After waving the boys off, they headed back to the lodge. 'Come on,' said Jack. 'Let's all get inside.'

Eva stumbled, unable to feel anything much from the knees down. Her sneakers were soaked through with freezing snow.

A strong arm came around her waist, supporting her just as she was about to pitch sideways again. Tucked against Jack's side, she put one numb foot in front of the other until they were safely inside the bottom door.

Jack lifted Poppy off his shoulders while Eva, using the wall as support, hobbled towards the staircase.

'What's wrong, Mummy?' Poppy asked, running up behind her while Jack locked the door.

Eva sank onto the bottom step and pulled at the wet laces, desperate to rid her feet of the soaked sneakers. 'My feet have gone numb.' Needles of pain speared through her lower legs as the feeling slowly started to come back. 'I'll be all right once I warm up,' she said, unable to suppress the violent shiver that shot up her spine. She did her best to smile at Poppy but only managed a grimace. 'I wasn't properly dressed for outside. My hands are stinging.'

Jack was back now, picking up the sneakers and looking down at her.

'Sit in front of the fire, Mummy,' Poppy said, helping Eva to rub her feet.

'The fire will be too much direct heat,' said Jack. 'Your mum needs a bath to warm up her core.'

Eva rolled her eyes at him. 'Like she knows what core temperature is.' Shaking her head and using the handrail to pull herself up, Eva began the long climb up the stairs, conscious of Jack and Poppy behind her.

'I won't be long,' she said when they reached the top.

He nodded, then looked down at Poppy. 'How about I get you breakfast?'

114

After adding more hot water, Eva sank deeper into the tub until the water lapped over her shoulders. Resting her head against the inflatable pillow, she closed her eyes, her mind wandering as the heat soaked into her bones.

She trusted him with Poppy. There was no denying that.

She wouldn't be lying here while he watched over her daughter if she had any lingering doubts about him. As he had done four years ago, Jack Walker had upended her life in twenty-four hours. Back then, they'd created new life, a child, something Eva had been told she would never conceive naturally because of her body's reluctance to ovulate. And now he was back, protecting that child from someone intent on harming her.

Eva shivered despite the heat of the water, the CCTV image of Gavin Hutton in a Goulburn street forming in her mind. Opening her eyes, she sat up, splashing water over the side, her gaze darting into every corner of the room. A man she didn't know was robbing her of her peace of mind, a man intent on cruelty was planning to take something infinitely precious from her.

She couldn't let it happen.

Back in her bedroom, she pushed aside the clothes in her wardrobe and stared at the safe in the wall. Reaching out, she rested her fingers over the combination lock, replaying her father's words in her head.

'*More feral cats?*' *she asked, leaning against the doorframe, and sipping her coffee.*

'*Take this with you, Evie.*' *Her dad closed the gun safe and straightened up, the pistol he'd taught her to shoot with and a box of ammunition in his hand.* '*It's registered. You may as well take it. It's yours.*'

Eva sighed. '*Oh, Dad, you know how I feel about guns. They're necessary out here on the farm, I understand that, but I'm a chef. When am I going to need a handgun?*'

'*I'll feel better if you have it, living alone in the mountains like that. Be sure to keep it in a safe, though. You remember what happened to Billy Burns when you were in year four.*'

'*I do,*' *she muttered.* '*That's why I hate them.*'

*Eva pushed off the doorframe as her father came closer. 'Take it,'
he said. 'You know we have others.'*

*'Yes, I know.' Eva put down her coffee mug and reluctantly took
the pistol she hadn't touched since high school. She'd never use it,
and she could always bring it home and make her father put it back
in the safe. Eva turned it over in her hand. Still, if it made him sleep
easier at night . . .*

She looked up at her father.

'I love you, Evie. I hope you never need it.'

Fifteen

Back in Flowers' room at The Loft Apartments, Ryder split the list Patricia Franks had given them three ways. There were companies specialising in field trips and leadership programs for high-school students, and then there were eco adventures, fly fishing and guided mountain walks. Not one of the operators they'd spoken to had heard of a security course being run anywhere in the Monaro area in the past.

Ryder was beginning to wonder if Kimberley Dickson had her facts straight about where this 'security course' had taken place.

Flowers hung up his phone and dropped his pen on the table. 'Horse riding, bird watching, four-wheel driving—everything except what we're looking for.'

Ryder tried to ignore the informational message playing in his ear for the eighth bloody time while he waited on hold. 'Hopefully Patricia Franks will come back to us this afternoon with her archived list.'

Flowers yawned and stood up. 'I'm making coffee. Any takers?'

'Yes, please,' said Sterling. 'Whatever you have is fine.'

'Instant, thanks,' said Ryder, losing patience when the message began to play again. He could recite it start to finish by now. Killing the call, he went to stand at the glass doors and looked out over a grey Lake Jindabyne. He was punching in the next number on his list, a company that ran white-water rafting adventures, when a call came through from Sergeant O'Neill at The Entrance.

'Sergeant, how are you?' Ryder switched his phone to loudspeaker.

'Ah, gettin' there,' the sergeant drawled. 'Sorry it's taken me a while. I've managed to get some information for you about Trevor Swan.'

'Great,' said Ryder, trying not to sound too impatient.

'Well, he's not at the boarding house anymore.'

'I'm not surprised. Did he leave a forwarding address, or has he kept in touch with anyone there?'

'This is where it gets interesting. The boarding house is still owned by the same bloke, so he remembers everything that happened.'

'What happened?'

'Swan went to visit his brother in the Philippines for a couple of weeks in 2017 and never returned. He didn't go back to his job either.'

'Hang on a moment, Sergeant.' Ryder spoke to Sterling: 'Check if Swan is listed as a missing person.' Then to Sergeant O'Neill: 'Did the landlord report him missing?'

'Nope, neither did the principal at the local high school where he used to do some casual work. They thought he must have met a woman and decided to stay illegally, so they didn't report it.'

'We'll check with the relevant authorities,' said Ryder. 'We know his brother arrived in Australia from the Philippines in 2017.'

'The landlord said Swan was a good tenant, always paid his rent on time and never caused any problems. That's why he kept some of his things in case he turned up one day out of the blue.'

'Things?' Ryder asked, a spike of adrenaline kicking his heartbeat along. 'Personal items?'

'Yeah, I thought you'd like that,' O'Neill chuckled. 'There's a cardboard box full of Swan's personal items in the garage. His clothes went in the charity bin a while back.'

'This is great news, Sergeant, thank you. We'll be up there tomorrow to take a look through that box.'

'Would you like me to take possession of it for you?'

'No, it can stay there. I'd like to have a talk to the owner. You can tell him to guard it with his life, though.'

The sergeant chuckled again. 'Will do. Stick your head in and say g'day if you have time.'

'He's not listed as missing, Sarge,' Sterling said when Ryder had hung up.

'Right. Call headquarters, Sterling. Speak to O'Day if you can, but if you can't, any of the others will do. Tell them to start calling the airlines. We need to know if Swan flew in on the same flight as Hutton. If not, find out when he flew back into Australia—if he did.'

'That could be why Swan hasn't called the hotline.' Flowers handed out the hot drinks. 'We were wondering why he hadn't claimed that reward.'

'*You* were wondering,' Ryder pointed out, picking up his coffee. 'You're obsessed with that reward.'

'I am not,' Flowers gave him a wounded look. 'But it's a lot of money on offer. Loyalty has its limits.'

'When did you become so cynical?' Ryder asked.

Sterling took a sip from her mug, swallowed, then grimaced. '*Ooh!* What is that?'

Flowers grabbed a packet and held it up for them to see. 'Tumeric latte. You can buy it in a packet now, Sarge.' Then to Sterling. 'Do you like it?'

'It's . . . interesting,' she said, taking another tentative sip. 'Have you tried it, Sarge?'

Ryder guffawed and took a sip of his instant black. 'Flowers knows better than to give it to me.'

While Sterling called Parramatta, Ryder studied an enlarged print of Thredbo Village. The information from the airlines and Trevor Swan's birth certificate could take another week to come through. Patricia Franks was searching the archives looking for the course Hutton had participated in, and the blood swabs taken from the campsite wouldn't be back in a hurry. Ryder studied the weather. The clouds had lifted, and the traffic heading up the mountain was moving at a good pace. It was time they got out in the field before heading back to Sydney this afternoon.

Twenty minutes later they were on the Alpine Way. The landscape flashed past: a winery, a guest house, a resort nestled around the shores of Lake Crackenback. Ryder followed the line of the ski tube up the mountain before it plunged underground and out of sight.

Flowers slowed the car at the Kosciuszko National Park gates, showed his badge to the woman on duty and they were on their way again.

Later they turned into Banjo Drive, took the loop around by the river and parked a short distance from the Thredbo Alpine Museum.

'Good afternoon.' A woman with spikey grey hair greeted them from behind the counter. 'Welcome to the museum. If you'd like to sign the visitors' book, it's right there,' she added, pointing to where a leather-bound book lay open on the glass counter.

'I'm Detective Ryder from Sydney Homicide Squad, and this is Detectives Flowers and Sterling,' Ryder began.

'Oh, good heavens,' the woman exclaimed before looking towards the back of the museum and calling, 'Chloe!' The woman looked back at Ryder. 'You're the detectives who solved that case up here a while ago. I remember seeing you on TV.'

'Yes, that was us,' Flowers said, moving up to stand beside Ryder. Sterling wandered off to have a look at the exhibits.

'Hello.'

Ryder turned to see Chloe Cambron walking towards them from the back of the museum, a delighted expression on her face, her lolly-pink hair shining under the lights.

'Remember us?' Ryder asked with a smile.

'Of course,' she said in her soft French accent. 'We haven't stopped talking about you since you made the arrest at Charlotte Pass. Helen and I boast to everyone who'll listen that the museum played a part in solving the crime.' She gave a soft laugh. 'We exaggerate, but it's good publicity.'

'We're hoping you might be able to help us again,' said Ryder.

Chloe clapped her hands. 'We'd be delighted, wouldn't we, Helen?'

The older woman nodded, her eyes shining.

'We're after information about a particular course or group activity that was run somewhere in the park, or its surrounds, some years ago. We believe it could have been slightly more hardcore than what's on offer now.' Ryder recalled Patricia Franks' words. 'Activities like canyoning, caving, mountaineering, abseiling.'

Chloe looked at Helen for several seconds. 'There was that one ...'

'Yes, I know the one you're thinking of,' Helen said, nodding.

Ryder waited, giving them time to think.

'I remember him,' said Chloe. 'We don't have any information about the company here at the museum, but his name was John. I never knew his last name.'

'Yes, John is right,' Helen confirmed. 'Bald.'

Chloe shook her head. 'Shaved. Aviator sunglasses, tall, well built, Australian.'

'I wish everybody had your memory,' said Flowers.

Chloe raised what appeared to Ryder to be tattooed eyebrows, and gazed at Flowers. 'I never forget a handsome face, Detective.'

Ryder smirked while Flowers grinned from ear to ear. Chloe's tendency to flirt hadn't lessened over the past year.

'The company was called Extreme something,' she said, 'Extreme *Adventures* maybe ...'

Ryder turned. Sterling was standing next to a rack of vintage skis. 'Can you do a business name and company search on your phone, please, Sterling?'

'Yes, Sergeant.'

'He came in here a few times looking at our maps,' Chloe went on. 'He took photos of some of them with his phone camera.'

'Do you remember which area he was looking at?' Ryder's heart began to thump hard. There was information to be learned from this instructor, and maybe from the others on the course as well.

Chloe's tattooed brows drew together as she thought back. She shook her head. 'I'm sorry, I can't remember where.'

'If you think of it, please, give me a call,' said Ryder. 'We've spoken to the National Parks and Wildlife office in Jindabyne. A staff member there feels this particular course catered to people with a military background. Is that your recollection?'

'There was a group of his students waiting for him outside once,' Helen said. 'They were carrying specialised equipment, like ice axes and crampons. I remember thinking a few of them had a military bearing, but not all.'

'Would you recognise any of them?' Ryder asked.

'Oh, no,' Helen said quickly. 'I didn't pay any attention to their faces.'

No use whipping out a photo of Hutton, then. That would spark false rumours and panic that the killer was in the area. Ryder could just imagine Inspector Gray's reaction.

'I want to say,' began Chloe, 'some of them were training for Kilimanjaro or maybe the walk to the Everest base camp. Anyway, he said they were getting in shape and acclimatising to the cold.'

Ryder glanced at Flowers. 'Sounds like the one we're looking for.'

'Extreme Adventures, you say?' confirmed Flowers.

Chloe nodded. 'I'm sure that's what he said when he rang and asked me about the maps, and again when he came in—Extreme Adventures.'

Ryder nodded. 'Well, thank you both. You've been very helpful.'

'Any titbits you'd like to share with us, Sergeant?' Chloe asked with a playful wink at Helen. 'We could keep our ear to the ground for you, so to speak.'

Flowers laughed. 'If we need an informant in Thredbo, you'll be first on our list, Chloe.'

'Merci, Detective,' she said, accompanying them to the door.

They bade farewell to Chloe and decided to stretch their legs with a quick walk through the village before heading back to Jindabyne. Ryder checked his watch. The display showed the temperature was an invigorating two degrees, the sun beaming from a cloudless sky. Ahead of them, a tall, rangy man in a button-down shirt, clearly accustomed to the cold, was sweeping the area in front of

CRACKENBACK

the newsagency. Further along, staff were dressing mannequins in the window of a ski-apparel store. Outside a bakery, a couple sat at a table, poring over newspapers, hot chocolates cradled between gloved hands.

Ryder walked on, leaving behind the enticing aroma of marshmallows and chocolate. While Flowers and Sterling lingered at a window display, Ryder's gaze tracked towards the golf course covered in snow after last night's dump, then higher to where Eva's lodge nestled among a thick expanse of trees. Over the years, Vanessa's sister had welcomed all manner of mountain bikers and climbers there as guests.

Maybe he'd give her a call.

123

Sixteen

In between patrols, Jack cleaned up the mess he'd made in the bathroom yesterday. Bending over, he picked up the pile of stiff clothing, pleased with his flexibility. Given a member of his regiment had suffered a similar injury years ago, Jack figured it would take around ten days to fully heal. Still, the skin was closing nicely, and the gnawing pain had lessened to an irritating soreness. Importantly, his body would be replenishing the blood loss while the antibiotics were keeping infection at bay.

Downstairs, he dumped the clothes in the washing machine and switched the setting to 'heavily soiled'. Back in the bathroom, he made sure every trace of blood was removed from the white tiles and basin, then washed the floor over with a mop he'd found in the laundry. Once the bathroom was restored to its pristine condition, he made his way to the Wisteria Suite where he'd put the rest of his things.

Eva had needed a distraction from the tense situation, so she was keeping herself busy making up the beds on the other side of the lodge. Earlier, he'd watched as she put butterflied lamb into the slow cooker before sliding a pie into the oven. Every time he did a perimeter check, the aroma wafting from the kitchen made his mouth water. Constantly hungry, he was yet to regain the weight he'd lost camping in the national park.

A door closed somewhere and then Eva appeared in the doorway, two folded blankets in her arms. 'Hey.'

'Hey,' he replied. 'Everything okay?'

She nodded, her gaze moving past him to the small, lightweight backpack open on the bed.

Jack pushed a hand into his hair. 'I put my stuff in here so it's out of your way. I didn't think you'd want to be looking at it all the time.'

'Here's as good as anywhere. It's not like I have guests.' She came into the room and put the blankets down on an armchair. 'What do you have in there?' she asked.

'Not much. I came in here to get the binoculars.' He held the backpack open for her to see. 'There's some dried food, chocolate bars and a plastic water bottle.' He'd been down to a day's rations when he'd lit the fire, a last-ditch effort to draw Hutton out. The knife had been a surprise, though, especially as the news reports said Hutton had beaten Burrows and Suter to death with his bare hands.

'How did you know Hutton was hiding out around Leatherbarrel Creek?' Eva asked.

He shrugged. 'I tried getting in his head. Where would I go if I were hiding out, getting ready to strike again?'

Jack didn't miss her sharp intake of breath. 'I wouldn't be in another town or State, that's for sure, especially with a bounty on my head. I wouldn't be too close to here either, where the locals know each other. There are campgrounds around Tom Groggin and Leatherbarrel. That means a food source and complacent tourists leaving cars unlocked. Hutton could scavenge a lot from those campgrounds.'

She raised her eyebrows. 'So, you went into the bush on a hunch?'

'I wish I was that good,' he said, unable to keep the rueful smile off his face, 'but we camped around Leatherbarrel and Dead Horse Gap before we came up here to the lodge. I'd given the students orienteering maps of the area.'

'So, you were right.'

It was more a statement than a question, so Jack didn't answer. With luck, his instincts would stay solid and Hutton would turn up here, giving Jack the opportunity to deal with him once and for all. Otherwise, everything he'd put Eva through yesterday when he'd burst in downstairs would be for nothing.

'That's it?' she said. She was peering into the backpack again. 'Is that all you had with you?'

'Pretty much. There's an extra pair of woollen socks in there, and a second pair of speedos. They dry quicker than undies.'

She shot him a look, then walked over to where his swag sat in a corner of the room. 'What about in there?'

He frowned. 'Only a sleeping bag. It's bulky at the moment. You can take it out and have a look if you like.'

She shook her head.

'What exactly are you looking for, Eva?'

She paused. 'Come with me. Poppy's having an afternoon nap, but she's a heavy sleeper. We won't wake her up.'

Wake her up? Doing what?

'Okay . . .' He followed her through the hallway and into the lounge room, where the fire had died down to a single lick of flame. Making a note to stoke it before it went out completely, he left the binoculars on the mantel and followed Eva to the door of her suite. She paused, then turned to face him as she had done four years ago, though not for a moment did Jack kid himself it was for a similar reason this time. Putting an index finger to her lips, she opened the door and beckoned him inside.

The wardrobe door stood slightly ajar. Eva pushed it wider then, standing on tiptoe, reached behind a stack of woollen sweaters to retrieve something hidden behind them.

Jack swore under his breath when he saw it. So that's what she'd been looking for in his backpack. He glanced across the room at Poppy. Thankfully, she was facing the window, her silky hair the only part of her he could see, her tiny, defenceless body a small bump under the flowery quilt.

Bringing his gaze back to Eva, he felt the weight of the steel-framed, compact Beretta the moment she gave it to him. He quickly checked the safety and magazine before shoving the handgun into his waistband and leaving the room.

'What the hell are you doing with a Beretta in your wardrobe?' he demanded the moment they were outside the room.

'It's mine—'

'It should be in a safe,' he snapped. 'Poppy—'

'I'm not that stupid,' she snapped back. 'It is locked up . . . normally.'

Jack watched as she walked over to the lounge and sank down in one corner, a box of ammunition magazines in her hands. 'There's a safe at the back of the wardrobe.' She raised her chin and looked him straight in the eye. 'I took it out after I had a bath this morning. I didn't have the opportunity to get it yesterday when you barged in here. You're lucky, otherwise I might have used it on you.'

Needing to gather his thoughts, Jack went to the fireplace and added two small logs before brushing off his hands.

'You don't have a handgun?' she asked.

'Nope.'

'Why not?'

'I don't need one. The majority of my work involves training corporations and their staff on how to *avoid* getting kidnapped. The negotiating work happens intermittently.' Jack manoeuvred the logs around with the poker so they didn't smother the flames, then sat down at the opposite end of the lounge. He glanced at the ammunition in her hands, relieved he'd only had to deal with something as dangerous as a doorstopper.

For a while they stayed silent, staring into the flames as the fire roared to life again, giving each other time to cool down.

'Is it registered?' he asked eventually.

She nodded. 'It's Dad's. He bought it for me, though. He taught me and Vanessa how to shoot.'

'Do you still practise target shooting?'

'No. Vanessa does. She'll be a third-generation farmer when Mum and Dad retire. Vanessa loves the farm as passionately as she loves skiing.' She looked down at the ammo in her lap. 'Dad wanted us to learn how to use a gun safely after a boy we went to school with accidentally shot his brother. We have rifles at the farm, for pest control, but with large animals, well, sometimes they need to be put down.' She shot him a glance. 'I only took it to make Dad feel better. He was worried about me living here on my own.'

When he didn't say anything, she asked, 'What about you, do you practise?'

'Yeah, at the shooting range.' Jack had never been able to imagine Eva as a country kid, though he'd known she'd grown up on a property. But he could see it now in the way she talked about the firearms kept at the family farm, and the way she'd calmly put the piece in his hand. 'You were never tempted to stay on the property?'

She shook her head slowly. 'I only ever wanted two things in life: to be a chef and to have a family.'

'You've achieved both of those.'

'I was lucky you came along.'

Jack swivelled around so he could look directly at her. He had no idea what she was going to say, but he sensed that whatever it was, it was big.

'When I was a teenager, I was told I had polycystic ovaries.' She waved a dismissive hand like she didn't intend explaining it. 'Short story is, I was never going to ovulate. I told you I was protected, but it wasn't by a contraceptive; I was told my body simply didn't work that way. All I had to worry about was you using a condom.' Finally, she turned to face him. 'I don't know why my hormones chose that moment to get in sync, but I'll be forever grateful they did. Poppy is my miracle baby, Jack, loved and cherished by my entire family.'

'I'm glad.' Jack swallowed hastily. She'd been honest with him. It was time he did the same. 'Look, after our conversation in the park, I went home, telling myself you were a lovely woman and you'd meet a decent bloke in time, one who'd be around for you and Poppy, a bloke who doesn't have one foot in such a dangerous occupation.'

'I don't need a *bloke*.' She got to her feet and stood looking down at him. 'I need Hutton out of our life. That's what you came here to do, isn't it? So use the Beretta if it gets to that point.'

❄

Eva sat drinking a glass of water at the kitchen table. She hadn't intended on telling Jack about her medical condition; the conversation had just gone in that direction. She put the glass on the table with a snap, then sighed as the swing door opened and he walked in. He didn't sit, just took the firearm from his waistband and laid it carefully on the table.

Eva raised her eyes to his.

'I'm going to try to negotiate with him. Hutton and I have a relationship of sorts. I've met him three times: here, in the Philippines and the other day at the campsite. If I can get him talking, I might be able to convince him to turn himself in.'

'You really think he'll come voluntarily?'

'I don't know, but prior to Hutton being kidnapped, I had a hundred-percent success rate, so I think it's worth a shot. I'll take him by force if I have to.'

He put his hand on the Beretta and shifted it closer to her. 'Normally, I'd dissuade any novice from handling a firearm regardless of the situation, but you're not a novice. You mightn't have kept up your level of accuracy, but you've been a shooter in the past and that's enough for me.'

Eva nodded. 'Okay.'

'You can use it as a last resort if Hutton gets past me, not that I'm expecting him to. You'll need to wait until the last possible moment, and fire at close range. It's the only way you'll hit him.'

Seventeen

Poppy had woken from a long afternoon nap around five asking if they could make cupcakes. Eva agreed, happy to keep their home life as normal as possible despite the ever-present threat of evil appearing in the form of Gavin Hutton.

'Can I swift?' Poppy asked. She was standing on a solid kitchen chair, a small wooden spoon in one hand, a container of sprinkles in the other.

'Sift,' Eva said with a smile, though it quickly faded as she remembered how easily Poppy had dragged the chair from under the table across to the bench. Her thoughts shifted nervously to the loaded handgun stowed in her wardrobe. Rationally, she knew Poppy wasn't strong enough to drag the cane chair across the carpeted bedroom, and even if she did manage to stand on it the way she was doing now, the shelf was too high for her to reach. But so ingrained in her was the responsibility to keep firearms locked in a safe, she felt totally reckless having the Beretta so accessible, even if it made sense to do so in this situation.

Eva tipped the flour into the sifter and held it steady while Poppy turned the handle.

You'll need to wait until the last possible moment, and fire at close range. It's the only way you'll hit him.

If she were forced to shoot Hutton, it would be in self-defence. Jack hadn't needed to spell that part out for her.

'Well done.' She smiled at Poppy and put the sifter on the bench. 'I'll fold the flour in, and then you can give it a stir with your spoon, okay?'

Poppy didn't answer.

'Okay?' Eva asked again.

'Okay.' Poppy screwed up her nose. 'I'm hungry already.'

'Would you like some sultanas? These won't be ready until after dinner.' Eva went to look in the pantry. 'Where are they?' she said, moving groceries aside on the shelves. 'I couldn't find them yesterday either.'

The oven beeped, having reached its required temperature. 'We can put the cupcakes in now,' she said over her shoulder. She straightened up, and put a hand on her hip. 'Well, that's odd.'

'What's odd?'

Eva gave a violent start and spun around, her heart racing. Jack was standing in the middle of the kitchen, a purple bath towel from the Wisteria Suite hanging over one shoulder.

'Don't sneak up on me like that.'

'I didn't,' he said, going to the sink and filling a glass with water. 'I just walked in, didn't I, Poppy?'

Poppy nodded, giggling like a co-conspirator.

'What's odd?' he asked again, his face covered in a sheen of sweat. Earlier, he'd wanted to know if she owned any free weights. She didn't, but she'd given him a set of resistance bands she'd bought on a whim and never opened.

'Sultanas, tinned berries, cashews. I know I bought them, but they're not here.' Eva went to pick up the sifter only to knock it into the sink where Jack was refilling his glass. She paused, willing herself to breathe while he fished it out. 'I was going to put berries in the pie this morning. I used apples instead, but I'm certain I bought berries.'

'Maybe you left a bag behind at the supermarket?'

Eva shook her head. 'I'm a chef. I check all the bags are in the trolley before I leave. I can't be running backwards and forwards to the supermarket when the lodge is full of guests.'

He leaned against the sink, watching her, his arms folded. Eva suspected his relaxed pose was for Poppy's benefit.

'I'll see if I can find the docket later. Poppy needs something to eat now.'

She watched him push off the sink. He went to the fridge and opened the door abruptly. 'How about yoghurt?' He held up the container for Poppy to see.

Poppy nodded enthusiastically.

Troubled by the missing groceries, Eva settled Poppy at the table, watching while Jack spooned yoghurt into a bowl. She was so used to doing everything herself, it was unsettling to see Poppy being cared for by her father.

'What do you do when you get home from shopping?' he asked, glancing at Poppy, who'd picked up some plastic blocks that had been left on the table. She was spooning yoghurt into her mouth with one hand while building a block tower with the other.

'I take Poppy upstairs and make her sit on the lounge while I bring everything up, usually two bags at a time.'

'Do you put the roller door down?'

'No.'

'Do you lock the car?'

Eva shook her head. 'Few people around here lock anything.'

'Tailgate up or down?'

'Up.' A chill ran through Eva's body. 'You're thinking what I'm thinking, aren't you, that someone . . . Hutton potentially . . . has—'

'The obvious thing is that you've left a shopping bag at the supermarket. But I'm not discounting what you're saying. I know Hutton watches people.'

'You need to tell me about the others he's . . .' She swallowed hard. She couldn't say 'murdered' with Poppy in the room, and up until now she hadn't felt ready to stomach the details.

'Where's your car key? I'll go and see if you've left it in the boot.'

Eva walked over to the ceramic bowl where she tended to dump everything after arriving home: keys, loose change, shopping dockets.

'Mummy, can I watch *The Wiggles*?' Poppy had finished her yoghurt and was sliding off the chair.

'Sure,' Eva said, relieved Poppy would be occupied so she could talk to Jack.

'Mummy, can I watch *The Wiggles*?'

Eva frowned. 'I already said yes, Poppy.'

'I can put it on for her,' he offered, his helpful tone suggesting it wasn't necessary she do absolutely everything. 'If you want to finish what you're doing here.'

Eva hesitated. She hadn't fully adjusted to this tense cooperation that existed between them. She put the car key in his hand. 'Thanks. I'll see you in the lounge room when I'm done.'

Ten minutes later with the cupcakes in the oven, Eva washed and dried her hands, thinking how Poppy had gone off with Jack without question. He'd won her over when he'd stomped on that juice box and, this morning, she'd been totally comfortable riding on his shoulders while the snowboarders wrestled with the ski racks. At times, Eva had caught Jack watching Poppy, and her. She would have liked to have known what he was thinking, but he'd simply looked away with a faint smile.

Leaving the warmth of the kitchen behind, she went into the lounge room to find him rebuilding the fire, the door to her suite standing open.

'The weather's getting worse,' he said as she sat down.

'Nothing in the boot?' she asked hopefully.

'No, unfortunately.'

Eva tipped her head to one shoulder then the other, stretching out the kinks in her neck. Wood creaked with every strong gust that slammed into the lodge from the south. In the lulls, the happy strains of Dorothy the Dinosaur singing about rosy cups of tea could be heard from Eva and Poppy's room.

'I definitely bought those things.' She waited until he sat beside her, then showed him the items she'd underlined on the shopping docket.

'They're all snack foods,' Jack said. 'No perishables.'

'I know.' She glanced at him. 'Do you think it's him?'

'It's possible, or it could have been an opportunistic thief passing by.'

Eva gave him a doubtful look. 'You said Hutton watches people.'

'He does his homework, that's for sure. It's the only explanation for him finding Julieann. Neither of us are on social media. I think he was watching me in Sydney, and then followed me to Shoal Bay. I bet he watched her movements before he turned up posing as a strata inspector.'

'So, he's strategic?'

He nodded. 'Very much so.'

Eva folded the shopping docket over and over until it was a tiny square in her hand. 'How did you work all this out, Jack?'

'Where would you like me to start?' He leaned back against the lounge but didn't move along to put space between them. 'Have you been keeping up with the news, about Hutton?'

'I don't always get time. I guess I've relied on Pierce to warn me if they think he's back in this area. I know he's killed two people.'

'I suspect he's responsible for the death of another person in Western Australia: Delores Taylor. Delores was the married sister of Roland Carr. I'd worked with Roland a couple of times. He was a money-drop veteran.'

'Was?' Eva asked, fearing Jack's former workmate had become another victim.

'Roland's retired in Fremantle. He was with us in the Philippines.'

'And you think Hutton killed his sister?'

'It's possible, but if he did, he used a different method. It was a hit-and-run. The two men were beaten to death.'

And now he had a child in his sights. Eva shivered and looked towards her room where Poppy was singing along out of tune. 'I've only heard about the two men.'

'That's Dominic Burrows and Fergus Suter. Dominic was the nephew of one of the underwriters for the insurance company,

Mike Joseph. Fergus was the partner of Will Guthrie, a hostage-retrieval expert. Will was with Roland and me in the Philippines.' Jack stretched his legs out towards the fire. 'Forget about Roland in Western Australia for now. His sister died, but there's nothing to link that death with the Hutton murders over here, at least not yet.

'As for Will,' he went on. 'He wouldn't have known Hutton's name, apart from being the serial killer the police were hunting for. In a hostage situation, especially if we're dealing with a group of kidnappers we're not familiar with, everything is kept on a need-to-know basis. Will and Roland were there on standby, but in the end they weren't needed.'

'So, they wouldn't have known that Gavin Hutton was the Australian hostage back then,' Eva mused. If that were the case, the Homicide Squad would be hard pressed to make the link between Hutton and the members of the crisis team. At last she was beginning to understand the reasoning behind Jack's thinking, although all of this could have been explained to Pierce.

They sat in silence, the light fading, the wind gusts coming in quick succession now.

'Will and Roland booked flights home as soon as they got word they weren't going to be needed. I was the only one on the team who'd had direct contact with the kidnappers, and I only learned that Hutton was wanted for murder when I came home from visiting my mother in Ireland and saw there was a reward out for him.'

'You never considered going to the police with this information?' Eva asked. Jack's reticence to involve the police was one of the things that had troubled her the most.

'I ran out of time.' He turned to look at her, his expression earnest. 'I began searching up everything I could about the murders in Sydney and Goulburn. It wasn't hard; there were articles, interviews and photographs everywhere. I couldn't believe that Hutton had murdered two people who were related to members of crisis teams I'd worked with in the past. I was in the process of getting all the information ready for the police when Julieann called.'

He hesitated for a few moments. 'I knew then he was coming for you, or Poppy.'

Eva brought a hand to her mouth, stifling the cry that threatened to escape.

'I packed some camping gear and jumped in the car,' he continued on. 'That's when I called Roland in Fremantle to see if anything like that had happened in his family. I asked him some roundabout questions and found out his sister had been killed.'

Eva lowered her hand and turned to gaze into the fire, nausea churning her stomach at the thought of what loomed ahead.

'It's not that I didn't want to tell the police,' he said, 'but I needed to get here quickly, and find Hutton, or head him off, or *something*. I'd already failed you and Poppy by not being around. I wasn't going to fail you again.'

Eva turned towards him in surprise, but he leaned back and closed his eyes like he'd made an admission and nothing else was up for discussion.

'Where did you leave your car?' she asked, hoping he'd keep talking if she switched the topic to something practical, like logistics.

'Bullocks Flat. I hitched a ride with some blokes coming up to Thredbo, camped out the back here for a few days and watched the lodge. Once I knew you were okay, I hiked towards Tom Groggin. I knew the police had been searching for Hutton along the Alpine Way last year.'

'What were you going to do?'

'I've got plastic zip ties in my swag.' He opened his eyes and turned his head to look at her. 'If he hadn't got me with that blade, I would have dragged him down to the Alpine Way, or into one of the campgrounds, and asked someone to call the police.'

'And that's what you intend doing here, if you can't talk him into giving himself up?'

'Yes.' He sighed and got to his feet. 'Hutton's left us until last because in his mind I'm the one to blame for what happened. But he's wrong, Eva. So, let him come.'

She watched him head towards the lobby, where he would begin his half-hourly perimeter check of the Golden Wattle.

There was a pop from the fire and a cracking sound from outside. Eva looked up, not sure if it was lightning she'd heard above the roar of the wind, or a branch breaking off one of the gum trees.

Then the lights began to flicker.

Eighteen

Ryder drove into the basement carpark to find Vanessa unloading
skis from the back of her SUV. She turned and waved, a sunny smile
lighting up her face. Ryder pulled in beside her car and lowered the
window. 'I'll give you a hand.'

'I meant to unload these yesterday,' she said as he climbed out,
'but I was so tired, I couldn't be bothered. Who knew I'd find driving
more tiring than ski patrol?'

She stepped in for a hug, and the tension melted away from
Ryder as he embraced her. 'Between the two of us we've covered
some ground in the last few days,' he said when they parted. 'I gave
Eva a call, but it went through to voicemail.'

'Did you leave a message?'

'No, we needed to get on the road.' Ryder looked at the skis.
'Which ones do you want me to carry?'

Vanessa pointed to two sets of skis propped against a wide cement
column. 'Those two?'

'Sure.'

'Be careful of the edges,' she warned.

'These are nice,' he said, looking down at a black pair with a
slight curve and a bright orange tail.

'They're racing skis. They don't flex easily.' She hoisted two pairs
onto her shoulder with the practised ease of someone who'd spent

years doing it. 'They might throw you around a bit,' she said with a grin.

'I'd probably kill myself.'

They loaded the rest of the skis into the elevator and Vanessa pressed the button for their floor. 'I don't like leaving them in the car,' she said. 'Are you sure you don't mind them being in the apartment?'

'Provided *you're* in the apartment, I don't mind at all.'

'Thank you.'

'Want a beer?' she asked when they were finally inside and the skis were stowed in the spare room.

'I won't say no,' Ryder said, sliding open the balcony door. He stepped out into the city air, so much warmer than in Jindabyne. To his left, lights shone from an adjacent apartment building, illuminating the kids' playground below. To his right, the Lane Cove River glimmered like a black ribbon in the darkness.

He turned as Vanessa stepped onto the balcony. 'I'm sorry we missed each other,' he said.

'Me too. Never mind.' She clinked her wine glass against his beer bottle and took a sip, her eyes shining at him over the rim. That was one of the things he loved about her, she never made anyone's bad day worse.

They sat down in the big, circular cane chairs she'd bought the week after she'd moved in with him. *I want to be able to sit outside, Pierce,* she'd said. Before that, Ryder hadn't bothered with outdoor furniture, but sharing a drink out here with Vanessa at the end of the day had become one of his favourite pastimes.

'So, you think Gavin Hutton is back in the Snowy Mountains?' she asked.

'Honestly, I don't know where he is.' Ryder told her about the false sighting on the beach at Jervis Bay. 'I still feel the most credible sightings of him were those along the Alpine Way this time last year. And yesterday, a whole lot of blood was found near a campfire not far from the Alpine Way.' Ryder took a pull on his beer. 'I wanted to make sure the sergeant down there was getting the forensics done properly.' He sighed. 'We did get some good news, though. Hutton has a brother.'

Vanessa raised an eyebrow. 'He does?'

'Yep. Flowers and I are off to The Entrance tomorrow to see what we can find out about him. Sterling should be okay in the office, I think. She's had a couple of solid days getting her head around the case. Anyway, enough about me. How did you go? Did you sell any skis?'

'I did. I took tons of orders from the ski shops.'

'That's great.' Ryder wasn't surprised at all by her news. Vanessa was an experienced patroller who knew everything there was to know about the ski industry. 'Where are the little ones you got for Poppy?'

Vanessa jumped up. 'They were the only pair I *did* bring up. Wait there.'

She came back carrying the shortest pair of pink skis Ryder had ever seen. 'Baby skis,' he said with a chuckle, turning one over in his hands. 'They're really nice.'

'I thought so,' she said, taking the ski back and putting it with its mate.

Later, they carried their drinks inside to the kitchen. Vanessa had picked up a marinara mix from the fish markets, so while she stir-fried the seafood in the wok, adding onion, garlic, white wine and tomato paste, Ryder put the spaghetti on to boil.

'What time are you leaving for The Entrance in the morning?' she asked, watching while he added salt to the spaghetti.

'Flowers is going to be here at seven. I want to be back at the station by lunchtime. The Inspector's after a progress report. What about you?'

'I'm here for the next two days. I have an online training course tomorrow, and the following day I'm doing bookwork. Can you imagine, *me* doing bookwork?' She grimaced and handed him the spaghetti spoon.

'You really hate bookwork that much?' he asked, serving the spaghetti onto their plates.

'I really do,' she said, standing on tiptoe and kissing his cheek. 'You're really lucky you're hot, Detective.'

Nineteen

Jack woke in the early hours of the morning to the sound of Poppy crying. Tossing the blankets aside, he sat on the edge of the rollaway bed and looked towards Eva's room. A faint strip of light shone from beneath the door.

The storm had raged throughout dinner and then for hours into the night. The torch they'd left on the coffee table was still there but, thankfully, despite several worrying moments, the power had stayed on. Everything was calm now, save for Poppy's intermittent cries. Jack stood up, hating the thought of Poppy in any kind of distress. He hoped it was nothing more than a bad dream.

An image flashed in front of his eyes. A man, lying face down in the dirt, the back of his skull missing. Jack blinked against the unbidden image that assaulted him when he was least expecting it, and went about rebuilding the dying fire. As Poppy's cries grew louder, he picked up the small broom and swept the hearth clean of the soot and ash blown by the wind down the chimney.

The door opened, and Eva appeared in a white dressing gown, her hair loose about her shoulders, Poppy on her hip. 'She's not well,' she said, carrying a whimpering Poppy closer to the fire.

'Would you like to put her down here?' Jack asked, grabbing a blanket off the rollaway bed and spreading it out on the lounge.

'Thanks.'

'Do you want a pillow, Poppy?' he asked gently.

At Poppy's nod, he fluffed up the pillow and put it on the lounge, then he straightened up and looked at Eva. 'Did she have a nightmare?'

'No, it's an earache. She suffers from them every now and then.'

'What can I do to help?'

'Could you watch her while I go and get some Panadol?'

'Sure.'

'Can I sit here until Mum comes back?' he asked Poppy, pointing to the corner of the lounge.

She nodded, her big eyes awash with tears, her face flushed as if she were running a temperature. 'Warm enough?' he asked, patting her feet, which were encased in fluffy penguin slippers.

Poppy nodded miserably, and two big tears slipped down her cheeks.

Shit. A painful lump formed in Jack's throat, and his eyes misted over. Poppy's tears and penguin socks were about to bring him undone. He swallowed hard, his chest physically hurting. 'Do you want me to get Rock-a-Billy Bear?' he asked, his voice thick.

'He's Rock-a-Bye Bear,' Poppy whispered, tugging at her earlobe.

'Huh. Rock-a-Bye Bear. Will I get him?'

Poppy nodded, and Jack got up just as Eva came back with the Panadol. 'She wants the bear,' he said, hooking a thumb towards her room, not wanting to appear presumptuous by walking in without permission, though the irony didn't escape him when he thought of how he'd strongarmed his way into the place yesterday.

Eva gave him a curious look. 'It's on her bed.'

The door was open. The bear was sitting in the middle of Poppy's perfectly made bed. Jack didn't linger in the girls' space, just picked up the furry bear and carried it outside before closing the door behind him.

Eva was giving Poppy medicine through a dropper. 'It's the orange-flavoured one. You like it.'

Poppy nodded and swallowed her medicine.

'Do you have ear drops?' Jack asked, relieving Eva of the bottle and putting it on the mantel. Poppy held out her hands and Jack leaned over and put Rock-a-Bye Bear in her arms.

Eva shook her head. 'I tossed them out a while ago. They were past their expiry date. She hasn't had an ear infection for a while.'

'Mummy . . .' Poppy began to cry again.

'Give the medicine time to work, sweetheart,' Eva said, rubbing Poppy's back. 'Try to go back to sleep.'

'What?'

'Try to go back to sleep.'

Jack tipped his head towards the stairs. 'I'll go for a bit of a walk.'

The stairs were freezing on his bare feet, the concrete passageway as icy as cold storage. Aiming the beam of torchlight at the lock on the external door, Jack thought about Eva's missing groceries. Had Hutton been watching her, and taken the things from the back of the SUV while she'd been upstairs? It would be easy enough. Less of a risk than coming into the lodge when this door was unlocked, the way Bede had the day before yesterday. There was always a chance of discovery with sneaking in, but the odds of getting away with it were good, especially between seasons, like now when there were no guests. If Hutton possessed enough bravado to talk himself into Julieann's apartment and pass himself off as a strata inspector, he wouldn't hesitate to open this door, climb the stairs, and . . . what? Steal food from the kitchen? A chill ran down Jack's spine. Or steal a key to the bottom door so he could let himself in whenever he chose?

Back upstairs, he asked Eva if Poppy was settling down.

She nodded and gave him a relieved smile.

'That door downstairs,' he said. 'It opens outwards. Does the snow build up against it on the outside?'

'Absolutely. It's the bane of my life, that door.'

'How much snow builds up?'

'A lot. If it's been snowing overnight it's the first thing I check in the morning, otherwise the guests can't get out with their gear. When it snows consistently I have to dig it out three or four times

143

a day.' She sighed. 'Ideally that door should open inwards, but they made the hallway too narrow when they built this place. You saw how hard it was for those snowboarders to get the ski racks out.'

'Well, I think it's working in our favour at the moment,' he said.

In the lobby, he grabbed a room key from behind the desk and then checked the front doors were secure. Downstairs again, he unlocked the external door and gave it a push. Sure enough, it didn't budge, the resistance of the built-up snow outside making it impossible to open. If Hutton intended to use this door tonight, he'd need to dig his way in.

Bypassing the laundry and equipment room, Jack went into the garage. He flicked off the torch as the sensor light came on. The woodpile. The SUV. The pegboard and tools. Nothing had changed since he'd come down looking for Eva's missing groceries.

Upstairs again, he unlocked the rooms with ceiling access, then relocked them. It took another ten minutes to check all the window locks, and then he was done.

Eva was standing in front of the fire, rocking Poppy to and fro, the little girl's head on her mother's shoulder. 'You were right,' he said, keeping his voice low. 'There's a ton of snow built up outside that door, so you can relax. No one is getting in here tonight.' He looked at Poppy. 'No better?'

Eva shook her head. 'If she doesn't improve, I'll have to take her to the doctor tomorrow.'

'Let's worry about that later. Would she come to me, do you think? You look dead on your feet.'

Eva turned and spoke softly in Poppy's ear. The little girl nodded and held out her arms to Jack. He picked her up, taking her weight on his forearm as she settled against his chest. Soft arms wound around his neck before her head came down on his shoulder. He winced as her knee pressed against the cut on his abdomen.

'Careful,' said Eva, watching his face. 'You're sure you're okay?'

'Yes.' The ache in his chest was worse than the one in his stomach. 'It's worth the pain.'

She smiled a little, and Jack could have sworn her lips trembled slightly, but she turned away before he could be sure. 'I'm going to make a cup of tea. Want one?'

'Yes, thanks,' he said, then watched her leave in the direction of the kitchen, wondering why it had taken a catastrophe to bring him back. A child's earache seemed trivial in comparison to his job, where he attempted to save lives and mitigate the worst of terrible situations. But it didn't mean he wasn't needed here.

It was cooler and darker away from the fire, so he tightened his grip on Poppy, and walked a circuit around the furniture. Jack had led men into battle, run interference, and come under enemy fire— but with his tiny daughter burning up in his arms, never had he felt this helpless.

❋

Jack lay beneath the surface of the water unable to breathe, the lead weight on his chest keeping him submerged. Above him, white clouds crept across an azure sky, the vital oxygen he so desperately needed mere centimetres above him. Lungs fit to burst, he kicked frantically, only to sink lower and lower. Unable to feel his legs, he watched the sky darken, and the sun disappear.

Jack sucked in a deep breath and opened his eyes. The weight on his chest was Poppy, snoring softly, her hair tickling his chin. Dragging oxygen into his lungs, he gave Poppy the gentlest of squeezes. He remembered her dozing off on one of his circuits around the lounge room. Careful not to wake her, he'd sat down in a corner of the lounge while Eva had curled up in the other corner drinking her tea. Somehow, lulled to sleep by the warmth of the fire, he must have sunk lower and lower until he was lying on his back, his left foot on the floor, his right leg bent and resting on the lounge.

Jack lifted his head, discovering the reason for his dream. Eva was lying on top of his leg, mercifully with a pillow beneath her head. Jack curled his toes to try to work some feeling back into both limbs. He jerked as pins and needles shot through his feet.

Eva stirred, pushing herself up with her hands, her hair tussled, eyes confused. 'Oh, I'm sorry. Here, let me take her,' she whispered, reaching for Poppy.

'She's fine,' Jack struggled into a sitting position. 'I can lie her down here, or would you like me to carry her back to bed for you?'

Eva checked that Poppy was still asleep. 'Bed would be great.'

Jack made sure the feeling had returned to his feet before he stood up. Poppy murmured something in her sleep.

In the bedroom, Eva pulled back the covers so he could put Poppy into bed. She rolled over but didn't wake up.

'I left the electric blanket on low,' Eva said, pulling the covers over the little girl before placing a hand on her forehead. 'The Panadol has taken the temperature down but she's still too warm.'

Jack glanced at the clock on Eva's bedside table. 'It's four-thirty. Try to have a few hours' sleep if you can. I've dozed off a couple of times already. You don't need to worry. I won't go back to sleep.'

'I'll try,' she said, and he didn't miss the relieved expression that crossed her face.

He nodded, and turned to leave.

'Jack?' She laid a hand on his arm. 'You shouldn't worry either.'

He frowned, not understanding.

'Kids get temperatures all the time,' she said, her eyes soft. 'Poppy will be okay.'

Twenty

'What's The Entrance like?' asked Flowers, as they wound their way through the seaside town of Long Jetty. 'I've never been up this way before.'

'Lots of pelicans,' said Ryder.

'Awesome.'

Ryder gazed out the passenger-side window. Though his parents had moved to Newcastle years ago, he'd grown up on the Central Coast, spending his youth playing footy and surfing McMasters, Shelly and Avoca. With the exception of larger shopping centres, taller apartment buildings and a hundred roundabouts, little else had changed along the string of beaches stretching from Pittwater in the south to Lake Munmorah in the north. Even the golf range at Bateau Bay was still there.

They took the streets by the coast, passing a blue-and-white art-deco surf club, the Norah Head lighthouse standing proud on a distant headland. The road curved and the bridge spanning The Entrance channel came into view. For as long as Ryder could remember, a dredge had been used to help the seawater flow freely into the Tuggerah Lakes. Now, the ugly piece of naval equipment sat defeated in the middle of the silted-up channel, a rusting casualty of the ocean's shifting shoals and currents.

The sprawling, single-storey boarding house stood on a corner, two blocks back from the main street. The owner, Barry Dollen, opened the front door the moment they rang the bell at 8.30 am, making Ryder think he'd been on the lookout for them for some time. Tall, a little stooped, with the ruddy complexion that suggested he enjoyed a few drinks, Barry led them down a long hallway devoid of furniture. 'We won't be disturbed in the kitchen,' he said, his long brown cardigan falling unevenly at his back.

In contrast to the rest of the house, the kitchen was all commercial-grade stainless steel, the floorboards scrubbed so thoroughly they appeared almost white. The faint tune of a nostalgic rock song played quietly from a radio on the windowsill, while an enormous pot of bolognaise simmered away on the cooktop.

Ryder handed Barry Dollen his card. 'What can you tell us about Trevor Swan, Mr Dollen?'

'He was harmless,' Dollen said without hesitation. 'He never caused a problem the entire time he was here. There aren't many I can say that about.'

'Did he get many visitors?' Ryder asked.

Dollen paused for a few seconds before replying. 'His elderly mother, Sissy, used to visit him every few months, but when she became ill Trevor started going to see her. Apparently, she'd adopted him when he was young. They loved each other, them two; I could tell. One time, he came back awful upset after seeing her.' Dollen shook his head. 'She didn't know him. Old-timers disease, you know. He was upset for weeks.'

'So, she's Sissy Swan?'

'As far as I know. I might have her name written in my old address book.'

'She was his only visitor?' Ryder asked while Flowers made a note of Sissy's name. 'We're especially interested in his brother.'

'Yes, Sergeant O'Neill said you were. Trevor thought the world of his brother, talked about him all the time. He was proud of him being a Corporal in the army.'

'That's Gavin?' Ryder asked.

'Yes, that's right, Gavin Swan. I was just tryin' to think of 'is name.'

'Actually, they have different last names,' Ryder said.

'Did he ever come here?' Flowers asked.

'I can't rightly remember. He could have. Trev was a long-term tenant.'

'How long was Trevor here?' asked Ryder.

Barry scratched his head. 'Ten years at least. Maybe twelve.'

'Did you have an emergency contact for Trevor?' asked Ryder.

'Yeah, it was his mother, Sissy. I didn't call her, though, when he didn't show up. She was in the nursing home, as I said, and couldn't recognise him. Didn't see the point.'

'You didn't report his absence to the police?'

'I thought about it, but I didn't want to get him into trouble, so I spoke to the high-school principal where Trevor did a bit of casual work, mowing the lawn and stuff. It was him who said he might have met a woman and decided to stay in the Philippines illegally.'

'So, neither of you reported him missing?'

Dollen shook his head. 'His rent was paid a month in advance.'

'You said he was proud of his brother. He must have talked about him a lot,' said Flowers.

'He made a point of telling people his brother knew how to handle a gun. I got the feeling he did that in case people were thinking of giving him a hard time. Trevor was always battlin', you know.'

Flowers frowned. 'Doing it tough?'

'Yeah, well, he had a bit of a problem.'

'What sort of problem?' asked Flowers.

'I don't know the proper term, but you could tell. Apparently, he had some kind of accident when he was a kid, too.'

'What kind of—'

'Was Trevor in good spirits when he left for the Philippines?' asked Ryder, cutting off Flowers' persistent line of questioning with a glance.

'Was he ever! He drove everybody mad talkin' about it. He was that excited to be getting on a plane for the first time. Gavin was working over there by then.'

Ryder caught Flowers' eye. It was the first they'd heard of Hutton being employed in the Philippines. 'He had a job? They didn't just meet up for a holiday?'

'No, he was working. I remember Trevor saying he would need to occupy himself while Gavin was at work.' Dollen raised both hands. 'I couldn't tell you where it was, though. It wasn't Manila. Trevor had to go further on from there.'

Ryder waited while Flowers wrote everything down in his notepad before asking, 'Sergeant O'Neill said you kept some of Trevor's things?'

'Yep, the box is in the garage.'

'We'd better have a look, then,' said Ryder.

Two large concrete steps led the way to a neatly mown back lawn. Clothes hung from a Hills hoist, the double garage at the rear of the property accessed from the side street.

'You've kept them for a while,' Ryder said as they crossed the yard.

'I was expecting him to come back. As time went on, I took the clothes to the charity bin and rented out his room. The furniture's mine. I put his personal items in here, though, in case he came back.'

'Have you ever done this before, for other people?' asked Flowers.

'Nope. Never needed to. Sometimes, if they don't pay their rent, or they can't get along with the others, they leave and they take their gear with them.'

The cardboard box was sitting on a line of cupboards.

'This is everything?' asked Ryder, looking at the single, solitary carton that represented Trevor Swan's life at The Entrance.

'Everything that was in his drawers is in there, except for a couple of packets of lollies I remember throwing out.'

'Did you keep his mail?' asked Flowers.

'Never received any mail that I know of.'

'Have you been through these items recently?' Ryder asked.

Dollen shook his head. 'To tell you the truth, I'd forgotten all about it. When Sergeant O'Neill came over, he told me not to touch anything. I haven't looked in there since I packed it up.'

Ryder nodded. He'd have to remember to thank Sergeant O'Neill for his thoroughness. 'Thank you, Mr Dollen. We'll come back inside when we're done.'

'All right. I'll go and see if I've still got contact details for Trevor's mum.'

Left alone in the garage, Ryder and Flowers snapped on latex gloves and then Ryder opened the box. A digital clock lay on top. After inspecting it, Ryder wound up the cord and slipped it inside the evidence bag Flowers was holding.

Next was an electric razor. 'This was probably too much hassle for him to take,' said Ryder. 'It's heavy.' Further down were men's handkerchiefs still in their cellophane packaging, and an open packet of plastic hair combs.

Ryder dug into the box again, bringing out a pen, a shoehorn and a coffee mug, all with the same branding, BHM Holdings. 'Search up this company, Flowers.'

Flowers did a quick search on his phone. 'One of their assets is a gold mine in the Philippines,' he said, scrolling with his thumb. 'Maybe Gavin worked there, and he sent this stuff to Trevor.'

'Hmm. So, Gavin comes home in 2017 and begins his killing spree, and Trevor stays on in the Philippines.'

'Maybe Trevor got himself a job at the mine while he was over there,' mused Flowers.

'That's possible. I'll contact the company and find out what I can about both brothers.'

'I wonder if Trevor knows what his brother is capable of?'

'Here we go: bank statements.' Ryder shook a wad of papers from a plastic sleeve and laid them out on top of the cupboards.

Flowers moved closer while Ryder scanned the dates for the most recent one. 'February 2017,' said Ryder. 'It looks like he's printed these from his phone or laptop.'

'It's looking more and more like Trevor didn't come back from the Philippines.'

'Yes, you'd have to think if he was living in Australia, he'd be accessing this account.' Ryder pointed to the bank statement.

'There's a recurring Centrelink entry. We'll get this information through to Parramatta when we're done here. The bank will be able to tell us which ATMs Trevor's been using to make withdrawals. Remind me to ask Dollen if Trevor had a laptop when he lived here.'

After gathering the papers and returning them to the sleeve, Ryder took a yellow plastic container the size of his palm out of the box. *Genevieve Gilmore* was written in gold lettering on the lid. 'Looks like the container I used to keep my mouthguard in,' he said, opening it up.

Flowers gasped. 'Holy shit!'

Ryder stared down at the acrylic half sphere.

Flowers took a step backwards. 'What the hell *is* that?'

'A prosthetic eye.'

'Far out,' Flowers exclaimed, moving forward again. 'It dead-set looks real.'

'They do a good job, don't they?' Ryder tilted the box a fraction so Flowers could see. The eye stared up at them, the iris light grey, the pupil a perfect black circle, the spidery streaks of red paint replicating veins on the white of the eye. 'Genevieve Gilmore must be the ocularist.'

'Never heard of it,' muttered Flowers.

'There aren't many. It's a specialised field.' Ryder put the lid back on the box and carefully held it out so Flowers could bag it.

'Why wouldn't he take his eye overseas with him?' Flowers shook his head. 'Christ, that sounded weird!'

Ryder smirked. 'Settle down, Daisy. It's just a piece of hollowed-out acrylic painted to match the other eye. Trevor must have a newer one if he's left this one behind. They used to be made of glass in the old days, but technology has improved them out of sight— pardon the pun.'

Flowers gave him a long-suffering look. 'How do you know all about false eyes and ocularists?'

'I was at an autopsy. The female victim had lost an eye to cancer earlier in life.'

'Oh, right.' Flowers glanced over his shoulder to make sure no one was in the yard. 'Maybe we should ask Dollen what kind of accident Trevor had when he was a kid,' he said in a low voice. 'Maybe it was an eye injury.'

Ryder paused. His partner's instincts were good, but sometimes he could get caught up in the moment and forget what they were trying to achieve. 'Look, we need to locate Trevor. That's a top priority. Once we do that, we can pressure him into telling us where this murdering brother he idolises so much is hiding out.'

'If he knows.'

'Yes, if he knows, and if he's willing to talk.'

Ryder watched as Flowers repacked the box with Trevor's meagre possessions.

'Forget about what kind of injury he had as a kid, and keep our focus on the prize,' he said as they emerged from the garage. 'Hutton under arrest. That's our end game.'

Twenty-one

Ryder and Flowers ordered coffee from a cafe near the bridge.

'I'll have a dozen oysters as well, thanks,' Flowers said to the woman in a flowery apron serving behind the counter.

'Go and sit outside in the sun, lovey,' the woman said. 'I'll bring them out to you when they're ready.'

'It's nine-thirty in the morning,' Ryder said as they sat at a small table in the sun.

'So what? I'm hungry.'

Ryder called Benson while they waited for their order to arrive. 'I'm sending you a photo of Trevor Swan's bank statement.' Ryder paused as a man walked by their table. 'Can you contact Centrelink, and the bank, see if they have updated details for Swan on their system?'

'Sure. What about ATM and branch activity?' Benson asked.

'Get that, too. I have a feeling Swan could be with his brother, or at least know where Hutton is.'

'Okay, Sarge, I'll get onto it.'

'Has Swan's birth certificate turned up?'

'Not yet.'

'Okay. We've found out that Trevor Swan was adopted, so you'll need to apply for a pre-adoption birth certificate.'

'Okay, Sarge. Oh, the National Parks and Wildlife office called,'

154

though. Patricia Franks is still looking for that company, the one the woman at the museum told you about.'

'Chloe?' Ryder paused again as the woman who served them put the coffees and oysters on the table. 'Extreme Adventures was the name, Benson.'

'That's the one. It rang a bell with Franks, too, apparently, but she hasn't been able to find it in the archives yet. She's still searching.'

'Okay,' said Ryder, then paused before he continued. 'Hey, Benson, sorry for asking over the phone but I've hardly been in the office. How's the move to Sydney working out? It can wait, if now's not a good time.'

'Fine.' There was a pause, then he asked, 'Why?'

'Just wondering.' He watched as Flowers squeezed lemon juice over his oysters. 'You've been a bit short-tempered lately. It's not like you.'

'Oh, yeah.' He heard Benson sigh. 'Truth is Sarge, I'm knackered.'

Ryder frowned at the unexpected answer. 'Have you seen a doctor about it?'

Across the table, Flowers stilled, an oyster shell in his hand.

Benson chuckled. 'I'm not sick, I can't bloody sleep. It's the traffic noise. I'm used to the country. Fair dinkum, I don't know how you put up with it.'

'Oh, okay. Still, lack of sleep's not good.' Ryder had imagined that, with five kids at home in Queanbeyan, Benson would be enjoying his best sleep in years. 'Have you tried earplugs?'

'I've been playing my music. I'm going to look around for somewhere quieter when the lease is up on this place, or at least move into an apartment with double-glazed windows.'

'I've noticed the change in him,' Flowers said when Ryder hung up. 'He's bitten my head off a couple of times.'

'I know. Having trouble sleeping apparently.'

'Tell him to get some of that sleep tea from the supermarket. It's great.'

Ryder picked up his coffee and looked out over the channel. Beneath the bridge, a tinny with an outboard motor puttered along sending wash towards a squadron of pelicans paddling towards the waterfront for feeding. 'I'll let you tell Benson about the tea.'

❄

Barry Dollen had never seen Trevor Swan using a laptop, but he'd given Ryder a mobile number for Sissy Swan before they'd left the boarding house. Ryder called the number as they headed back to Sydney along the Central Coast Highway.

'This has been my number for about eighteen months now,' the young man who answered the phone told Ryder. 'In the beginning, a lot of calls came through for her, but you're the first one to phone in ages.'

Ryder's conversation with the school principal turned out to be just as fruitless. As Dollen had already told them, the two men had discussed Trevor's absence and decided it wasn't their place to notify the authorities when it appeared that Trevor hadn't returned from the Philippines. 'Trevor was employed on a casual basis,' the principal said. 'I noted it down as an abandonment of employment and left it at that.'

When Flowers joined the line of semis and B doubles on the M1 heading south, Ryder called Sterling.

'Morning, Sarge.'

'How are things going, Sterling?' Ryder asked. It was only eleven o'clock, but Ryder wanted to check that her first morning in the office with the task-force boys was going smoothly.

'Everything's going well. I've been given plenty to do.'

'Don't worry, they'll keep you busy. Just write this name down for me, will you? It's Genevieve Gilmore. She's an ocularist.' Ryder spelled out the name and the occupation. 'Find out where Genevieve Gilmore practises, and make an appointment for me to talk to her as soon as possible. She'll probably need to block out some time.'

'Will do, Sarge.'

'Thanks, Sterling. We should be back shortly after midday.'

They made good time, only slowing when they turned onto Pennant Hills Road. The traffic was backed up bumper to bumper in parts, the congestion so heavy they were forced to stop at nearly every red light. Facets of the case circulated in Ryder's mind as they crawled through one northern suburb after another.

'Check out that Lego art,' said Flowers when they were pulled up at yet another red light. 'That's a character in a video game I play.'

Ryder gazed in awe at the monster filling the entire window of a hobby shop. 'You'd need the patience of a saint to build that. What game is it?'

Flowers mentioned a name that Ryder didn't recognise, his attention switching to a collection of toy road signs displayed in the hobby shop's second window. One was a drawing of a koala with the word 'Xing' underneath. The one beside it was identical except for a kangaroo. Koala crossing, thought Ryder, looking at how the X replaced the word 'cross'.

'That could be it,' he murmured, cutting off whatever Flowers was saying about his favourite game.

'What could?' Flowers asked as they began to move again.

'Hang on a minute. I need to ring Sterling.'

She answered on the second ring.

'Extreme Adventures, Sterling. Have you tried dropping off the "e" in your search?'

There was a pause, then: 'Sorry, Sarge, I don't—'

'The "e" in extreme, I mean, so the word begins with an "x"?'

'Oh, I get it. No, I didn't think of that.'

'Can you do it now?'

'Sure.'

Ryder waited, tapping his foot to the sound of Sterling typing on her laptop. Silence followed, then: 'There's one here that could be it.'

'What is it?'

'Xtreme Aussie Adventures. Extreme with an X.'

Ryder smiled. 'Call Chloe at the Thredbo museum and Patricia Franks at the National Parks and Wildlife office in Jindabyne. With luck Chloe might have forgotten "Aussie" was part of the business name. Ring me straight back and let me know if I'm right.'

'Yes, Sarge.'

Ryder ran a hand across his jaw as Flowers powered through the intersection and the traffic began to flow freely again. 'Hopefully, this is the business we've been looking for.'

'Nice work, Sarge.'

Ryder nodded and looked down at the phone in his hand, willing Sterling to call back with good news. For months, the task force had been slogging away at their desks, chasing numerous false sightings and hitting dead-ends at every turn. Now, there were multiple lines of enquiry for them to investigate.

Was their luck finally about to change?

Twenty-two

Poppy's ear was still giving her trouble, forcing Eva to give her the prescribed dose of Panadol when it was due.

'Two-thirty was the earliest I could get her in at the doctor,' she told Jack as she made coffee in the kitchen. After their disturbed night, she and Poppy had slept in. 'I can take her into Jindabyne after lunch. You can stay here if you'd rather wait . . .'

Jack looked up from the table where he was playing Feed the Woozle with Poppy. 'We don't split up. We go together.'

Eva held his gaze, wondering if he still didn't trust her not to do a runner, or to call the police.

'The weather's supposed to get worse,' he said. 'Do you have chains in the car?'

'I don't need them. I've already had my winter tyres fitted,' Eva said, pleased when he looked suitably impressed.

'It's your turn, Walker,' Poppy said softly, tugging at her earlobe. Eva had given up trying to get her to stop.

'Mine again?' Jack rolled the dice across the table. 'Three.'

Eva sipped her coffee while Poppy loaded Jack's spoon with three treats that were really only small cardboard discs. Poppy's excitement level was more muted than normal, but even so, the game was a handy distraction for all of them. Another front had come in, bringing dark skies, heavy snow and wind. Eva wasn't looking forward to the drive into Jindabyne.

'You have to feed the woozle the snacks now,' Poppy instructed, pointing to the cardboard monster on the kitchen bench.

'You mean I have to get up?' Jack frowned.

'That's the game. You have to get off that chair.' Poppy giggled while Jack rose and carefully carried his spoon across to the bench. He paused, then none too gently shoved the spoon into the monster's mouth. 'Have another cupcake, greedy guts.'

Poppy dissolved into giggles, then clapped a hand over her mouth and looked at Eva, her blonde eyebrows raised as though she'd suddenly remembered something important.

Eva lowered her coffee cup. 'What?'

Poppy pointed to the cardboard monster. 'The woozle was the one who ate my sultanas!'

Eva gave an uneasy laugh. So, Poppy *had* been paying attention while she and Jack had discussed the missing groceries.

'Can you blame him?' Jack said quickly. 'I wouldn't like eating these cardboard things for dinner.'

'Me either,' said Poppy, and giggled again.

'Okay, I think the woozle's been fed enough today,' Eva said. 'How about we pack this game up? Poppy, would you like to play with my jewellery until we have to get ready?'

Poppy climbed off the chair and went to the kitchen door, the earache and woozle thief forgotten for the moment.

'I'll be there in a minute,' Eva called as Poppy left the room.

'We shouldn't underestimate her,' Eva said, glancing at Jack. 'She's bright enough to know a piece of cardboard with a monster face painted on it doesn't eat real food. It shows she's been thinking about it.'

'She's obviously processed what we were saying,' he agreed. 'You did the right thing, though, by distracting her with the jewellery.'

'I don't want her frightened.'

'We'll have to watch what we say when she's in earshot.'

Eva nodded, realising for the first time they were jointly discussing Poppy's wellbeing.

Eva's phone rang, the melodic notes echoing throughout the kitchen. The screen lit up with Logan Clarke's name. 'It's my landlord,' she said.

'Any idea what he wants?'

Eva's heart sank. She had a pretty good idea what Logan wanted. 'I'm not sure. It could be something to do with the property. He's also asked me out a few times.'

There was a long-ish pause. 'He has good taste. How about you let it go to voicemail?'

Eva nodded. Recently, she'd been thinking about accepting one of Logan's invitations. Suddenly, the idea held no appeal.

'Nice guy?' Jack asked.

Eva hesitated. Logan *was* a nice guy. Logan *wasn't* Jack Walker. 'He's a good landlord.'

The computerised voicemail did its thing and then Logan's voice reverberated around the kitchen. 'Hi, Eva. I'm in the village for a few days. If you fancy a coffee, give me a call. I'm staying at the Alpine Hotel. Cheers.'

'I'll call him back and tell him Poppy's sick,' she said, hitting the redial button. 'It's the truth.'

'Would you like some privacy?'

'It's fine, I'm not interested in going out with him.' She put the phone on loudspeaker as Logan picked up. 'Hi, Logan. How are you?' she asked.

'I'm well. I've just wrapped up a court case, so I'm here helping a mate out with a few things.'

'Oh, right. Well, thanks for the invite but I can't make coffee. Poppy's sick. I need to take her to the doctor.'

'How about tomorrow, then?'

'I can't promise anything because I don't know how she'll be. Maybe next time. Sorry, Logan, I'm flat out. I have to run.' Before he could reply she hung up and put the phone back on the bench.

'Harsh,' Jack said, his blue eyes dancing with amusement.

'Let his mate keep him company,' Eva said, heading for the door and hoping the warmth in her face wasn't obvious. 'He didn't even ask what was wrong with Poppy, or how sick she was.'

Twenty-three

'I'm sorry, Sergeant, there's no one here at the moment who can take your call.' The operator's voice came down the line from the Philippines. 'If you give me your details, I'll have the Human Resources manager call you back as soon as possible.'

'Thank you.' Ryder looked at the evidence bag containing the BHM Holdings pen, shoehorn and coffee mug they'd found among Trevor Swan's possessions. 'If you could stress that it's urgent. As I said, we're looking for an Australian citizen, Gavin Hutton, who may have been employed by your company around 2016 to 2017.'

'Uh-huh. I've written all that down.'

Ryder gave the operator his contact details and said he would forward an email to the company as well.

The minute he hung up, Sterling came over to his desk. 'Excuse me, Sarge?'

'Yes, Sterling?'

'Trevor Swan's pre-adoption birth certificate came through.' She put the printout on the desk so he could look at it. 'It's as we thought, he and Hutton share the same mother but different fathers. Trevor's father is Kyle Robert Simpson. Simpson has a long record, mostly for armed robbery, so I was able to track him down. He's been in prison in Western Australia for nine years.'

'Maybe Trevor was in an orphanage and adopted from there,' she went on.

'Possibly. He could have been fostered by Sissy Swan years before she formerly adopted him, too.' Ryder handed the printout back. 'This is good work, Sterling. I want you to get in touch with Corrective Services and try to set up a Skype meeting with Kyle Simpson. He might know where his son is and, more importantly, he might be able to tell us something about his half-brother.'

'Yes, Sarge.'

'And Sterling—' Ryder handed her the evidence bag containing the branded items '—could you take these to forensics, please? See if they're able to lift any prints off them.'

'Okay.'

'Any luck with Xtreme Aussie Adventures?'

'Not yet. I've carried out ASIC searches and found that the business is owned by a private trust. I'm making further enquiries to try and find a name.'

'Hmm.' Ryder leaned back in his chair. He had a feeling they could be heading for another dead-end. God only knew what the former operator was doing now, and even if they managed to find him, what were the odds of him remembering anything about Hutton? 'Look, keep digging, but if something more urgent comes up we might have to sideline it.'

Sterling nodded. 'Okay. You also have a Facetime call at four-forty-five with the ocul . . . oc . . . the eye woman,' she finished in a rush.

'Genevieve Gilmore?' Ryder smiled. 'Good. Thanks, Sterling.'

O'Day was the next to stop by Ryder's desk. Immigration had no record of Trevor Swan re-entering Australia, despite the return date on his paperwork stating he would only be away for three weeks.

'Okay.' Ryder sighed. 'Can you call the Registrar of Deaths Abroad and see if they have anything on record about Swan?'

O'Day nodded. 'Can do, Sarge.'

'And what about the mobile-phone providers? Has Swan taken out a new phone plan?'

'Not yet. Benson just called. He's on his way back but he wanted me to pass on that Swan's benefits are still being paid by Centrelink, but there's been no activity on his bank account since he left for the Philippines. The only withdrawals have been bank fees.'

❋

Ryder had just hit send on his email to BHM Holdings when Flowers ambled into the office with a large folded sheet of paper tucked under his arm and two takeaway coffees. He looked at Ryder. 'Got a minute?'

'If one of those is mine, I've got five.'

Flowers raised his eyebrows. 'Tumeric Latte?'

'Nah, forget it.'

'Kidding,' Flowers laughed. 'I got you a flat white.'

He handed Ryder his coffee, then brought over a chair for himself. The deceptive thing about Flowers, Ryder had discovered, was the sheer volume of work he could get through in a day without ever looking busy.

Ryder recapped what he'd learned from O'Day.

'Maybe Swan *is* working in the Philippines, and he's happy to let his bank account here mount up.' Flowers' foot jigged up and down, the way it did when he was thinking. 'He'd have to be doing it off the books, though. He doesn't have a working visa.'

'If he's even alive,' mused Ryder.

Flowers' foot stilled and he looked up. 'That crossed my mind too.'

Ryder ran a hand around the back of his neck where the tension had started to gather. He'd been confident of a breakthrough when they'd left The Entrance earlier that day, but in a matter of hours they were back to hitting dead-ends at every turn. 'I've asked Sterling to contact Corrective Services to set up a conference with Swan's father to see if he has any idea where his son is.' Ryder took a sip of his coffee. 'I'm hoping Hutton sent those BHM marketing things to Trevor. Sterling has taken them down to forensics. If he did, there's a chance his print could be on one. Forensics lifted a ton of prints off the cenotaph in the Goulburn park.'

'Yep, Fergus Suter's body was lying beside it.' Flowers drained his coffee and dropped the paper cup in Ryder's bin. 'A fingerprint match would put Hutton right at that second murder scene, and give weight to the CCTV footage of him coming out of the Snake Pit pub.'

'Excuse me, Sarge.' It was Sterling again. 'A message just came through from Gilmore. She's had a cancellation. She can talk to you now, if you're free.'

'Yep. Tell her I'll call in a couple of minutes.'

Flowers stood up. 'I'm keen to have a look at this,' he said, holding up the sheet of paper he'd put on Ryder's desk. 'It's the locations of the burned-out cars. Sergeant Cooper just sent it through.'

'Good. I'll come around and have a look after I've made this call.'

Genevieve Gilmore was around fifty with red hair past her shoulders, her frames so large she looked like she was going to a 3D movie.

'We're trying to locate Trevor Dylan Swan,' he said, after they'd exchanged pleasantries. 'We think Mr Swan might be able to help us with one of our investigations.'

Gilmore nodded. 'I have his file here with me. I haven't seen Trevor since his last appointment in 2017.'

'He's missed some scheduled appointments, then?'

'Yes, but only for his annual clean. He's not due for an eye replacement for a couple of years yet.'

'Okay.' Ryder read out the address of the boarding house at The Entrance, and Gilmore confirmed it to be the same address she had on file.

'You don't have a forwarding address for him?' she asked.

'No. He went overseas for a holiday. Since then we haven't been able to trace him.'

'Oh, dear, I do hope he turns up,' she said. 'I hate the thought of something happening to Trevor. He's such a sweetheart.'

'Anything you can tell me about him would be helpful.'

'Yes, of course. I saw Trevor on a more regular basis when he was a child and a teenager than I do now. I remember his mother telling me he'd never had a prosthetic eye when he was with his biological mother, which was really sad. One of the first things she did when she adopted him was to address that.'

'How did Trevor lose his eye, Ms Gilmore?'

'It was an accident with a ruler when he was very young.'

'That would have been an extremely traumatic experience.'

'Yes, absolutely. And Trevor already had other issues to contend with. I don't think he was ever formally diagnosed with foetal alcohol syndrome, but my understanding is he suffered from a mixture of developmental problems due to his biological mother's heavy drinking during pregnancy.'

Ryder nodded. This information fitted with what they already knew.

'Trevor was very lucky, Detective. Sissy adopted him when he was about five, I think. She was able to give him a stable, non-violent upbringing and arrange for the interventions and medical help he needed, the prosthetic eye being one of those things crucial for his self-esteem.'

Ryder nodded again, a picture forming in his mind of a little kid whose opportunities in life had been diminished before he was even born.

'He had some coordination problems, which I understand contributed to the accident, but he wasn't aggressive or hyperactive. He was quite gentle, he got along well with people. I'm sure that was all due to Sissy. As I said, he was very lucky.'

'And unlucky in other ways.'

Genevieve Gilmore nodded. 'Yes, unlucky in other ways.'

'Did he ever talk about his brother?' asked Ryder.

Gilmore frowned. 'I don't think so . . .' She shook her head. 'No, I don't think I knew he had a brother.'

'His name is Gavin.'

She gave a definite shake of her head this time. 'No . . . no, Gavin doesn't ring a bell at all with me.'

Ryder's hopes sank even lower. 'Well, I appreciate your time. If anything comes to mind, even if you don't think it's important, please call. You can get me on this number.'

'I'm sorry I couldn't be more help, Detective. I really hope you find him safe and well.'

Ryder hung up and dialled Harriet Ono's number. His call went straight to voicemail.

'Hey, Harriet,' he said in his most upbeat voice, knowing it would get under her skin. 'Pierce Ryder here. How are you? Listen, I know how you love to prioritise my requests, so I thought I'd let you know it was me who asked Sergeant Cooper at Jindabyne to send those swabs taken from the Kosciuszko campsite to you.' He paused, imagining her at this point in the message, rolling her eyes and saying, *That'd be right, the impatient bugger* to anyone within earshot. Ryder grinned at the thought. 'Anyway, I look forward to getting the analysis as soon as possible. Thanks, Harriet.'

He pocketed his phone and went in search of Flowers. Walking through the general office, he saw Benson back at his desk. He headed towards the meeting rooms, catching sight of his reflection in the window. It made him think of Inspector Gray, standing upstairs and gazing out onto the street. Anytime now Gray would be on the phone asking for the formal report Ryder had promised to have to him yesterday.

He found Flowers in one of the smaller meeting rooms.

'I've enlarged it again,' he said as Ryder sat down. It was a map of the Monaro area from Queanbeyan to the Kosciuszko National Park.

'Look.' Flowers pointed to various x's marked on the map. 'These show the burned-out cars, and she's written the date they were found beside each one.'

'Good on you, Cooper,' Ryder said, poring over the map. 'The sites are pretty well spread out from Cooma to Bredbo all the way up to the national park.'

'Some of them go back a long time,' Flowers said, pointing to a mark on the map with his pen. 'This one's from ten years ago. We know Hutton was deployed with the army at that time. He flew back into Australia in 2017, so I've put red dots on the ones from that year on.'

'Okay, let me see.'

'I don't know the scale of the map,' said Flowers, 'but I've drawn a circle around the ones with the red dots, and it looks like they're all between Thredbo Village and—' he squinted at the map '—Tom Groggin Station?'

Ryder smiled. 'Jack Riley country.'

'Who's Jack Riley?'

'A famous stockman, said to be the inspiration for "The Man from Snowy River".'

'Cool. I know the poem,' said Flowers. 'I haven't heard of Jack Riley, though.'

'Riley spent a lot of time around Tom Groggin Station. Have a look at your streaming service, they might have the movie.'

'Yeah, I'll watch it when I have all that time off.'

Suddenly, a line on the map caught Ryder's eye and he leaned closer. 'So, between Thredbo and Tom Groggin, you say? Look at this. That broken line is the Victorian border. What was the name of the creek Cooper mentioned, near the campsite?'

'I've got it in my notes. She said it was near the border. *Leather* something?'

Ryder clicked his fingers a few times. 'Leatherbarrel!' He scanned the map more closely. 'Here it is!'

Flowers leaned forward, almost bumping heads with Ryder. 'Those dumped cars look like they're in that general area.'

'Yep.' Ryder leaned back in the chair and shook his head. 'This feeling I have that Hutton's been in the Snowy Mountains keeps bugging me, but we still have no hard evidence. We've had car break-ins with blankets and sleeping bags taken, but no money. We've had sightings of a man sleeping in barns and sheds last year. And I'm convinced Hutton steals cars and burns them out because . . . it makes sense. Why risk someone recognising you?'

'Especially with everyone on the lookout.'

'Right. And we know he did this extreme course down there, but we're not sure where.'

'It's more than a hunch, Sarge,' said Flowers, 'but you're right, there's nothing concrete. Still, by the looks of this map, these dumped cars are in the vicinity of where the blood was found at that campsite.'

'See how far Thredbo is from Tom Groggin.'

Flowers' thumbs were a blur on his phone screen. 'About nineteen kilometres.'

Ryder stared at the map. 'For all we know, these cars could have been stolen in Victoria, brought across the border into New South Wales, stripped for parts and then burned out.'

A knock came at the door. Ryder looked up to see Benson standing there.

'Sarge, Glebe Police are on the phone. A student at the University of Technology walked into the station about fifteen minutes ago and reported a break-in. They think you need to see him in a hurry.'

Ryder frowned. '*I* do?'

'Yep. They're not a hundred percent certain, but they think it has implications for the Hutton case. His name is Brandon Moss.'

❄

Ryder guessed Brandon Moss to be in his mid-twenties. The computer-science student wore skinny jeans, a retro Donkey-Kong T-shirt and a pissed-off expression. When Benson brought him into the inter-view room, Moss gave Ryder and Flowers the once over.

Ryder waved him into a chair. 'I'm Detective Ryder and this is Detective Benson, and Detective Flowers. What seems to be the problem?'

'I already told them at the other station there's some dude stealing my shit.' The young man tucked a lock of chin-length hair behind his ear. 'I don't know why they brought me here. All I'm asking is for you guys to do something about it.'

'All right, take it easy,' Ryder said. 'You're presently residing in Ultimo?'

'Yeah, but that's not where the break-in happened.' The young man held up his phone. 'It's at home.'

'Where's home?'

'About ten k's past Thredbo on the Alpine Way.'

Flowers sucked in a breath.

'Okay. What's on the phone?' Ryder asked.

'Him! The arsehole who's been nicking my stuff. The window has been busted for years, that's how he's been getting in.' Moss worked the phone with his thumb. 'I put a camera in my room the last time I went home, so I could catch the loser once and for all.'

Ryder took the phone off Moss, his heart thumping hard. 'When did you first see this?'

'When I woke up.' Moss leaned over and set the video in motion. 'Finally, I had proof.'

Ryder stared at the screen, elation racing through his body. A shadowy figure was climbing through a low window. Once inside, the man shone a torch around, the beam highlighting his features for a second or two. 'One side of his face is banged up, but that's him,' he said to Benson and Flowers.

'You *know* this guy?'

Ryder watched while Hutton moved around the room like he owned the place, going directly to a desk drawer and taking out a chocolate bar.

Moss shook his head. 'The fucker even used my shower.'

'Is this a family property?' Ryder asked, the adrenaline pumping hard now. This was the first image of Hutton they'd seen since the CCTV footage from Goulburn in March 2019.

'Yeah, that's the old house that was on the property before Mum and Dad built the new one. They let me move into it when I turned sixteen, kind of like a bachelor pad. It's empty a lot of the time now because I'm in Sydney at uni.'

'Where's the new house?'

'Closer to the road. This one is set back.'

'Have you called your parents?'

'No!' Moss's eyes rounded. 'I don't want my dad going down there to sort him out. My dad can't land a punch to save his life. Can't you guys send someone around?'

Ryder gave the young man's phone to Flowers, and tipped his head at the door. 'Get Inspector Gray down here.'

'Hey!' Moss rose from his seat. 'I need that.'

'Sit down! The man's a killer.'

Moss sat.

Ryder put his mobile on the table. 'Call your folks and put it on loudspeaker. I want to talk to them.'

Moss tapped the number into Ryder's phone with an unsteady index finger.

'What took you so long to come in?' Ryder asked as the phone rang at the other end. 'It's after one.'

'I only woke up at eleven-thirty.'

'Hello, Edward Moss speaking.'

The young man visibly relaxed at the sound of his father's voice.

'Hello, Mr Moss. This is Detective Sergeant Pierce Ryder from the Sydney Homicide Squad. There's no reason to be alarmed. Your son is safe. He's here with me at Parramatta police station.'

'What's happened?'

'Brandon has filmed someone breaking into the old house at the rear of your property.'

There was a pause, then: 'I beg your pardon.'

Ryder took a breath, understanding the man's confusion. 'Brandon tells us the last time he was home he installed a camera. He's been able to watch the room on his phone screen.' When Edward Moss didn't say anything, Ryder went on. 'The man who broke into Brandon's room is extremely dangerous and wanted by police. I want you and your wife to get your wallet and keys and leave the property immediately. Don't pack anything, just go. He could still be in the vicinity.'

There was a longer silence this time, then: 'Is this a hoax?'

Ryder looked at Brandon and motioned for him to do the talking.

'Hey, Dad, it's me. It's true what he's saying. I noticed some of my stuff was gone the last few times I've been home. I didn't want to worry you and Mum. I thought it was probably just kids, so I rigged up a camera.'

'Good grief.' Edward Moss sounded totally flummoxed. 'All right then, we'll do as you ask, Detective.'

'Head to the Jindabyne police station and ask for Sergeant Cooper. Don't hang around, leave right away.'

Twenty-four

With the weather worsening by the hour, Jack was keen to leave for Jindabyne with plenty of time to spare before Poppy's appointment. The Alpine Way would be treacherous, but on the upside, he was confident Hutton would be sheltering somewhere until the worst of the storm was over. After all, he'd taught him how to survive in this climate.

While Eva dressed Poppy, Jack secured the lodge as best he could. Going into Jindabyne was far from ideal when they should be hunkering down and lying in wait for Hutton. Of all the situations Jack had anticipated dealing with at the Golden Wattle, having to choose between Eva and Poppy's long-term safety and Poppy's immediate health hadn't been one of them. In the end, he had no choice. Poppy had burrowed her way inside his heart, and seeing her unwell was excruciating. There was no choice but to get her medical help.

He smothered the fire and was picking up his jacket when Eva emerged from her room carrying Poppy and an enormous tote bag. Eva wore a long black quilted jacket over her jeans and jumper, an animal-print beanie and matching gloves. Jack froze, a sudden wave of longing crashing over him. Standing within reach was all that he'd given up, and everything he'd missed out on since.

Eva was looking at him strangely.

He swallowed, shrugged his jacket on hurriedly and looked up.

At her faint nod, he slipped inside the room, took the Beretta down from the wardrobe, checked the safety and stuck it in his waistband. He waited while Eva locked the door to her suite. 'All set?'

'Would you mind driving?' she asked. 'Poppy just vomited.'

Poppy looked at him through bleary eyes, her red nose the only bright spot in her otherwise pale face. 'Where's your Rock-a-Baby Bear?' Jack asked, but Poppy was in no mood to humour him, merely pointing towards Eva's room.

'Do you want me to fetch him?' Jack asked.

Poppy nodded.

'I'll sit in the back with her,' Eva said when Jack came back with the bear, but when he went to give it to Poppy, she shook her head and rubbed her eyes with her fists.

'He can wait on the lounge,' Jack said, putting the toy down and reaching for Eva's tote. 'Let me take that.'

'What's in the bag?' she asked, pointing to the green shopping bag in his hands.

'The room keys,' he said, signalling for her to go ahead of him down the stairs. 'I locked all the doors.'

'And you're bringing them with you?'

'Yep. If he breaks in while we're gone and is lying in wait for us, I know he won't be in any of the rooms.'

Moments later they stepped into the garage, the frigid air a shock after the warmth inside the lodge. 'Do you remember the code?' he asked, pulling the door closed behind them. The bulky keypad with the manual buttons mounted on the wall didn't inspire confidence.

'I had to look it up in my password book, it's been so long since I used it. It was such a nuisance, malfunctioning in bad weather all the time.'

'Let's hope it works today,' he said, watching as she punched in the code with a gloved finger. The alarm had been no help to them in the past few days. Its inability to isolate sectors of the lodge made it useless when anyone was inside. But with luck . . .

There was a sickly beep, followed by another, and another. 'That'll do. Come on. Let's get Poppy in the car.'

The SUV was cold and jumpy, but by the time Eva had strapped Poppy into her booster seat, and was settled in beside her, the engine was idling smoothly. Jack engaged the central locking, hit the magic button for the roller door, and began to reverse. A faint high-pitched shriek signalled activation of the alarm system. With luck, it would stay on.

Out on Crackenback Drive, the visibility was so poor he switched on the fog lights and put the car in snow mode for better traction. With the wipers working at high speed, they crossed two bridges without passing another vehicle, the Thredbo River shrouded in an eerie mist. Jack turned on the hazard lights, his eyes briefly meeting Eva's in the rear-view mirror.

Minutes later, they were on the Alpine Way, passing the site of the Thredbo landslide, the wind buffeting the SUV at the higher elevation after the comparative shelter of the village.

❄

Eva watched as Jack pulled into a park directly below the doctor's surgery and cut the engine. The outdoor shopping centre was built on a hill and surrounded by a wide, wooden verandah. 'Are you coming in?' she asked, unbuckling her seatbelt.

He twisted around in the seat, and Eva didn't miss the slight grimace the action caused him. 'I think it's best if I stay here. There's a chance someone might recognise me and want to talk.' He hesitated. 'It's better if that doesn't happen.'

'Okay. You'll freeze in the car,' she warned, unbuckling Poppy. The drive from Thredbo had lulled the little girl to sleep, but she was now beginning to stir.

'Don't worry about me,' he said, getting out and coming around to hold the door open for her.

'Okay, I won't. You survived Iraq; you'll survive the Jindabyne carpark.'

Poppy scrambled over the seat and Eva swung her up onto her hip as Jack reached in and retrieved the tote. He touched Poppy gently on the cheek with his thumb. 'Be a good girl for your mum and the doctor.' Then to Eva: 'I'll be waiting.'

Twenty-five

Ryder sped along the Hume Highway in the unmarked four-wheel drive, the red and blue emergency lights flashing. Flowers was in the passenger seat. Sergeant Thalia Cooper was on the other end of the line from Jindabyne.

'The first thing is to close the Alpine Way to traffic between Thredbo and Tom Groggin Station,' Ryder said, accelerating past the line of traffic that had reduced speed and veered left in response to his emergency lights and siren.

'I'll get the road closure done as soon as I possibly can, Detective Ryder. We have perilous conditions right now. Most of my officers are responding to road accidents. A number of four-wheel drives have hit black ice and slid off the road.'

Ryder's expectations slipped a notch. 'Okay, officers from Queanbeyan and Cooma will reach you soon, so you'll have more manpower. In the meantime, put out a general broadcast. People in properties along the Alpine Way and Thredbo Village need to be aware a wanted criminal is in the area, and that they should lock their doors and shelter in place.'

'Yes, Detective.'

'Also, stress that no one, under *any* circumstances, should approach this person. Community safety is our number-one priority.'

'Got it.'

'Ask the radio stations to continually broadcast the road closure to avoid traffic backing up, especially if the weather is as bad as you say.'

'That won't be a problem, Detective. The Alpine Way is often closed because of heavy snowfall. What is your recommendation for Jindabyne?'

'Jindabyne residents should heed the warning and stay vigilant but are free to move around town. Hutton avoids busy places. The property he broke into was quite remote.' Ryder swore under his breath and moved up behind a B double, forcing the stubborn truck driver to yield. 'Just a minute, Cooper.'

'You'll be hearing from us later,' Flowers muttered, giving the driver the death stare as they sped past. Ryder checked his rear-view mirror. Two police four-wheel drives rounded a bend about two hundred metres behind them. Benson and O'Day were in one car, Brown and Sterling in the other.

'Sorry, Cooper. How'd you go with Brandon Moss's parents?'

'They've been in and handed over the keys to both dwellings on the property. They're now comfortably ensconced in a motel by the lake.'

'That's good.'

'What's your ETA, Detective?'

'I'm hoping we'll be there before dark. We're just about to turn onto the Federal Highway.'

'We'll be expecting you around five, then. Come to the Jindabyne Memorial Hall. We're assembling there.'

❄

Vanessa called as they skirted around the Lake George shoreline. 'I got your message, Pierce,' she said, the concern evident in her voice.

'Hi, Vanessa,' said Flowers before Ryder could answer. 'Just letting you know I'm here, and listening.'

'Hi there, Mitch,' Vanessa said with a laugh, the warm, familiar sound giving Ryder's spirits a much-needed boost. 'What's happening?' she asked.

Ryder quickly filled her in. 'I think you should call Eva. Tell her to lock the doors and for her and Poppy to stay inside.'

'Oh my God, I will. She's so busy, she never has the TV or radio on during the day, and she's rarely on social media. She'd probably have to hear it from Bede.'

'The weather's bad up there apparently, which is good from a safety point of view. I'm expecting most people will be inside already.'

'It'll make your job more difficult, though, trying to catch him. Please, take care, both of you.'

'We will,' said Ryder, knowing she wanted to say more but wouldn't with Flowers in the car.

'How's the new job going, Vanessa?' Flowers asked.

'It's not too bad, Mitch. Different from what I'm used to. I'm working in the apartment for the next two days doing bookwork of all things. At least I'll be able to keep the TV on, so I can watch the news. Anyway, I'd better call Eva.'

'Bye, Vanessa,' said Ryder. Then, not caring that Flowers could hear: 'Love you.'

'Love you, too.'

To his credit, Flowers stayed silent. Ryder could only assume that, like him, the seriousness of what lay ahead was weighing heavily on his mind.

'Sounds as if she likes her new job,' Flowers said eventually.

'Yeah, she says she does, but it's so different to being a ski patroller.'

For a long while after that they travelled in silence, until Ryder finally asked, 'Did you eat lunch?'

'Nah, didn't have time. You?'

Ryder shook his head. 'We'll stop at Maccas in Cooma. Who knows when we'll next eat?'

❄

In Michelago, large rain drops fell from a gunmetal-grey sky, splattering onto the windscreen.

Mutual hunger added to their solemn mood, as did the many road casualties dotting the shoulder, large crosses painted on their furry backs, indicating an animal rescuer had already checked for young.

'Ever hit a roo?' Ryder asked, stifling a yawn. It had been a long day, and it was about to get longer.

The peal of Ryder's mobile phone cut off Flowers' response.

'Hello, Detective. It's Clayton Rose calling,' said a man with a New Zealand accent. 'I'm from the legal department in BHM Holdings, the Philippines.'

'Yes?' Ryder shifted in the driver's seat. Three hours ago, the lawyer's call would have been the cause of much excitement, so desperate was Ryder for a lead on Gavin Hutton. But thanks to Brandon Moss's hidden camera, the call wasn't so vital now.

'Human Resources said you requested information about a former employee of ours, Gavin Hutton?'

'That's right. I appreciate you calling back.' Ryder grimaced at the terrible connection making it difficult to understand what the lawyer was saying. 'You've already answered the first question I was going to ask—did Gavin Hutton work there?'

'He did. He was employed as a security guard for around eleven months.'

'What about his brother, Trevor Swan?'

'No, he just happened to be visiting his brother at the time.'

Ryder frowned. 'At the time of what?'

There was silence at the other end. Spotting a driveway up ahead, Ryder pulled over into the loose gravel. 'Mr Rose, Gavin Hutton is wanted for the murder of two men in Australia. We know these crimes occurred after he came home from the Philippines. If you have any information that is pertinent to our investigation, I urge you to tell me.'

'I see. I had no knowledge of that. I assumed you were calling about the kidnapping.'

Ryder began to record the conversation on his phone. 'We're not aware of anyone being kidnapped. Could you give us a brief rundown, please, and just to let you know, we'll be recording the conversation.'

'Of course. Back in March 2017 we were forced to deal with an awful situation. There's nothing unusual, or wrong, about our employees going into town for a day or two when they have time off. On this occasion, though, they were targeted by a group of criminals who took them hostage.'

'How many people were taken?' asked Ryder.

'Three of ours, including Gavin Hutton, and Mr Hutton's brother. It was particularly bad because they were kept in atrocious conditions for almost three months, deprived of adequate food, and given no access to medication. It was a terrible time for all involved, and particularly tragic when Mr Swan was killed.'

Ryder looked across at Flowers. The younger man's eyes widened. 'How did he die?' Ryder asked.

'The kidnappers became desperate. Eventually, they lost patience with the negotiator, and executed Mr Swan to send a message.'

Flowers' chin dropped to his chest and he shook his head.

'Who was the negotiator?' asked Ryder.

'An Australian. Hang on a minute.' There was a rustle, like the sound of pages being turned. 'I have the reports here from the debriefing. They're quite extensive. Here we go: it's signed Jack Walker, Crisis Team Negotiator.'

'Would you be able to email me copies of those reports?'

'Of course.'

'Any intel we can get from you, or any insight into Gavin Hutton's state of mind, would be helpful for when we're dealing with him,' Ryder said, before reciting his email address.

'I do know he came out in better shape than the other two, but he didn't return to work here. There was a police investigation in the Philippines, but it was pretty clear what had happened. What else?' Rose muttered. There was the sound of him flipping over more pages. 'Mr Hutton left for Australia after his brother was cremated. Anyway, you can read it all in the report, Detective Ryder. I must say I'm shocked to hear what you've told me.'

No more shocked than Ryder was to learn that Hutton and his brother had been kidnapped. 'You've been extremely helpful,' he said, checking over his shoulder and pulling onto the road when there was a break in the traffic.

'You have my number now. If there's anything else you need to know, feel free to call.'

'Thanks. You've tied up some loose ends already, particularly in regard to what happened to Trevor Swan.'

'Yes, that was incredibly sad. Unfortunately, he was in the wrong place at the wrong time.'

❄

Ryder asked Flowers to play back the conversation he'd recorded. Though slightly echoey and scratchy, the phone had managed to capture the gist of his conversation with Clayton Rose.

'Send a copy of it through to Inspector Gray,' Ryder said as they joined the line of cars at the McDonald's drive-through. 'He's waiting on a report from me. This might keep him off my back for a while, and you can send it through to the task force as well.'

'Will do.'

'And Flowers? You're the one with your eye on becoming a police prosecutor, so I'll give you those reports from BHM Holdings when they come through. You can give me the rundown on them.'

'Yes, Sarge.'

They were about sixth in line from the first window when the four-wheel drive with Brown at the wheel turned into the carpark. 'You can drive from here, Flowers,' Ryder said, throwing open his door. 'I want to have a word with Sterling.'

The rush of freezing air brought Ryder wide awake after the recirculated heat in the car. Alighting from a police car always attracted curious glances from the public, but Ryder took no notice as he strode towards the four-wheel drive now joining the queue. Sterling lowered the passenger-side window as Ryder approached.

'How's it going?' he asked, leaning down so he could talk to Brown as well.

'No problems,' said Brown.

'How far behind are the others?'

'Ten minutes, max. They stopped at Queanbeyan so Benson could grab a couple of things from his place.'

'Ah, okay. Hey, listen, we've just learned that Trevor Swan died in the Philippines.'

'No shit?' said Brown. 'How?'

'Flowers is sending you a copy of a conversation I had with the company lawyer. That'll bring you up to date.'

'It just came through now,' said Sterling, looking at her phone.

'Good. I just wanted to tell you that Swan's death certificate would have been issued in the Philippines, so you can tell O'Day he can expect a copy to come through from the Register of Deaths Abroad.'

Sterling nodded. 'I'll do that, Sarge.'

Brown pointed a finger over the steering wheel. 'Flowers has reached the ordering window. Does he know what you want, Sarge?'

'We've already ordered, on the app.'

'There's an app?' exclaimed Sterling.

Ryder grinned and tapped his hand on the sill. 'See you up there.'

Twenty-six

'She'll need nasal spray, antibiotics and a decongestant, Eva,' said Dr Helen Ives. 'The decongestant will make her sleepy, so don't worry.'

'Thanks Helen. She hasn't had an ear infection for a while, so I was out of drops. We've had a few disturbed nights.'

'I'll give you more repeats. It's a good idea to have some handy.'

'Thanks.'

'I'm going to refer her to a paediatric ear-nose-and-throat specialist too. It'll mean a trip into Canberra.'

Eva looked at the older woman, her stomach churning with sudden anxiety. 'So, it's not a straightforward ear infection? Poppy does have some hearing loss?'

'It's associated with the sniffle she has. The hearing loss is a result of her eustachian tubes being blocked, which happens a lot in toddlers and children because they haven't fully developed. Most likely, by the time you get an appointment, the spray will have already unblocked them. Still, I fear she has the start of glue ear.' Helen smiled at Poppy. 'If a child can't hear, it delays their development.' She glanced at Eva. 'Purely precautionary.'

'Thanks, Helen. I'll make an appointment right away.'

'Ring me if you're worried about anything.'

'I will.'

Eva paid at reception and put the referral letter into her tote bag.

'Let's get your beanie on, sweetheart,' she said after she'd zipped up Poppy's jacket. She slid the woollen hat over Poppy's hair, making sure her ears were well covered. 'There we go.'

Outside, she found Jack leaning against the surgery wall, his dark blond hair standing up in the wind. 'Would you like me to put her in the car?' he asked, his blue eyes searching her face.

'That's probably a good idea,' she said, letting him take Poppy. 'I'll be as quick as I can.'

The pharmacy was a few shops along from the surgery. Eva unzipped her jacket and pulled off her beanie, the central heating like a sauna after the subzero temperature outside.

While they made up Poppy's prescriptions in the dispensary, Eva browsed the shelves, putting a packet of strong painkillers into the basket for Jack, along with lozenges in case they succumbed to whatever bug Poppy had picked up. Determined not to think about whether Gavin Hutton was anywhere near the Golden Wattle, she added a tube of antiseptic gel, surgical cotton squares and antibiotic cream to her basket. Jack was getting stronger every day—the dehydration, blood loss and lack of food no longer an issue—but she had no idea how his stomach wound was healing.

A picture of Gavin Hutton, a knife glinting in his hand, came to mind. Eva pushed it aside. Here in the brightly lit pharmacy, she could pretend for a little while that everything was normal.

'Eva?'

She swung around to see Bede standing there, a pharmacy bag in his hand. 'Oh, hi, Bede.'

'I thought it was you.' He glanced at the array of items in her basket. 'Are you all right? You look as white as a sheet.'

'I'm fine.' Eva smiled, hoping it was convincing enough not to pique Bede's curiosity further. 'Poppy's not well. I've had her at the doctor.'

As if to verify what she'd just told him, the pharmacist called out Poppy's name. Eva signed for the medications before paying for everything at the front counter. When she went to leave, she was dismayed to find Bede waiting for her at the door.

'What's wrong with the munchkin?' he asked, holding the door open against a strong gust of wind. Snow blew off the roof and landed on a four-wheel drive parked directly below them in the carpark. They walked together towards the stairs, melting clumps of snow dragged in on people's boots making the boards slippery and wet.

Eva relayed what the doctor had told her.

'Oh, the poor little tyke, where is she?'

'In the car,' Eva said, with a nod towards the SUV, 'with Jack.' It would be silly to say otherwise. Bede knew her too well to know she would never leave Poppy alone in the car.

Bede's eyebrows shot up. 'Oh, she's with her father?' he said quietly.

Eva nodded.

'Do you mind if I come and say hello?'

Eva shook her head. 'Of course I don't mind.' Resigned that there was nothing she could do, she followed her friend down the wooden steps. 'Are you feeling okay, Bede?' she asked.

'Yes, I'm just a bit chesty. It's the sudden change in temperature, I think.'

'I'm sorry I didn't let you know I was coming to the shops like I said I would,' she apologised. 'We wanted to get Poppy to the doctor as soon as possible.'

'Of course. Don't give it a second thought.' He watched while Jack lowered the window then propped an elbow on the sill. 'G'day, I'm Bede. I own the Willy Wagtail. It's the lodge closest to Eva's.'

'Jack Walker. Good to meet you.' Jack gave Bede a friendly smile. 'Thanks for sending those boys around to help with the racks.'

'No dramas. We help each other out around here, being a small community.'

'That makes sense. It's a harsh climate.'

'Especially for a woman on her own,' Bede said pointedly.

While Eva cringed inwardly, Jack simply nodded once, his face unreadable.

Bede peered into the back seat. 'You get that ear better, hey, poppet? No more headbanging.'

Poppy didn't answer, just shifted restlessly in her car seat.

Bede straightened up and looked at Eva. 'Take care on the way back. It's carnage out there on the roads.'

And that was the lesser of the dangers facing them. 'You too,' she said, sorry to see Bede go, sorry to have to leave the safety of the bustling town brimming with so many familiar faces.

'Bede's old-school,' she said, sliding into the back seat beside Poppy and slamming the door. 'Don't take offence.'

'I didn't,' Jack said, his focus on the reversing camera as he backed out. 'He's protective of you. Seems like a decent bloke.'

'He is. Bede's too polite to pry into people's private lives, and I never felt the need to explain anything. He knows your name, that's all.'

Jack's mouth curved in a smile. 'No wonder he came down to see for himself then.'

❄

The conditions had worsened during the time they'd been in Jindabyne. Despite flashing signs warning of black ice, two four-wheel drives had skidded off the bitumen into ditches before they'd reached the Alpine Way. Police and road-service vehicles were on the scene.

Eva tucked a blanket around Poppy. She'd slipped into an exhausted sleep five minutes after taking her medication. Eva leaned forward, peering through the gap between the seats. The speedometer showed they were travelling at twenty-five kilometres an hour, the only indication of the traffic up ahead slowing, the red glow of tail-lights from the vehicles ahead.

'I'm pulling into Bullocks Flat carpark,' Jack said suddenly, turning on the indicator. 'I'll grab a few things from my car while we're here. It's not like we're going anywhere fast.'

'Do you remember where you parked?' Eva asked a little while later as they passed row after row of snow-covered vehicles.

'Yep. I just hope it's not completely under snow.'

As it turned out, the Toyota 4Runner was only partially buried. Jack was able to get access through the passenger side, which had been protected from the elements. Eva watched from the idling SUV while he opened the passenger door and pulled something out from under the seat. He slipped the object into his jacket pocket, slammed the door closed, then climbed into the rear seat.

Eva threw open the door of the vehicle and stepped out into the snow, watching while he collapsed one of the rear seats before dragging a backpack in from the boot space.

While he went about locking the car, she opened the tailgate so he could put the bag inside. She'd ride up front now Poppy was sound asleep.

'Do you have a phone charger?' he asked as they drove back towards the Alpine Way.

Eva pressed down on a section of dashboard fascia, and a hidden compartment popped open. 'There's an iPhone connection in here.'

One hand working the wheel, Jack reached inside his jacket and took out a phone. Eyes glued to the road, he handed it over.

Eva stared at the iPhone in her hand, the moment not lost on her. The first thing he'd done when he'd bulldozed his way into the Golden Wattle was to take her phone. Now he was handing her his. She unwound the charger cord and plugged in his phone.

'Thanks,' he said as she slid it into the cupholder near the gear stick. Big, fat snowflakes continued to fall as they re-joined the line of traffic on the Alpine Way. 'There must be another accident,' he said, looking in the rear-view mirror. Moments later a highway patrol car, its blue and red lights flashing, overtook the stationary line of vehicles.

'Looks like we're staying here for a while.' Jack put the SUV in park and pulled on the handbrake.

Eva yawned and leaned back against the headrest. 'Can't say I'm sorry. For the first time in days I feel safe and relaxed cocooned in here.'

There was a long silence.

Eva turned to look at him. He was staring through the windscreen, one hand caressing the gearstick, an elbow propped on the sill, his wrist resting on the top of the steering wheel.

'I'm sorry I've brought all this on you and Poppy,' he said, his apology weighted with emotion. 'A man is supposed to take care of his family. *Christ*, even my father did that, in his own strange way.'

'You're here now,' Eva said, instinctively reaching out and laying a hand over his.

He nodded, a muscle working in his cheek.

Suddenly embarrassed, Eva went to withdraw her hand, but he caught it in his, lacing long fingers through hers.

Pure pleasure spread through Eva's body, stoking in her the same crazy longing as when he'd first touched her four years ago. 'I should apologise, too,' she said, 'for hitting you when you were already hurt, and for my intention to clobber you with that doorstop.'

Jack looked at her then, a different emotion, admiration maybe, replacing the pain in his eyes. 'You were protecting our child. I wouldn't have expected anything less.'

Before she had a chance to reply, the car in front moved off, and Jack had to let go of her hand.

Eva turned to look at Poppy, happy to find she was still sound asleep in her car seat. When she turned to face the front, Jack was switching on his phone. It took a while for him to get a signal, but soon he was unlocking it with the eye scanner and dialling into voicemail on loudspeaker.

You have one new message. Message received on the ...

'It's me,' a woman said. 'I'm relieved you reached the lodge. FJ was here yesterday. He's taken it. He'll hold onto it until it's needed.'

Eva turned to Jack in confusion, watching as he deleted the message. 'Reached the lodge? How did that woman know—'

'It's Julieann,' he said. 'I emailed her from your computer right before I locked it in the drawer in the lobby.'

Eva thought back to those first terrifying hours when she'd been certain Jack was there to take Poppy.

'Remember how I told you about the photo Hutton saw when he was in Julieann's apartment?'

'Yes, that's how he found out about me and Poppy.'

Jack nodded. 'Julieann said he picked up the photo frame and was holding it while he was talking to her. It's made of brushed metal. Anyway, I told her not to touch it because there's a strong chance he's left a print. It's with a man I can depend on. He has no idea what's inside the package Julieann gave him, but he trusts me.'

'Why didn't you keep the photo frame yourself so you can give it to the police?'

'I wasn't even sure I was looking for Hutton in the right place, and anything could have happened to me out there in the national park.'

'It did,' she said dryly.

'I wanted the print to be in the hands of someone who could get it to the police no matter where I was. With a fingerprint, and Julieann as a witness, he could at least be charged with acts of intent to commit murder of you or Poppy. It's important we show premeditation.'

'You sound like you have it all worked out.'

He leaned forward and pressed the button to turn down his heated seat. 'Maybe now, after spending weeks out there thinking about it. I didn't have time to see Julieann before I raced down here. I told her not to touch the photo frame, and that I'd contact her when I found Hutton. At that point she could ask FJ to come and get it.'

Eva didn't ask who FJ was. She wasn't sure he'd tell her if she did. 'What if the police charge Hutton with the murder of the other two men in the meantime?'

'I hope they do. What I have is corroborating evidence that would support the charge of intent. We can't have Hutton being released, ever.'

❄

To Jack's way of thinking, something else was going on aside from the inclement weather. While Eva dozed, the number of vehicles travelling in the opposite direction had increased, as though they were being turned around and sent back to Jindabyne. So, it came as no surprise when he rounded the final bend to see barricades blocking the road a short distance on from the Friday Flat entrance to the village. An electronic sign announced that the Alpine Way was closed beyond Thredbo. A highway patrol car, its lights flashing, was parked to one side of the barricades.

Eva stirred in the passenger seat as the car came to a stop. 'What's going on?' she asked, staring at the patrol officer approaching the car.

Jack lowered the window. 'I don't know.'

'Afternoon,' the officer said, peering into the interior. He looked at Jack, then Eva, before scanning the back seat where Poppy was still sleeping. 'Where are you folks off to?'

'The Golden Wattle Lodge, in Thredbo,' said Jack.

'Are you staying there?'

Eva leaned forward so she could speak to the officer. 'I live there. I'm the lessee.'

'Are you planning on going anywhere tonight?'

'No, we've just had our daughter at the doctor's,' said Jack. 'What's going on?'

'We believe there's a wanted criminal in the area. Residents and guests can access the village via Banjo Drive. People planning on travelling to Victoria are being turned around in the Friday Flat carpark, so try to avoid that side of the village.' The officer waved an arm, and a second officer waiting near the stationary police vehicle shifted aside one of the barriers. 'Stay home and lock your doors. Keep a radio or the TV turned on, and if you see anyone acting in a suspicious manner don't approach them, call triple zero and ask for the police.' The officer stepped away from the car and waved them on before moving on to the next vehicle.

Jack drove carefully through the gap in the barriers, watching in the rear-view mirror as the car behind them turned down the hill towards Friday Flat.

'I didn't call them,' Eva said. 'Just so you know.'

Jack glanced sideways at her. 'I know. I trust you.'

There was a long silence while Jack wound his way through the narrow streets. Snowbanks had built up at the side of the road, frozen walls of ice illuminated in the sweep of fog lights.

'This will derail everything, won't it,' Eva asked, 'just as you feared it would?'

'If he gets away,' he said, hating the fear in Eva's voice. 'But that's always been the risk.'

'I don't want to go into protective custody with Poppy, or for us to live in fear of Hutton, but I'll need to make a choice one way or another if he gets away, won't I?'

'Let's hope the police get him. Whatever intel they have, I hope it's sound.'

In his peripheral vision, Eva gave a distracted nod.

'The most logical explanation is that someone has seen Hutton around Leatherbarrel Creek,' Jack said as they climbed higher. 'The damage I did to his face could have been severe enough to force him out of the bush. There are campgrounds around there.'

'Maybe he was making for the lodge, and somebody saw him.'

Jack had been wondering that, too. He nodded, feeling the intensity of her gaze in the shadowy interior of the car.

When the steep driveway came into view, he flicked on the indicator and left the road. The tyres skipped a little before gripping the ice, the gum trees along the boundary sagging under the weight of the snow. Ahead of them, the lodge stood marooned in a sea of white, the build-up on the roof at least ten centimetres thick. Jack scanned the area around the garage while Eva pressed the magic button for the roller door.

'Everything must be all right,' she said. 'I can't hear the alarm.'

Jack pulled into the garage, the sensor light flickering on and showing everything was as they'd left it. Putting the car in park, he kept watch in the rear-view mirror until the roller door closed with a definite thump.

Cutting the engine, he looked at Eva. She turned huge hazel eyes on him, her white face framed by the turned-up cuff of the animal-print beanie. 'All good so far,' he said, refusing to let the jolt of electricity that scorched through him every time he was close to Eva distract him. 'Let's get inside. I'll carry Poppy.'

The little girl stirred as he lifted her out, her hands coming up to cover her eyes against the sudden glare of light. With Poppy slumped on one shoulder and his backpack slung over the other, Jack watched as Eva punched the number sequence into the keypad. The alarm disarmed with two anaemic beeps.

'I can't believe this old rattler held up,' she said.

Reassured that the lodge's defences hadn't been breached, Jack led the way into the frigid hallway.

'Brrr,' he heard Eva say as they traipsed up the stairs. 'I'll get the central heating going, the last thing we need are frozen pipes.'

✳

While Jack checked the interior of the lodge, Eva managed to rouse Poppy for long enough to give her a small amount of custard, a little water and her antibiotic drops.

'Let me get these clothes off before you get into bed,' she said when they were back in her room. Poppy swayed sleepily while Eva unbuttoned her daughter's coat and wrestled it off her shoulders. As Poppy crawled towards the bedhead, Eva managed to drag one boot off her small foot, then the other. 'Hang on,' she said, tugging back the covers so Poppy could slide underneath.

'Go back to sleep,' she said with a smile, tucking the doona around her daughter and kissing her forehead, pleased her skin was feeling cooler now. 'You can sleep in your leggings and sweater tonight.'

Eva switched on Poppy's night light, then moved over to the window. Raising a hand, she touched her fingertips to the freezing glass, looking for footprints in the clearing like the ones she'd noticed the other day. Though it was almost dusk and the light rapidly fading, she could see that the snow-covered ground was unmarked.

Eva drew the curtains across the window, her attention drawn to the icicles hanging from the eaves. She tiptoed from the room and quietly shut the door. She should take a look at the verandah, too.

Icicles tended to form on the eaves once the water in the gutters had frozen.

By the time Eva came into the lounge room, Jack had the TV tuned to the local channel, and a fire roaring in the grate. A Breaking News panel along the bottom of the screen confirmed what the policeman on the Alpine Way had already told them.

Eva went to stand beside him, grateful that the central heating was cranking up. The weather bar on the screen showed the temperature had fallen to minus six. 'Any more news?' she asked.

He shook his head. 'There's a police update in twenty minutes.'

'If the signal hasn't been knocked out by then,' said Eva dryly. 'Do you have a radio?'

She nodded. 'It's more reliable than the TV. I'll get it.'

'I'll go. You warm up in front of the fire. Where is it?'

'In the kitchen, on the corner of the bench, next to the pot plant.'

While Jack went to fetch the radio, Eva stood close to the fire, imagining Gavin Hutton roaming the mountains, slicing open Jack's skin, inside a woman's apartment, his murderous hands holding a photo frame while he gazed down at the picture of Eva and Poppy. He'd violated the home of a woman Eva didn't even know, a woman who treasured a photograph of her and Poppy because of her love for Jack, a woman who would have died, too, if not for that photograph.

Needing to break the repetitive cycle of her thoughts, Eva looked around the room for a distraction. Surely something in here needed to be put back in its place, or straightened or tossed in the bin. But the room looked orderly. Remembering the icicles hanging from the eaves outside her bedroom, she headed over to the window, the same one through which she and Jack had watched Randall reverse his trailer when he'd delivered the firewood. Was that only a couple of days ago? The clearing would be in the dark shadow of the hill now, so she flicked the switch for the verandah light and shifted aside the curtain.

She looked up towards the eaves and gasped, a scream building in her throat.

Twenty-seven

Jack dropped the radio and moved, wrenching open the kitchen door and pulling the Beretta from his waistband. Flicking off the safety, he raised the pistol to shoulder height, steadying it in a two-handed grip.

In the lounge room, he swept left, noting the door to Eva's suite remained closed, then right, beyond the dining table to the top of the staircase.

Stepping lightly, and using the massive fireplace in the middle of the room as cover, he moved forward. Logically, he knew there was no one in the lodge, he'd checked it minutes earlier, but Eva wouldn't have screamed without a reason.

A soft sound had his heart crashing against his ribs. He rounded the fireplace to find her backing away from the window.

He lowered the pistol. 'What's wrong? Are you all right?'

She nodded. 'I'm sorry; I couldn't help it.' She pointed to the window as he came closer. 'Out there.'

With the pistol held against his shoulder, Jack approached the window from the side, parting the curtains when he was close enough.

A macabre figure gazed back at him.

A snowman had been built on the verandah, though not the friendly type children liked to make. This snowman was a grisly construct, staring at him through the glass—hatless, one eye a round stone, the other eye disturbingly real. Jack's stomach gave a sickening churn. *Was it?* He couldn't tell from where he stood on the other side of the glass, though the knife that served as a nose was chillingly real. The handle had been pushed into the snow leaving the blade exposed.

Jack let the curtain fall into place and went to Eva. 'What made you look out the window?' he asked, shoving the pistol into his waistband. 'Did you hear a noise?'

She shook her head, her face devoid of colour. 'I was looking to see if there were icicles on the eaves. I opened the curtain and saw it.' She licked her trembling lips. 'He's out there—'

Jack pulled her against his chest, his heart rate slowing now he knew Hutton could have been there and gone already. 'He's messing with us,' he said, rubbing a hand over her back, knowing she would be more terrified for Poppy's safety than her own.

She nodded against his chest.

'Listen.' He took hold of her shoulders and gently set her away from him. 'He may have left by now. He's trying to scare us.'

Eva gave a watery smile. 'It's working.'

He released her and looked towards the window. 'There's evidence out there that I need to bring in.'

'No, Jack! Are you crazy?'

'Probably. Do you have ziploc bags in the kitchen?'

She nodded.

'Can you grab some for me, please? It'll save me time looking for them.'

'Here,' she said, handing him the plastic bags a few minutes later.

'Make sure you have your phone,' he said. 'And hold onto the Beretta.' He took her hand and laid the butt of the pistol in her palm. 'Safety's on.'

'You're the one going outside. You should take it.'

'He's not after me. Sure, he attacked me down at Leatherbarrel, but he didn't know it was me then, and he used a knife because he wouldn't have wanted his hideout found. It's you and Poppy he's after. He wants *me* to suffer.'

'Okay.'

'If something does go wrong, I want you to take the phone and gun, and lock yourself in the room with Poppy. Call triple zero. The police are up on the Alpine Way and at Friday Flat. They could even be in the village by now. They'll be here in minutes. All set?' he asked, not wanting to give her time to dwell on what might happen.

She nodded. 'All set.'

'Lock the door behind me,' he said, leading the way through the lobby and into the vestibule. 'When I come back, I'll give three quick raps on the door, and say the name of the lodge.' He looked down at her, impatient to get out there, needing to be rid of Hutton once and for all.

She nodded, but when he turned away to unlock the door, he felt the pressure of her hand on his forearm. She was staring up at him, her eyes wide with worry, and while she didn't say anything, he could see she was trying to.

Jack laid a hand over hers and gave it a gentle squeeze.

He was halfway out the door when he heard her say, 'Be careful. We've just got you back.'

❄

With a deep sense of unease, Jack waited until the door closed behind him and the lock engaged. Two porch lights, positioned just above eye level and mounted on either side of the main doors, cast a bright light over the verandah and partway into the clearing. Seconds ticked by slowly as he scanned the perimeter where light faded to dark.

With unhurried, deliberate steps, he walked towards the roughly made snowman, the quiet of early evening broken only by the sound of his footsteps on the wooden boards and the occasional rustle of wind in the trees. Hutton would have spent a considerable amount of time in the open, given the snow it had taken to build the gross figure.

Using one of the plastic bags as a glove, Jack worked the knife free and bagged it, the below-zero temperature like a blast of dry ice on his face. Scanning the clearing a second time, he leaned closer to study what looked like a human eye. Burrowing his hand into the snow underneath the object, he scooped it out and slid the whole lot into another bag.

Straightening up, he looked around again. Was Hutton out there, or had he found shelter somewhere and settled in, waiting to return later?

'Gavin!' he shouted as he walked towards the door. 'I'm here if you want to talk about Trevor.'

Standing in the pool of light, he gazed across the clearing and into the blackness beyond. Then he rapped three times on the door, and said, 'Golden Wattle', for Eva to open up.

❄

'Was he out there?' Eva asked, bolting the door, her palms clammy, her legs shaky.

'I hope so. I hope he heard me.'

'Who's Trevor?' Her heart had jumped into her throat when she'd heard him hailing their adversary.

'His half-brother.' Jack gestured with his chin, the way he had the other day when he'd muscled his way in downstairs. 'Let's go into the kitchen.'

'I want to check on Poppy first,' she said.

While Jack headed towards the kitchen, Eva slipped into the bedroom, the fairy night light casting a soft glow around the room. She tiptoed over to the bed, relieved to see Poppy still asleep. A part of her longed to stay, to slip into bed and feel safe, to read a book to Poppy and smile together at the illustrations. But the other part kept her where she was, anxious to get back to Jack, knowing the life she was desperate to hold onto depended on what they did next. She turned to go, the clock's luminous hands pointing to just after seven.

The plastic bags and their ghastly contents were on the kitchen bench. Jack had the tap running.

When he saw her he came closer, and they studied the eye inside the ziploc bag. The snow around it had already begun to melt. He pushed it gently with an index finger, his hand red from the cold. 'That's a flexible material. It's false.' He looked at her. 'Do you have a container I can put this stuff in? It's a long shot, but the knife could have a print on it.'

Eva found a container while Jack ran his hands under the warm water. 'He must have held it by the blade and pushed it in,' she said, putting a plastic box and lid on the bench.

'Yeah. It's weird. I wanted to kick the snowman in, but it's so damn cold it's practically frozen solid.'

A chill ran down Eva's spine, her gaze drawn once more to the contents of the plastic bags. 'This is really messed up, Jack.'

He turned the tap off and dried his hands with paper towel. 'I know.'

'What's his half-brother got to do with it?' Eva asked. 'Why do you want to talk about him?'

He didn't answer right away but balled up the paper and tossed it in the bin. 'Trevor was in the Philippines visiting Hutton. He was kidnapped, too, along with the others.'

'He was unlucky?'

'They were all unlucky.'

Eva frowned. 'You told me there was a Swedish guy in the group. Why didn't you tell me one of the others was Hutton's brother?'

'Because Trevor didn't make it. They executed him.'

Eva drew in a sharp breath. 'Executed?'

Jack nodded. 'To send me a message. Pay up or we'll kill another one.' Jack ran a hand down his face. 'Hutton blames the crisis team for his brother's death, and me more than the others.'

A shiver ran down Eva's body like someone had traced the curve of her spine with an icy finger. She'd never understood Hutton's thirst for revenge when he'd *survived* the kidnapping. She'd assumed he'd lost his mind. Now she understood. He was seeking revenge for his brother's death.

'They shot him while I was on the phone to them,' Jack said, his voice turning a little husky, 'like one of those horrific news reports you see on TV where people are begging for their lives.'

Eva swallowed. 'Oh, Jack, that must have been horrendous.'

'That's why I didn't tell you. You were terrified in those first few hours, thinking I was here to try to take Poppy away from you. It was difficult enough explaining my work and how all that tied in with Hutton. I was injured. There was a lot going on. Killing Trevor was a message that they were out of patience, and they chose Trevor Swan because his life had the least value.'

Eva watched as he put the bags inside the container. 'Is this another message for you?'

He glanced at her and snapped on the lid. Then he nodded. 'An eye for an eye.'

Twenty-eight

Plain-clothes detectives, uniformed officers and members of the dog squad unit gathered inside the Jindabyne Memorial Hall where Sergeant Thalia Cooper gave an initial briefing on the planned police response.

'As of four this afternoon, in response to credible information received from a member of the public, the Alpine Way has been closed between the Victorian border and Thredbo Village. Police patrols have been stationed at both Thredbo and on the border, and there are a number of patrols stationed intermittently along the closed section of road. This number will increase as more personnel arrive this evening. Media broadcasts have been released, particularly for Thredbo Village, Crackenback Resort and all other properties along the Alpine Way from Thredbo to Jindabyne. Any suspicious behaviour is to be immediately reported to police.'

Ryder listened from a far corner of the hall where the Homicide task force had chosen to congregate. Standing beside him was Sterling, then further along were Benson, O'Day and Brown. Flowers was sitting behind them, reading the reports that had come through from the mine's legal department on his phone.

Sergeant Cooper cleared her throat. 'A number of residents along the closed section of the Alpine Way have chosen to evacuate. Others have decided to shelter in place. The patrols I previously mentioned will have two tasks: the first is to respond to calls from residents along the closed section, and the second is staying vigilant for any sign of Gavin Hutton.'

'At first light tomorrow, the dog squad will attend the property of Mr and Mrs Moss, where hopefully the dogs will pick up the scent from inside the old house at the rear of the property, after which our forensics team will enter the premises to brush for fingerprints and collect any other DNA evidence.'

Sergeant Cooper looked up from the microphone. 'At this point, I'll hand you over to Senior Sergeant Hanlon of the dog squad. If you could take it from here, Senior Sergeant?'

Someone bumped Ryder's elbow. He turned to see Harriet Ono standing beside him, a black forensics bag slung over the Canberra pathologist's shoulder. 'Stop requesting me, Pierce. People are starting to talk.'

Ryder smiled at the woman, who only came up to his shoulder. 'Harriet, I knew you'd hate to miss out on all the excitement.'

'Humph! I get enough in the lab.' She stood on tiptoe, trying to peer through the mountain of police in front of her. 'What's happening?'

'An initial briefing for first light tomorrow,' Ryder said, keeping his voice down. 'You get access to the property straight after the dogs. There'll be air support, too, weather permitting.'

'And what are you and boy wonder over there going to do?' she asked, glancing at Flowers, who was yet to look up and notice her. 'Walk around in your suits looking hot while the rest of us do the hard work?'

Ryder smirked. He could always count on Harriet and her smart mouth to keep the energy up in the room.

'I've got something for you.' She dug in her bag and took out an envelope. 'It's a copy of the blood analysis you requested from that campsite. You'll want to see it.'

Ryder slid the report out of the unsealed envelope and quickly skimmed the contents. Two human blood types found.

'No animal, huh?' He looked at Harriet. 'There were two people at that campsite?'

She nodded.

He skipped to the bottom of the report where she'd highlighted a paragraph stating that DNA found at the campsite matched DNA found at the Burrows crime scene in Sydney.

'That match has got to be Hutton,' Ryder said.

'Yep. Again, he doesn't have a record, so he's not in the database. You're going to have to catch the guy to prove it was him.'

'Tell me something I don't know,' he said, feeling a small measure of satisfaction that her report confirmed he'd been right all along in thinking Hutton had been hiding out in the Snowy Mountains. It would justify his investigative process to Inspector Gray prior to Brandon Moss's video taken in the old house.

'No hits on the other blood sample either,' he said, going back to the report.

When there was no answer, he looked up to see Harriet threading her way through the crowd. Ryder sighed, wondering who else had been at that campsite, and where they might be now.

His phone buzzed, breaking into his thoughts. Vanessa's name lit up the screen. Leaving the others to listen to the remainder of the briefing, he left the hall, answering the phone as he walked out into a carpark overflowing with police vehicles. 'Hi.'

'Hi, Pierce. I'm really sorry to interrupt, I know you're really busy.'

'Actually, everything's going pretty smoothly at the moment.' He shivered as a gust of wind penetrated his clothing. 'Jindabyne Police have put a lot in place already. We're hitting the area at first light tomorrow. Is everything okay there?'

'I'm fine. I'm having trouble getting through to Eva, though.'

'Oh, you haven't spoken to her yet?'

There was a pause, then Vanessa asked, 'What did you say? I can't hear you over the background noise.'

'It's the wind. Hang on.' Ryder moved around the other side of the building. 'Is that better?'

'A bit. I've left a couple of messages for her, but she hasn't returned my call.'

'She's normally quick getting back to you, isn't she?'

'She is. I didn't want to bother you, but it's a bit out of character.'

'It's no bother. We're in Jindabyne now. There's a briefing happening in the hall. Keep trying to get hold of her, and I'll call you when we're done here. If you haven't heard back from her by then, Flowers and I will take a trip up to the lodge.'

'Oh, thanks, Pierce. Any other time I'd call Bede and ask him to walk over, but with the order to shelter in place I wouldn't put him in that position.'

'Vanessa, this is your family. I'll check it out, okay?'

'Thank you.'

'No worries.' He grimaced as another gust of wind caused the phone speaker to crackle in his ear. 'I'll call you back soon.'

Ryder returned to the hall, only to run into Patricia Franks in the small entryway. A relieved smile lit up her face when she saw him.

'Hello, Detective Ryder. I hope I'm not in the way.'

'Not at all, Patricia. Nice to see you again.'

'I was looking through the door wondering how on earth I was going to find you in the crowd.'

Ryder smiled. It was a miracle he'd recognised her, bundled up in a long puffer jacket, the fur-lined hood drawn tightly around her face. He looked down at the plastic sleeve she was holding. 'Is that for me?'

'Yes. You may not even need it now, but I found this document when I was looking for something else. It had been filed incorrectly.' She slid the piece of paper out of the sleeve. It was a permit of some kind that Ryder didn't bother reading. It wasn't even the name Xtreme Aussie Adventures that caught his attention. It was the signature that interested Ryder; the name Sterling hadn't been able to find from all her searches.

'John Walker,' said Franks. 'That was the name I was trying to remember. It's such a common name, too.'

'In my experience, it's the common ones we tend to forget.'

'I sent you an email earlier with the document attached, but then I saw on the news you were back in Jindabyne, so I thought I may as well bring it down on my way home.'

LEE CHRISTINE

'Thanks for this, Patricia,' Ryder said.

She waved a hand. 'You can keep that one. It's a copy.'

'I appreciate it.' After thanking her again for coming out in the cold, he went to find Flowers. His partner was standing with the rest of the task force listening to the ongoing briefing. He looked around as Ryder joined the group. 'Hey, Sarge.'

'Have I missed anything important?' he asked.

'They're showing us the terrain we'll be covering tomorrow. It's an overview only. There's a final briefing at five in the morning.'

Ryder nodded. 'You and I won't be part of the ground search, Flowers.'

'What about the rest of us?' asked Benson, peering around Sterling and keeping his voice low.

Ryder nodded. 'I want you, O'Day and Brown out there. I'll be depending on your experience. You can take Sterling with you.'

Sterling's face lit up and she almost clapped before hastily lowering her hands to her sides. Ryder looked at each of his team members in turn. 'Flowers and I will be in radio contact tomorrow, ready to move in as soon as Hutton is found.'

Brown gave one of his rare smiles. 'Good to see you're full of confidence, Sarge.'

'I am,' said Ryder. 'I've got a good feeling about this one.'

206

Twenty-nine

Jack came back from the kitchen carrying two steaming bowls of food. 'I heated up this chicken pilaf you had in the freezer,' he said. 'Try to eat something.'

Eating was the furthest thing from Eva's mind, her stomach churning every time she thought of Gavin Hutton being outside her front window. 'What did you do with the plastic box I gave you, the one with the knife and other things off the snowman?' she asked.

He set her meal down on the coffee table and handed her a fork. 'I locked it in the room with my stuff.'

'Thank you. I don't want to look at it, and I don't want Poppy finding it either.'

He sat on the lounge, and though he kept to the other end, he wasn't as far away this time. 'Hmm. This is really good,' he said, tasting the pilaf and glancing at her out of the corner of his eye.

'It's Poppy's favourite. I always keep some in the freezer,' she said, working a little pilaf onto her fork.

For the next few minutes, they ate in silence, and to Eva's surprise she found she was hungry. 'Jack,' she said, a little later as she took a break to let the food settle. 'There's something I want to say.' There was no better time than now to say what was on her mind.

He lowered his fork. 'Yeah?'

'If something happens to me—'

207

'Nothing's going to happen to you,' he said quickly.

Eva held up a hand. 'Just let me—'

'Sorry.'

'Vanessa is Poppy's legal guardian, just so you know.' Eva took a deep breath and steadied herself. 'I'm not saying this just because she's my sister, but you wouldn't meet a better person.'

There was a long silence, the only sound the music playing quietly from the radio.

He leaned over and put his bowl on the coffee table. 'A sense of security is vital for a child. I would never take Poppy away from a family she loves and trusts,' he said, his voice turning a little hoarse. 'I'll be honest with you, though; I've loved making a connection with her over the past few days.'

'I know.' Eva fixed her gaze on one of the wooden chess pieces, needing to get the words out as soon as she could. 'What I'm saying is, Vanessa is a reasonable person. If you wanted to be in Poppy's life, I'm sure you'd be able to work something out.' She turned to look at him then. Jack was leaning forward, staring into the fire, his elbows resting on his knees. 'Just in case,' she said softly.

❄

While Eva put the dishwasher on and went to check on Poppy, Jack grabbed the torch and began his routine check. With the exception of the kitchen light, Poppy's night light and the fire, the lodge was in darkness. If Hutton were planning on coming back, he'd need a torch or night-vision goggles.

Shining the beam around the garage, Jack thought about what Eva had said. She'd taken him by surprise, forcing him to confront the worst possible outcome, something he hadn't let himself do. He knew how to save lives; he'd been doing it in one form or another since he'd held Julieann up in the surf, and he wasn't about to let anything happen to the mother of his child. Hutton's warped desire for revenge could never match Jack's willingness to lay his life on the line for his own. That had come as naturally to him as breathing.

Climbing the stairs, his thoughts stayed with Eva. Was there another message in what she had said? By telling him Vanessa would be open to him being involved in Poppy's life if something happened to Eva, was she indirectly opening a door for him now, if they all made it through unscathed? Jack indulged himself for a few brief seconds then suppressed his hopes. It was too soon for expectations of that kind.

A little while later, he was stoking the fire when Eva came out of her room. 'How's Poppy?' he asked.

'She's still asleep.'

'The medication must have knocked her out.'

'She hasn't slept well the last few nights either.'

'Why don't you try to get some sleep as well?' he suggested.

'Oh, I couldn't.' She held up her hands and shook her head. 'I'm too freaked out to go to sleep. Just the thought of Hutton being out there on my verandah—no. I'd rather stay out here and help you keep watch.'

'Okay, you take the lounge, then. That way, it doesn't matter if you nod off.'

Eva curled up in a corner of the lounge and looked at him. 'I wish I could have a glass of wine,' she said, 'but I'm too scared. What if he got in here and I had to shoot him?' She laughed a little shrilly. 'I'd be lucky to hit him sober.'

Jack stood up. 'There's zero chance of him getting in. Stay there.'

He remembered seeing an open bottle of Semillon in the fridge; in fact, he'd been tempted to down a good portion of it himself the day he arrived, before Eva had given him painkillers.

In the kitchen, he poured out one-third of a glass and carried it back to the lounge room. 'A small amount will take the edge off, but you're right, you don't want too much.'

'What about you?' she asked.

He shook his head and sat down. 'When this is all over, maybe.'

As Jack watched her sip her wine he couldn't help but remember the time he'd stayed here. Every night at dinner, she would explain what wine they would have with their meal. On one occasion a

LEE CHRISTINE

vigneron from a local winery had joined them, and talked about the variety of grapes that grew well in the cooler climes of the Snowy Mountains region. Jack watched Eva now, tasting the wine and savouring it. After a while, her breathing slowed as she started to relax.

'Tell me something about your job,' she said, looking up and catching him watching her. 'It's so far removed from most people's experience. I'm curious.'

'What do you want to know?'

'Well, for instance, how does it start—do you just drop everything when you get word that there's been a kidnapping?'

He nodded. 'I always keep a bag packed and ready to go, the way you always have Poppy's pilaf made and in the freezer.'

She smiled, and Jack thought how lovely she was with her hazel eyes and fair hair pulled up into a high ponytail.

'Just a slight difference there,' she said, holding the glass by the stem and turning it around slowly. 'So, you fly to wherever the family are located?'

'Mostly, but in this instance Hutton had no family, and the kidnappers had unrealistic expectations of the ransom they would get. Right from the beginning, I felt it had the makings of a perfect storm.'

'Really, why?'

Jack took a breath and told Eva the story.

❄

From the first-floor window of Jack's apartment, Centennial Park stretched before him, an oasis of green in the middle of metropolitan Sydney. Below at street level, riders from the nearby equestrian centre sat astride their mounts, waiting to cross at the lights. One big bay was moving around restlessly, keen for the morning's exercise.

Jack enjoyed watching the daily practice when he was home, like now, waiting for the call the insurance company had told him to expect. His phone lit up at the exact moment the lights below turned red. He waited, counting silently before answering so as not

210

to appear too anxious. Down on the street, the riders nudged their horses into a walk. Jack turned on the recording equipment and answered the call. 'Hello.'

'Who am I speaking to?' The man spoke with a heavy south-east Asian accent.

'Who is this?' asked Jack.

There was a pause, then, 'You can call me Angel.'

'You can call me Jack.'

'Jack?'

'Jack.' Angel was nervous, a worrying sign. Hostage negotiations were notoriously unstable at the best of times and especially when dealing with a novice.

'We have two Australians. We want two million in cash.'

Jack hung up. Jotting down the time and duration of the call on his legal pad, he tried to imagine the criminal's shock. Angel was about to learn the way things worked in the world of kidnap insurance. He picked up his personal mobile and called Mike Joseph. 'Find out what we know about a bloke called Angel.'

Jack hung up again, went into the kitchen and poured his second cup of coffee for the morning. He'd give Angel ten, maybe fifteen minutes at the most. Back at the window, he caught sight of the horse's rumps, their tails swishing just before they disappeared beneath the canopy of green.

Angel turned out to be more patient than Jack had given him credit for. He called back in twenty.

'One and a half million,' he said.

'Ten thousand dollars, and we'll need proof of life. That's our first and only offer.'

Jack ignored the stream of expletives being shouted down the line, then just as Angel calmed down enough to start talking, he hung up.

Time to play the long game.

❄

Jack looked at Eva and shrugged. 'Normally, I might make a few phone calls while I'm getting my things together. It's not as exciting as it sounds. I think being a chef on a super yacht is a lot more glamourous.'

Her expression turned downcast, and she sighed. 'It *was* fun, until it *wasn't.*'

'What happened? Did you strike bad weather?'

'I struck a bad egg.'

'Oh, geez.'

'Hmm.' She glanced up at him. 'It was terrifying, because I was trapped, surrounded by ocean, with nowhere to run.'

'I can imagine. You worked on that yacht for a few years, didn't you?' he asked.

She nodded. 'Everything was great until the owner's brother decided to join us on board for a couple of weeks. The crew were fantastic. They could see what was happening and they ran interference and kept him away from me during the day. The nights were the worst. I had to lock myself in my cabin.'

'Did you report it?'

'I reported it to the owner.' She shook her head slowly, as though she still couldn't believe what had happened. 'He wouldn't hear of it. He inferred I was making it all up. I felt so unsupported, so *betrayed.* I'd worked for him for years without incident. I needed him to intervene because his brother wouldn't take no for an answer.' She swallowed. 'That hurt.'

'I'm sorry that happened to you.' Jack shook his head in disgust. 'He was a coward for not standing up. Did you report it to the police?'

'No, I walked away. I did make a promise to myself, though, that if I disembarked unscathed, I'd never work for anyone else again. I would always be my own boss.' She took another sip of wine before looking up. 'Anyway, that's in the past. I'd seen everything I wanted to see. I was done travelling by then.'

'So, you found this place and put down roots?'

'I did, as far from the ocean as I could get.' She shifted onto the edge of the lounge and leaned forward to put her glass on the table.

'Here, I'll take that,' he said, standing up.

'Oh, thank you.' She looked up at him, her fingers brushing his as he took the glass. 'I love it here, Jack,' she said huskily. 'I don't want to leave.'

Jack couldn't help it. He reached out and gently ran the back of his fingers along her jawline, exactly as he had four years ago. She turned into his touch, just has she had back then, and with a groan he turned and put the glass on the table. When he turned back, she was standing up, her eyes gleaming.

'It would be crazy to do this now,' she said.

He nodded. 'It would . . . though it's killing me to say it.'

She smiled. 'Maybe one little kiss?'

Jack dragged in a deep breath and raked back his hair. 'Yeah . . . but, no.'

'You're right! Bad idea.' Eva glanced towards her room where Poppy lay sleeping before moving away from him. 'If it's anything like last time . . .'

Jack ran a hand down his face then gestured over his shoulder. 'How about I go and make us both coffee?'

'Good idea, Jack.' Eva folded her arms across her body and sat down on the lounge again. 'We can't lose focus.'

❄

'Eva!' Someone was shaking her shoulder. 'Eva!'

Eva opened her eyes. Jack was leaning over her, an index finger pressed to his lips.

She came instantly awake, sitting up so quickly her head spun. He didn't need to say anything. She could tell from his grave expression that Hutton was nearby.

Jack had turned off the radio, the room quiet now save for the odd crackle of the fire and the sound of her own breathing. Jack took the Beretta out of his waistband, and with a silent nod he put it in her hand. Eva glanced at the bedroom door, which was still firmly closed, praying that Poppy stayed asleep.

Jack moved through the darkened room like a silhouette. She followed, sliding the Beretta into the front of her jeans. Putting a finger to his lips again, he moved to the window where earlier she had pulled aside the curtain and discovered the snowman.

Eva moved closer to him, her ears straining, the room cooler away from the fire. But it wasn't the chill closer to the windows that sent a shudder through her body, but the cruel heart and twisted mind of the man outside, hell bent on taking away everything she loved.

A footstep.

A creak.

The faint rustle of clothing.

Eva held her breath, her heart pounding.

A slow creak of board under a definite footstep. Fainter, as though he were moving away. Louder as he came back towards them.

She moved closer to Jack. 'What's he doing?' she mouthed.

He put his mouth to her ear. 'He's walked up and down a few times. I'll see if I can get him talking when he comes close to the front door. I don't want to wake Poppy.'

She nodded, watching as he turned on his phone torch. With the beam aimed at the floor, he led the way into the lobby, and through the glass doors into the vestibule. 'Ready?' he mouthed.

Eva nodded. She wanted this over and done with.

Thirty

The tiny cloakroom worked well as a makeshift office. Ryder pulled down the window shutter then slid the lock across the door. While Flowers got the two-bar strip heater on the wall going, Ryder hung his overcoat on one of the empty coat-stands.

'What's going on?' Flowers asked, pulling out a chair and sitting at the counter next to Ryder.

Ryder took Harriet's report out of the envelope. 'Good news here. DNA profile taken from the campsite at Leatherbarrel Creek is a match for blood swabbed at the Sydney crime scene.'

'That's awesome news. So, that would be Gavin Hutton's DNA? When we apprehend him, we can prove it?'

Ryder nodded, pausing as people walked through the entryway talking. The shutter muffled most of the noise, but he didn't want anyone overhearing what they were discussing. 'There were two lots of human DNA found in the samples, but no animal blood.'

Flowers frowned. 'So, what does that tell us, that Hutton has murdered someone in the National Park?'

'I don't know. No one's filed a missing person's report, and there hasn't been a body found.' Ryder put the forensics report back in the envelope and slid the plastic sleeve across the counter for Flowers to see. 'Patricia Franks turned up earlier with this, too. Take a look at the name of the owner.' Ryder pointed to the name printed under a scrawled signature.

'John Walker?' Flowers looked at Ryder. 'John. Jack. It's got to be the same guy.'

'Is Walker's signature on any of those reports that came through from the Philippines? If it is, we can compare it with this one.'

'I'm sure I saw it on the last page. His report's the most harrowing of all the ones I've read so far.' Flowers picked up his phone. 'It might take me a while to find it, Sarge, there are so many attachments. I wish I had hard copies. But if we're right, it would mean Hutton and Walker knew each other before Hutton was kidnapped.'

'Walker could be former army,' mused Ryder. 'He had a business that was popular with military types.' Ryder stood up. 'Look, it's almost ten, I need to call Vanessa. I'll get Sterling to come in here. She can go through some of the attachments for you. She has the reports on her phone.'

Flowers nodded. 'Thanks, Sarge.'

Once Sterling was settled in the cloakroom with Flowers, Ryder exited the hall. Bending his head to the wind, he strode through the carpark, the Milky Way on full display in a cloudless night sky. Ryder called Vanessa as he rounded the corner of the building, but the call went straight to voicemail.

'Hi, it's me,' he said after the beep. 'Just wondering if you'd managed to talk to Eva.' He paused, gazing up at the expanse of night sky. 'I'm outside at the moment, in the freezing cold, inhaling pure oxygen. You should see the sky. It's incredible. I know you've seen the Milky Way lots of times before, but it's great. It's like an enormous chandelier.' He paused again, his finger hovering over the end-call button. 'Anyway, that's about as poetic as I get, so let me know if you got onto Eva. Bye.'

There was a message from Inspector Gray requesting an update, so Ryder spent the next ten minutes responding to his rapid-fire questions. By the time Ryder rang off, his eyes were watering from the cold and his face had turned numb, but the Inspector was satisfied.

Flowers was waiting for him in the entryway when he got back. One look at his partner's face and Ryder knew it was something big. 'You need to look at this, Sarge,' he said.

The urgency in Flowers' voice sent a chill through Ryder colder than the night air outside.

Inside the cloakroom, Flowers gestured to Sterling. 'Show Sarge what you found.'

Sterling picked up her phone. 'I was opening the attachments looking for the one with Walker's signature, when this one came up.'

Ryder leaned forward, squinting at the small print.

'It's only general information.' Sterling held up the phone for Ryder to see. 'It's the names of the Crisis Response Team appointed to Hutton's kidnapping case.'

Ryder read the names. 'Jack Walker. Well, Clayton Rose told us he was the negotiator. Roland Carr?'

'Look at the next two, Sarge,' urged Sterling.

'William Guthrie!' Ryder's heart gave a single leap. '*Michael Joseph!*'

'I know.' Flowers' voice was shaky with what Ryder assumed was a massive hit of adrenaline.

'Jesus!' Ryder stared at the names. 'Hutton's not a serial killer. This is strategic. He's murdering people close to the crisis team.'

Flowers and Sterling looked at each other. 'That's what we think, too,' said Flowers.

Ryder inhaled then blew out a breath. 'Great pick up, Sterling, especially when you're not as familiar with the case.'

Sterling beamed. 'I'd not long finished reading through the files you gave me, Sarge. Michael Joseph is the first victim's uncle, isn't he?'

Ryder nodded. 'What I can't understand is why Will Guthrie and Mike Joseph both lied to the police. We've interviewed them more than once. They knew Gavin Hutton was our prime suspect, and yet they said nothing about working on his kidnapping case.'

'Yeah, it's strange they'd cover that up,' agreed Flowers. 'Bereaved family members are usually desperate to have the killer caught.'

'Makes me wonder what they're hiding,' said Ryder.

'I did a bit of reading before, when I got bored out in the hall,' said Flowers. 'They're an elite group, these crisis teams. The positions are highly sought after, and super competitive, always someone ready to step into their shoes if they screw up. And as Clayton Rose told us on the phone, this hostage crisis went wrong in a big way.'

'Maybe they didn't want the publicity,' Ryder said, nervous energy pumping through his system. 'Maybe they thought they'd already lost their loved ones, and there was no point losing their high-flying jobs as well.'

'So, their job takes precedence over helping the police find a killer?' asked Sterling, aghast.

'Look, I'm wondering what they've got to hide, too, but we need to move on.' Ryder leaned a hand on the counter and looked down at Flowers' phone. 'You'd better find that signature on Walker's report. I want to know for sure if he's the same bloke who ran those courses down here.'

Ryder's phone rang.

'Hi, Vanessa,' he said, accepting the call. 'Did you get on to Eva?'

'No, I didn't, so I rang Mum and asked her in a roundabout way if she'd spoken to Eva. She said about four or five days ago. I mean, that's not unusual, but it *is* unusual for Eva not to call back. She hasn't answered an email I sent her either, or been on our family chat.'

Ryder could hear the worry in Vanessa's voice. 'We need to check on her. Flowers and I will take a trip up there.'

'Sarge?' said Flowers.

'Can you hang on a minute, Vanessa,' Ryder said. 'I won't be a sec.'

'Sure.'

Ryder leaned over and peered at Flowers' phone, comparing the signature on the bottom of Jack Walker's report to the one on the form from the National Parks and Wildlife office. In his mind, there was no doubt.

'They're identical,' said Flowers.

'Yes, they are. Jack Walker and John Walker are the same person.' Ryder put his phone to his ear. 'Yeah, sorry Vanessa.'

'That's okay.'

'We've got a lot going on right now.'

'Sounds like it. You didn't put me on hold.'

'Oh, right—doesn't matter.'

'I heard you talking about Jack Walker?'

Ryder froze, his mouth turning dry. 'Yeah. Do you know him?'

'Well, I know *a* Jack Walker.'

'How?'

'It's probably not the same one. I mean, how many Jack Walkers would there be in Australia?'

'Just tell me how you know him. It could be the same one.'

'Poppy's father is Jack Walker.'

'Poppy's father?' Ryder gripped the phone harder, aware of Flowers and Sterling watching on. 'I didn't think he was on the scene.'

'He's not. I haven't actually met the guy. I only know what Eva's told me about him.'

'Where does he live?' he asked casually.

'I don't know where he is now, but he was based in Sydney. He used to teach extreme sports and survival skills in the Blue Mountains. But in winter, he'd shift the courses to the snow. That's how Eva met him.'

'Okay,' said Ryder, endeavouring to sound as natural as possible. 'I don't think that's the guy we're looking for; as you said, it's a common name. Anyway, Flowers and I are just about to head off. How about I give you a call when I'm at Eva's?'

'That would be great. Thanks, Pierce. Take care.'

❋

Ryder braked in front of the community hall just long enough for Flowers to jump into the passenger seat.

'Sterling's joined the others,' Flowers said, pulling on his leather gloves. 'I told Benson we're going to check something out, and to watch his phone in case we need back-up.'

'Good.'

Flowers dragged the seatbelt across his body, clipped it in, then pressed the button for the heated seat. 'Far out,' he said. 'So, Jack Walker is Poppy's father?'

'Apparently. And Gavin Hutton has already murdered two people with close ties to members of the crisis team. What if Jack Walker's the next team member on Hutton's hit list? You can't get much closer than a daughter.'

'Oh, Jesus, not a little kid.'

Ryder turned left onto the Alpine Way and switched on his police lights. For a long while they drove in silence. When they passed the turn into Crackenback Resort, Ryder said, 'Eva hasn't returned Vanessa's calls or emails for a few days. It's out of character.'

'It doesn't sound good, Sarge. Maybe we should call for back-up now.'

'No, you've put Benson on notice. I know Eva's been teaching a cooking class the last few days, and the weather's been wild. She could have trees down, power problems—anything could have happened.'

Ryder drove on, wishing he felt as optimistic as he sounded. The Alpine Way was all but deserted save for a couple of highway-patrol cars travelling in the opposite direction, their lights flashing. Static from the police radio filled the car.

At the Thredbo turn-off, a line of road-closure barriers prohibited access further along the Alpine Way. Ryder waited while an officer headed for the driver's side of the car, a torch in hand.

Ryder lowered the window and held up his badge. 'Detectives Ryder and Flowers, Sydney Homicide. We need to go to Thredbo Village.'

The officer stepped away from the four-wheel drive and waved them on towards the Banjo Drive entrance. In the village, streetlights shone onto narrow, winding roads, the only sign of life an occasional light shining from the window of a ski lodge.

Ryder's phone rang.

Vanessa.

Hesitating, he glanced at Flowers as they crossed the Thredbo River, before accepting the call. 'Hi.'

'Oh, Pierce, I'm glad I got through,' Vanessa said, sounding a lot more upbeat than when he'd last spoken to her.

'What's up?'

'I called Bede to ask if he'd spoken to Eva.'

'Has he?' Ryder asked, the anticipation unbearable as he waited for her answer.

'Yes, he ran into her in Jindabyne this afternoon. Poppy's been sick, so Eva took her to the doctor. I'm so relieved.'

A little of the tension drained from Ryder's body. 'That is good news,' he managed to say.

'I know. Have you left yet? I was hoping you hadn't gone too far. I wanted to save you a trip.'

'That's all right,' Ryder said, hating that he was about to lie to Vanessa for a second time. 'We'll turn around and head back to the hall.'

'Okay. I'm sorry to be a nuisance, but with that dangerous guy on the loose down there, I was really starting to freak out.'

'Don't worry about it. You can sleep well knowing everything's okay.'

'I will. Drive safely.'

'Bye, Vanessa.'

Flowers stretched out his shoulders and shifted in his seat. 'Well, they were okay this afternoon, but we're still going up there, aren't we, Sarge?'

Ryder nodded. 'There's a lot more going on around here than we know. And we're not going back to Jindabyne until we find out what it is.'

Thirty-one

'He's messing with us again,' Jack whispered, stopping her when they reached the lobby. 'I'm going to try to talk to him from inside. If I can convince him to give himself up, that would be the best outcome. It's a long shot but it's worth a try.'

Eva nodded, glancing down at the firearm in her hand. 'Anything is preferable to violence. You have the skills, Jack, you may as well use them.'

'I'll aim to keep things calm, and talk him down if the volatility goes up. If I can make lots of small, nonaggressive points, they can add up and hopefully subtly influence him.'

'Change his thought process?'

'Yeah, even if it's only for a minute or two. It'll be a start.'

'Do you have the zip ties?'

He nodded once and touched his jacket pocket. 'If he doesn't respond, I'm going out there. If he does respond but things aren't going well, or he starts breaking down the door, or I think he's going to run, I'm also going out there, and you have to lock the door.'

'What if he has a gun?' she whispered.

'We can't know that. If he does, he mightn't be planning on using it. A gunshot brings people running, and remember, he's not after me, he's after you or Poppy. Keeping me alive is part of his plan.

He wants to watch me suffer over the loss of you or Poppy. That's what's driving him on. Okay?'

She nodded. Despite her fear, she knew that Jack was the best person to capture Hutton.

He laid a gentle hand on her shoulder and looked into her eyes. 'Ready?'

This time, it was Eva who covered his hand with hers, squeezing it firmly. 'Ready.'

He led the way through the glass doors and into the vestibule. 'Stay back here,' he said, before moving towards the wooden doors leading onto the verandah.

Eva did as Jack asked, watching as he put his ear to the door. While he listened for Hutton's footsteps, she silently took off the safety. If Jack got in trouble, and she had a clear shot at Hutton, she would take it.

Eva knew every creak and groan the place made, and she stiffened, her fingers tightening on the pistol when she heard Hutton coming closer to the front door. The verandah was built of solid hardwood, the boards safe but noisy due to decades of expansion and contraction.

Jack looked up. 'Hutton?' He spoke in a relaxed manner as though he were answering a telephone call. 'Can you hear me?'

Eva waited, her heart hammering.

'Gavin?'

Seconds of silence followed, then, 'Yeah?'

Eva stiffened.

Jack looked around and gave her the thumbs-up.

'I can hear ya.'

'Gavin. I think we should talk about how we can resolve this situation.'

'I don't give a shit what *you* think, Walker.'

A second thumbs-up from Jack.

'Are you willing to talk? Yes or no?'

A long silence, then, 'You invited *me*.'

So, Hutton *had* been watching when Jack went out to the snowman. He'd heard him call out. Eva's scalp crawled as she imagined Hutton creeping around in the dark outside. Where had he been hiding? Near the picnic tables? Near Poppy's swing?

'Have you thought about giving yourself up?' Jack asked.

Hutton laughed.

Terror raced through Eva's system at the unhinged sound. The thought of him being anywhere near Poppy . . .

'Give myself up? That would make it easy for you, Walker, wouldn't it?' Hutton said, in what Eva thought his most chilling answer yet.

'It would make it easier for *you*. A warm bed. Three meals a day. Access to medical care. Things you don't have now if you're living out near Leatherbarrel Creek.'

'You talk shit. Your shit talk is what got Trevor killed.'

Eva watched as Jack considered his response.

'The kidnappers became desperate,' he said in a calm, unhurried tone. 'They refused to take part in further negotiation. Their appalling decision resulted in Trevor's death.'

There was a long period of silence, the atmosphere so taut with tension Eva could hardly bear it.

'Someone's got to pay,' bawled Hutton suddenly. 'An eye for an eye's the only way.'

Jack didn't respond immediately, and in the quietness that followed, Eva turned towards the glass doors, hyperaware of Poppy sleeping not far away.

'The men responsible for Trevor's death *are* paying,' Jack said eventually. 'They've been charged and jailed in the Philippines.' He paused.

Eva gripped the Beretta, silently willing Poppy to stay asleep.

'Will you do the right thing and give yourself up?' Jack asked. 'I doubt you can last much longer out here.'

Another interminable silence. Eva watched Jack, her nervous system charged with tension, the muscles across her shoulders fraught with strain.

'Gavin? What would it take for you to turn yourself in?'

The wail from a siren cut through the night.

Eva jumped, looking at Jack as his head snapped up, his face like granite.

The siren cut out.

In the silence that followed, footsteps could be heard retreating from the verandah.

'Gavin? *Gavin!*'

Shouting an expletive, Jack unlocked the door and raced into the night. Eva moved, heart thundering, legs heavy as though weighed down with water. When she reached the front door, she could see Hutton illuminated in the strobe-like flashing lights of a police four-wheel drive parked at the corner of the building. He was near the picnic tables, heading towards the track the snowboarders had come down.

'Hold it there, Walker!'

Eva stepped onto the verandah to see that Pierce Ryder and his partner had their firearms trained on Jack, who was running through knee-deep snow in pursuit of Hutton.

'He's getting away!' Jack hollered.

'Pierce!' Eva's scream was ripped from her throat. 'Don't shoot! Jack's after Hutton!'

Ryder lowered his pistol and looked towards her, though Flowers kept his gun trained on Jack.

'Poppy and I are fine,' she yelled, looking back at Hutton, and raising the Beretta. In her peripheral vision, she saw Ryder run to the back of the car and take something from inside before shouting to Flowers, 'Secure the lodge! Look after Eva and Poppy!' Then: 'Okay, Walker, I'm right behind you!'

Hutton had reached the start of the track when the clearing lit up like someone had switched on flood lights. Ryder held a powerful torch while Jack was centred in the spotlight like a spider in a web.

A calmness came over Eva, and she steadied the pistol in a two-handed grip. With her shoulders level and her elbows locked, she aligned the pistol with the centre of her chest, pushing forward with her strong hand and pulling back with her support hand. *You won't hit anything with a limp wrist, her father said.* She firmed her wrists and lined up Hutton.

'Eva,' someone said quietly, 'put the gun down, please.'

Eva ignored the voice, her wrists locked, her index finger on the trigger. Jack was gaining ground but, any second now, Hutton would be lost in the trees.

'Eva? I need to check that Poppy is okay.'

Eva blinked; her concentration broken. She hesitated, then slowly lowered the gun. Mitchell Flowers was standing at the bottom of the steps.

'Can you show me where Poppy is?' he asked.

She nodded and put the safety on.

'Thank you.'

Eva looked towards the clearing. Jack had followed Hutton up the slope. Pierce was only steps behind. 'I had one clear shot, and I didn't take it. I hope I don't live to regret that.'

'Is the gun loaded?' Flowers asked, ushering her inside and locking the door.

She nodded. 'We've been keeping it on the mantel.'

When he didn't say anything, she led the way through the lobby and into the lounge room.

'Is it registered?'

'Yes. It's mine.' Eva stared into the dying fire. She needed to rebuild it for when Jack and Pierce came back. Tears pricked the backs of her eyes as she put the Beretta on the mantel. 'They'd better come back,' she said, unable to keep the tremor out of her voice, terrified for them both, and for Vanessa. How could she face her sister if anything happened to Pierce because of her?

'They'll come back, Eva,' Flowers said, his eyes serious. 'Sarge won't let Hutton get away.'

She smiled then. She'd only met Pierce's partner a couple of times, but she liked him. 'Neither will Jack. Come on, I'll show you Poppy.'

Eva waited outside the room while Flowers checked that Poppy was still sleeping soundly.

'Just following orders,' he said, with an apologetic smile as she closed the door quietly. 'How many external entrances are there?'

Eva gave him a rundown of the layout, and the steps Jack had taken to secure the building.

'Right.' Flowers nodded his approval. 'Sounds like he's been pretty thorough.'

Eva almost told him what Jack had told her a dozen times, that there was no way Hutton or anyone else could get into the lodge, but she bit her lip. Flowers had a job to do.

'I'll start on this floor,' he said.

The muscles in Eva's chest tightened, forcing her to pull in some long, deep breaths then slowly release them. After a while, the constriction in her chest eased and she moved towards the fireplace where one tiny lick of flame burned in the grate. Opening the lid of the wood box, she took out paper and hurriedly scrunched it into a ball, her ears straining for the slightest noise that would tell her Jack and Pierce were returning with Hutton in handcuffs, or zip ties.

Gripped by a sudden irrational fear that if she let the fire die everything would be lost, she threw the balled-up paper on top of the flame, watching as it quickly caught alight. Choosing some small pieces of kindling, she fed the fire, waiting until the twigs were well alight before adding a small piece of firewood, then another. By the time Flowers had checked both wings of the building, one of the logs was burning.

'Just going downstairs, Eva,' he said with a smile.

With Flowers checking the lower level, Eva gravitated towards the windows, avoiding the one that looked out onto the bizarre snowman. Shifting aside the curtain, she gazed across the verandah towards the wooded hillside. High on the slope, almost at the point where the trees met the ski run, she could just make out a moving light.

A sudden thump had her spinning around, her heart leaping, the nerves in her scalp tingling. She knew that sound. It was the bang of the bottom door hitting the wall when the wind caught it.

'Detective Flowers!' she called, hurrying to the top of the stairs. 'Don't open that door.'

No answer came back.

'Detective?' she called again.

But the only thing that greeted her was a rush of freezing wind, and she didn't call again, knowing in her heart it was already too late.

❄

Ahead of Ryder, Jack Walker moved like a mountain goat, sticking to the edges of the icy track where he found footholds in the soil, rocks and exposed tree roots.

Ryder's thighs burned, his only respite from the punishing pace Walker set when he stopped every thirty steps or so and waited for Ryder to shine the Maglite into the snow gums. So far, the only signs of life they'd spotted were the glowing eyes of ground-dwelling nocturnal animals.

'Any sign of him up ahead?' called Ryder, ignoring the lactic acid burning his thighs and calves. It was warm in the trees, sheltered and quiet, with zero wind chill. Ryder would have expected to hear Hutton moving through the undergrowth, but other than the sound of their heavy breathing and the faint stir of leaves, the hill was silent.

Walker stopped suddenly. The terrain had evened out for a few metres. 'Want me to take that torch?' he said.

Ryder passed it over. Walker was a big unit, about an inch taller than Ryder and ninety-odd kilos of muscle. 'He's got to be in the trees,' Ryder said, scanning the gums as Walker shone the torch around.

'I agree,' said Walker. 'That track's like an ice rink. He'd need crampons to get up there, and there are no holes in the cover.'

'Let's keep climbing, then,' said Ryder. 'With luck we'll find tracks.'

Walker shone the torch ahead of them and started to move. 'Up here the track doglegs to the left.'

'Okay, keep going.'

Five minutes later they stepped out of the trees, an expansive area opening up in front of them.

'It's a ski slope,' said Ryder, catching sight of a snow-gun machine across the other side of the run. This had to be the spot the guests from the Golden Wattle exited the slopes at the end of the day and followed the trail to the lodge.

Walker shone the torchlight up and down the deserted run but all was quiet, no sign of movement. 'Damn! I think we're on the Supertrail. He could have gone anywhere,' he said, kicking a lump of snow in frustration. 'We've lost him.'

Thirty-two

Eva backed away from the stairs, then turned and ran to the fireplace. Grabbing the Beretta, she flicked off the safety.

Where was Detective Flowers? And where were Jack and Pierce? Questions ran through her mind as she raced back to the top of the stairs.

Secure the lodge, Pierce had yelled.

Flowers had been downstairs. She'd told him about the layout, so there was no reason for him to open that door, and yet the intermittent bang as it struck the wall, and the draft of frigid air blowing in from outside, told her it was definitely open. Had Flowers received a call on his radio from Pierce and gone to their assistance? Eva's entire body trembled. What was happening? Was someone lying wounded? Jack? Pierce? She looked down at the gun by her side, the barrel shaking. If Hutton had won, she was the last line of defence standing between him and Poppy.

Footsteps on the cement floor.

Eva looked up, hoping it was Flowers at the bottom of the stairs.

A stranger appeared.

Staring up at her.

Lean. Long hair. Damaged face. A gun in his hand.

Eva stared in horror. Where was Jack? Pierce? And Flowers?

Sorrow washed over her, bringing with it a strange, removed

calmness. Time slowed down. He hadn't moved, content to leer at her.

He hadn't seen the pistol at her side.

When one corner of his mouth curved in an evil smile, Eva raised the Beretta and pulled the trigger. The shot was like a bomb going off, the bullet ricocheting off the solid concrete walls enough times to make Hutton retreat. Eva glanced over her shoulder. Poppy was nowhere in sight.

She looked down the stairs again. Hutton had the harder shot, firing up the stairs, but right now he was in the passageway surrounded by concrete. A ricocheting bullet in the confined space could easily hit him.

Jack's voice played in her head. *You'll need to wait until the last moment, and fire at close range. It's the only way you'll hit him.*

He laughed. An unhinged sound that had Eva retreating. How long could she keep him trapped in the concrete hallway before he took a risk and charged up the stairs, firing?

Turning, she fled through the lounge room, dragging her door key from the pocket of her jeans with her left hand. Slipping inside her room, she closed the door silently and put the Beretta on the floor. In the glow of Poppy's night light, she slid the key into the lock and turned it.

Praying Poppy wouldn't wake, she hurried to switch off the night light, plunging the room into darkness. After moving the panda onto Poppy's bed, she picked up the chair and carried it carefully through the darkened room to the door. Setting it down quietly, she abandoned the idea of wedging it under the doorknob; if Hutton had made it up the stairs by now, any sound she made could draw his attention. Of all the locked rooms in the lodge, he couldn't possibly know which one was hers.

All she had to do was keep Poppy silent.

She picked up the Beretta with one hand and pulled her mobile phone from the back pocket of her jeans with the other as she crept across the room, glancing over at Poppy every few seconds to make sure she didn't wake her up. Only when she was as far away from the door as she could possibly get did she unlock her phone and call triple zero.

While Poppy lay sleeping, Eva stood in the shadows whispering to the operator, while Ryder's four-wheel drive stood at the end of the driveway, its doors open, its police lights flashing.

Jack took off at the sound of the gunshot before the echo had fully died. One look at the detective's face and he knew he was thinking the same thing: Hutton had doubled back to the lodge.

Choosing a direct line of descent, Jack kept the torch beam low. With the detective on his heels, he launched into the trees, slipping and skidding his way downhill. Thrashing through the snowy undergrowth, he covered the distance in a fraction of the time it had taken for them to climb up.

A branch slapped him in the face, pitching him sideways, his boots sliding over small, loose stones. Correcting himself, he pushed off a jagged rock before seeking out the wet patches of bare earth and grass.

Two-thirds of the way down, he glimpsed the clearing below. Veering back towards the frozen track, he covered the rest of the way down slipping and sliding on his butt, until the icy track spat him out into the clearing.

The detective slammed into his back.

Jack hauled himself to his feet, heard the detective doing the same. Lungs burning, he ran through the knee-deep snow. The lodge was in darkness save for a pool of light shining through the bottom door, which stood open.

Dread settled over Jack, not an unfamiliar feeling to him, but far more painful because this time it was personal. This time it was *his* family.

Beside him, the detective drew his pistol as they reached the building.

A dark figure lay slumped in the snow.

232

The detective got there first, crouching beside his partner. 'Oh, Jesus, Mitch,' Jack heard him say as he raced into the building. He had his foot on the bottom stair when he was pulled backwards and slammed against the concrete wall. The detective was in his face.

'He's got my partner's gun,' Ryder growled. 'Listen.'

In the distance, they could hear the wail of sirens.

'My kid's up there,' Jack said, biting out the words and shoving the detective away at the same time. Pivoting, he grimaced at the burning pain tearing through his gut, and bolted up the stairs.

Halting at the top, he waited for his eyes to adjust after the bright-ness of the torch. Ears straining for the faintest sound, a breath, a sigh, a scuff on the floor, he walked slowly towards the fireplace, wondering if Hutton had been and gone, dreading what could be waiting for him if he had.

Jack glanced towards Eva's door, desperate to know if she and Poppy were safely inside, but his fear of alerting Hutton to the location of Eva's room outweighed his need to know. If Hutton were still in the lodge, the approaching sirens would be dividing his focus.

Jack scanned the room, searching for anything out of place. The rollaway bed, the blanket draped over the back of the lounge where Eva had been sleeping, the fire stoked, the Beretta gone from the mantelpiece.

Jack drew in a breath. Everything was as it should be.

And then he saw it.

On the other side of the fireplace, propped up on the dining table, was Poppy's Rock-a-Bye Bear. Jack's stomach twisted into a sicken-ing knot. They hadn't used that table in the time he'd been there, and he remembered Eva putting the bear on the floor when she lay on the lounge.

Hutton, trying to psych them out as he'd done with the snowman, luring Jack with his daughter's toy.

Instinct told him his adversary was on the other side of the fire-place. Jack glanced around the room for something to use. His gaze landed on the large wooden box on the coffee table. Eva's chess set.

He could hear the detective requesting paramedics, and disembodied voices filtering up the stairs from the police radio. As the approaching sirens grew louder, Jack quietly moved to pick up the box and open the brass latch. Heart thundering, he returned to the edge of the fireplace until the dining table was once again in his line of sight.

He could live with Hutton touching Poppy's bear, but the thought of him touching his daughter, or Eva . . .

Fury drove strength into Jack's muscles, and he hurled the box towards the dining table, moving the other way the instant it left his hands. As chess pieces bounced and scattered in every direction, he snatched up the brass poker and rounded the fireplace.

Hutton realised a fraction too late what had happened, wheeling around as Jack raised the poker and brought it crashing down on his forearm. Hutton bellowed and dropped the police gun. Jack took a step and kicked the gun out of reach while Hutton bent at the waist clutching his injured arm and howling.

Glancing over his shoulder, Jack shouted for Ryder.

A sharp sting stole his breath. Jack stepped backwards, staring down in horror at the slim knife embedded in the back of his left hand.

Hutton slowly straightened, leering at Jack in the gloomy light. His nose sat off-centre, and he watched Jack through his good eye, the other blackened and swollen from their fight in the bush. A malicious smile split his damaged face.

'Have another go, Walker, why don't ya?'

Jack punched him with his right fist, the impact cracking bone and sending Hutton staggering backwards and crashing into the table.

Jack watched, pulling in deep breaths, his left hand numb and useless at his side. 'It's over, Hutton. The police are everywhere.'

Using an elbow, Hutton levered himself up off the table, and straightened again. Only then did Jack see the modified ice axe in his hand.

A gun shot exploded the moment Hutton charged, the bullet tearing through his pants and shattering his femur. He bellowed and dropped the ice axe, then fell to the floor clutching at his leg.

Jack turned to see the detective standing at the top of the stairs. Ryder came towards him, his firearm still trained on Hutton while he scooped up his partner's gun and the shortened ice axe. He glanced at Jack. 'Are you okay?' he asked, putting the weapons well out of reach.

Jack lifted his injured hand, too lightheaded to say anything.

'Jesus!' he heard the detective say. 'Paramedics are on their way.'

With Ryder standing guard over Hutton, Jack walked unsteadily towards Eva's room. Resting his forehead on the door for a bit, he dragged in some deep breaths then, clenching his good fist, found the strength to thump twice on her door. 'Eva?'

There was no answer, no movement from within.

No.

Tears pricked the backs of his eyes. Behind him, he could hear the detective barking orders to the reinforcements charging up the stairs. Terrified of what he might find if he opened the door, he thumped on the door again. 'Eva?'

The doorknob moved a fraction, followed by the sound of a key being inserted from the other side. Jack lifted his head and, bracing his good hand on the doorframe, watched as the door slowly opened.

❄

Ryder pointed to Hutton on the floor. 'He's not going anywhere, Benson, but cuff him all the same.'

'My pleasure,' said Benson, pulling out his handcuffs. O'Day went with him.

'I need paramedics up here,' Ryder shouted, giving Walker and Eva a few minutes before he went over. Walker had his good arm wrapped around her, holding her as she buried her face in his chest, her arms linked around his waist. Blood dripped from Walker's hand to form a pool on the carpet.

'How's my partner?' Ryder asked as the first paramedic arrived. 'Has he come to yet?'

'He's woken up, but he's in Disneyland,' a thickset bloke who looked to be in his early thirties told Ryder. 'They've got him on a stretcher now.'

Ryder relaxed a fraction and pointed the paramedic towards Hutton before going over to see Eva.

'Oh, Pierce,' she said, taking his hand and holding it tight. '*Thank* you.'

'I'm glad you're all okay,' he said, glancing at Walker. 'You've had a lot of people worried.' He looked past Eva's shoulder, but the room was still dark, and he wasn't able to see Poppy.

'Poppy's asleep,' Eva said, following his line of vision. 'Thank God she has glue ear. She slept through everything.'

Ryder allowed himself a smile. 'Gotta be grateful for small mercies,' he said, looking down at Walker's hand. 'You'd better get that looked at, mate, or you'll lose the use of it for good.'

Eva looked down, seeing for the first time what Walker had been hiding from her. 'Oh, God, Jack,' she cried, staring at his hand in horror. 'You need to go to the hospital.'

She stepped away from him, and it was then that Ryder noticed the blood on the front of her jumper where she'd been pressed up against him. Walker's skin had turned an unhealthy shade of grey. In Ryder's estimation, only the doorframe was holding him up.

Ryder moved through the lounge room, catching sight of Harriet Ono, who was standing by patiently, her forensics bag slung over her shoulder.

'Harriet. We'll set up a crime scene as soon as the injured are out of here,' he said, turning away and glancing around the room. 'I need the paramedics here now,' he hollered. 'And someone get those front doors open.'

'I'll see to it, Sarge,' said Sterling, already running.

Ryder watched her disappear into the lobby. When he got back to Eva, Walker had slumped to the floor.

Thirty-three

Eva sat in the waiting room at Canberra Hospital, watching the breaking news reports coming out of Thredbo.

Jack had been flown to Canberra to have microsurgery on his hand and to repair the re-opened stomach wound. By the time Sterling had dropped her and Poppy at the hospital at the end of the two-and-a-half-hour journey from Thredbo, Jack had already been in surgery for an hour and a half.

Eva sipped her coffee, her eyes gritty from lack of sleep, her nose blocked from an air-conditioning vent blowing cold air onto her head. No matter which chair she chose to sit in, she couldn't escape the chilly draught, the cold seeping into her bones despite being wrapped in her warmest coat.

Poppy, on the other hand, was wide awake and full of energy following her marathon sleep, asking Eva to count how many times she could hop around the coffee table.

Eva looked around as someone came into the waiting room, her heart swelling with relief and gratitude at the sight of her younger sister.

'Here you are,' Vanessa said as they hugged each other tight. 'What is it with the two of us and Canberra Hospital?' she asked.

Eva gave a watery smile, remembering her mad dash to the hospital last year to visit her injured sister. 'I'm hoping after this one, I won't see this place for a while.'

Vanessa released her to pick up Poppy. 'Hey, kiddo,' she said, tickling Poppy's tummy and making her giggle.

'Are you staying with us?' Poppy asked, looking hopefully at Vanessa.

'I am,' said Vanessa with a smile. 'I'm staying in the hotel next door, and I've booked a room for you guys as well.'

'Thanks, Vee,' said Eva with a grateful smile.

'Auntie Nessa, is that game still on your iPad?' Poppy asked, losing interest in the sleeping arrangements. She put an index finger in her mouth and pushed out her cheek.

Vanessa took her iPad from her tote and switched it on for Poppy. As the little girl settled down to play the game, Vanessa turned to Eva. 'What happened? Pierce rang and asked if I could come down. He didn't have time to talk, just told me to turn on the radio while I was driving. Oh, and that it wasn't you or Poppy in the hospital.' Vanessa took a breath. 'God, Eva, how did Gavin Hutton end up in your lodge? The news reports are saying details are sketchy.'

Eva took a deep breath and ran through the events of the past few days, Vanessa's face growing more incredulous as the story went on.

'You *fired* at him? In the lodge?'

Eva nodded. 'With my old Beretta.'

'Did you hit him?'

Eva shook her head. 'Pierce shot him, after Hutton stabbed Jack in the hand.'

Vanessa gave a small gasp, before pressing her hand to her mouth.

Eva leaned over and put her arms around her sister. 'Pierce is fine. I spoke to him while he was organising for the helicopter to pick up Jack. I'm sure he'll call you again when he can.'

'Is Jack going to be all right?' Vanessa asked, after a while.

Eva nodded. 'I'm worried about the damage to his hand, but he's going to live.'

'Just as well. It's about time I met this guy.'

Eva smiled. If anyone could cheer her up, it was Vanessa.

238

'I'm serious, Evie. You've always been cagey about him.'

'There wasn't much to tell, I hardly knew him,' Eva protested, then lowered her voice as Poppy looked up.

'I bet you know him a hell of a lot better now,' Vanessa said. 'How do you feel about him bursting into the lodge like that and taking things into his own hands?'

'Honestly? I'm grateful.' Eva lowered her voice to a whisper. 'Poppy and I mightn't be here now if he hadn't worked out what was happening.' She reached out and laid her hand over her sister's. 'He was going to go to the police with what he knew, but he ran out of time. I'm not sure if he'll be charged with anything.'

Vanessa shook her head. 'It's like something out of a movie.'

'I know.'

'And he's a *ransom* negotiator?'

Eva nodded. 'Crazy, hey?'

'So, do you have feelings for him now?' Vanessa asked gently.

'I do, I *like* him. I liked him before, too . . . a lot.' Eva looked over at Poppy, her lips trembling. 'And we made this beautiful child together . . . and he's so good with her.'

'Do you think things will change after this?'

'I'd like them to.' Eva pulled a tissue out of her tote. 'But he still has the same dangerous job, so I'm not getting my hopes up.'

They sat for a while, and when they tired of watching the same news story play over and over, Vanessa went in search of coffee and came back with two lattes and three muffins.

At 2 am a nurse came into the waiting room and told them Jack was expected to be in surgery for a few more hours, and after that he would be taken to recovery. 'You should go home and get some sleep,' she said.

'Come on, Eva,' Vanessa said. 'If you won't come with me, at least let me take Poppy.'

'You promise you'll call?' Eva asked the nurse, not wanting to leave Jack alone in the hospital. He'd saved her life, and the life of their child, and despite the horror of their ordeal, there had been pockets of joy, too, as they'd cared for and watched over Poppy.

After everything he'd done, she hated the thought of him waking up after surgery and no one being there for him.

'There's a change of shift at seven,' the nurse said. 'I won't be on duty when you come back, but I'll make sure they know to call you when he starts to wake up.'

With Vanessa holding Poppy's hand, Eva wrapped her coat tightly around her body, and reluctantly left the hospital, knowing the surgeons were still at work fighting to save Jack's hand.

❄

At 6 am Ryder unlocked the door and slipped quietly into the hotel room. As Vanessa had promised, the bathroom light was burning and the door stood slightly ajar, making it easy for him to find his way around the unfamiliar hotel suite.

While he waited for the shower to heat up, he undressed slowly, his body bruised and aching from the punishing downhill descent. Wincing as the hot water spray hit his back, he braced a hand on the tiles and closed his eyes. For years, Ryder had lain awake at night wondering where the hell Gavin Hutton was. This morning, he didn't need to wonder. Hutton was lying in a hospital bed under heavy police guard, probably not far from Jack Walker. Thanks to an exhaustive investigation process, and an ounce of luck, there was every chance Gavin Hutton would be put away for life.

For the next few minutes, Ryder let the water cascade over him, before eventually opening his eyes and reaching for the body wash.

Ten minutes later, he slid into bed beside Vanessa, curling his battered body around her fragrant softness. 'Do you want to talk?' she asked, her voice husky with sleep.

'Later,' he said, wrapping an arm around her waist, knowing she hadn't left the hospital until after two.

He closed his eyes, couldn't help the exhausted sigh that escaped his lips.

'Are you okay?' she whispered.

'I am now.'

Thirty-four

Eva knocked on the door of Jack's private room to find him sitting up in bed. His left hand was heavily bandaged, raised and resting on a pillow.

He smiled as she came into the room, his blue, almost Nordic, eyes watching her as she put a few sports magazines on the bedside table. 'I would have preferred to make you something delicious to eat, but I haven't been back to the lodge yet.'

She dragged up a chair and sat down, suddenly nervous of how things might be between them now their ordeal was over.

'It's a nice thought. Thanks.'

'How are you feeling?' she asked. 'They told me not to come in until noon. They said you had a lot going on with your hand.'

'Yeah.' He looked at his bandaged hand. 'Just as well I'm right-handed, hey?'

She managed a smile. 'Still, it affects everything. Have they told you what to expect?'

'A minimum six weeks' rehab in Sydney, and that's if everything goes well. A second or third operation could be on the cards, if there are complications. The knife severed tendons and nerves,' he said, looking at his hand again with its boxing-glove-sized bandage. 'I look like Mickey Mouse.'

'What about the stab wound?'

'They think it will heal up fast now it's been properly fixed.'

'Well, that's good news,' she said brightly, though inside she was disappointed he would return to Sydney sooner rather than later. She looked around the room, silently chiding herself for getting her hopes up. Jack had left them once before, when she was pregnant, and if the past few days had proven anything, it was that Jack had valid reasons for making that decision. Surely those reasons still held.

Eva cleared her throat. 'So, how long will you be in here for?'

'Three to five days, apparently.'

'Oh, will you be able to manage?' she asked.

He smiled then and reached for her hand. 'I've had war wounds worse than this, and I've always managed.' He threaded his fingers through hers, sending spikes of pleasure through her body. 'Come on, everything's going to be all right.'

Not for her it wouldn't. Not when he walked out of their life again because another Gavin Hutton might come along.

'I'm sorry,' she said, embarrassed as tears began to well in her eyes. 'When I think of what could have happened . . .'

'You did great, Eva. It was a smart decision retreating to the room when you did.' He lay back on the pillows. 'Where's Poppy?'

'Vanessa's looking after her. She came down from Sydney early this morning. I was going to bring Poppy, but I thought it might be too much for you today. Would you like to see her tomorrow?'

He nodded, his eyes slowly drifting closed, before he opened them wide again. 'Sorry,' he said, trying to wake himself up.

'Jack, go back to sleep,' Eva said, rubbing the back of his good hand. 'I'll be here when you wake up.'

❄

Eva found Ryder at the coffee machine.

'Hey,' he said when he turned around and saw her. 'I was just about to stick my head in. How's the patient?'

'Tired, and pumped full of painkillers. He's just gone back to sleep.'

'Was the operation a success?'

'It's a wait-and-see situation, apparently.' She put her coins in the machine and pressed the button for a latte. 'Did you manage to get any sleep?'

'I caught a couple of hours this morning.'

'I was so happy to see Vanessa. Thank you for calling her.'

'Well, I figured you two would like to be together.'

Eva nodded. Vanessa had chosen well. Pierce Ryder was good guy. They stood for a while, drinking their coffees.

'Have you charged Hutton yet?' Eva asked after a while.

'Not yet. I'm waiting on the forensic report, and for Flowers to arrive. He was discharged from Cooma Hospital this morning.'

'He's not driving, is he?'

Ryder shook his head. 'The detective who brought you here last night, she's bringing him in.'

'She's been doing a lot of driving,' said Eva with a smile.

'I think she likes it. She's also a speedboat driver.'

'Really? That's different.'

'I know.' Ryder looked at his watch. 'Hey, Eva, I was thinking, I need to get a statement from you at some point. If Jack's asleep, does it suit you to get that out of the way now?'

Eva took a sip of coffee. She'd told Jack she would be there when he woke up.

'The hotel has a couple of conference rooms,' Ryder said. 'We can see if one's free.'

Eva hesitated. It was convenient for her to do it now, and for all she knew Jack could sleep for a couple of hours. Tomorrow, she'd bring Poppy in to visit him before heading back to the lodge to see what needed fixing. Later today, she would be emailing her guests, reassuring them that the Golden Wattle would be open for business as usual.

'Okay, let's do it now,' she said, not wanting to waste the final few days she would have before Jack left the mountains again.

Ryder's phone rang as he walked back to the hospital with Eva. Signalling that he'd take the call outside, he gave her a wave and answered Harriet Ono's call.

'Hello, Harriet,' he said. 'Speak only if you have good news.'

'Hutton's forensics are back. You'll have your fifteen minutes of fame with this one, Pierce.'

'It's the only reason I do this job—to see my face on the TV.'

'Well, get ready for the publicity, Detective, because Hutton's DNA matches the blood taken from the crime scene near Central Station.'

'And . . .'

'And his fingerprint matches a partial print lifted from the cenotaph in the park in Goulburn.'

If he hadn't been standing outside a hospital entrance, Ryder would have punched the air. 'That's great news, Harriet. Thanks.'

'Hang on a minute, there's more. His DNA also matches the blood at the campsite, and I lifted a ton of his prints from Brandon Moss's place and the Golden Wattle Lodge, too. You'll need those if you're going to charge him with entering premises with the intention of committing a criminal offence.'

'He'll be charged with that one and multiple other offences. Gavin Hutton is going away for a long, long time.'

'Congratulations, Pierce. I was starting to think you'd never get him.'

Ryder smirked. 'Geez, thanks for the vote of confidence, Harriet.'

'No problem. You'll never get a big head with me around.'

A text message from Flowers beeped through as he ended the call.

Hey, Sarge, I'm back. I'm having something to eat in the coffee shop upstairs.

Disinclined to wait for the lift, Ryder ran up the stairs to the third floor. He saw Flowers' immediately; he was the one with the bandage around his head.

'Hey, Daisy,' he said, sliding into the booth opposite and stealing a piece of the banana bread Flowers had cut into small squares. 'How's the old noggin'?'

'Seen better days, Sarge.'

'Great Pete Murray song that,' Ryder said. 'No long-term damage, then?'

'I bloody hope not. Did you find out what the mongrel hit me with?'

'According to Brown, it was a snow shovel.'

'Shit! They'll be giving me crap about this for years.'

'They found it down the side of the lodge. It came from the neighbouring lodge, the Willy Wagtail.'

'Whacked with a shovel from the Willy Wagtail. What a story.'

Ryder smiled, wondering when he'd become so fond of his police partner. He didn't want to suffer another fright like the one he'd had last night.

'Remember when Vanessa rang last night, when we were almost at the lodge?' Ryder asked.

Flowers frowned then stared at the plate of banana bread.

Ryder watched. Just how much memory had Daisy lost?

Flowers looked up. 'Who's Vanessa?'

Ryder must have looked alarmed because Flowers burst out laughing almost immediately. 'Bam! Got you that time.'

Ryder rolled his eyes. 'I admit, you had me worried for a while.'

When they'd sobered enough to talk again, Flowers said, 'Yeah, I remember. She said she'd talked to Eva's neighbour, Bede. He'd seen her and Poppy in Jindabyne.'

'Right, well, I just took Eva's statement. She said while they were in Jindabyne at the doctor, Hutton had come to the lodge and built a snowman on the verandah.'

Flowers picked up another piece of banana bread. 'That's a creepy thing to do.'

Ryder nodded. 'Hutton had used one of his knives as the nose, and one of the eyes was prosthetic.'

'Oh, that's bad. One of Trevor's?'

'Probably. Anyway, I think he hit you with the same shovel he used to build that snowman.'

Flowers expression turned rueful. 'Whacked with a Willy Wagtail shovel that was used to build a snowman. This gets better and better.'

'Stop feeling sorry for yourself. Walker went out there and brought the eye and knife inside. They're in a container up at the lodge.'

'What do you want me to do? I can't drive.'

'Nothing. Brown and O'Day will get it. I'm just letting you know.'

'You could have kept that one from me until I was feeling better.'

Ryder told him about the DNA matches Harriet had found. 'Hutton's going to be a guest of Her Majesty for decades to come.' He shifted his aching legs under the table. He was going to be even sorer tomorrow. 'There's one thing I need to know.'

Flowers looked up. 'Yep?'

'Why'd you open that bottom door?'

Flowers looked at him, a confused expression in his eyes. 'I didn't. It was locked when I went down. I went into the garage and had a look around. When I came out, that door was open.'

'You're sure?'

'Positive.'

Ryder's scalp crawled. There was only one explanation for that: Hutton had a key.

Just then Ryder's phone rang. 'Here we go,' he said, looking at the name on the screen. 'It's the Inspector.' He glanced around the cheerful coffee shop, pleased to see the place was empty except for three people sitting at another table. He swiped his thumb across the screen. 'Afternoon, Inspector,' he said quietly.

'The press are camped outside the building, Ryder. Can you at least give me some idea of what charges you'll be expecting to lay?'

'A number of serious ones.' Ryder pulled his notepad from his coat pocket. 'One charge of assaulting a police officer,' he said, looking at the bandage covering much of Flowers' head. 'Two charges of assault with malicious intent, with an instrument, to cause grievous bodily harm.' While the Inspector took his time writing down what Ryder was saying in his usual longhand, an image of the knife embedded in Walker's hand came to mind. 'One charge of gaining access to premises through deception.' He and Flowers would need to take a trip up to Shoal Bay at some point to get a statement from the woman Eva had told him about, Julieann Bower.

'Go on,' said the Inspector.

An image of Brandon Moss came to mind. 'One charge of break and enter and one charge of entering premises with the intention to commit a criminal offence.' Ryder could see Eva and Poppy, locked in their room, while Hutton hunted them down in their own home. A chill ran down Ryder's spine as he waited for the Inspector to catch up.

'Yes.'

'And two charges of murder, of Dominic Burrows and Fergus Suter.'

❄

Ryder took a call from Benson as he was leaving the cafe. They'd found Hutton's dugout.

'It was hidden in a rocky hillside,' Benson said. 'It didn't take long for the dogs to find it once we reached the area where Walker said he was holed up.'

Ryder ducked out of the way of a hospital trolley coming towards him down the corridor. 'Good work.'

'He was pretty well set up. We'll be down here for a while. You should see the stuff he had.'

'Yeah?'

'Swag, full goose-down sleeping bag, strap-on spikes, even climbing crampons and fishing gear. He knew what he was doing.'

'It must have been a reasonable space,' said Ryder, finding an empty waiting room where he could talk without being overheard.

'Big enough to keep him out of the wind, and more. We've already matched a few things up with items that have been reported stolen. Beats me what he survived on, though.'

'Lots of trout and fruit, I'd say.'

'Maybe,' said Benson, pausing as something set the dogs off barking. 'Hang on, I'll just move away.' Another pause, then: 'Oh, and Hutton had another one of those little yellow boxes.'

Ryder frowned. 'From the ocularist?'

'Yeah. Nothing in it, though.'

Ryder moved to stand in a patch of sunlight coming through the window. 'My guess is he brought Trevor's eye back with him from the Philippines.' He told Benson about the snowman on the verandah.

'That is totally messed up.'

Ryder nodded in silent agreement. 'It sure is. Anyway, keep me up to date.'

'Will do, Sarge.'

Ryder left the waiting room and made his way to the hospital wing where Hutton was being kept under police guard. Amid the chaos of his arrest, Ryder had only looked the killer in the eye for a second after discharging his weapon, and then Hutton had crumpled to the floor. Ryder showed his badge to the uniform police on guard outside the room before going in.

He approached the bed slowly, flexing his hand where the Glock's recoil had caused a blister to form in his palm. Hutton was unconscious, attached to numerous IV lines, his leg in traction, one wrist handcuffed to the steel bed. Monitors blinked in the shadowy room.

Ryder stood looking down at the felon he'd been after for so long. He looked small, clean shaven and washed, hardly threatening in the large hospital bed. But Ryder knew otherwise. Hutton might appear insignificant, doped to the eyeballs and with his lids half open, but he was still a danger.

Taking a deep breath, Ryder stepped away. They had him now. They had all the time in the world to interview him and to organise their evidence. As he left the room, he thought to himself, it wouldn't be the last time he would come face to face with Gavin Hutton.

Thirty-five

Jack looked up as Eva came into the room. For a few moments, he allowed himself the simple pleasure of looking at her, something he hadn't been able to do during their time in the lodge. She wore a pale-blue jumper over blue jeans, her fair hair pulled up in its usual high ponytail, and silver hoops in her ears. As she came towards him, he smiled at her sneakers, white with glittery blue dots. She was lovely, but so much more. Little wonder he'd fallen for her all over again.

'Hey,' she said. 'You're awake.'

Jack wished he looked better for her, wished he wasn't stuck in a hospital bed attached to intravenous drips, wished he didn't have a bandaged hand the size of a table-tennis bat. 'I'm more alert than I was earlier. How're you doing? You've had a rough few days.'

'Me? I came out unscathed, and so did Poppy. We're alive because of you,' she said, sitting down and staring at him with wide hazel eyes.

Jack reached out with his good hand and stroked her cheek with his thumb. She turned into his touch like she had before, and he smiled. What kind of fool was he to have stayed away from Eva and Poppy for years?

'I had to give a statement to the police about everything that happened,' she said, taking hold of his hand and holding it in both of hers. 'I told Pierce the truth, Jack. The way I saw everything.'

'That was the right thing to do.'

'He asked me if I wanted to press charges against you.'

'I'm not surprised.'

She nodded. 'I said no. I told him my first thought was that you were going to take Poppy, but after that, I realised there was something bigger going on.'

'Thanks for not pressing charges, but it could still happen. The police can charge me, too, and if they decide to do that, I'm prepared to wear it. Hutton's going to jail. That's what's important.'

'Pierce Ryder's a good man,' Eva said, 'a reasonable man. He's my sister's partner.'

'Well, that'll make for good family relations,' he said, seizing the opportunity to test the water.

Eva held his gaze for a long moment before she finally spoke. 'Is that something you want, Jack?'

Her forthright question took him by surprise. A lump formed in his throat, preventing him from speaking right away. Finally, he got himself under control and nodded. 'It is.'

He wanted to say more, that Poppy wasn't the only one who'd found her way into his heart, but now was not the time to push his luck.

'What's really changed?' she asked, staring at him with troubled eyes. 'When I told you I was pregnant, you said it would be better if you weren't involved. I know now that you were referring to the new job you'd committed to, and the risks associated with that.'

Jack nodded, deflated by the doubt he read in her eyes. 'I thought it best at the time for a number of reasons. I'd just signed on for a job that could take me anywhere. I'd signed a stack of confidentiality agreements. Even when I was home, I wouldn't have been able to talk to you about where I'd been or what I'd done.'

Eva shifted in her chair. 'Back then, I wasn't asking you to have a relationship with *me*, only whether you wanted to be involved in Poppy's life, whether that was co-parenting, or access, or . . .' She faltered. 'Had you considered having a relationship with me?'

Jack released her hand. 'Of course I had. Why wouldn't I? You're amazing.' He closed his eyes, trying to find the best way to explain it.

'Leaving aside the dangerous nature of my job, I didn't think my being away for months on end with no guaranteed end date, and not being able to discuss my work with you when I did come home, was a good foundation on which to build a relationship.'

She nodded. 'You were probably right.'

Jack dragged in an unsteady breath. 'That's what I was attempting to say the other night when you jumped up and said you didn't need a bloke. Back then, rightly or wrongly, I felt certain you'd meet a decent guy who'd be around a lot more than I would be.'

'Well, you were wrong.'

He narrowed his eyes deliberately. 'Have you given anyone a chance?'

'Not really.' A soft smile curved her lips then Eva asked, 'Should I have?'

'Not really.'

When her eyes began to glisten, Jack took his chance. 'Is it something you'd consider, having a relationship with me, not for Poppy's sake but for the two of us? Correct me if I'm wrong, but I don't think the attraction angle needs work.'

'I'd do more than consider it, I'd say yes,' she said, her voice turning husky. 'But I'm scared, Jack. Your job is no less dangerous today than it was back then, and Poppy's safety has to be my first priority.'

The tension left Jack's shoulders, and for the first time since he'd burst into the ski lodge, hope unfurled in his chest. Could this turn out to be the best day of his life?

'Eva,' he said gently, 'when I took that job in kidnap insurance, I signed a non-disclosure agreement of the existence of the policy itself, and its contents. I also signed a non-disclosure agreement about the reimbursement of money to the affected families. A breach of either of those agreements makes the policy invalid.'

When she didn't say anything, he went on. 'I tore up every confidentiality agreement and every contract I'd signed the moment I forced my way into your lodge and told you all about Gavin Hutton. The negotiation work ended then.'

She smiled. It was the first full-on, delighted smile he'd seen since all this began, and the smile that had knocked him for six over four years ago. 'I can't believe it,' she said, rising from her chair.

'Believe it. That decision was made the minute I decided to go after Hutton.'

She stepped towards the bed before bringing her hands up to cup his face. 'Don't you dare move,' she whispered, before leaning over and placing her lips on his.

❄

Jack opened his eyes an hour later to find Detective Ryder standing over him. He blinked hard, then used his good arm to hoist himself higher in the bed.

'I've got a bone to pick with you,' Ryder said before Jack could even open his mouth. 'What the hell were you thinking?'

Jack had been expecting this. The detective had a right to be angry. 'All I was thinking about was saving Eva and Poppy.'

'And you assumed you were more qualified to do that than the police?'

'Not more qualified, less noticeable, disguised as a camper in the bush. I had a history with Hutton, too. I figured I was ahead of you guys.'

The detective's face flushed a dull red. 'It was a *bad* decision, Walker. You went vigilante and he stabbed you.'

'If I hadn't flushed Hutton out of the bush, you wouldn't have him on some kid's phone now. He'd still be in his hole.'

'How the hell do *you* know about that?'

'I was flown here, remember, and Hutton's here under police guard. I overheard a couple of them talking about why the search party centred around a farmhouse had been called off.'

Ryder cooled down a little, as though he accepted what Jack had said. 'Look,' Jack said, loath to argue with the bloke who'd put a slug in Hutton's leg, 'you don't know how I feel about Eva and Poppy.'

'I know you haven't been around.'

'I had my reasons,' Jack shot back. 'I was always there if they needed me, and I was there when it counted.'

There was a pause. Jack braced himself for what the detective was going to say next, probably something about him being a less than ideal father. But Ryder surprised him.

'If you'd come forward with your information,' he said, 'my partner wouldn't have sustained a serious head injury, and Eva's ski lodge wouldn't look like a blood bath.'

Jack paused. He regretted that those things had happened, but he wouldn't do anything different if he had his time over again. 'I weighed up the risks, but I feared you'd hit the area with your dogs, sirens and air support and drive Hutton deeper into the bush. If that happened, he could have come back for Eva and Poppy any time. I also thought I had a good chance of talking Hutton down, maybe even persuade him to turn himself in.'

Ryder didn't look convinced. He shook his head and paced the room for a bit, his hands in his trouser pockets. 'Eva's not pressing charges against you, but I'm going to have to charge you with something,' he said eventually. 'Your blood's up at that campsite. It proves you were there and that you failed to come forward with information about an ongoing investigation.'

Jack frowned. 'Just do whatever you have to do.'

'You know, it's people like you who make our job harder, Walker.'

'Yeah, how's that?' Jack snapped, finally losing his patience.

'Mike Joseph and Will Guthrie, for starters,' Ryder said. 'Why don't you tell me about them?'

Jack shook his head. 'I think I know where you're going with this, and you're wrong.'

Ryder walked closer to the bed and looked down at him. 'We interviewed Guthrie and Joseph numerous times. They knew Hutton was our prime suspect and neither admitted to a link. Were they protecting their well-paid jobs because there's a line of people waiting to take their place?'

'No.'

'Why then? Why were they prepared to put the wider community at risk from Hutton?' Ryder pushed back his suit coat and put his hands on his hips. 'Come on, Walker, make my job easier for once.'

'Mike wasn't there, and Will and Roland didn't know. They never learned the names of the people who were held in that shed. I was the only member of the crisis team who had direct contact with the people who took them. Will and Roland were on standby in a hotel ready to hand over the money and retrieve the hostages, but the Swedes cut a deal first. Everything's done on a need-to-know basis. As soon as they were told our deal was off they left for the airport.'

'So, they never knew the names Gavin Hutton or Trevor Swan?' Ryder asked.

'Not in relation to the kidnapping.' Jack paused, then asked, 'How did *you* find out about Trevor Swan?'

The detective told him how Swan had been Hutton's emergency contact in Zimbabwe, and how marketing items from BHM Holdings had been found at a property where Swan had once lived. 'We suspected Hutton had sent those things to his brother and was likely to be employed in the Philippines.'

'Okay, I'm following you.'

'BHM Holdings sent us copies of the kidnapping reports. Your signature matched one that was on a form at the National Parks and Wildlife office as the owner of Xtreme Aussie Adventures. We knew Hutton had been a participant on one of your courses. So, any day now you would have been hearing from us, demanding you tell us everything you knew about Hutton. If you'd cooperated, we would have surrounded the area at Leatherbarrel Creek where you used to take the participants, and brought him in.'

Jack had to give it to the guy, he was one hell of a detective. 'Perhaps I underestimated you, Detective Ryder.'

Ryder was quiet for a while as though weighing up what Jack had said before coming to some sort of decision. 'Eva tells me someone you know has a framed photo of her and Poppy,' he said eventually. 'Do you suspect it has Hutton's print on it?'

Jack nodded. 'I'll bring it into Parramatta when I get back to Sydney.'

'That was good thinking. The more offences we can charge him with, the better.'

Jack huffed out a breath. 'Don't tell me we're agreeing on something?'

The two men regarded each other for a bit.

'There is one thing I'm worried about,' Ryder said. 'My partner said he didn't unlock that downstairs door. He checked that it was locked before going into the garage. When he came out, it was open. Naturally, he went to try to close it, and that's when Hutton hit him.'

'I knew it.' Jack rested his forehead in his palm in an effort to stop the headache he could feel coming on. 'Eva has old-fashioned keys for that downstairs door. They go missing all the time. The first thing she should do is up the security. I'll talk to her about it.'

'Thanks.'

They were making progress. The detective was even thanking him now.

Jack made a decision. 'There's something you might want to see. It's not pleasant. It's not evidence to support your charges, but you've spent years hunting this guy, and . . . it might be of some benefit.' Jack pointed to the bedside table. 'Will you hand me my phone?'

Ryder did as he asked, and Jack scrolled through his phone until he found the recording of his conversation with the kidnappers. 'I have all the recordings, but I copied this one so I could have on hand the final minute or two.' He put his phone on loudspeaker and hit play.

Jack had lost count of how many times he'd listened to the breakdown in negotiations that night. Now, he watched as Ryder listened to the rising volatility of the group holding the hostages. They weren't speaking English among themselves, but you didn't need words to understand how fraught with danger the situation had become. Jack listened again to the conversation between him and Angel, the rising threats, the banging door, a man begging, someone shouting, 'Goose! Goose!'

Ryder raised a querying eyebrow at Jack.

'Trevor Swan's nickname,' he said.

There were several seconds of silence during which a first-time listener might imagine that the recording had finished. And then Jack heard his voice again, asking Angel to calm down. And then a gunshot cut off the conversation. Ryder stiffened as he had last night up on the hill above the Golden Wattle Lodge.

'That was the moment Trevor "Goose" Swan died,' Jack said, scrolling through his phone until he found the photo he was looking for. 'As I said, it's not pleasant.' He held up the phone so Ryder could see the photo of Trevor Swan sprawled face down in the dirt, a gunshot wound to his head. 'They sent this through to me within minutes of the execution. I believe Hutton's misguided thirst for revenge began here.'

Jack gave the phone to Ryder, who put it back on the table. 'I couldn't show any of that to Eva. It's too awful, too graphic.' He looked at Ryder. 'In the end, I think she just had to trust me.'

Ryder stared at him for a long while as though weighing up his thoughts. 'You're lucky, Walker,' he said eventually, an unreadable expression in his eyes. 'It's a privilege being a father, and you have a second chance with your daughter now. Don't throw it away. Not everybody gets that.'

'I don't intend to,' he said, watching as Ryder turned away and headed for the door.

Jack frowned. 'So, what are you charging me with?'

'Lighting a fire in a national park,' Ryder called over his shoulder. 'You'll probably get off with a warning.'

Thirty-six

'Have they taken up the carpet in the lounge room yet?' Eva asked as Vanessa came into the kitchen.

Vanessa nodded. 'They're about to put down the underlay.'

'Did you look to see if the floorboards are stained?'

'There's not a mark on them. As soon as the new carpet is down, the lounge room will be as good as new, except for the different colour, which I like, by the way.'

'I'll go and have a look once it's down.'

Bang!

Eva gasped, her heart racing so fast she could barely draw breath.

'It's the staple gun,' Vanessa said hurriedly, looking at her with worried eyes.

Bang!

Eva jumped again. 'Shit!'

'Hang on.' Vanessa hurried from the kitchen, and came back through the swinging door a minute later carrying a bottle of bourbon and two crystal tumblers. 'I raided your liquor cabinet,' she said.

Eva watched while Vanessa sat opposite her and poured them each two fingers of bourbon.

Vanessa picked up her glass, wincing as the staple gun went off again. '*Salut.*'

Eva frowned and moved her glass aside. 'Sorry, Vee, the smell alone is turning my stomach.'

'It's the stress of being back here for the first time since it happened. It's only been a few days. How did you go with the counsellor at the hospital? Was she any help?'

Eva nodded. 'She was the one who suggested Mum and Dad come and get Poppy and take her to the farm. I'm supposed to be concentrating on myself.'

'That makes sense. Poppy isn't going to have any repercussions, but you will, and you won't know for a while how they will manifest.' Vanessa picked up her glass and downed the contents. She stilled, then blew out a long breath. 'That'll put hair on your chest.'

Eva couldn't help but laugh. 'Spoken like a veteran ski patroller.'

'You can take the patroller out of the bar, but . . .' Vanessa said with a chuckle.

They sat in silence for a while, listening to the intermittent shot of the staple gun.

'Did you take Poppy in to see Jack before he was discharged?'

Eva nodded. 'We didn't get any one-on-one time, between Poppy and the doctors, nurses and physios. But he's been calling every day.'

'I thought you were going to tread lightly at first?'

'That was our intention, but . . .'

'It's got hot and heavy really quickly?'

'I think it would if we had the chance, but with everything that's happened, and with Poppy around, and now his hand.' Eva shrugged. 'We haven't decided anything. We're going to take it as it comes.'

'When am I going to meet him?' Vanessa grumbled. 'It's not fair that Pierce has met him, and I haven't.'

'I don't know. We're not even sure yet when he'll make it back here.'

'Pierce told me there's one good thing that's come out of all this, besides Hutton being captured,' Vanessa said eventually.

'What's that?'

'Brandon Moss, the software design student who rigged up those cameras, he's getting all that reward money, and he's only twenty-one.' Vanessa laughed. 'Pierce said Flowers is so jealous.'

Eva smiled. 'I wonder what he'll do with it.'

'He's planning on using it for a tech start-up. Apparently he's had an idea for ages, and now he has the money.'

'The counsellor said I should think of all the good things to come out of this, like getting back together with Jack, and now that kid getting the reward.'

'And Poppy having those blocked ears,' added Vanessa. 'How lucky was that?'

'I know. I keep thinking about it.'

Vanessa leaned across the table and patted her hand. 'Try not to worry about her. Mum and Dad will be looking after her. You and I need this time to get things ready for the opening weekend.'

'You didn't have to take the week off, Vee. You've only been in the job six months.'

'They were perfectly fine with it, and if they hadn't been, well, too bad.'

'Aren't you enjoying it?'

Vanessa shrugged. 'It's all right, but you know me, I love being outside. I never saw myself as a *salesperson*.'

'Does Pierce know how you feel?'

'I think he might have a suspicion it's not my cup of tea ... Oh, speaking of tea!' Vanessa stood up and went over to the bench. 'I'll boil the kettle and make you a nice cupppa. It'll make you feel better.'

Eva laughed. Their mum had always subscribed to the belief that *a nice cup of tea* made everything more bearable. 'I think I'm turning into Mum. I've been downing copious amounts of tea these past few days.'

Vanessa picked up Eva's untouched glass of bourbon and downed it. 'This works better for me when I'm traumatised.'

'That's not a smart way of drinking,' Eva scolded, realising too late her tone of voice sounded as though she were chastising Vanessa.

'Honestly, I don't care. My sister shoots at a killer, the killer stabs Poppy's father, and then my boyfriend shoots the killer, all on the other side of that wall. If I can't down two shots after all that, when the hell *can* I?'

'You're right.' Eva covered her face with her hands, then took them away and looked at her sister. 'Honestly, I'm not myself.'

'No one expects you to be.' Vanessa dropped a teabag into the mug and poured boiling water over the top. 'I'm glad Hutton didn't ... you know ... die in here. As well as being a horrendous experience for you personally, it could have affected the business you've worked so hard to build up. Can you imagine the ghost stories? People would say the place was haunted by a killer.'

Eva nodded. 'I'm sure I would have accepted Bede's offer.'

'Bede told me he'd offered you a job.' Vanessa put her tea in front of her. 'When was that?'

'It's been a standing offer for ages.' Eva blew on her tea before taking a sip. 'Bede's finally realised he's going to have to open the Willy Wagtail year-round. It's too difficult to make a living if you only open in winter. He asked me if I'd like to manage it.'

'Bede's a good bloke,' said Vanessa. 'Nice of him to lend you a dining table while yours is getting repaired, too.'

'Yeah, he's lovely, and he'd be a great boss, but I don't want to manage a large bar and restaurant, and spend my time sampling craft beers and booking live band gigs.'

'Sounds like the perfect job to me,' Vanessa said with a laugh. 'If I wasn't in Sydney, I'd apply for it.'

Later, after the carpet layers had left and all the furniture was back in place, Eva stood surveying the lounge room. 'It does look lovely. The new carpet has given the room a real lift.'

'As long as you won't be frightened here,' Vanessa said.

'Why would I be frightened?' Eva said with a frown. 'Hutton's in police custody. I think I'd be more freaked out if this had been a random attack. That would have made me worry that it might happen again because the lodge is so isolated. But this was premeditated and carried out by someone seeking revenge. It's over now.'

'That's the spirit,' Vanessa said, throwing an arm around Eva's shoulders. 'I'm still sleeping in Poppy's bed tonight, though.'

Epilogue

Jack turned left onto the Alpine Way and headed towards Thredbo. It was the first time he'd been back to the mountains since Gavin Hutton had been captured. He hadn't intended to stay away from the Snowy Mountains for so long, but his rehabilitation had been more onerous than he could have imagined in those first few days when he'd lain in a Canberra Hospital bed.

Yesterday, he'd passed a milestone, which meant today he was back behind the wheel. The temperature gauge on his dash showed it was one below zero, warm for a winter morning in the middle of July.

The Bullocks Flat carpark was packed with vehicles, the day trippers already lined up and waiting for the ski tube to haul them up the mountain to Perisher Valley. As he passed the resort at Lake Crackenback, his mind turned to the last time he'd driven on this road with Eva and Poppy, not knowing what awaited them on their return to the lodge that night. But excitement was the only thing charging around Jack's system as he paid his fee at the park gates, Poppy's new Rock-a-Bye Bear on the passenger seat beside him, the original now part of police evidence.

In Thredbo, the roads had been ploughed, and the Golden Wattle's driveway was clear. Leaving the car in front of the garage, he walked to the corner of the building to gaze across the expanse of snow, more compacted than it had been the night he and Ryder had chased Gavin Hutton into the night.

Breathing pure oxygen into his lungs, his let his gaze track upwards. Beyond the clearing, the tree-covered terrain sloped up towards a backdrop of white-capped mountains.

A Christmas tree stood in the lobby, decorated with baubles Eva had collected from her travels. He glanced at the fire, pleased to see that it was well stoked. He knew where she would be, cooking up a storm in the kitchen in preparation for tonight's Christmas in July dinner.

Eva was standing at the bench, wearing skinny jeans, an over-sized jumper and après boots. She turned to see who it was, and immediately dropped the wooden spoon she was holding. She met him halfway and he caught her to him, closing his eyes as they held each other tight for a long time.

'You surprised me. I didn't think you were coming until next weekend,' she said when they finally broke apart.

'I know you love Christmas in July and I didn't want to miss it,' Jack said, smiling down at her, 'so I worked extra hard on my rehab, putting myself through an enormous amount of pain so I could drive down and be here with you.'

'Thank you.' Eva smiled up at him, closing her eyes as he lowered his head for a long overdue, lingering kiss.

'I won't ruin the sleeping arrangements, will I?' he asked when he raised his head.

'Not at all. Actually, Vanessa owes me a big favour, so Poppy can sleep in her room tonight.'

'Way to make me popular with the sister I'm yet to meet.'

Eva laughed. 'Actually, we're going to have to convert one of the suites into a room for Poppy anyway, now that you're going to be a permanent resident.'

Jack smiled; happy Eva had already thought about that. They had a family life to look forward to now, something Jack hadn't had for a very long time. Even his work situation was settled. While the negotiation side of his business was finished, the demand for corporate training was solid and consistent.

'Did you see Poppy?' Eva asked, breaking into his thoughts. 'She's outside with Vanessa and Pierce.'

'No. I was wondering where she was.'

'Vanessa was going to give her another ski lesson. They must have been downstairs getting their gear together when you came in. Come on.' She took hold of his good hand and pulled him towards the door. 'Poppy will be so excited to see you, and Vanessa can't wait to meet you.'

He'd caught up with Ryder a few times in Sydney as they'd sorted out bits and pieces to do with the Hutton case. In Jack's opinion, he and Ryder had reached the stage of mutual respect, and that suited Jack just fine. But now he was about to meet Vanessa, merging the professional relationship he shared with Ryder with the personal, Eva's sister. The nerves fluttering in Jack's stomach surprised him.

'Coded security door,' Eva said, punching in the numbers then holding the door open for him. 'And I'll show you the new alarm system later.'

'Very good.'

'How's the hand?' she asked, looking up at him and they walked up the slight rise together.

'It's great.'

'Jack. How is it really?'

He smiled. 'It's slow progress, but it's getting there.'

'Walker!'

Jack looked up to see Poppy. She was standing at the top of the rise, dressed in a puffy ski suit and pompom-topped beanie with matching goggles, and had a pair of pink skis strapped to her feet. About ten metres down the slope, a woman with her hair pulled back in a ponytail almost identical to Eva's except darker, straightened up and looked at him. She was taller, a little younger than her sister, and she gave him the once-over when he joined them. This had to be Vanessa.

'Walker, look at me!' Poppy yelled.

'Hi Poppy,' he called out. 'I'm watching.'

'Okay, Pop.' Vanessa waved her arm to get her niece's attention. 'What shape are you going to make with your skis?'

'Pizza!' Poppy called back.

'That's right. A pizza shape. When you're ready.'

'Walker, watch!' Poppy hollered.

'I haven't taken my eyes off you yet,' Jack hollered back, and they all laughed.

After checking that he was watching, Poppy bent her knees and began to glide down the slope in a straight line. When she picked up too much speed, she brought her knees together, pushing the tails apart and bringing the tips together into a snow plough.

As she neared the bottom, still upright, they all cheered. Vanessa caught her niece under the arms and put her down next to Jack. 'Maybe your dad can catch you, too, when his hand gets better,' she said.

Jack smiled, not sure whether Vanessa's use of 'dad' was deliberate or accidental. Not that he minded. He *was* Poppy's father.

'Jack, this is my sister, Vanessa,' Eva said quickly. Then to Vanessa: 'I'd like you to meet Jack.'

'Hi, Jack,' Vanessa said with a cheeky smile at her sister. Jack didn't know if that was a good sign or not, so he said hello and then nodded to Ryder.

'Much traffic on the road?' Ryder asked.

'It wasn't too bad; I took it pretty easy. It feels good to get out of the city, though.'

Ryder nodded. 'Every time I come up here, I find it harder and harder to go back.'

'Mummy?' Poppy said softly, though she was staring at Jack, a confused expression on her face.

'Yes sweetie.'

'Auntie Nessa said Walker is my dad.' Poppy put her finger in her mouth and pushed out her cheek, the way she did when she was really concentrating.

The group fell silent.

'Is he?' Poppy asked, peering up at Eva through her coloured ski goggles.

Jack looked at Eva for direction, his heart beating hard. She nodded at Poppy. 'He is,' she said simply.

Taking his lead from Eva, Jack gave a quiet nod, too.

'Do I have to call him Dad?' Poppy asked in a soft voice. 'Because I like Walker better.'

Suddenly Jack had something in his eye. Blinking, he crouched down so he was on her level. 'Hey, Poppy. You can call me whatever you like, okay?'

'I'll call you Walker. *Everybody* has a dad,' she said as if it were the most boring thing in the world.

Jack reached out and jiggled the pompom on her beanie before straightening up. 'Well,' he said, looking around at the others and putting his arm around Eva, 'now we've got the easy stuff out of the way, what else do you have in store for me?'

Acknowledgements

To my beloved family and friends who are a constant support to me always, thank you.

To Annette Barlow and the entire team at Allen & Unwin, you are an absolute pleasure to work with. Many thanks also to Nada Backovic for her amazing cover design.

To Bernadette Foley and the Wednesday Workshop ladies, thank you for reading my words and giving me your honest feedback. I always look forward to our monthly meetings.

To Anna Clifton and Linda Hills for reading my first draft, thank you. And to Paula Anicich for her help with research for this story.

And to my friend, who prefers to remain unnamed, and who patiently answers all my police-related questions, many thanks again.

And finally to my readers. You give me the inspiration to keep writing. Thank you.

Coming February 2022

Dead Horse Gap

LEE CHRISTINE

When a light plane crashes at night in the New South Wales Snowy Mountains, Sydney Homicide's Detective Sergeant Pierce Ryder and Detective Constable Mitchell Flowers are sent to investigate possible foul play.

As Ryder and Flowers look into the crash, they expose a generations-old feud between two local families. Could the bitterness that has been carried through the years have anything to do with the death of the pilot?

Meanwhile, Detective Constable Nerida Sterling is already deep undercover in the Snowies, her assignment to infiltrate a drug ring operating in the mountains and to ultimately hunt down a murderer. As her cover becomes more and more tenuous, to what lengths will Sterling go in order to get the information she needs?

ISBN 978 1 76106 607 8

Prologue

They didn't call him cowboy for nothing.

Most pilots would have aborted the landing on the tiny airstrip, unwilling to descend over the mountainous terrain in the dark, but he knew the runway was there, and he was confident he could make it. He should have landed hours ago, but a blizzard had forced him to fly around the weather. Now, long after darkness and aviation last light, the pilot made a bumpy approach into Khancoban Airport in the Snowy Mountains. He was accustomed to night flying thanks to years of crop-dusting after dark, and he had confidence in his Cessna. He had checked it prior to departure, checked he had enough go-juice, checked that he himself was fit to fly.

Fierce gusts buffeted the light plane as he worked the throttle, controlling his descent. Focused on his instruments, his mind totally in the cockpit, he checked the plane was straight and level, checked his airspeed was good, checked his altitude and GPS track. He looked up, scanning the darkness for the visual cues he needed to put the light plane safely on the ground. The clouds parted, and in the momentary wash of moonlight he glimpsed the three-kilometre stretch of water he'd been searching for. He closed the throttle, raised the nose and extended the undercarriage, slowing the Cessna before it dropped into the bank of fog hovering over the Khancoban pondage. He switched on his landing lights. Two bright beams appeared on each wingtip.

Tension gathered at the top of his spine. In the reflection of his landing lights, he could see the strands of fog becoming thinner.

Now. Any moment now.

The pilot let out a triumphant whoop. He was over the water, flying at a slow 70 knots and one minute away from landing. He chose full flap before opening the throttle to maintain his approach as the flaps ran to position. The airstrip was short and devoid of runway lights, but it was there, waiting in the darkness, just on the other side of the concrete spillway.

Five seconds to landing, and the pilot glimpsed the turbulent water below, gushing from the spillway and flowing into the Swampy Plain River. Then he was touching down, applying the brakes as soon as the wheels struck solid ground.

Euphoria raced through his body but it was immediately replaced by horror at a looming shape blocking the runway. Unable to stop in time, he wrenched the plane to the left, hoping to ground loop whatever it was. Time slowed. The plane careered to the left, a tyre exploding like a bomb. Above the blood pounding in his ears, he heard the grating, tearing sound of metal as the right wing clipped the tractor and was torn from the plane. The engine hit the ground, flinging fuel across the airstrip and sending the control column slamming into the pilot's chest. With the breath punched out of him, he groped for the Cessna's door handle, sparks spraying like fireworks all around him.

One

Detective Constable Mitchell Flowers had never been a fan of light planes. As a passenger, he worried about the single engine failing, or the lone pilot suffering a medical emergency. But as he walked across the part-asphalt part-grass runway of Khancoban Airport, it was clear that neither of those things were responsible for this accident. The burnt-out tractor with a slasher on the back in the middle of the airstrip was quite obviously the culprit.

It was 6.45am and first light in the Snowy Mountains in New South Wales, two degrees above zero, minus six with the wind chill. Flowers had woken with a dull headache brought on by too many hours in front of a computer screen and too few hours' sleep. Negotiating the snowy hairpin bends along the Alpine Way had intensified the headache into a painful throb on the left side of his skull. He reached into his coat pocket for a tab of anti-inflammatory tablets, popped out two and swallowed them dry.

As he neared the wreckage, a uniformed officer straightened up from where he'd been taking photographs of a landing wheel that had rolled some distance away. Bald and heavy-set, he had the kind of bushy moustache blokes his age had grown in the seventies and never shaved off.

'Sergeant Walt Collins, Khancoban Police,' the officer said, hitching up his pants by the belt.

Flowers held up his ID. 'Detective Constable Mitchell Flowers, Sydney Homicide.'

'Sydney?'

Here we go, thought Flowers, not missing the officer's unimpressed expression at a wet-behind-the-ears detective with a full head of hair homing in on his turf.

'That's right.'

'I asked for the Queanbeyan boys.'

'I was in Queanbeyan for a court case,' Flowers replied, careful not to sound defensive.

It had just gone midnight last night when Inspector Gray had called his mobile and told him to get himself to Khancoban. *A plane has crashed on the Snowy Hydro airstrip. Possible sabotage according to early reports. The pilot's dead.*

Sergeant Collins looked past Flowers to the gravel road where a small group of onlookers had gathered outside the locked gate. 'So, you're it?' he asked.

Deal with it, Flowers wanted to say. Instead, he answered calmly, 'My partner will be here soon.' How soon that would be Flowers had no idea, so he took out his notepad and pen and asked, 'So, what happened here?'

Sergeant Collins gave a heavy sigh and gazed at the two blackened vehicles roped off with police tape. 'The plane came in late last night. The airport manager heard it and raced down here. He did his best but there was nothing he could do. Fire and Rescue put out the blaze.'

Flowers followed the sergeant's gaze. A fire truck was parked on the other side of the airfield, its two crew members on watch.

'What state is the body in?'

Sergeant Collins shook his head slowly, his eyes grave. 'Burned to a crisp.'

Flowers jotted down shorthand in his notebook. Just his luck he was on his own at his first plane crash, and one where foul play was suspected. He shivered inside his heavy-duty police jacket and wondered what Detective Sergeant Ryder would do if he were here.

No doubt his more experienced partner had attended multiple plane crashes in the past. He'd done everything else.

Flowers glanced back towards the burnt-out vehicles. 'Why was the tractor on the runway?'

Collins spread his hands. 'Nobody seems to know.'

'Who had access to it?'

'Only the bloke who does the mowing, apparently.'

Flowers nodded. 'I'll figure out what other resources we'll need to bring in, and I'll get in touch with the Coroner's office.' Beyond the wreckage, several large pieces of jagged metal and other general debris were scattered across the grass, torn from the aircraft before it had been engulfed in flames. 'Do we know who the pilot is—*was*?'

'We're pretty sure it's Art Lorrimer. The wreckage is consistent with a Cessna 210, which he flies. He was due to land here yesterday, but the weather turned bad.'

'Is he local?'

'Not to Khancoban,' Collins said. 'The family have a grazing property down Tooma way, White Winter Station.'

'Have they been notified?'

'Not as yet.'

Flowers looked at the growing number of people gathering at the gate. A sign bearing the Snowy Hydro logo warned: Khancoban Airport, No Entry, Authorised Personnel Only.

'Was anyone waiting here for him to land last night?'

'Not to my knowledge.'

'How long does it take to walk into the town? Five minutes?'

'If that.'

'So, maybe he wasn't getting picked up, maybe he intended on walking into town. I'll make some enquiries, see if he booked a room anywhere.' Flowers pocketed his notepad and pen, the acrid smell of burnt rubber and aviation fuel surrounding the wreckage turning his stomach. 'I'd better take a look at the body,' he said, glad he'd decided to skip breakfast.

With Sergeant Collins close behind, Flowers ducked under the police tape, the stench poisoning the otherwise pristine breeze blowing off the pondage on the other side of the spillway. As they moved carefully towards the burnt-out vehicles, it became clear from the angle of the plane that the pilot had attempted to turn away from the tractor. The right wing had detached from the fuselage while the undercarriage looked to have been ripped out, possibly from colliding with the tractor's slasher. But that would be for the Australian Transport Safety Bureau to work out.

'You have photographs of all this?' Flowers asked, burnt grass crackling under his boots.

'Yep.'

As they drew closer to the plane, Flowers held up a hand for Collins to stop. He could already make out the charred skull and torso from where they stood and, to his mind, there was no doubt how the pilot had died. 'We need to leave this to forensics,' he said, turning away from the grisly scene. 'We touch any part of that and it could crumble to black ash.'

As they walked back towards a large, corrugated-iron shed, the lone building gracing the airport, Flowers phoned Harriet Ono in Canberra. She was Ryder's most trusted forensic pathologist.

'Boy Wonder!' Harriet's voice reverberated in his ear. 'Why are you calling me?'

Flowers winced at the nickname she'd bestowed on him when he'd first been partnered with Ryder. 'Shouldn't you be in an autopsy or something? I was getting ready to leave a message.'

'I couldn't resist answering when I saw it was you. What's up?'

Flowers gave her a rundown of the situation. 'I need a team up here real fast. Can you do it?' He watched as Sergeant Collins headed into the shed. Both roller doors were open and two men were sitting at a table inside, deep in conversation. 'I think a rep from the Transport Safety Bureau could be here already.'

'Probably, they're based in Canberra as well. What's the weather like?'

Flowers surveyed the sky. 'Fine, partly cloudy with a light breeze coming from the south—'

'Righto, smart-arse. Listen up, the local police or emergency services can cover the crash site if there's strong wind or rain threatening. That's it, until the body is removed. I don't want anyone contaminating my crime scene.'

'So I'll take that as a yes?'

'Of course it's a yes,' she said irritably. 'Where's Ryder? Is he okay?'

'Fine. Busy juggling court appearances and a whole bunch of other stuff. I'll tell him you were worried though. Thanks, Harriet, see you when you get here.' He hung up before she could give an outraged reply. Hiding an amused smile, Flowers went to join the others, relieved that the crime scene would soon be in the hands of one of the best police pathologists in the business.

The shed was part office, part rec room and part hangar. A yellow plane, hardly bigger than a toy, was parked at the far end. Flowers sat down at the table and Sergeant Collins made the introductions. Zane Alam from the Transport Safety Bureau was slightly built with shiny black hair. By contrast, Benjamin Hoff, the airport manager, was blond and lanky and dressed in pilot's white.

No chance of mixing these two up, thought Flowers, despite their identical aviator sunglasses. Taking out his notepad again, he spoke to Ben Hoff first.

'Why was the tractor parked in the middle of the runway?'

'I have no idea. When I left, it was parked beside the shed, like it always is.' Hoff's reddened eyes shifted to the blackened scar on the airstrip. 'It's *never* left on the runway—for obvious reasons.'

Flowers turned to Zane Alam. 'Do you think the pilot made an emergency landing?' Despite the tractor and slasher, it seemed an obvious question to ask.

'That will all come out in our investigation,' Alam said. 'From initial reports, and these are purely anecdotal, Detective, the pilot may well have landed safely if it weren't for the tractor. Several members of the community heard the plane come in, as did Ben. No one reported hearing engine failure.'

Flowers noted this down, nodding for him to continue.

'The pilot wouldn't have seen the tractor until after he'd touched down,' Alam went on. 'This airstrip doesn't have runway lights that can be switched on remotely from the plane. If it had, they might have given him a slightly better chance of seeing the tractor sooner and taking evasive action.'

Flowers frowned. 'Pilots can turn on runway lights?'

Alam nodded. 'Not all airports are big enough to have control towers, but some do have runway lights. The pilot tunes in to a particular radio frequency that allows him to switch them on. This pilot would have approached slowly because of the short runway and lack of lighting. When he touched down, he'd have lost too much speed to get the plane back in the air, but he'd still be travelling too fast to avoid a collision. Everything would have happened in seconds.'

Silence fell over the group. Flowers stared at the grey tabletop and tried to imagine the pilot's panic when he realised the runway was blocked. 'Where are the keys to the tractor kept?' he asked after a while.

Hoff turned and pointed to a desk barely visible under multiple stacks of paper. 'In the desk drawer, over there. It's still locked, and the shed wasn't broken into.' The skin on Hoff's left cheek was raw, as though he'd been singed by the fire.

'Who else has access to this place, and to the tractor key?' Flowers asked.

'Besides me, there are two other pilots,' said Hoff, before reciting their names and phone numbers.

Flowers nodded and wrote down the details. 'Who was the last person to use the tractor?'

'Our regular maintenance man, Orville Parish. He's been cutting the grass here for over ten years. You wouldn't find a more responsible person.'

Flowers made a note of the name. 'Is the key in the drawer the only one you have?' he asked.

'Yes,' Hoff confirmed. 'As I said, the tractor was parked in its usual spot when I left the airport around five.'

Flowers wrote down *hot-wired*? 'Has anything unusual happened lately, anyone hanging around?'

'Nope. It's been pretty quiet.'

'What about kids?' To Flowers' way of thinking, joy-riding on a tractor at night might be something kids would do.

'Haven't seen any. The local kids know better, but we have a lot of tourists in town now with the ski season under way.'

'Any CCTV cameras?' Flowers hadn't sighted any, but it was always good to check. Plus he'd be reporting all this to Ryder, so he needed to be thorough.

Hoff shook his head again. 'No, we don't have cameras here.'

'What's this airport mainly used for?' Flowers asked with a frown, gazing out at the short runway.

'A bit of everything,' Hoff said. 'Private planes are able to land here, and the National Parks and Wildlife fly out when they do weed control. Of course, the Snowy Hydro use it, and sometimes a resident needs to be flown to hospital.'

'That's probably my team,' Alam said suddenly.

Flowers looked up. Sure enough, the recognisable sound of a helicopter rotor cutting through the air could be heard in the distance.

'That chopper isn't going to land here, is it?' he asked, surprised that he sounded a lot like Ryder. 'I won't risk the crime scene being compromised.'

Alam shook his head. 'There's plenty of space for it to land on the other side of the road.'

'Good.' Flowers stood up. 'Nothing happens until the police forensics team gets here. Our investigation takes priority.'

Two

Detective Sergeant Pierce Ryder kept his eyes on Nerida Sterling's olive-green jacket and black helmet. Detective Sterling was two places ahead of him in the chairlift queue at Thredbo Ski Village in the Snowy Mountains, standing alone with her snowboard. The Chili Peppers' 'Higher Ground' blared from a speaker overhead, enhancing the holiday atmosphere. Ryder slid forward on his skis, using his poles to stop him from running into two young snowboarders in the line in front of him. They were brimming with excitement about how much air they'd caught on their last run down.

'Excuse me fellas, I'm a single,' said Ryder, his neck warmer pulled up to the bottom of his goggles. The pair cordially parted, giving Ryder the space he needed to move ahead of them. He glided past, nodding his thanks, but they took no notice, already discussing which run they were going to take next.

Ryder drew level with Sterling. Careful not to let his left ski drift anywhere near her snowboard, he stared straight ahead. Her right foot was free of its binding in readiness for the ride up, and the last thing he wanted to do was trip her.

An empty chair rounded the corner, scooping up the couple ahead of them. 'Have a good one guys,' the liftie called before beckoning Sterling and Ryder forward.

With his poles tucked under one arm, Ryder glided towards the designated red line stating 'wait here' then watched over his shoulder as another empty chair approached from the rear. To anyone watching, they were strangers about to share a ride up the mountain, not two members of the Sydney Homicide Squad. When the chair nudged them in the back of the knees, they sat simultaneously.

Ryder brought down the safety bar, watching Sterling from the corner of his eye. 'How was your counter surveillance?' He spoke quickly, conscious of their limited time.

'Safe. I made sure I wasn't followed.'

'I'm glad we were due to meet today,' he said, pulling his neck warmer down so his voice wasn't muffled. The day was mostly clear but a chilly four below zero. Ryder's lips were already stinging. 'Flowers is in Khancoban.'

Sterling stilled for an instant then wrangled her snowboard onto the footrest. 'Right now?'

Ryder nodded. 'As we speak.'

'For the plane?'

'Yes. Did you hear it come in?'

'No, the sirens woke me up though. I thought it was a road accident until I saw a post on the Khancoban Community page saying it was a plane. Why are Homicide involved?'

They were high on the chairlift now, with no chance of being overheard. Even so, Ryder looked straight ahead, disguising their conversation to anyone who might be watching.

'A tractor was left on the runway and the pilot was killed. If it was intentional there'll be an investigation. So don't worry if you see us around town.'

'Okay.'

'How're things otherwise?'

'The same. I have nothing new to report.' Sterling curled her mitten-covered hands around the safety bar. 'If someone's dealing drugs in the pub, it's not happening on my shift. Maybe it's time I put the word out that I'm looking to score a hit.'

Ryder took a deep breath. He could sympathise with her frustration; he'd been undercover himself several times and it was tough and lonely work.

'Listen to me, Sterling, it's your first assignment and it's normal to be frustrated, but it can be dangerous to try and *make* things happen. Buying drugs and having them in your possession creates a whole new set of problems. If you buy marijuana, what are you going to do if they insist you smoke it with them, or if they want you to take some other drug?'

When Sterling didn't answer, he went on.

'Disposing of the drugs becomes a problem too.'

Sterling nodded. 'I hadn't thought that far ahead.'

'That's why we have these meetings. You've been undercover for eight weeks. I know that feels like a long time when nothing's happening, but don't lose sight of the fact that it's been six *months* since Scruffy Freidman's body went floating down the Thredbo River. That day, the drug squad lost whatever information they thought they'd get from him and the trail went cold on my investigation here. So don't feel pressured to make things happen.'

Just then, the chairlift came to a sudden stop.

'Someone's probably fallen over on the unloading ramp,' Sterling said.

'That's good,' said Ryder, as the chair swung gently, 'maybe we'll get an extra minute.'

'Someone found out Freidman turned, Sarge.'

'No doubt.'

Freidman had approached the drug squad and offered to turn informant in exchange for protection. In a show of good faith, he'd tipped them off that a murder was imminent in the Snowy Mountains. But it was Freidman who'd turned up dead.

'The way I see it, Sterling,' Ryder went on, 'you're in Khancoban to make connections and build relationships with the locals and regular visitors. You're a woman spending a season in the snow, improving your snowboarding on your days off, like thousands of others.'

'I understand. I'm just worried that half the ski season is over and I haven't learned anything useful.'

'I'm not saying there won't come a time when asking to buy drugs is a reasonable course of action, but now is not the time. In my experience, it's usually the little things that crack the case open, not something big like you see in a TV drama. A guy talking himself up in the pub, and you overhear him and think *ah ha*! Or the same thing could happen when one of us is listening to an intercepted phone call. When you hear it, you'll recognise it for what it is.'

'Thanks, Sarge. What you're saying makes sense.'

The chairlift began to move again.

'How are you, otherwise?' Ryder asked the same question every time, concerned for the young detective's mental health. It took nerve to pretend you were someone else while remaining strong and focused. For reasons unknown to Ryder, Sterling had been hungry to take this assignment, fully aware she would be separated from her family, friends and co-workers for months. It was up to her to prove she had the mettle for it.

'My head's fine, Sarge.'

'If you need to be pulled out—'

'No worries there.'

They were drawing closer to the station. Whoops of laughter rang out from the slope below as the chair in front moved over the safety net.

'Stay safe,' he said, dragging up his neck warmer.

When Ryder's skis hit the snow, he stood up, Sterling half a second ahead of him. Once clear of the unloading area, he watched her head to a safe place where she could sit down and buckle in her loose boot. He skied past, cruising along the top of the track while looking for an easy entry into the run. Ryder's girlfriend, Vanessa, was a ski-patrol officer at Thredbo, but despite her intensive tuition, he was an average skier at best. He looked for a groomed run to take him all the way down the mountain, recounting Vanessa's instructions in his head. Somewhere behind him, Sterling would be taking her time adjusting the bindings on her snowboard before heading in a different direction.

Ryder pushed off down the slope, his weight on his downhill ski despite how unnatural it felt. He made a wide turn, picking up too much speed before he remembered his edges. Pointing his skis a little uphill, he transferred his weight and made another wide radius turn. Someone shot past in a blur and Ryder's nerves tingled as he tightened his grip on his poles. Colliding with someone at speed would put him in a hospital bed quick smart.

Aside from the physical risk, it had made sense for him to meet Sterling in Thredbo. He was staying at the Golden Wattle, the ski lodge in Thredbo that Vanessa's sister Eva managed, while he was attending court in Queanbeyan. Eva's ski lodge was a convenient midpoint between the court and Sterling's Khancoban operation.

After a few more turns the run levelled out to a gentler slope. Confident on the easier gradient, Ryder glanced around but the area was deserted save for a ski instructor surrounded by a group of primary-school-aged kids. Reaching up, he slid open the vent on his helmet. The ski apparel was another reason for them to meet on the mountain—the helmets, goggles and face coverings made it almost impossible for anyone watching to recognise them.

Ryder relaxed, his body no longer needing his full concentration to stay upright. He exited the trees halfway down a wide run and traversed to the other side, careful not to miss the narrow trail that would take him through the trees again, and down the slope to the Golden Wattle Lodge.

❋

Vanessa was outside the lodge near the bottom-floor exit, her back to Ryder as he skied across the clearing. Dressed in her red ski-patroller's uniform, her hair pulled up in its usual high ponytail, she was moving between a couple of trestle tables she'd set up in the snow. As he came to a stop beside her, she looked around and took out her earbuds.

'Hi. How did you go?'

To anyone within earshot, the question was a simple enquiry about how he'd handled the conditions, but Vanessa was fully aware he had a member of his squad undercover, and the movements and responsibilities that went with it.

Ryder clicked out of his bindings and leaned over to pick up his skis. 'I didn't stack it, so on the whole pretty good,' he said, his thighs burning from the continuous snowplough he'd used to get him safely down the last section of track in one piece.

'I told you we'd get those old footballer knees loosened up,' she said with a smile.

'Careful, not so much with the old. What are you up to?'

'Waxing my skis. I don't start until eleven and they needed it. Want me to do yours?'

Ryder looked at the skis clamped to the trestle tables. Vanessa was dripping hot wax from a block onto the undersides of the skis. The process looked a lot more complicated than waxing a surfboard.

'Will it help my skiing?'

'It'll make you go faster.'

'No thanks.'

She laughed, and Ryder learned over and kissed her gently on the temple, happy she was enjoying working in the snow again. After meeting while Ryder was investigating a case in Charlotte Pass, Vanessa had given up her ski patrolling to move to Sydney with him, but she'd hated being stuck in a sales job demonstrating skis rather than using them. Eventually, she'd made the decision to return to Thredbo for what would be her final season, while Ryder stayed working in Sydney.

He watched as Vanessa continued waxing her skis. As it turned out, with him in Queanbeyan for court, they were seeing a lot more of each other than they'd anticipated. But their permanent move to the country once the season wrapped up was looming large in Ryder's mind. With Vanessa's parents retiring, the time had come for her to take over the running of the family property, as she'd promised them she would. And Ryder had promised Vanessa he'd be right there beside her.

He sighed and touched her lightly on the back. 'As much as I'd love to stay and watch this fascinating process, I need to shower and change.'

She turned to look at him enquiringly, as though she were trying to read his thoughts.

'Drive safely,' she said quietly, 'and say hello to Mitch for me.'